BEHEMOTH

BY

HP NEWQUIST

A RELAYER BOOK

The Relayer Group
New York, NY

Copyright © 2019 by HP Newquist

All rights reserved.

No part of this book shall be reproduced, stored in a retrieval system, or transmitted by any means, electronic, mechanical, photocopying, recording, or otherwise, without written permission from the publisher. No patent liability is assumed with respect to the use of the information contained herein. Although every precaution has been taken in the preparation of this book, the publisher and author assume no responsibility for errors or omissions. Neither is any liability assumed for damages resulting from the use of the information contained herein.

This book is a work of fiction. Names, characters, places and incidents are either a product of the author's fertile imagination or are used fictitiously. Any resemblance to actual events, places or persons, living or dead, is entirely coincidental.

Second Edition
RELAYER Books, 2022

ISBN-13: ISBN-13: 978-0-9885937-5-6
ebook ISBN: 978-0-9885937-4-9

Cover Design © 2019 by Mikio Murakami
http://www.silentqdesign.com/

Previous Edition: ISBN-13: 978-1-947522-27-5
ISBN-10: 1-947522-27-2

For information, address The Relayer Group at info@relayergroup.com.

*To Trini
For being there*

THE BEGINNING

Behold now the Behemoth that I have made along with Man.
Its limbs are as strong as copper, its bones as a mass of iron.
It ranks first among God's works . . .
Nothing on earth is its equal—a creature without fear.

The Book of Job, 40:15

There be creatures that are created for vengeance, which in their fury lay on deadly strokes. In the time of destruction they pour out their force and appease the wrath of Him that made them.

Ecclesiasticus, 39:28

The people shall be wasted with hunger, and devoured with burning heat and bitter destruction, and the teeth of beasts will I send upon them.

Deuteronomy, 32:24

.

CHAPTER 1
APRIL 4
THURSDAY, 10:30 PM

The last shards of winter cold clung to the night air, like small steel hooks gripping flesh. The calendar said it was spring, but jagged sharpness remained in winter's feeble bite.

People in the small towns from Morris to Ashford were inside their homes, fireplace embers fading, blankets wrapped tightly around sleeping bodies. Quiet enclosed each house like a cage.

A single car careened through the towns along an empty road. Its headlights sliced erratically through the night air.

"Give me a colder beer this time," said Terry Moran, tossing an empty can over his shoulder. It landed in Charlie Bedecker's lap.

"Jesus, you drink fast. You'll finish before Kevin and me get ours," whined Charlie.

"Yeah, well, maybe you should learn to speed it up," Terry replied. "My baby sister can drink faster than you guys."

The three boys laughed. Another round of cans popped open in the car.

Terry Moran sat behind the wheel of his father's Lexus. Kevin Parelli was in the passenger seat, with Charlie Bedecker lounging in the back. The case of beer they had stolen out of Kevin's garage was on the floor.

The boys drove through the dark drinking beer because there was nothing else to do. They were seniors in high school with nowhere to go, nothing to see. It was hardly after ten, and everything in the county was closed. Driving and beer were the only ingredients available to produce excitement on a school night.

"We could drive to Wilburn," suggested Charlie, burping. "They might have a bar still open."

"Fuck that," said Kevin. "That's a half hour drive. Let's just drink what we have."

They wandered the back roads of the soundless towns, making random turns and looking for long stretches of road. They roared down straightaways and cut across farm roads—little used tractor paths barely suitable for cars. They had no idea where they were.

Winding along an unpaved road under a thick canopy of trees, the boys found themselves in a town darker than the sky. It looked abandoned.

Kevin stared out the window. "Hey, we're in Morris," he said, almost to himself. "I've never been here after dark."

"Nobody's ever here after dark." Terry sucked on his beer, watching the road over the top of the can. "This town is deader than Bambi's mom once the sun goes down."

They glided down the unlit main street, past a looming church. The car's headlights flared against it, lighting up its towering stone spire. The windows were boarded up. Its doors were chained shut.

Kevin peered into the gloom. "The church looks like something out of Frankenstein," he said, his voice low. "It's fucking creepy."

"My mom says that people in Morris never go out after dark because they turn into witches," Charlie said.

Terry snickered. "No offense or anything, Charlie, but your mom isn't exactly the sharpest tool in the shed. Doesn't she still believe in the Tooth Fairy?" Kevin laughed up his beer.

Charlie let it go. "Yeah, well, how come nobody from Morris goes out at night?"

"Nobody in any of these shit towns goes out after dark." Terry smirked. "Besides us, there isn't anybody on the road for twenty miles. Morris isn't any different. It just has the weirdest reputation."

Kevin turned up the radio. The music rumbled loudly, rattling them in their seats.

The people in Morris heard the car as it drove by. No one opened their windows to look.

Terry wound through the shadowy village. Once the houses were in his rearview, he headed in the direction of the interstate road.

Staring out the windshield, the lines on the road got fuzzy and wavy. He blinked his eyes, trying to focus through all the beer. It didn't help.

Suddenly he found himself at a dead end. A concrete barrier blocked the way.

"What the Hell is this doing here?" he asked. He expected an answer.

"Don't know," slurred Kevin.

"Morris puts up roadblocks against the state road at night," said Charlie. "It keeps people from driving around town. Looking for gas and stuff. Waking people up." He slumped into the safety of the backseat. Terry and Kevin turned to look at him. "At least that's what my mom says."

"Well, Charlie, your mom might have finally gotten something right," Terry said, throwing the car into reverse. "We'll just go around this thing and get on the state road with a little four-wheeling."

Kevin scrunched up his face. "This isn't a four-wheel drive."

"It's my dad's car. Not mine. I don't have to worry if the transmission holds up. So I can make it anything I want. Right now, I want it to be a Jeep."

With that, Terry Moran pointed the Lexus toward the shoulder of the road. Toward the field beyond.

CHAPTER 2

APRIL 4
THURSDAY, 11:05 PM

The Lexus nosed down sharply over the shoulder without slowing. The boys saw that the long grass in the field ahead was as tall as the car. The headlights reflected frenetically off the weeds.

"This shit's too deep. I can't fucking see a thing!" Kevin said, his head craning close to the windshield.

"Neither can I and I'm fucking driving!" Terry shot back. "Give me a beer. We'll be out of this in a second." The car bounced over stones and old corn furrows.

"Maybe you oughta slow down," Charlie said. "Or better yet, stop and make sure we're going the right way."

"We're going the right way," Terry snarled, accelerating through the enveloping grass. "I aimed towards the road when I went over the edge. It can't be more than a couple hundred fee—"

The Lexus imploded.

Crashing brutally into something invisible in the night, the car crumpled in on itself.

Airbags burst open. They did not prevent Charlie from becoming a projectile. He was thrown over the front seat, smashing Kevin's head into the windshield, crazing the glass. Terry's chest rammed into the steering wheel as Charlie's shoulder smashed against the back of his skull.

Suddenly, the car was silent and dark. A thin whistle of steam exhaled from the radiator.

The crash was over in the moment it happened.

The lights on the dashboard had gone out. The headlights were dead.

Shrouded in blackness, none of the boys made a sound. Slowly, painfully, they took stock of themselves. Each touched his own head, arms, chest, and just to make sure, his testicles.

Charlie spoke first. His voice was a groggy whisper.

"Are you guys alive? Kevin? Terry?" He had come across the top of them and was now lying in their laps, his right arm twisted behind him.

"I think I cracked my head open," moaned Kevin. "I feel . . . blood on my face."

Terry made a spitting sound against the steering wheel. "I lost a . . . coupla teeth. My . . . chest . . . hurts."

Charlie attempted to roll off them to the floor. He let out a piercing scream as he banged his side. "Ahhhhh, fuck! My fucking arm! It's broken!"

Kevin forced the passenger door open. He let himself fall out into the grass. "Hold on, Charlie," he winced. "I'll help you in a second. Lemme sit for a second."

Terry leaned towards his door and found it already open. He stood up carefully, touching his mouth gingerly with one hand. "This fucking . . . sucks." He looked around and then back into the car. "Charlie, can you sit up?"

"No. Everything hurts too much." Charlie began whimpering.

"Shit," murmured Terry. He sucked the night air into his lungs. It soothed his head and throat but burned in his chest. "I gotta see what happened."

Unsteadily, he walked to the front. "Kev? Kev, you okay?"

Kevin groaned back. "I think so. Feels like someone hit my head with a fucking rock."

"Did you see anything? Do you know what we hit?"

"Uh uh." Kevin tried to stand. "Must have been something in the grass."

"No shit, Sherlock," Terry replied. "Can you come around to the front?" He coughed up some blood, and what felt like a little bit of tooth.

"Yeah, but I can't see anything," said Kevin. The stars and the night sky did nothing to illuminate the trees and grass around him. "You got a light on you?"

Terry checked his phone. No power, no light. He could feel the cracked glass face. He thought for a moment. "The old man has a flashlight under the seat. Hold on."

Terry pushed through the grass and bent into the car. He felt Charlie's head on the seat. "You still with us, Charlie?" He tried to smile, then realized Charlie couldn't see him. It was utter blackness out here.

"Fuck, I don't know. My legs are messed up. My arm hurts really bad."

"Okay, hang on. Me and Kev are gonna check the damage." He leaned down to feel under the seat and felt pressure on his lungs. His fingers scrabbled around on the carpet until he felt the cylindrical shape of the flashlight. As he stood up, his lungs felt better.

"Whew," he wheezed. "I'll be right back."

"I'm not going anywhere," Charlie slurred, his voice trailing off.

CHAPTER 3

APRIL 4
THURSDAY, 11:10 PM

Terry could barely make out Kevin on the other side of the car. He switched on the light and shone it over the hood at Kevin's face.

His friend's head was smeared in blood, making his face shine bright red. The sight of it made Terry want to throw up.

"Are, are . . . you okay, Kev?"

"Why? Does it look bad?" Kevin self-consciously touched his forehead.

"Maybe it looks worse than it is."

Terry flashed the light around the car's hood and saw that it was cleft into a perfect V. Lying in front of the grille was a rectangular stone, maybe three feet long. The impact of the car had knocked the stone on its side—after the stone had stopped the car dead in its tracks. Terry tapped the rock with his foot. "What is this? A gravestone?"

Kevin shook his head slowly. Droplets of blood sparkled as they fell through the flashlight beam before sinking into the grass. "I don't think so. It's like a milestone marker. Or a historical marker."

"You mean I totaled my dad's car on a fucking marker?" Terry whined, his voice rising. "What's it doing out here?"

Kevin stared blankly at the stone. It was dark black and smooth, and obviously heavy enough to go head-to-head with Mr. Moran's Lexus. And win.

"Let me have the light," Kevin said, extending his arm.

They bent down to examine the marker. Its four sides tapered into a small pyramid at the top. Rubbing his hand over its flat coolness, Kevin's fingers stopped over deep grooves. He pulled the grass away and held the light up to the stone.

"It's got words on it," Kevin said. He was having trouble seeing; the blood streaking his face made his eyelids stick together.

"What's it say?" Terry sneered. "I Killed Mr. Moran's Car?'"

Kevin squinted in the light. "It has . . . a little cross. Let's see. It has . . . oh shit! It has the name of a priest. Father Timothy Moynihan. And . . ." Kevin wiped the blood out of his eyes with his sleeve.

"And what?" asked Terry, a sliver of panic gilding his voice. "What? Did I knock over a priest's grave? Jesus, dude, I'll go to Hell for that."

"I don't think it's a grave," Kevin said slowly, squinting again. "The other thing it says is 'One of Five.'"

"One of Five?"

"One of Five. That's it."

"That's it?"

"I just said that was it," Kevin snapped.

"One of five whats?" demanded Terry.

"How should I know? Maybe one of five markers. Maybe it's part of a series. Like baseball cards. I don't know. Don't fucking ask me." Kevin's skull throbbed where it had smashed against the windshield. The air was turning icy and he was shivering. He wanted to go home.

From inside the car, Charlie moaned softly. "Are you guys getting us out of here? I need to go to a doctor."

"What are we going to do?" Kevin asked.

"I don't know," sighed Terry, feeling small and lost for the first time since he was in grade school. "My phone shattered."

Kevin fished his phone out of his pants pocket. It lit up, then he cursed. "No service." He slapped the phone against his thigh.

Terry looked at the sky. "Maybe we should just stay here and wait until morning. We can walk back into Morris then."

"We can't stay here," said Kevin. "My mom'll freak. If I don't call her, she'll kill me." He looked wistfully towards the road. "You think anyplace out here still has pay phones?"

Terry shrugged. "If you want to walk ten or so miles in the middle of the night, go ahead. But Charlie's not in any shape to walk."

"Let him stay here and sleep," Kevin said. "You come with me; we'll call his parents. And a doctor. He'll be okay. But I'm not doing all the talking." In the dark, Kevin's voice was accusing. "It's your car. You should do some explaining."

Terry let out a hissing sound from his nostrils. "Okay, okay. I'll go with you. Let's tell Charlie."

Aiming the light into the car, they explained the plan. Terry didn't like the way Charlie's limbs looked, contorted in horrible angles.

"Here, drink another beer real fast," said Kevin. "It'll kill the pain." He popped a can and held it to Charlie's mouth. Charlie guzzled quickly; most of the beer ran down his mouth and neck. He sputtered.

"I'll be okay, guys," Charlie coughed. "Hurry back. Really. Hurry."

Charlie started to drift off. Kevin gave him a pat on the shoulder. Terry tousled his hair.

Then Charlie's two friends were gone.

CHAPTER 4
APRIL 4
THURSDAY, 11:30 PM

Charlie didn't know how long he'd been asleep. Maybe minutes, maybe hours. It was very dark and so very cold. He awoke with a hazy start, thinking he heard screams—maybe Terry's, maybe Kevin's. His eyes fluttered open, and he called out. His voice was a croak, not even a whisper. "Terry? Kevin? Guys?"

No response.

He'd been dreaming. From where he lay on the seat, Charlie could see stars twinkling through the open window. His brain was foggy from so much beer. He tried not to think of the pain in his arms and legs.

They would be back soon. They promised.

Charlie started to black out.

As his eyelids shut, he saw a tremendous hand, like a claw, reach into the car and grab his chest. *It must be the paramedics*, he thought dreamily. But where were the flashing lights? There were no ambulance lights. No sound. No sirens.

He could feel his rescuers pulling him out of the car. He looked at them through blurring eyes that couldn't focus. Their hands felt like talons. Their distorted faces looked like a horror movie monster peering in at him.

This is going to be a fucked-up dream, Charlie told himself as he slid back towards sleep.

He let out one last breath as his flesh was torn off his body.

CHAPTER 5

APRIL 4
THURSDAY, 11:55 PM

It was almost midnight in Ashford. Billy McGrath walked alone down the middle of Main Street, weaving. He needed fresh air, cold air. He needed it to infuse his body and needed it to clear his head.

Hands deep in his pockets, Billy squinted against the wind and the cold. His eyes watered and glistening tears froze at the corners of his eyelids. His brain ached from his wife's yelling.

Christ. They'd been married two months and she was already bitching at him. Tonight it was about how much time he spent playing video games. Billy decided that instead of yelling back, he would go for a walk. Because if he didn't get out of the house, he might throw something at her. And that something might be heavy. And it might be his fist.

Ashford was empty. It always was after nine o'clock. The town's traffic lights had switched over to blinking yellow caution mode. No green, no red.

Everything was closed, including the town's three restaurants and four fast food places. Even the convenience store shut down at 10:30, belying a promise to be open from seven to eleven.

Nothing in town moved. Nothing but shadows that danced a two-step as yellow traffic lights flashed in a blaring throb of silence.

Billy wanted to see if the door to the store was unlocked—he could use another beer, even if he had to steal it. Barely anyone locked their doors in Ashford. Not like over in the village of Morris. People in Morris supposedly triple-locked their doors at sundown. And they stayed inside till after sunrise.

Billy didn't know why he was thinking about Morris. But it took his mind off the beer. He decided not to rob the convenience store.

He'd heard that Morris people didn't trust anybody from outside their town. They were snooty, anti-social, and paranoid.

Maybe you could only understand Morris if you lived there, he said to himself.

Still and all, nobody in Ashford cared about what went on in Morris. Billy certainly didn't.

That was about to change.

There was a car accident in Morris tonight. A bad one. The car was sitting wrecked in a field, radiator still steaming. It wouldn't be discovered until tomorrow morning.

There had been three boys in the car. What remained of them wouldn't be found until much later.

Billy McGrath didn't know about the accident.

He walked to the end of Main Street and turned down Salisbury Road. That was where all the hardware stores and lumber sheds were. Big yards with chicken wire fences encircling pipes, bricks, and concrete sacks stacked high on palettes. He walked past them, away from the town center and deeper into the darkness.

Salisbury Road dead-ended into barren lots and scrub bushes. It was a flat expanse of nothing—an abyss.

Off in the distance were houses. All dark. Not even the wraith flicker of TV lights.

Billy gazed into the blackness. He thought he'd be able to see the lights of his house from here. He couldn't.

Resting a moment, he leaned against the chicken wire fence. His head began to lighten, as if toxin was seeping out of it. He could feel it. The walk was doing him good.

Something growled.

Cocking his head, Billy heard gravel rattling on the far side of the empty lot. He squinted and peered. It sounded like a dog tramping around one of the contractor sheds.

The noise it made was strange, though. A little creepy. It was a hollow grunt, a snarl.

Billy walked on, more slowly. His thoughts returned to more important things. "Goddamned wife, man, she's driving me nuts . . ."

He watched his steaming breath as it wisped out against the black sky. He tried to blow smoke rings that vanished too quickly.

The odd noise came again.

Louder.

This time it echoed. Like several low voices murmuring. Wariness crept into his head. One dog was fine, but more could be a problem. He'd once seen a pack of wild dogs tear up a full-grown elk while he was hunting . . .

He heard clumps of gravel skittering across the ground. Moving towards him.

Billy caught his breath, and it trailed away in a truncated puff of air. *Freakin' dog*, he thought to himself, trying to calm down. If he had to, he knew he could run back up the street and get up over a fence. Hopefully, it wasn't a wolf or a coyote. That would suck.

The growling noise was louder and closer. He heard something else in the grunting now, something wet. Dripping.

Billy started walking backwards. He eased toward the pulsing light of the intersection and the false safety of the deserted storefronts.

He tried to imagine what was making that noise in the dark.

It sounded bigger than a dog. Much bigger.

Maybe an escaped animal. From a zoo or a circus or something.

The sound. Again.

Grinding.

Closer.

Louder.

The sound swelled around him.

The hair stood up on his neck. The skin on his arms crawled.

A monstrous thing stepped into the street.

It rose over him, blocking the light.

Billy saw his stalker. He whimpered out loud—unable to help himself.

He almost got enough air into his throat to scream.

Almost.

The thing attacked him.

For ten seconds. Twenty. Thirty.

Then Billy was gone.

Forever.

That night, he was the only one who saw exactly what death looked like.

Even those three boys, whose car now sat empty and quiet in a Morris field, hadn't seen the horror coming.

CHAPTER 6
APRIL 5
FRIDAY, 8:06 AM

The ruined Lexus was still hidden in deep grass far off the road at eight o'clock the next morning. That was when Robert Garrahan drove into Morris.

Garrahan had never been to Morris before.

He was getting an early start on his weekend, driving upstate from New York City. Garrahan had a small vacation home in Ashford, the next town up from Morris.

He also had a book he was supposed to be writing. The book wasn't moving forward. This was the third straight Friday he'd taken off work from the *New York Globe*, where he was editor-at-large. That title—and his part ownership of the business—meant he never physically had to be in the office. He could work anyplace he wanted. Days like today were supposed to be days where he chipped away at the book. Instead, Fridays had become little more than unproductive vacation days.

On this Friday morning, his car's gas gauge flashed ominously at him. Christ, he'd forgotten to gas up. He was running on fumes and still had ten miles till Ashford. The turnoff to Morris, little more than a sign with an arrow, beckoned.

As he drove the winding road, Garrahan was struck by how colonial the village of Morris was. A majestic church with a high steeple, another building that looked like town hall, a row of houses curving up over a low hill, and a handful of shops. In the foreground, a much-needed gas station.

Garrahan eased his car into the station. It was a tiny white stuccoed storefront with two pumps outside and automotive parts hanging in the window. More of a house than a traditional gas station. The second story had white lace curtains in the windows—probably where the owner lived. A toolshed sat beside the house with rusting tools and machines of indeterminate vintage leaning up against it.

It was like stepping back in time.

He turned the car off and climbed out, taking his time to stretch and look around. An old couple sat in the window seat of a diner two doors down. Kids laughed over by the church. There was morning frost on the grass in the park across the street.

As he walked towards the station door, a young girl came hurrying out. She was nine or ten and wore overalls and a parka.

"Can I help you?" she asked, eyes squinting in the cold sun. She cocked her head to the side the way that kids do when they hope adults will not want too much from them.

He smiled. "I'd like to get some gas."

She frowned. A little. "That's my job. I'll pump it for you."

Garrahan shrugged. "Okay, thanks."

The girl got the gas going and looked at Garrahan. "We don't get a lot of out-of-towners here," she said.

"Yeah? What do you get?"

"Mostly people from here in Morris, a few from up Ashford way."

"From up Ashford way? You make it sound like it's far away. It's barely ten miles." He smiled again.

She couldn't tell if he was joking. "It is up over the hill, on the other side of the forest."

"It's a lot closer than Manhattan."

"Is that where you're from?" Her curiosity was piqued.

"Yeah, when I'm not hanging out 'up Ashford way.'"

"I've never been to New York City," she said, glumly.

"It's not far. Maybe your parents will take you someday."

"Maybe. We don't travel much." She sighed and shrugged in a single movement. "People here never go anyplace."

Garrahan looked up and down the street. As if to confirm his status as "someone not from around here," he now saw that there were people standing in their front yards. They were trying hard not to look at him. All were failing.

"What's your name?" he asked the girl.

"Abby."

"Nice name."

"Thanks." She pulled the hose from the car and hung it up on the pump. "That'll be fifty-five dollars."

He smiled again. "Your prices are as high as they are in the city. I guess it's not as quaint here as I thought."

She shook her head as he handed her the cash. "It's not quaint. It's boring."

"Boring is all inside your head," he answered. He climbed back into the car and turned the ignition. His radio began blaring, loud and noisy.

Her eyes widened again. "That's a cool song. Is that your player or the radio?"

"Radio. It's the only station you can get from New York this far out."

"Could I get it on my radio in my room?"

"I don't see why not. Here." He grabbed a business card and wrote down the station's call letters. "Tune it in to that number. It'll make you feel like you're in the big city." He put the car in drive. "See you, Abby."

She waved demurely. He drove off.

The people of Morris watched Robert Garrahan drive away.

When he was out of sight, they gathered together to talk about him.

CHAPTER 7
APRIL 7
SUNDAY, 8:45 AM

Garrahan heard the thump of a newspaper landing on his porch. He hadn't paid for the paper in more than a year, and yet the kid still delivered it every Sunday.

Making toast for breakfast, he sat down and perused the paper. He read that Billy McGrath, the local handyman, had disappeared. Without a trace, the paper said. Big surprise there; Garrahan had heard the gossip. At the tender age of twenty-seven, Billy was a barely functioning alcoholic, and had married a certified bitch two months ago. Everyone in town had commented on it. The wife, whom no one ever spoke kindly of, reported Billy missing after he went for a walk Thursday night.

There was a brief article on the death of three boys in Morris. The kids were from Ashford but were driving drunk through Morris after midnight. Their car had hit the concrete barrier the town put up every night. Making it worse, coyotes had gotten to the dead boys during the course of the night. It had been so grisly the coroner serving Morris refused to let the parents see the remains.

Garrahan checked the date of the accident. Same night Billy McGrath disappeared.

All the other crime news was basic small-town stuff. Kids caught throwing rocks at cars from a bridge. Someone hunting without a license. A phone stolen from John DeGarmo's old Buick.

That afternoon, Garrahan went into town to pick up a frozen pizza for dinner. At the market, he saw Mary McNeeney sitting on a stool chatting with Ruth Bihlman. The two women said hello as he put his groceries on the counter.

"Sounds like you had some excitement up here the last few days," he said off-handedly.

"Oh, you mean Billy," Mary said, stating it as a fact.

"Well, yeah, that. He come back yet?"

The women exchanged glances. "No one's heard from him since that night. A'course, no one would blame him, but even his folks haven't heard from him. Gone into thin air."

Garrahan arched an eyebrow. "Really? No word?"

"Not a peep," Ruth said.

"Weird," said Garrahan. "What about the accident over in Morris?"

"Well, that's just teenagers getting into trouble, isn't it? I feel bad for 'em, but they shouldn'a been drinking and driving. And their poor mothers, not even getting to see the bodies before they put 'em in the caskets. Horrible coyotes." Mary McNeeney shivered.

Garrahan looked at the women. "Both things happened the same night."

"Oh, yes," exclaimed Ruth Bihlman. "You know, they say trouble comes in threes, like when famous people die. They always die in threes. I hope nothing else terrible happens."

Mary McNeeney finished bagging Garrahan's groceries and handed them over with a smile. "You be careful, Mr. Garrahan. Don't want you to be the unlucky third."

Garrahan grinned. "I won't be. Nothing exciting ever happens to me."

CHAPTER 8

APRIL 13
SATURDAY, NIGHT

A week went by. The nights were already less chilly.

A woman named Dorothy Flick lay on her front porch swing. Curled up with her knees tucked against her stomach. The calm of the night kept her motionless.

Dorothy shouldn't have been sleeping outside, in the dark. She was too old, and her memory too far gone, for the night to be safe. It was worse because of her dementia. Sometimes she woke up and didn't know where she was. Or who she was.

The night had never been dangerous for Dorothy. She didn't live in Morris where she'd heard they had laws about the night. Rules about staying inside after dark.

Those rules no longer mattered.

Not anymore. Not since the accident.

Dorothy didn't know about the car crash. She had stopped watching TV and listening to the radio a decade ago. She couldn't concentrate—everyone spoke so fast and the stories were too short. She couldn't make sense of them.

Dorothy had intended to go inside and go to bed. That's what she always did. Tonight, she had stared at the sky for a long time. She fell asleep. She didn't mean to.

Her sleep was labored. It was tough to get comfortable on the porch swing. And at eighty-two years old, her breathing sometimes stopped suddenly, yanking her out of even the deepest dreams.

Dorothy had been asleep for several hours—sometimes waking up without even knowing it—when she sat bolt upright in the swinging chair. Something was not right.

At first, she didn't know whose house this was or how she'd gotten there. Confused, she peered into the emptiness of her unfamiliar backyard. She knew something or someone was out there. It had made a noise to wake her out of sleep. Snapped a low branch perhaps or kicked a stone along the path.

Maybe it was her son, Dorothy thought. No, she realized. He had died a long time ago. Years ago. She shook her head. Maybe the neighbors were coming to visit. She didn't remember inviting them. And it was so late. If they were coming over now, they were being rude.

Suddenly, the sound was close. Right near the porch. And still Dorothy couldn't see it. If only she could turn on the light.

Switch on the light. Of course. That was easy. She stood up to do just that.

Dorothy was slammed violently to the ground.

It happened so quickly she didn't even cry out. An unexpected sharpness pierced her face and neck, and something stabbed deep in her side and stomach. More than one stab. Many.

She felt herself being lifted up. The colors in her head went from the black of night to bright red. Then a bright orange flare splashed through Dorothy's brain.

In the space of seconds, without uttering a sound, the woman was dead. And dragged away.

CHAPTER 9
APRIL 20
SATURDAY, 9:10 AM

Garrahan made it a point to go to Morris a couple of weeks after his first stop. It appealed to his sense of what an old village should be. Old villages, to Garrahan's mind, being distinctly different from modern villages. Modern villages were places where the inhabitants petitioned Walmart to come in and make their roadside havens a shopping destination for everyone within twenty miles.

Abby was standing at the gas station pump, like she'd never left. As Garrahan pulled in, she smiled.

"Hello, Mr. Garrahan."

He was amused. "You remember me?"

"Sure!"

"I'm impressed," he said. "Especially since I didn't tell you my name."

She grinned wider, a kid outsmarting an adult. "Yeah, but you gave me your business card with the radio station number on it."

He smiled. "So I did. You ever listen to it?"

"Every day. Need some gas?"

"Sure, fill it up." Exactly as he had two weeks before, Garrahan watched the people come out from their homes to populate the idyllic scene—and to look at him. Probably idle curiosity on a Saturday morning. It felt intrusive.

He ignored them. "What songs do you like to listen to on the radio?" he asked her.

"Just about everything," Abby replied, watching the numbers click on the pump.

Garrahan noticed that she glanced up the street every few seconds, eyes darting from the pump to the people in their yards.

A man appeared at the door of the station. He was about Garrahan's age, maybe a little older. He walked over, wiping his hands across his pockets. He addressed Garrahan in an even voice. "Thanks for stopping by my station. Appreciate your business. We don't get . . ."

"Many out-of-towners here. I know," Garrahan said. "Abby told me."

The man nodded. "You're the guy that gave her the name of that radio station in the city."

Uh-oh, here it comes, thought Garrahan. Do a kid a favor, and her father decides that you're messing with his child.

"Yeah. I did. Guess I should've thought a bit more about it first."

Abby's dad smiled. He had all his teeth—which for some reason, Garrahan didn't expect. They were straight and white.

"Nah. Glad you did. Thanks." The man reached over and playfully tugged on Abby's ponytail. "We don't travel much, and things like a decent radio station or a good movie keep a kid from going stir crazy in a place like this." The smile faltered so briefly that Garrahan wasn't sure it actually had. "Stuff like that kept me sane when I was growing up."

Garrahan was relieved. "You grow up here?" Garrahan asked.

The man nodded, looking embarrassed. "Lived my whole life here. My grandfather built this station."

"Wow." Garrahan didn't know what else to say. He'd never known anybody who hadn't moved at least once in their lifetime.

"That's what I think sometimes, too. Wow!" The man laughed. "We're pretty busy, though, so we don't get down to New York or over to Boston as much as we could. Fact is, I don't remember the last time I went down to New York . . ."

"It's still there."

"Yeah, yeah. You're right. No hurry, no worry." His grin turned lopsided. "Well, hey. Thanks again for your business, uh . . ."

"Robert. Robert Garrahan."

"Nice to meet you. I'm Bruce Donahue. You've met Abby." His daughter grinned and pulled herself close.

"I have." Garrahan winked at her. "You've got a good worker there." He got in his car. "Nice meeting you, Bruce. Abby, good to see you again." Garrahan drove off as they waved.

Abby and her dad turned to go into the station.

"See? I told you he seemed like a nice man," Abby said, looking up at her dad.

"Yes, he does." Bruce Donahue nodded. He watched the car as it wound down the road and into the woods. His neighbors edged back into their homes.

"If he's a smart man, he won't come back."

CHAPTER 10
APRIL 27
SATURDAY, 9:15 AM

Garrahan did come back. A week later, he stopped at the gas station in Morris, dust skittering behind his wheels as he pulled in next to the pump. He liked this new routine.

He clambered out of his car, expecting Abby to walk out.

She didn't come.

He waited a second. And another. Still, she didn't come out. Neither did her father.

Strange, he thought. *They were always right there, ready to work.*

Nothing.

He thought he should honk his horn, but that would be rude. He walked towards the front door of the station.

A weather-beaten man, maybe in his late sixties, stepped quickly through the door. He wore the de rigueur coveralls and baseball cap of a garage mechanic. They were spotless. He looked like somebody pretending to work at a gas station rather than someone who actually worked there. Like a dress-up version.

The man wiped his lily-white hands on a spotless rag. "Help you?" he asked with a bright smile.

"Uh, yeah. I need some gas." Garrahan glanced around.

"Looking for something?" the man asked.

"There's a girl that works here. Her father owns this place. I expected to see her."

"Can't help you there," the man said, jamming the nozzle into Garrahan's car. "I just started coupla days ago. Don't know nobody here from before."

"You know the owner, right?" Garrahan asked.

"Yeah, I met him. Old man Pienazak. He came down from East Janesville to give me the keys. Showed me how to work the register."

"Pienazak? No, no." Garrahan shook his head. "No. The Donahues. Bruce Donahue. He owns this place. His family has for a long time."

"Donahue? Don't think so. But . . . wait a minute. I saw his name on some receipts I found in a drawer. He must've sold to Pienazak. Old man has eight or nine stations from here to New Hampshire."

"So you don't know the Donahues?"

"Can't say as I do."

"Aren't you from around here?" Garrahan asked suspiciously.

"Family is," the man said. Without missing a beat. "I been living in Mercer for the last twelve years. Helping my sister take care of her son. She's all alone, and the kid is hydrocephalic. I haven't been around much." He attempted a grin. It looked like he was physically forcing it on his face.

The man topped off the tank and holstered the nozzle. With nothing left to say, Garrahan paid him and got back into the car.

This isn't right, Garrahan thought.

Something happened here.

He shrugged. *It's none of my business. People move all the time. They didn't owe me a change-of-address card.*

His tires squealed as he pulled out of the station. The attendant, whose name was Earl Pittsley, watched him go.

In a room above the gas station, Abby Donahue's mother scratched at the window as Robert Garrahan drove away.

She cried into her hands.

She missed her daughter and husband.

She wanted them back.

CHAPTER 11
APRIL 28
SUNDAY, 5:17 PM

Garrahan spent a restless weekend. He wondered if Abby and her dad were the newest additions to the list of people who had gone missing around Morris.

Sunday evening, on the way back to New York, Garrahan stopped at the gas station to see who was there. He couldn't help himself. He wanted the nefarious small-town thoughts to stop skittering around his brain.

Please don't let it be the old guy again, he thought. *Let it be someone else. Anyone else.*

It wasn't anyone else.

The crusty guy walked out, rubbing his clean hands with an even cleaner towel. Garrahan made up an excuse for his return.

"Car's been leaking oil. I want to add a quart before I drive to the city."

The man looked at him with the same plastered grin he'd had on Friday. "Coulda gotten it cheaper up in Ashford."

The remark surprised Garrahan. And how did this prick know he was up in Ashford? "I didn't think of it in Ashford." Garrahan said, letting his irritation show. "Are you going to sell me some oil, or do I have to go back to Ashford?"

The man spread his hands wide. "Just trying to help the customer get the best deal. Like Santa in 'Miracle on 34th Street.'"

"I'll take two quarts." Garrahan smiled tightly.

"Comin' right up."

Garrahan looked around, hoping to see Abby or her dad or any other face. No one.

He completed the transaction and drove off without a thank you. As far as Garrahan was concerned, he wasn't stopping in Morris for gas anymore. Its quaintness had evaporated in the patina of a fake smile and poor customer service.

He watched Morris disappear in his rearview mirror.

CHAPTER 12

APRIL 28
SUNDAY, 5:25 PM

Above the station, Elizabeth Donahue lay on her bed, dreaming of her daughter and husband. She was too drugged to rouse herself when she heard Garrahan's voice outside. She wanted to run downstairs and into the street after his car, beg him to stop. Beg him to help.

She couldn't do that. Not during the day. Everyone would see her.

She could go outside after dark if she wanted. They'd let her do that. No one in their right mind went out after dark. Ever.

But she might have to. For Bruce. For Abby.

She stared out the window until sunset. As the purple sky draped itself over the forest, she pulled the shutters closed.

And bolted them.

CHAPTER 13

APRIL 29
MONDAY, 10:45 AM

Garrahan sat in his office on Monday morning, writing his column for the *New York Globe*. The door was closed, and he was trying to concentrate.

He gazed out the window of his tenth-floor office. The cars below skittered and scampered around each other in a never-ending game of hopscotch.

Nancy Hempel threw open the door and strode into his office. Without knocking. Garrahan hated that. It didn't matter that they were in a relationship; she was supposed to knock like everybody else. If Garrahan's mother worked here, he would make her knock.

The problem was that he liked Nancy a great deal. More than he had expected to.

"So, we on for lunch?" she asked, leaning so far over his desk that his nose almost disappeared into her cleavage.

"Nance, how many times have I asked you to knock when the door is closed?"

"Maybe a thousand times. I keep forgetting." She was unrepentant.

"Or you just don't care."

"It's your stupid quirk." She said it with a pout. He found that maddening. Also endearing.

"Well, it's my quirk and it's my office. I'm serious. It drives me nuts when you—or anyone else—barges in . . ."

"Okay, okay," Nancy said, waving him off. "I'm sorry already." The pout got bigger. "Are we having lunch or not?"

They were back where they started. He had lost again. She wasn't ever going to knock when his door was closed.

"Yes. We are. How about one o'clock?"

"Fine. See you downstairs. Did you make reservations anywhere?"

"No. Did you?"

She rolled her eyes. "You said last night you would pick a place."

Garrahan whirled his chair around to his computer. "I didn't. Go ahead and pick someplace. Anyplace." He was tuning out.

Nancy knew Garrahan was already back in his column. "I'll make reservations at Burger King, then. Okay? Table for two?"

Garrahan peered at the screen. "Uh-huh. Perfect. Sounds great. See you then."

Nancy walked out of the office. She left the door open behind her. On purpose.

He hated that.

She flashed a smile at him as she walked down the hall.

At lunch, Garrahan was more distracted than usual. "What are you thinking about, Robert?" Nancy asked, pointing her fork at him.

"Nothing, really. My column. The fact that I need a haircut. Getting a security system for the place in Ashford. A traffic accident over in Morris. A little of everything."

"Jeez. You need to focus. And why do you need a security system for the house? Nothing ever happens up there."

"I know. But this past month, some kids got killed in a car wreck. Supposedly coyotes got them. Plus, a guy who lives in town is missing. And I told you the gas station family in Morris moved out after being there forever." He paused. "I think I should have an alarm. This weekend felt kind of creepy." He stared at his untouched food. "Maybe I'm getting old and nervous."

Nancy picked at her pasta, skating it around the dish with her fork. "You should get rid of that place. It's in the middle of nowhere. You might as well have a weekend place in Malaysia for how far away it is."

"That's exactly the point."

"I know, but still. You're not getting anything done up there, are you?" Nancy asked, gently. "Think about it. How many chapters have you written?"

He didn't want to answer, in part because she had a point. Garrahan had been working on his book about New York architecture for three years. A small publisher was interested in it but wanted to see the finished manuscript. He didn't tell the publisher he was only a quarter of the way through it.

"Besides," she prodded "Wouldn't you be more inspired if you were actually around architecture while you were writing about it?"

Nancy didn't understand. Garrahan needed to get away on the weekends. The city and the newspaper and the insistent pace crowded his thoughts during the week. He needed the silence to decompress.

Her point was valid, though. The drive was getting to him, little events were annoying him, and the new gas station guy in Morris had pissed him off. Maybe he should rid himself of the house.

When he got to the office, Garrahan decided to put the events in Ashford out of his mind. He walked into the maze of cubicles and poked his head into Dave Vanukoff's space.

Vanukoff was the Globe's suburban reporter, primarily for crime reporting. Garrahan was Vanukoff's boss, although he never seemed able to boss Vanukoff around.

He expected to find Vanukoff working on his next post. Instead, Vanukoff was looking at a swimsuit pictorial on his computer screen.

"Hate to disturb you, Dave," Garrahan said softly.

His presence didn't faze Vanukoff, who continued to peer at the photos. "What can I do for you, Robert?" he asked, adjusting his glasses with his forefinger.

"I've got a story I'd like you to check on."

Vanukoff tore his gaze away. "What kind of a story?"

"A few strange events upstate. Sort of a human interest in a small-town thing."

"Yeah, what sort of strange events?"

"A couple of disappearances, a car crash, that kind of thing."

"Doesn't sound like much."

Garrahan knew that. "Nothing ever happens up there, so it could be interesting."

Vanukoff shrugged. "'Up there' meaning where?"

"Do you know where Morris and Ashford are?"

"Not without a map."

"They're a couple of little villages right around where New York, Vermont, and Massachusetts meet."

Vanukoff winced. "Crap, Robert. Do you think you could send me any farther away?"

Garrahan smiled. "Not without a plane ticket."

"Grand. Any deadline on this?"

Garrahan hesitated. He didn't want to appear overanxious. This was more a scouting mission to ease his own mind than a real city newspaper story. "Um, how about end of next week?"

"Okay. Anything else?"

"That should do it for now."

"Great. See ya." Vanukoff pushed his glasses back up his nose and returned to the bodies on his screen.

CHAPTER 14

MAY 3
FRIDAY, 1:56 PM

Four days later, Vanukoff knocked on Garrahan's office door. Garrahan looked up to see him slouching against the doorframe, tablet in hand.

"You're lucky you caught me in," Garrahan said. "I was going to work from home today."

Vanukoff smirked. "The joys of running an online establishment."

"Not sure I would call it joy," Garrahan responded. "What's up?"

"I went to Ashford."

"That was fast." Garrahan was ready for a revelation. "And?"

"There's no story."

"What do you mean, "no story?"

"Just what I said. No story.

"How can there be no story?"

"Because there isn't." Vanukoff looked at his tablet. "You've got a car accident. Three drunk kids die when their car hits a historical marker. In the middle of a field, no less. They get picked over by coyotes in an area known for its wild animals. The local doctor recommends that the families not look at the remains. To spare them the pain."

Garrahan grimaced. "I heard the parents were pretty upset about that decision."

Vanukoff arched his eyebrows. "Did the doctor make the right call? Maybe yes. Maybe no. But there's nothing sinister about it."

"I thought the boys hit a road barrier, near the highway. You said it was a marker?"

"Yeah. They were driving in a field. Apparently so drunk they thought they were still on the road. They hit a historical marker. A small monument or something."

"A historical marker in the middle of the field? That's strange."

Vanukoff sighed. "I didn't put it there, Robert. Maybe it's a war monument or a gravesite. I'm just telling you what I found out."

"Seems a little weird, that's all . . ."

"Fine. It's weird. Can I continue?" Vanukoff asked. "Next, you've got a missing husband. This guy Billy McGrath. He married a ballbuster. Even her own father doesn't like her. Nobody blames the guy for taking off. Almost everyone expects he'll show up in a few weeks. Speculation is he's down in Florida fishing and getting drunk. That's where he's originally from."

"But . . ."

Vanukoff held up his hand. "Not finished. As for the old lady, Dorothy Flick. She was eighty-two years old. She has, or had, Alzheimer's. She also had some form of Parkinson's. She should not have been living alone, but her son and daughter in Boston wouldn't put her in a care facility. So she shuffled around town. Picked up at least twice in the last year by the cops while walking through a cornfield in her bathrobe—once while carrying a broken toaster. As far as anyone knows, she up and walked away and got lost. If she doesn't turn up alive, she'll certainly turn up dead. She might have wandered into a field or the woods and just died. Nobody's surprised that she's gone. They expected it sooner or later."

"Those are interesting stories."

Vanukoff frowned. "Yes they are, Robert. They are very interesting stories. But only if you happen to live next door to these people. If you live in New York City, they are merely curiosities. A kid falling out of a ninth story window in the Bronx—that's an interesting story. Especially for our site."

Garrahan leaned forward and splayed his fingers on the desk. "I guess there's no story."

"Now you've got it." Vanukoff smirked. "How'd you hear about that stuff, anyway? Those towns are in the middle of fucking nowhere."

"I've got a weekend house there. I've been going up to work on my architecture book." He tried not to sigh. "Last few times, I heard people talking. I thought there might be something to it."

"Well, maybe you ought to get a place closer to the city. Where the real stories are." Vanukoff unslumped from the doorway and shuffled back to his cubicle.

Garrahan decided Vanukoff was right.

CHAPTER 15
MAY 3
FRIDAY, NIGHT

The farmhouse was illuminated by a single outdoor light. It was a solitary sentinel that did nothing for the people sleeping in the house. It provided no warmth, and certainly no protection. The feeble light was barely able to hack through the shadows cloaking the house.

There were four people inside. They breathed deeply, each in their own pattern and rhythm. The parents slept in the one room upstairs. The two children had their small bedrooms on the ground floor. All the windows were open, allowing the barest of cool spring breezes to pass through the rooms.

Something moved towards the lamp post and slapped the light bulb from the night. The tinkling of glass fell to the ground and was gone. The yard became nothingness.

The white siding of the house faded into invisibility. The windows dark rectangular stains. No light emanated from inside.

Two quiet circuits were made around the outside of the house. The location of each of the inhabitants was noted. The smallest child, a boy, was the easiest target. He slept underneath a window on the far side of the house.

The parents' window faced the opposite direction. They would likely hear nothing.

The boy slept fitfully, the rustling of his thin blanket audible outside the window. An involuntary sigh came from his room, perhaps the vestige of a bad dream. It broke the litany of the never-ending cricket chirps and rhythmic frog grunts in the grass.

There was a pause outside the window, to make sure the boy was in the depths of his sleep. It would be terrible if he was to awaken and cry out too soon.

No one in the house moved.

The boy's breathing was heavy again.

It was time.

With violent force, screens were ripped from his window. Strong hands reached into the room and down to the bed. The boy was grabbed, still wrapped in his blanket. He woke up as his body hurtled out through the window. Into the darkness. A guttural shriek cut through the night before the air was choked out of his mouth.

A light went on in the upstairs bedroom. The adults responding to the sound.

They were far too late. Their child had been carried off. Dragged into a blackness that surrounded their house like an impenetrable prison wall.

The boy, who tried to scream as all the sharp things entered and re-entered his chest, would never be seen again.

CHAPTER 16
MAY 4
SATURDAY, 11:40 AM

Garrahan went to Ashford on Saturday morning, determined to write at least twenty pages of his book. He left Nancy in New York after an early breakfast. She wasn't pleased about it, but she understood.

He wrote exactly two pages before he wandered over to the market.

Ruth Bihlman sat behind the counter by herself. Her erstwhile counterpart, Mary McNeeney, had flown to Indiana to visit relatives.

"I read there's a child missing over in Sycamore," Ruth said as Garrahan walked in. Her head nodded knowingly.

"And that's supposed to mean what?" he asked, displaying a trace of irritation. He knew she was only making small town gossip. He knew there was nothing to it, but it was getting to him. These conversations and thoughts wormed uselessly around in his brain, looking for a place to take up residence. It was stupid. Garrahan had had it with Ashford, Morris, and weekend getaways. He had a book to write and a new girlfriend that needed tending to.

"Doesn't mean anything," she replied laconically. "Is what it is."

He bought a carton of juice and left without saying anything else. He drove to his house and looked at his computer. He accepted the fact he was not getting anything done.

He threw the computer into his backpack, locked the doors, and headed to New York. He had made a decision. It was time to sell his place.

Garrahan skimmed along the highway, thinking "I will not drive through Morris. I will not drive through Morris. I will not drive through Morris."

He drove through Morris.

He couldn't help himself. He made the turn off the state road. "One last look, one last time. To see if Abby and her dad came back."

He drove slowly by the gas station. Beyond the station window, he saw Earl Pittsley with his feet on a desk, watching TV. Garrahan, disappointed, kept driving.

He realized he'd never driven past the station into town. Now he found himself gliding up the gently rising hill of Morris's main street. Orderly Victorian houses sat on his left, the village green on his right. The houses were fronted by sloping little lawns that ran to the street, their porches were ringed with flowers.

At the end of the green was the church, its steeple a poking fingernail in the expanse of bright blue sky. It was constructed of stone that had darkened over the years. The church wasn't like the clapboard houses of worship that dotted the northeastern United States like whitewashed stalagmites. It was dark and imposing, even Gothic. Some of the upper stained-glass windows were boarded over. Garrahan saw a chain and lock around the front door.

When he reached the end of the street, he encountered a small nondescript building with a sign on the lawn that said, "House of Prayer." *What a shame*, he thought. *A stunning cathedral in the middle of town, and these people used an Elk's Lodge knockoff for their church.*

He turned the car around and headed back the way he came. He noticed two things.

The first was that all the front doors on the homes were big and metal. No nice wooden doors with glass panels or decorative trim. They looked like blast doors, the kind installed on warehouses.

The second thing was that along the sidewalks in front of the houses were large concrete bowls. They looked like they should cradle sprays of flowers or ornamental planting. But they were empty. Some were cracked, others were chipped along their rims. They were all painted a bright red. Garrahan counted a dozen of them. *Maybe they were for recycling or garbage*, he thought.

He passed the station and glanced in again. Pittsley wasn't there. And the TV was off. In the four minutes that it had taken Garrahan to drive by and turn around, Pittsley had gone.

Garrahan didn't slow down. He kept driving. He was done with this odd little town.

From the window above the station, Earl Pittsley watched Garrahan's car roll by. Elizabeth Donahue sat in a chair in front of Earl, eyes wide, looking out the window.

Earl's manicured hand was wrapped tightly around Elizabeth's mouth. She had no way to scream.

CHAPTER 17
MAY 4
SATURDAY, 3:55 PM

Nancy was curled up on Garrahan's couch when he arrived at his apartment. It was four in the afternoon.

"What are you doing home so early?" she asked, not getting up.

"Couldn't get any work done," he said. "No use wasting time there. Might as well loll around here." He tossed his duffel bag into the closet. "How was your day?" he asked.

"Same old stuff. Spent my time missing you." She smiled. "Hoping you'd come to your senses and come home early."

Garrahan laughed and looked at the wall clock. "You want to go do something? Bike over to the park? Hit a museum? We still haven't seen the Dreyfus show at the Cooper-Hewitt."

"Sounds good. Let's do it."

He nodded and went to change his clothes.

"So, are you getting rid of the Ashford place?" she asked, bending down to lace a sandal. There was no malice in the question. Garrahan bristled just the same.

"I don't think so. Not yet." Then he decided to answer honestly. "Maybe it is too far away."

"I believe I've told you that a time or two," she said, standing up.

"Or a time and a hundred."

"Why couldn't you get any work done?" she asked.

"I don't know. Preoccupied, distracted."

"Distracted? There's nothing up there!"

There was no way she was going to understand his fixation on the idiosyncrasies of Ashford and Morris. Especially the gas station. He didn't understand it himself. It was nearly an obsession. Maybe he was getting compulsive as he aged. Wasn't he washing his hands more lately, too? Jesus, he was getting older—and weirder.

He didn't tell her that. "Lot of stuff on my mind." He looked at the clock again. "Anyway, I'm here now, and we have a few hours of daylight left. Let's go." He grabbed his keys.

"Oh," Nancy said, and pulled up short. "You had a call earlier. I answered it, kind of on instinct." She grinned sheepishly. "I hope you don't mind."

He smiled. "I'd only mind if it was one of my other dates calling." So few people ever used the phone anymore. It was almost old-fashioned.

"That's why I thought I should answer it. To help coordinate your schedule."

Nancy had a wry sense of humor. He truly appreciated it. "Good thing I have you to manage my schedule," he grinned.

She grabbed her jacket and walked to the front door. Garrahan followed her, keys jangling.

"By the way, who was it that called?" he asked, locking the door behind them.

Nancy shrugged. "No one I knew. A man named Bruce Donahue."

CHAPTER 18
MAY 4
SATURDAY, 4:00 PM

As each day of Spring passed, the sun pounded with greater ferocity through Elizabeth Donahue's windows. She had lost track of time. She had no sense of how long Bruce and Abby had been gone. Maybe a few weeks. Maybe a month. All she knew was that they were still gone.

Edward Malden sat next to her, as he did every day. It was part of his job to be here.

Malden was the town's minister, a position that also made him the town's equivalent of assemblyman, selectman, and mayor. More than that, he was the protector of the town. Keeper of its secrets.

A tall, gaunt man, Malden leaned his angular face into Elizabeth's. He began his daily ritual, asking the question. Over and over.

"Where did Bruce go, Elizabeth? Where did he take Abby?"

Elizabeth didn't know.

So she couldn't answer.

Elizabeth believed she would die in this room. In this house that sheltered her husband's family for generations. This house that had reinforced metal bracing on all the doors and windows. This house that had protected her family when the sun went down.

It was a good house. It had the scars, the gouged wood, and the teeth marks across its outer face to prove it. This house had been her family's sanctuary.

Now she was its prisoner.

Edward Malden was her jailer. He whispered in her ear.

He told Elizabeth he would soon be her executioner.

CHAPTER 19
MAY 4
SATURDAY, 4:22 PM

"What did Bruce want?" Garrahan asked Nancy. He wanted to hear every word Donahue had uttered.

She answered by not answering. "Who is he? I've never heard you talk about him."

"Oh, he's . . . a guy who owns a house near me in Ashford."

There was immediate suspicion in Nancy's voice. "He sounded in a rush," she said.

"Why don't you tell me what he wanted and maybe I can tell you why he was in a rush." The beginning of a standoff.

"He didn't say. He said he was in New York. He'd like to see you if you were available."

"Did he say when?"

"Tomorrow."

"Did he say where?" This was like Twenty Questions, only more annoying.

"At your office."

"Did he leave a number?"

"He didn't."

"Hmmmm . . . " Garrahan dropped into silence. She should have gotten the number.

What could Bruce Donahue want from him? Tips on touring New York City?

"So what does he want?" Nancy pried.

"I have no idea," he answered.

By Sunday night, he'd put it out of his mind.

CHAPTER 20
MAY 6
MONDAY, 11:03 AM

The phone rang in Garrahan's office at a minute past 11 AM on Monday morning. He was reviewing an abysmally written letter to the editor from a Staten Island congressman.

"Robert Garrahan," he barked.

There was a hesitant silence on the other end. Then, "Mr. Garrahan?"

"Yes. Who is this?"

"Mr. Garrahan, this is Bruce Donahue. We met . . ."

Garrahan sat up, dropping the letter into the waste basket. "Yes, of course. At your gas station. With Abby." Garrahan felt giddy; one mystery in his life was about to be solved.

He could hear relief in Donahue's voice. "You remember. I'm glad." He paused. "I tried to reach you at home this weekend. I hope that's all right."

"No problem." Garrahan got up and closed his door. "How are things?"

"We decided to move."

"And you're in the city now?"

"Yes, I am." Another pause. "Look, would it be okay if I came and talked to you today?"

It didn't sound like Bruce Donahue wanted touring tips for Manhattan. "Certainly. Anything in particular?"

"I'd rather talk about it in person."

"Come to my office. Do you know where we're located?"

"No. I don't know my way around New York."

Maybe he needed sightseeing recommendations after all. "I'm at One Penn Plaza, the big black building next to Madison Square Garden. 34th Street between 7th and 8th." He looked at the clock on his wall. "How about, say, two o'clock?"

"Thanks, Mr. Garrahan. I'll see you then."

"You know, Bruce, you can call me Robert . . ."

The phone line was already dead.

CHAPTER 21
MAY 6
MONDAY, 2:00 PM

At precisely 2 PM, an intern led Bruce Donahue to the door of Garrahan's office. Donahue stood stiffly with a baseball cap rolled up in his hands.

"Welcome," said Garrahan, extending his hand."

Donahue shook it. He sat down in a chair facing Garrahan's desk.

"Thanks for seeing me, Mr. Garrahan."

"It's Robert. My pleasure." He paused. "How's Abby?"

Bruce frowned, creating lines in his forehead. "That's kind of why I wanted to talk to you."

"Really?" Garrahan leaned forward. "Is she okay?"

"Yes. No. I mean, there's a problem that, well . . . Abby and I have a problem, and I wanted to ask you something." His looked out the window towards the Statue of Liberty and the shore of New Jersey.

"What kind of problem?"

Bruce shifted in his seat. "I'm not sure where to start. I've never talked about this before." Again his gaze drifted away. "No one ever has."

"Talked about what?" Garrahan's interest ratcheted up.

"What happens in Morris." Donahue's hands were shaking.

"And what is that?"

A stifling pause. "There are things . . . things that go on, things that we do . . . that that . . ." Donahue stuttered like a guilty kid.

"Look, Bruce, if . . ."

"No, it's okay. I need to tell someone. I can't talk to anyone in Morris." He made a low giggling noise. An odd sound for a man to make. "You're the only person I know outside of Morris."

"Me?" Garrahan cocked an eyebrow. "You've never talked to anyone outside of Morris? What about in other towns? What about . . ."

"I've never been outside of Morris," Donahue blurted out.

"Ever?" Garrahan was surprised.

"Ever. We're not allowed to . . . I mean, we're not supposed to leave."

Garrahan couldn't believe that. "What do you mean, not allowed?"

"Look," Donahue put his cap on Garrahan's desk. "Morris is an old town. One of the oldest in the country. Our families have lived up there for hundreds of years, and we never leave. We can't. If anyone left, they would destroy their friends. The ones who stay."

Garrahan shook his head. "You're losing me. You're here now, so obviously you could leave."

Bruce shook his head. "No, no. I snuck out. At dawn. A few weeks ago. I had to. I had to get away with Abby."

"Get away where? Is she here?"

"She's at the hotel. At the Lowell."

"You left her there alone?"

"I had to. I couldn't risk anybody seeing her while I came here."

Garrahan stood up. This was starting to sound more sinister than interesting. Donahue was on the run.

Garrahan ran his hand through his hair. The online edition of The Globe had to get posted in the next three hours. Time to cut to the chase.

"I have to say that you're not making much sense."

Bruce's eyes closed. He took a deep breath. "I know." His eyes popped open. "Listen to me. Please. We have a ritual. It goes back almost forever."

He struggled with his words as if he didn't want to say them—but couldn't stop himself. He looked like a man who wished he had the option of cutting his own throat rather than admit the things he had been part of.

"And part of . . . that ritual . . . is a . . . a . . ."

"A what?"

Bruce spoke quietly. "A sacrifice."

Garrahan's eyes narrowed. "A sacrifice to what?"

"I can't explain it. It's, um, it's like . . ." Again Bruce turned to the window.

"Like what?" Garrahan resisted the urge to drum his fingers on the desk.

Bruce locked his gaze on a boat crawling up the Hudson River. "The ritual is . . ." His body sagged. "Look, do you know the Old Testament verses?"

"Not off the top of my head, no." Garrahan answered.

Bruce sighed. "In Morris, our community has always believed in specific tenets of the Bible. Especially those in Book of Job and Deuteronomy. If you recall verses . . ."

Garrahan interrupted. "I don't know the verses, so we can skip that."

"The thing is, sacrifice is essential to our faith."

"What kind of sacrifice?"

"A sacrifice to remind us of how insignificant man is in God's eyes."

Garrahan suddenly saw Bruce Donahue as a rural man who might not have all his wits about him. In fact, despite having all his teeth, he might be a few fries short of a happy meal.

This is bordering on serious crazy. I'll give him two more minutes. Then he's got to take this show somewhere else.

"I have no idea what you're talking about," he said.

Bruce's chest heaved. The words came out slowly.

"Our faith requires that we show God that we are humbled by him and his creations." His voice dropped so low he was whispering.

"We do it by sacrificing a child."

Garrahan didn't hide his shock. "Wait. Are you talking about the boys in the car accident?"

Bruce nodded. "In a way. We didn't actually . . ."

"Those boys died in a crash. Animals got them."

"No," he replied. "They were killed."

"You don't know that."

Bruce nodded again. "I do." He cleared his throat. "They were killed, but not in the ritual." His head dropped, and it looked like he was going to cry. "They aren't part of our community, our religion. Those boys were in the wrong place at the wrong time. They weren't the ones supposed to die."

"Who was supposed to die?"
Bruce was crying. "My daughter. And her friends."

CHAPTER 22
MAY 6
MONDAY, 2:10 PM

"Say that again." Robert leaned forward against his desk.

"We sacrifice our children," replied Bruce.

"What does that mean?" Garrahan heard a faint buzzing in his brain.

Bruce wiped his mouth with the back of his hand.

"What I said. Sacrifice."

Garrahan's eyes were wide as he shook his head.

"You sacrifice children in Morris? As in, murdering them?" He scoffed without meaning to. "You know that's not believable."

Bruce tightened his grip on his cap. "I know, I know. It's been a secret for a long time. But when the boys in the car were killed . . ."

"You say they were killed. Everyone else says it was drunk kids who hit a stone and got eaten by coyotes." He wanted to say, "Happens every day."

Bruce shook his head. "They weren't eaten by coyotes."

"I read the news, and I had someone check it out. According to the local doctor, it was coyotes."

It was Bruce's turn to scoff. "The doctor is paid by the village council. Of course that's what he's going to say. You think he's going to announce to the world what really happened?"

Garrahan rubbed his eyes. This was like doing an interview for a conspiracy magazine.

"Bruce," he sighed heavily. "I'm having a difficult time with this. I mean, I don't know you. Hell, even the new guy at the gas station said he doesn't know you."

Bruce lurched forward, as if someone had punched him in the back of the skull. "You've been back to Morris?"

"Yes. I stopped a couple times. I asked the new guy if he knew what happened to you. He said that . . ."

Bruce jumped out of his chair. "You asked about us?!?!" he screamed.

Garrahan recoiled. "You weren't there. I was curious."

Donahue's face went red and he covered his mouth with his hand. "They'll know I'm here," he muttered.

"How are they going to know that?"

"Because you asked. They're probably waiting for me . . ." Bruce stopped with a jerk. His face went from red to white so quickly that Garrahan thought it was an illusion.

"Oh my God. Abby," he whispered.

Donahue turned and lurched out of Garrahan's office into the newsroom. Garrahan grabbed his shirt by the sleeve.

"Wait. Slow down. No one is . . ."

"LET ME FUCKING GO!!!" Donahue yelled, ripping his arm away from Garrahan. The news staff turned its collective head towards the editor's office. Garrahan saw the surprised look on their faces, and hesitated. Then he followed Bruce to the elevator.

"Let's talk about this." Garrahan wiped a bead of sweat off his upper lip. For some reason, he was beginning to feel guilty.

"Look, lots of people from out of town must go to your gas station. I'm sure you talked to lots of . . ."

The elevator door opened. Donahue dashed in. "No, no, we never talked to anybody from out of town," he said. "You talked to Abby, and I made sure she didn't say anything she shouldn't. That's why I was always around when you came by. I thought it was good for her, but . . ."

Garrahan slipped in next to Donahue. The elevator door sealed shut.

"Why did you come to see me?" Garrahan asked.

"I was going to ask you to help me find a hiding place for Abby. I've been staying in different places since we left. I didn't know where else to go and I can't keep going."

"Why do you need to hide Abby?"

Donahue fixed his eyes on the changing numbers in the elevator. "When the boys died that night, everything went wrong. The church elders need to make it right. They'll take our daughters and put them out at night until it returns."

Bruce's voice trailed off. He was crying.

"Wouldn't your neighbors stop that?"

A torrent of words gushed from Donahue's mouth. "Are you kidding? My neighbors won't do a thing. We've given our daughters to the town every year for decades. Since before I was born. It's a lottery. Abby wasn't picked on her tenth birthday, so she was safe. But now the council wants to use every girl, even if they were passed over before. They want Abby."

The door opened. Bruce looked around the lobby and pushed through the revolving doors. By the time he got to the sidewalk, he was almost running. Garrahan hurried to keep up.

They weaved through the crowd that clogged 34th Street until they reached Madison Avenue. Bruce, looking confused for a moment, turned left and headed uptown. Garrahan spit out questions that Bruce grunted answers to.

"Did anybody else leave with their daughters?"

"No. Just me."

That was interesting. Bruce is the only person who's out and about telling this story.

"So they've got everybody else. Why do they need Abby?"

"It's not even about Abby now. It's the fact that she and I left. No one is supposed to leave Morris."

"Does someone think you're going to reveal this secret? And that people will actually believe you?"

Bruce turned to him, slowing for a moment. "It's true. As God is my witness. It's all true. Every word." He picked up the pace.

Garrahan rolled his eyes. "Okay, okay. So it's true. And people in Morris are going to do everything they can to stop you from telling anybody. Right?"

"Right. Now you know."

They stopped at the crosswalk that stretched across 42nd Street. They were only a block from the hotel. Taxis passed so close that Bruce was nearly sideswiped. He didn't move; his eyes were focused on the far side of the street.

Garrahan, looking at Bruce's tortured face, had heard enough.

"I'm sorry about this, Bruce. I am. But I don't believe you. I can't. I hope it all works out for you." He turned to go back to his office. Once there, he would call the police. It was obvious that Bruce shouldn't be taking care of Abby right now.

Especially not in New York City, where he was probably more lost than his daughter.

The thought angered him. Garrahan choked it down. "If there is anything else I can do, something more reasonable, you can call me."

"You've done too much," Bruce said, not looking at him. The light changed, and Bruce stepped into the crosswalk.

Garrahan walked away. Behind him, he heard a screech of tires and the dull crunching thud of metal against bone and meat. Followed by screams.

In the instant it took to whirl around, he knew what had happened.

A major intersection at midday, lots of people, a nondescript car.

Bruce Donahue's body lying broken on the grimy pavement.

CHAPTER 23
MAY 6
MONDAY, 2:42 PM

Garrahan's first instinct was to run to Bruce. He took a step forward and stopped suddenly, nearly toppling a woman next to him. A crowd was gathering around Bruce's bloody body. There was no way he had survived.

The car had raced on ahead, darting in and out of traffic. Whoever was driving was moving quickly. Traffic was just heavy enough to provide cover, but not heavy enough to trap the vehicle in a jam. It was out of sight in seconds.

More ominously, it must have been following Bruce. And Garrahan.

People shrieked and jammed their fingers against their phones in a mad dash to request help.

It was fruitless. Bruce was gone. The one who needed help was . . .

Abby.

She was alone in the hotel. Her dad was dead.

Whoever had killed Bruce would want Abby.

And might want Garrahan.

He pushed through the thickening throng and raced up the street. His shoulder smashed into other shoulders as he dashed along the sidewalk. He hit the revolving door at the Lowell with so much force he felt the glass panel give.

Sweating through his shirt and breathing hard, he yanked a house phone off the counter.

"Bruce Donahue's room, please."

"Thank you. I'll connect you."

Please let her answer the phone, he thought. *Don't let her be . . .*

"Hello?" It was Abby.

He took a deep breath. "Abby, hi. It's Robert Garrahan. Your dad just came over to my office . . ."

"Hi, Mr. Garrahan. How are you? You'll never guess which radio stations I've been listening to since we got here."

He tried to keep calm. "You're right. I'll never guess. But you'll have a chance to tell me. I'm in the lobby. Come on down."

"Great! Are you with my dad?"

Oh shit. How to deal with this? "Yes. I mean, no. He's at my office. He didn't know his way around, so I said I'd come get you. What floor are you on?"

"The sixth. Room 623."

"Can you come down really, really fast? Like, on the stairs? Do you know where they are? They're faster than the elevator."

"Sure, I'll be right down. Should I bring a key?"

"Um, yes. That's a good idea. But hurry. Fast as you can."

"Okay." She slammed the phone down.

The concierge was staring at him. Garrahan realized he was sopping wet from his run. He straightened up and walked to the entrance, looking for anyone else racing to get into the hotel.

"Hey, Mr. Garrahan!" Abby's voice echoed across the marble lobby. She must have leapt all the way down from the sixth floor.

"Hey, Abby!" he said, looking around furtively, feeling exposed. "How are you?" He stuck out his hand to shake hers, but she hugged him around the waist.

"I'm great," she exclaimed. "New York is really cool."

"Yes, it is. We need to see more of it. Right away. Let's go."

He steered her from the main lobby towards the hotel restaurant. He took her hand and guided her through the tables towards the restaurant's entrance. It opened to the far side of the building.

"We picking up my dad?" Abby gazed up at Garrahan, and then to the buildings towering over her.

"Yep. Let's get a cab. We'll get there faster." They would go to his apartment until he could think this through.

Three cabs passed before one picked them up. He gave the driver his address on the Upper East Side.

Garrahan looked at Abby. She was craning her neck to see the tops of the skyscrapers.

"What's been your favorite part of New York so far?" he asked nervously, needing time to concoct a story.

"All the stores and all the movies on TV. I can't believe it. We don't have any of this stuff up in Morris."

"Not many places have the stuff New York has. It's as different a place as you'll ever visit." He tried to keep his tone flat, hoping she wouldn't hear the fear.

"I think it's great. I wish my friends could come here someday." She frowned, and then resumed her sightseeing.

Garrahan looked at the cabbie, who was busy talking on his phone in some language he would never understand. "Abby, do you know why your dad brought you to New York?" he asked quietly.

"Sure. To tell you about the ritual. And the Behemoth."

Garrahan wasn't sure he heard correctly. "The what?"

She turned to face him in the seat. "The Behemoth. I know I'm not supposed to talk to anybody about it, but my dad said he was going to tell you, so I guess it's okay."

"What's the Behemoth?"

"You know. The creature from the Bible. The monster in the woods."

Garrahan racked his brain, but it was coming up blank. He didn't know about any monster in the woods. "What do you know about the . . . the Behemoth?" he asked.

"Only what they teach us in Sunday school. That it waits. It feeds. It reminds us."

"Reminds you of what?"

"Of how God is both a loving and terrible God. Of how we must always remember that there is something more important and more powerful than us." She giggled. "This is like the questions on the Bible test."

That was too much. This little girl had been brainwashed, too?

Garrahan wiped the sweat off of his lip. Christ, this is insane. What have I gotten myself into? he wondered. I need to call the police. Maybe I'll turn Abby over to them.

The cab pulled up to his building. "I didn't know they had neighborhoods like this," Abby said, getting out. "I thought it was all just offices and hotels."

"Nope," he smiled, or at least tried. "A million people live here. We're all stacked up like ants in a colony." Abby giggled again.

"Is this where your office is?"

"No, this is where I live. I've got to get some things." His voice cracked ever so slightly.

"What about my dad?" Garrahan heard concern creep into her words.

"We'll get to him. Don't worry." He had no idea how he was going to address that subject with her.

"Okay. I've never been away from him for this long."

"Never?"

"Nope. My mom, neither."

Garrahan had never thought about Abby's mother. He'd assumed she was dead, and that Bruce was raising Abby himself. "Um, your mom? Where is your mom?"

"She's in Morris."

That's a relief, he thought, the air rushing out of his nostrils. At least there was a relative he could contact. "Why isn't she with you?"

Abby looked at him quizzically. "She had to stay behind while we escaped. Didn't my dad tell you that?"

"No, no he didn't."

"Did he tell you we have to go back and save her?"

"No. He didn't tell me that either. Save her from who?"

She stared at him. Her eyes moistened with a child's fear. Her lip quivered.

"I'd really like to talk to my dad now, okay?"

CHAPTER 24
MAY 6
MONDAY, 6:50 PM

Garrahan sat on the couch in his apartment, his elbows perched on his knees, hands and fingers tracing through his hair. In the next room, Abby's choking sobs were loud enough to hear through the closed door.

He didn't want to listen to Abby. Or look at Nancy.

It had not gone well with Abby.

The two of them had lunch and watched some TV. He tried to tell her about her father's accident as gently as possible. The little girl had broken down completely. Garrahan had no experience with situations like this. Not only did he not deal with children very often, he'd never seen anybody get killed before. He had to try to explain that reality to a child.

While Abby was sobbing into the pillow in the bedroom, he called Nancy. She showed up in twenty minutes. Garrahan told her the whole story.

"I don't believe I'm hearing this!" Nancy said, trying not to shout. "These words are actually coming out of your mouth!"

She flung her arms wide like a giant bird and then planted her hands on her hips. "Do you realize how bizarre this sounds?" she asked, her voice quietly shrill.

Yes, it sounded bizarre. He knew that. There was no way he could make Bruce Donahue's story believable.

"Look," Nancy continued "if he was killed by a hit and run driver . . ."

"Nance, there's no disputing that he was killed. I saw that."

"Regardless, I'm sure the police are already on it. They've probably contacted his family and are looking for this girl." She pointed to the bedroom with a shaky finger. "You've got to call the police and tell them you have Abby."

"If I do that, I think she will die," he said softly.

"How do you know that!?" Nancy asked plaintively. "All you know is that this girl's father was run down, and she has a mother in Morris. You need to take her to the police!"

He sighed, heavily. "I don't know if I have a choice."

"You're right, you don't have a choice! Call the police."

Returning her to Morris seemed like a bad idea. That's what the police would do.

Abby's crying grew quieter in the next room. Garrahan thought she might be trying to listen to them.

"We'll let her decide," he said.

"She's ten years old, for God's sake! She can't make a rational decision about this!" Nancy was beginning to fume. "You . . . you . . . you aren't making any sense!" Her hands came off her hips and covered her face. It made her look afraid. "Are you going to hide her forever?"

Robert shook his head. "I don't know what I'm going to do. We need to talk to her about it."

She sat down in a chair. "You have to rethink this," she said softly. "This is a little girl's life . . ."

He nodded as his thoughts raced. What if someone was looking for Abby? What if someone was looking for him?

There was suddenly a strange quiet as Abby came through the door of the bedroom. Her face was wet and red. She was forcing herself to stand up straight. She didn't look at Garrahan or Nancy. She looked at the floor.

"I have . . . to go . . . to my mom," Abby said, her voice lurching in sobs over the syllables.

Nancy arched her eyebrows at Robert, as if to say, "What did I tell you?"

Garrahan stood up and walked to Abby. "Are you sure?"

She didn't reply.

"Abby?"

"If I stay here, they'll find me, and they'll find you. They'll hurt all of us, like they hurt my dad." Tears rolled down her cheeks. "When they get me, I want to be with my mom. She and I will go together."

Nancy leaned towards her. "Go where together, Abby?" Garrahan was surprised at how gentle Nancy sounded.

Abby looked Nancy hard in the eyes. Suddenly she looked very grown up, a weary maturity masking her ten years. "We'll go to the forest. And we'll wait."

Nancy knew where this was going and didn't want to follow it. Garrahan did.

"They'll make you go, won't they?" he asked.

"Yes, and they'll lock all the doors in town so we can't get back inside." She wiped her nose. "Then we'll be gone, like all the others." She began to cry, loudly. "I thought I would never have to go." Abby blurted the words out. "I didn't get picked! It's not fair! I'm not supposed to have to go!"

Nancy was puzzled. "What do you mean, 'picked'?"

Garrahan scowled at her. "The lottery for girls. I told you."

"Oh, uh. Yes, right." Nancy nodded, frowning. "What if we call your mother first?" she suggested.

"My daddy tried. They won't let her come to the phone."

"Maybe they'll let her talk to someone who's not your daddy." Nancy shifted her gaze to Garrahan.

"You think they're going to let her to talk to me?" he exclaimed, throwing up his hands.

"Don't tell them it's you. Pretend you're from the phone company or a survey group or something. Try selling them credit cards. Just see if you can get her mom on the phone." Nancy shrugged. "We should contact her. The police certainly will."

"Fine," said Garrahan, defeated. He walked to the phone. "Abby, do you mind if I try?"

She shook her head.

"I need the number. Do you know it?"

Abby recited it slowly, and Robert punched the digits on his phone. After two rings, a man answered. "Yes?"

Garrahan cleared his throat. "Yes. I'd like to speak to uh . . . Mrs. Donahue?" He hadn't thought this out enough; he should've gotten her first name from Abby.

"May I tell her who's calling?" the man asked.

"Yes. This is a promotional call from American Express."

The man was abrupt. "She's not available right now. Try back later."

The line went dead in Garrahan's ear.

CHAPTER 25
MAY 6
MONDAY, 7:30 PM

Abby started crying again and went back into the bedroom.

"What are you going to do? Hide her here?" Nancy asked, her voice quavering nervously.

Garrahan shook his head. "I'll take her to her mother in Morris. But I've got to figure out how."

"You think they'll hurt a little girl?" Nancy asked.

"They killed her father, for Christ's sake. He told me they sacrifice a girl every year. I can't ignore that completely since he got killed immediately after telling me."

"All because they worship a monster from the Bible?"

"There is no monster." He rubbed his eyes. "It's a cover for something else. Has to be." He paused, trying to tie his thoughts together. "People there are hiding something. Who knows what it is? Maybe they're abusing kids. Maybe the whole town is a meth lab. I don't have any fucking idea. I do think they are capable of hurting Abby. And her mom." He stared at the ceiling. "Maybe I can get her mom out of there."

"Call the police."

He shook his head. "No. If this has been happening for years, the Morris police must be in on it."

Nancy let out a loud sigh. "This isn't a government conspiracy, Robert. Abby's mother is in a little house in a little town a few hours away. That's the story. How horrible could it be?"

CHAPTER 26

MAY 6
MONDAY, 8:00 PM

The broken tooth skyline of the Bronx jutted up around them as Garrahan drove north on the Bruckner Expressway. It was like driving out of a slavering mouth. The evening traffic was thick, like congealing sludge.

Abby sat in the front seat, her head leaning against the window. Her eyes were glazed. She rarely blinked.

"Do you want to get anything to eat?" he asked.

"No. Thank you."

"We could wait and do this tomorrow," he ventured. That's what Nancy had suggested before he and Abby drove off, leaving her alone in the apartment. He wished Nancy was with them now.

Abby shook her head, barely moving it from where it was pressed against the window. "I should go back tonight. That way, it'll be real quiet. I'll go into the house through the back door. Maybe there won't be a big fuss."

"Who would fuss?"

"Whoever's with my mom. I don't want to attract attention."

"We'll be quiet. It'll be late enough that the neighbors shouldn't hear us.

"I don't care about the neighbors. I care about the Behemoth."

"Why are you worried about the Behemoth? It's a creature from the Bible. From thousands of years ago."

She shrugged. "Maybe. But since it got out, it hasn't been in Morris. I should be okay." He could feel her shudder through the fabric of the seat. "At least for tonight."

Garrahan rolled his eyes. She was as hard to understand as her father. "What do you mean, since it got out?"

Abby turned to him. Her eyebrows creased. "I don't want to sound mean," she said darkly, "but didn't my dad explain anything to you?"

Robert felt embarrassed. "He told me a little. Not very much."

"But he was going to ask for your help. He should have told you all this."

How was Garrahan going to tell Abby that he had shut her father up by saying he didn't believe any of this story? That Bruce had stormed out without getting the chance to explain? "Most of our conversation was about your safety. He wanted to get back to you."

She looked at him suspiciously. He peered through the windshield, trying not to notice.

"It doesn't matter anyway," she said, her head rolling to the window.

"Yes it does," he said. "I need to know what I'm taking you to."

I also need to know what I'm getting into, he thought to himself. He couldn't drop her off on a corner and then slink away.

She sighed. "What do you want me to tell you?"

"Everything you know."

Abby knew a lot. About the Behemoth. About the ritual. About the five dead priests and the stone markers in the field.

She told it well, like a well-rehearsed actor.

Garrahan almost believed her.

Almost.

CHAPTER 27
MAY 6
MONDAY, 8:20 PM

As Garrahan and Abby drove towards Morris, Leonard Smeak was sitting at the Donahue's dinner table. He was listening, impatiently, to Ethan Landrieux recount his adventure in New York City.

Ethan had gotten lucky: he'd tracked Bruce for two days and ran him down at a crosswalk. A remarkable bit of good fortune.

Edward Malden had been supremely unhappy with Ethan for not finding the Donahue girl. Malden was sending Leonard and Ethan back to New York to find her.

Leonard was one of a select few people in Morris who could be trusted to take trips like this. Ethan was another, but he had inherited the honor: his great-great grandfather had single-handedly buried five dead priests all those many years ago. The night those priests died had been a defining moment for the town.

Leonard came by his privilege personally, although one might say it was part of a birthright as well. It was Leonard, like his father before him, who took the girls out to the forest every year. He left them there for the ritual. And if he touched the girls a few times before he chained them up, well, it wasn't like they were ever going to tell on him.

The fact that Edward Malden was thinking about sending Elizabeth Donahue out to the forest especially interested Leonard. He'd never taken a grown woman out there, and Elizabeth was a looker—even if she was a pain-in-the-ass bitch. He kept himself from grinning while thinking about it.

"Mr. Malden says we have to go back right away," Ethan said. "There's no telling where Abby might go. Or if this Garrahan guy is hiding her."

Leonard took a long drink from his glass of milk, wiped his mouth with a napkin, and pushed his plate to the middle of the table. He ran his hand over his smooth head, which he shaved twice a day. It resembled a shiny hollow-point bullet. "Go upstairs and tell old bag Bower to listen for the phone. Then let's ride."

Later in the night, Leonard and Ethan drove past Garrahan and Abby on opposite sides of the highway, neither aware of the other's presence.

CHAPTER 28
MAY 6
MONDAY, 11:49 PM

It was nearly midnight when Garrahan turned his car off the highway and crept towards Morris, easing around the concrete night barriers. In front of him, the village was small and dark. The streetlights were off. There was only the occasional glimmer of light through cracked shutters.

It looked fake, like a set for a model railroad.

Garrahan turned off the headlights, driving blindly in the dark. He hoped to God he didn't hit anything or drive off the road.

He looked at Abby. In the light of the dashboard instruments, her face was a pale green, her eyes wet and neon-colored.

"Turn left before the gas station," she said softly, as if worried someone else might hear.

They had agreed to go into her house through the back door to avoid attracting attention. Abby was sure that the neighbors would be asleep, but Garrahan wanted to make as little noise as possible.

He could hear the car's tires crunch over the gravel in the back alley, sounding like firecrackers. He was more nervous than he thought he would be.

His original plan to leave her at the door had gone out the window as he listened to her sobs on the trip up. He decided there was no harm driving Abby and her mom out of town. This new plan required details he didn't like, especially if someone else was inside with Elizabeth.

The car stopped behind the Donahue's house. Abby and Garrahan got out quickly, shutting the doors quietly. He stood next to her, barely able to see the outline of her face, and put his hand on her shoulder. She was more ready to do this than he was, he realized.

"I'm okay," she said without being asked. "Are you?"

"Not really," he whispered, trying to be funny. "But I'm ready."

"Okay," she answered. "Remember, after you go in, the first door on the right . . ."

". . . on top of the cabinet. Got it," he said. The part of the plan he didn't like.

They tiptoed to the back door. The world was empty around them—no sounds, no lights, no movement. Clear, crisp blackness. When they reached the steps, Abby stooped down in the dark, dipping her hand into an empty flowerpot. She extracted a house key.

Garrahan couldn't see Abby in the shadows, and she was right next to him. He imagined that this was what it was like to be legally blind. He heard the key click against the doorknob as she searched for the lock. When she turned the bolt, Garrahan thought the whole town could hear it.

A thin breath of air escaped from Abby's mouth. She pulled the door, its weather stripping hissing as it scraped against the steps.

They were in.

A nightlight from the end of the hall silhouetted Abby. A tiny bulb that threw everything into relief. She touched Garrahan's arm, gently guiding him to a room on the right. This was her part of the plan.

Garrahan took two steps into total darkness. He reached his hands out in front of him, moving in baby steps. His fingers, trembling from fear, searched for something solid. He was now truly scared.

Behind him in the hall, he could hear Abby breathe. There was no sound from his own lungs; he was holding his breath.

His hands bumped the wall, and his fingers crept eagerly against it like a pair of lost spiders. His fingertips traced along a high shelf. Everything was exactly as Abby had described it.

Garrahan touched some boxes. Laundry detergent. He gently slid them sideways, a few millimeters at a time. He walked his fingers to the back of the shelf, feeling blindly for something that wasn't wood or cardboard. Something hard, metallic.

The gun.

His fingers touched the barrel and pinched it. He tugged it towards the edge of the shelf, past the soap boxes. His other hand joined in, steadying the shelf and the gun until he pulled it down.

Garrahan let out his breath.

He couldn't see the gun in his hand, but it was heavy and cold. He didn't dare check the chamber to see if it was loaded, for fear that its metallic rasp would wake whoever might be in the house.

Garrahan went into the hall. He could see Abby in the nightlight. She walked towards the stairs.

He was committed. He had promised Abby that if they found her dad's gun, he would help her confront anyone who was in the house . . . even though he wanted to run screaming back to his car and drive towards the safety of New York.

He kept his hand on her shoulder and crouched down, trying to keep himself behind her tiny frame. She led as they walked into the living room where the nightlight was. They circled left up the stairs.

Abby's first step on the bare wood resounded like a rifle shot. The creak from her weight made Garrahan jump, and he brought the gun up quickly in front of him. His fear made it shake.

He counted each step as they moved quickly upwards. There were twelve. Each creaked a little less as they got to the top.

Abby made a right at the top. She moved swiftly into what she told Garrahan would be her parents' room. He followed on tiptoe.

His eyes had adjusted to the timid glow of yellow light from the downstairs nightlight. He could make out the shape of a woman lying in bed. Abby immediately huddled over her, as if attempting to cover the woman with her body. The bedsprings rocked slightly. He heard Abby whisper. "Mom. Mom. Wake up. It's me. Please wake up."

Garrahan walked to the shuttered window and looked through a slat. He could see the street and the gas pumps of the station immediately below him. Nothing else. Everything beyond was swallowed up in darkness.

Abby touched him and he nearly smashed into the window out of fright.

"My mom won't wake up," she said, her voice trembling.

He wanted to ask, "Is she alive?" and thought better of it. He went to the bed and leaned down to Abby's mother. Her breathing was deep—she was alive. He shook her gently, then harder, trying to wake her without making any noise. She didn't move. Maybe she was drugged.

"Fuck this," he whispered, suddenly wishing he hadn't said it. Abby was standing next to him. "I'll carry her," he whispered.

He put the gun on the bed near Elizabeth Donahue's feet. He reached under her neck and knees to hoist her up. He was going to dispense with niceties and toss her over his shoulder so they could get out of there fast. No need to do the superhero thing and carry her out in his arms like a damsel in distress. A solid fireman's carry would do. He started to lift her.

The lamp next to the bed flared on.

A sharp jab of light ripped at his eyes, and he recoiled.

He went from blind to blinded. He dropped Mrs. Donahue back on the bed.

Abby choke backed something. A scream, a cry.

Someone beyond the light screamed at him.

"What do you think you're doing?!?!"

CHAPTER 29
MAY 7
TUESDAY, 12:13 AM

The voice screeched again, angrier.

"Answer me, Abby! What do you think you're doing?"

Abby stammered. "I, um, I . . ."

"Well?"

"I just, um, decided to come home."

"In the middle of the night? Sneaking up the stairs?"

"Please, Mrs. Bower. I wanted to see my mom."

Garrahan could barely see through his squinting eyes. A stocky woman was blocking the door. She had a very long knife in her hand. He guessed that was for him if the occasion arose.

"You scared me half to death coming up here like that, Abby," the woman said harshly.

"I'm sorry."

"And who is this man?" Mrs. Bower hissed, pointing the knife at Garrahan. "He has no business here." She looked quickly back over her shoulder, down the stairs. "Where is your father?" she asked.

"He's dead, ma'am," Abby said, her voice steady.

Garrahan could see the woman falter, apparently not wanting to believe what she heard. "No, child. That can't be. They would never . . ." Her words faded out.

Garrahan didn't wait to hear the rest. Pivoting, he grabbed the gun. He took two steps forward and pointed it at Mrs. Bower's mouth. In the same instant, he pushed Abby away.

He was, admittedly, scared shitless.

"You shut the fuck up, whoever you are, or I will blow your head through the wall." The words came out of his mouth so forcefully that Garrahan thought his throat had ripped. He didn't know where the words came from; certainly he'd never used them before. He imagined they were from a movie.

Mrs. Bower dropped the knife and brought her arms up to her face.

"No, no, no . . . please!" she begged, dropping to her knees.

Garrahan took another step forward, slid the knife back with his foot, and pushed the woman's head down with the gun. Just like in the fucking movies.

"Mr. Garrahan, don't. She's . . ." Abby blurted.

"Don't worry, Abby. This'll be fine."

Mrs. Bower tried to cover her head.

Garrahan pushed the gun hard against the woman's skull. "I don't want a word out of you. Do you understand?" he barked. Bower nodded and began sobbing. "I will kill you if you make a single sound." He backed up to the bed. Breathing hard.

"Get the knife, Abby. If she moves, stab her."

Abby looked at him in pain.

"It's her or your mom," he said.

He walked to the far side of the bed and hiked Elizabeth Donahue over his shoulder. She was bony and didn't weigh much under her nightgown. He pointed the gun again. "You first, Mrs. Bower. Abby, follow her down. We'll go out the way we came in, and we'll go fast."

Mrs. Bower got to her feet. Slowly. She shuffled down the stairs. Abby walked stiffly, clutching the knife close to her chest.

Outside, Mrs. Bower looked around anxiously, stopping to listen. The street was quiet, and the town was quieter still. There weren't even any insect sounds to fill the emptiness of the night. Abby pushed past her to the car.

"Move it," Garrahan demanded. Mrs. Bower stepped towards the car, walking as if she might get attacked at any moment. It wasn't Garrahan she was afraid of. Her head swiveled back and forth, like waiting for a car to come and hit her.

"Take the gun, Abby," Garrahan said. Handing it to her, he tried to delicately ease Abby's mom into the rear seat. In the dark, the delicate part didn't work so well.

"You," he said to Mrs. Bower, "get in the back. Abby, in the front. Give me the gun and use the knife. If you have to."

"What are you going to do with me?" Mrs. Bower asked.

"I'm going to take you down the road until we're out of town, and I'll let you go."

"Outside? In the night?!?!" She choked on a shriek.

"Of course, outside."

"I can't . . ." She started crying.

"Shut up and get in the car."

Abby tugged at his sleeve. "We can't leave her outside. The Behemoth might get her."

Robert was incredulous. "Nothing is going to get her. And she might scream loud enough that someone could chase us."

In the dark, he could see Abby's head and hair flip side to side. "No one will chase us. Not this late." She looked up the alley. "No one has opened their shutters. They'll leave us alone."

"Then she's going with us. We'll drop her someplace safe along the road if you want."

He grabbed Mrs. Bower's shoulder and pushed her into the car. Abby climbed into the front and sat on her knees, facing her mother and the older woman. Garrahan jumped in and screeched backwards out of the alley.

Out in the middle of the street, he felt foolish for an instant, as if getting ready for a car chase that was only happening in his mind. The town was as silent as when they had driven up—he looked at the clock on the dashboard—eight minutes ago. Seemed like forever.

He sped out of Morris with his foot pressed against the accelerator. He saw no lights and heard no sounds. Nothing.

After getting onto the highway, he pulled over to the shoulder of the road. Vehicles sped past them. He turned to Mrs. Bower. She sat motionless in the backseat. He could see her face from the lights of passing cars.

"Give me one good reason why I shouldn't make you get out right here," Robert said, holding the gun on top of the seat.

"Because I could die," Mrs. Bower said. "And I don't deserve to." She started crying, a sound that turned into a keening shriek.

"That's going to be annoying," Garrahan muttered.

He drove for half an hour towards New York City. Finding an all-night truck stop, he made Mrs. Bower get out. How she got home from there was her own business.

An hour later, Garrahan pulled into a rest area. There, he and Abby—and Elizabeth Donahue—slept through the night in his car.

CHAPTER 30

MAY 7
TUESDAY, 7:49 AM

Garrahan woke slowly. He opened his eyes, trying to estimate the time without moving. The sun was already warm. *Maybe seven o'clock*, he thought.

He turned to look at Abby and her mother in the backseat. Abby sat, wide awake and eyes wide open, looking at Garrahan. She cradled her mother's head in her lap.

"Are you okay?" he whispered.

"I think so," Abby whispered back.

"Has your mom woken up at all?"

"No. But I think she's okay."

"Good."

Garrahan looked at his watch. It was a few minutes before eight o'clock. Christ, it had been less than twenty-four hours since Bruce Donahue had been in his office. In that time, he'd left New York, barreled up to Morris, and was already returning to the city.

"Where are we going?" Abby asked.

Garrahan hesitated. "I don't know. I haven't thought that far ahead." He rubbed his hands across his face.

Mrs. Donahue stirred. Abby patted her mother's head, and Robert saw Elizabeth's eyelids flutter. The woman tried to roll over in the cramped space of the car.

"Do you want me to tell her, you know, about everything that's happened?" Garrahan asked gently.

Abby shook her head. "I better do it. She doesn't know you."

Garrahan felt a twinge of hurt at Abby's words. *She may not know me*, he thought, *but I may have just saved her life.*

The pettiness of that thought embarrassed him.

Mrs. Donahue stretched, and her eyes opened. For an instant, she stared around. Garrahan saw slow confusion in her eyes. Her head jerked up, as if that would help her to take in her surroundings. Then she saw her daughter's face.

"Abby!" she shouted and pulled the girl towards her. She hugged Abby greedily, her body heaving with sobs as she cooed over her daughter.

Again, Garrahan felt embarrassment. This time because he was intruding. He turned to look out the window.

In a moment, he heard Mrs. Donahue's voice. "Where are we, honey? And where's your father?"

It was time for Garrahan to leave this part of the story to Abby. Time to exit. He looked back at Mrs. Donahue. "Um, hello. I'm Robert Garrahan. I've been helping Abby out for, um, the last few hours."

Mrs. Donahue's eyes narrowed. "Yes, I remember your name. Abby had it on a business card. Her radio card."

Garrahan smiled. "Yes, that's right." The radio card. That really was a long time ago.

"Anyway," he continued "You and Abby need to talk for a while. I'll give you some time alone." He grabbed the door handle. "I'm going for a walk. I won't be far."

With another smile at Abby, he climbed out of the car and walked to a group of deserted picnic benches. The air was cool, and the sound of traffic rushed over him. He sat down and watched the highway. Occasionally, he glanced back at the two people who had become his charges.

.

CHAPTER 31
MAY 7
TUESDAY, 8:01 AM

Garrahan could see Abby gesturing with her hands, and her mom gesturing back. From this distance, he couldn't hear any sound coming from the car. The constant din of eighteen wheelers was a pummeling roar that drowned out everything.

After twenty minutes, he began to get fidgety. He got up and walked around.

Abby and her mother talked for a half hour, and then got out of the car. Mrs. Donahue moved slowly and brushed tears away. Garrahan walked over to them.

"Thank you," Elizabeth said. "I appreciate what you've done." Her eyes were wet.

"You're welcome," Garrahan replied. He didn't have anything else to say.

"We can't go back," Abby said, taking her mother's hand and looking at Garrahan. For a moment, it was hard to tell which was mother and which was child.

"Okay . . ." he replied, letting the word drag out. "Where do you want to go?" He was uneasy about what the answer might be.

Elizabeth shook her head. "We don't know. We've never been out of Morris."

This admission was as strange coming from her as it was from her late husband.

"We weren't supposed to leave. We didn't." Elizabeth said, her eyes clearing.

"So I've heard."

"What have you heard?" she asked, her head tilting.

"Only what I heard from Bruce and Abby." He held her gaze.

"Hard to believe?" she asked, pursing her lips.

"Yes it is," he nodded.

"Do you believe it?" Her eyes were piercing. "Any of it?"

He looked at Abby and tried not to wince. He was thinking of things that the "monster" could be a disguise for.

"No. I don't."

Elizabeth pulled the blanket tight around her shoulders. "That's okay. We don't expect outsiders to believe." She looked at her daughter and sighed. "Would you be opposed to taking us to New York? We'll make our own way once we're there."

Garrahan stared at them. His original plan was to take them to the nearest police station and be done with it. Instead, he nodded.

They climbed into the car. No one spoke as they merged onto the highway.

Once he was cruising at a comfortable speed, he dialed his phone. He called the office and listened to a message from Dave Vanukoff. He transferred to Vanukoff's line.

"Jesus, Robert, where are you?" Vanukoff hissed, his voice a harsh whisper.

"I'm working out of the office."

"That's not what I mean. Where are you geographically? There were three state troopers in here looking for you. They wanted to talk about that guy in your office yesterday."

Garrahan's hand slid off the steering wheel. He caught himself and grabbed the wheel tighter. "What about it?"

"I don't know. They wouldn't tell me anything. They asked about the guy and said something about his wife and daughter being kidnapped. He was in a hit and run. It's a fucking soap opera. They want to hear what you know about it."

"I don't know anything about it," Garrahan said dryly. How the Hell had word about the Donahues already made it to the cops? Somebody was spreading news with incredible speed.

"I'm sure you don't. They said the kidnapped girl was from Morris, and her mother went missing last night. After her husband died yesterday. Coincidentally, you happen to be out of the office today. Also coincidentally, you asked me to look into stuff going on in Morris just a few . . ."

"It is a coincidence." There was no conviction in Garrahan's voice.

"I'll pretend to believe that, even though it can't be true." The accusation hung without malice.

"Is Nancy around?" Garrahan asked.

"No. The troopers talked to her, and she left. She was pretty rattled." He paused. "What does she know about this?"

"Nothing," Garrahan lied. "I'm going to call her."

"You coming in?"

"Maybe tomorrow."

Vanukoff cleared his throat. "Not that this means anything, but here's an interesting update. After the cops came in, I searched for any weird shit I could find about Morris. Not the stories you wanted—other stuff."

"And?"

"I found references to the town founder, Clifford Morris, going back a few hundred years. There was a writ for him back in England to stand trial on a variety of charges—fraud and piracy among them."

"What does that have to do with anything?"

"Not sure. But it could tie in with something else. Your little town of Ashford once had a nasty reputation for slavery. Right up into the 1920s."

Garrahan sighed. "Most towns in America had slavery at one time or other."

"Yeah, but Ashton's problem wasn't garden variety slavery—it was also kidnapping. A group of businessmen kidnapped little girls, usually Native Americans, and shipped them to Europe as slaves." He let that sink it. "And since the talk this morning in law enforcement circles was about a kidnapping..."

"That's Ashford. It's not Morris."

Vanukoff scoffed loudly. "Like town boundaries up there make a difference? There were reports as recently as the 1980s of kids being abducted for..."

Garrahan interrupted. "Look, I've got to go." Vanukoff's story made a strange kind of sense.

"Fine by me. Can I do anything?" Vanukoff asked.

"No. I'll call the cops and tell them what's going on." Garrahan felt pain in his skull.

"Whatever you say." Vanukoff hung up.

CHAPTER 32
MAY 7
TUESDAY, 9:25 AM

Elizabeth stared out the car window in silence for half an hour. The hills and farmland had given way to suburbs and houses with attached garages. Abby was asleep.

Garrahan watched Elizabeth in the rearview mirror.

"How are you doing?" he asked quietly.

Her voice was soft. "Fine. I guess." She stroked Abby's hair.

"Can I ask you a question?"

"Of course," she replied, turning her eyes to him in the rearview.

"Abby told me a story about the Behemoth. A creature from the Bible. Why do you and your church tell her such things?"

"About the Behemoth?

"Yes."

"Because the story is true."

"You mean it's true if you have faith that it's true?"

She shook her head. "Listen, I'm not a religious person. I don't need faith to believe in the Behemoth. It exists." She held his look in the mirror. "You cannot say that about any other religious artifacts. The Holy Grail, The Ten Commandments."

"The Behemoth is a religious artifact?" Robert asked.

"Icon might be a better term."

"You're not religious? Every single thing I've heard over the last twenty-four hours has only been about religion."

She let her gaze wander across the horizon as she considered her response. "Religion was different for me. My mother wasn't from Morris. She was born in Easton. Her father—my grandfather—was a grain purchaser. He took her on trips to Morris for the corn auctions. It's one of the few times during the year that outsiders go to Morris and mingle with the people. It's always tightly controlled. At one of the auctions my mother met my father, who was a born-and-bred resident of Morris. They saw each other in Morris over the course of a few years. Eventually, my father asked her to marry him. Surprisingly, she said yes. It meant her moving to Morris and becoming part of an isolated community. It also meant leaving her own family behind. But she was in love. So she bought into everything. Lock, stock and barrel."

"Including the stuff about the rituals and the Behemoth?"

"Certainly. But she had experience in the real world. She knew that other places were not like Morris. She taught me that."

"If your mother knew all this, why didn't she leave?"

"Why should she? She married a wonderful man, my father. She had a child—me—and had a nice life. There was no reason to leave." Garrahan saw something dark pass briefly over Elizabeth's eyes: a sinking of her brow, a slitting of her eyes. "Plus, people are encouraged to stay in Morris."

"You mean they aren't allowed to leave."

Elizabeth shrugged. "That's a reasonably accurate statement, yes."

"You see things differently than Bruce does." He didn't want to say, "than Bruce did."

"I have a bigger world view."

"Then why didn't you run away with Abby? Why Bruce? You better understood what it's like out here."

That look again on her face. "I've always been considered my mother's daughter in Morris. She was one of the few outsiders allowed to marry and move into town. Every few years someone does marry in—it keeps the gene pool safe to swim in, if you get my meaning." She laughed bitterly.

"Up until she died, people viewed her with suspicion. That suspicion still applies to me, even after all these years. Bruce and I decided when it was time to take Abby away—after the council decided to round up girls—that he would go.

"If I had gone, townspeople would have considered it inevitable, that I was going back to the world from which my mother had come. They would have chased after me in minutes once they noticed I wasn't around.

"But if Bruce left . . . well, that was unthinkable. His family has been in Morris for hundreds of years. People might have thought he was out in the fields, or down in the basement working on the gas pumping equipment. They would believe anything except him running away. I covered for Bruce for three days before they went after him."

Tears welled up. "Now he's dead."

She brought her eyes to Garrahan. "You were the only person he'd ever spent any time talking to who didn't live in Morris. A contact with the outside world. I don't know what he expected. We didn't have time to plan anything. All we wanted was for Abby to be safe."

"What about you? What was supposed to happen to you?" asked Garrahan.

"We never got a chance to talk it through." She blinked back a tear. "I didn't think they'd kill Bruce. I thought maybe I'd be locked in the house, and he and Abby would be someplace far away and safe . . ." Elizabeth slumped against the door.

"If we had made a plan," she said, choking up, "none of this would be going according to it."

CHAPTER 33
MAY 7
TUESDAY, 9:30 AM

Leonard and Ethan arrived in New York before dawn. Leonard wanted to check out Garrahan's apartment later in the morning, when Garrahan should be at work. Or possibly be home, hiding the girl.

They had a few hours to kill. Leonard found a strip club to occupy their time. Ethan almost asked Leonard if they could go to the American Museum of Natural History. He desperately wanted to see the dinosaur skeletons he had seen in books, but he knew Leonard would make fun of him. Plus, Leonard had a reputation as a gabber. He would probably snitch and say something to Malden.

As the morning rush hour wound down, they drove to Robert Garrahan's apartment, parking at the end of a long row of brownstones. Leonard got out, sizing up the people nearby. He strolled down the sidewalk with his hands in his pockets, whistling nonchalantly. Ethan kept up, trying to hide his nervousness.

At the entrance to Garrahan's building, Leonard motioned for Ethan to sit on the steps. They made small talk until a young man came out of the building, and Leonard—smooth as a shadow—caught the lobby door before it closed. Ethan was impressed. For a weird old guy, Leonard was slick.

They checked Garrahan's name on the lobby mailbox and walked the three flights to his floor. They knocked on the door, not expecting him to be there, but making sure . . . just in case.

Leonard rapped on the door several times. After a moment, it rattled slightly from the inside. Ethan's eyes bulged. A woman called out, startling them both.

"Yes? Who's there?"

Leonard cleared his throat. "Hi, we're looking for Robert. Robert Garrahan?"

The voice from inside. "He's not here. Can I take a message?

Leonard shook his head vigorously. "Uh, no. We'll just come back."

He tugged on Ethan's sleeve and dragged him down the hall. When they got to the stairs, they heard the door open behind them. A young woman appeared at Garrahan's door, leaning out into the hall.

"Hey!" she yelled. "What do you guys want with Robert?" Leonard started to walk towards her.

"We want to ask him some questions," he said, lazily.

She straightened up in the doorway. "Does this have anything to do with what's happening in Morris?" She asked it hesitantly.

"Why, yes it does," Leonard replied.

Ethan, not moving, watched the two of them. Sweat broke out on his face like hives.

"Has he told you about it?" asked Leonard.

As the bald man walked towards her, Nancy became immediately uncomfortable.

"A little bit. Not much," she said, her voice faltering.

This guy was rough looking and too—what was the word?—weathered to be a cop. She wrapped her hand around the doorknob. "I told the state troopers what I knew this morning."

She began to move back into the apartment.

"Wait . . . who are you?" Her eyes went wide, and she thought—ever so quickly—about Bruce Donahue getting run down. Getting murdered.

"You're the ones looking for Abby . . ." she breathed.

Without a sound, Leonard reached inside his coat pocket.

To Ethan, it looked like Leonard was getting ready to toss something to the woman.

A gun appeared in his outstretched hand.

The piercing *whumpf* of the silencer discharge caught both Nancy and Ethan by surprise. Ethan jumped . . . and Nancy fell. She was bleeding from above her eye.

Before her body hit the floor, Leonard was pushing Nancy into the apartment. Soundlessly, Ethan rushed in and closed the door.

Leonard dragged Nancy into the living room. He dropped her unceremoniously on the floor. Her head thudded dully.

Ethan's mouth was dry. "Is there anybody else in here?" he worried.

"How the fuck should I know?" Leonard asked, stepping over Nancy and striding into the bedroom. "You've been with me the entire time. Figure it out for yourself."

Ethan looked in the bathroom, in the shower, in the hall closet. No one.

He looked down at the woman. Her head was framed in a near-perfect circle of expanding blood. Leonard came out of the bedroom. He tapped her breast with his shoe.

"Really no choice here, right Ethan?" Leonard asked, a statement of fact. His grin twisted into a leer. "She saw us. She could identify us in the future."

Something ugly in that look, Ethan thought. He'd heard things about Leonard. Nothing you could ever ask him about.

"Right," Ethan said, nodding. "She knew too much. That's the answer, right?"

Leonard nodded. "You are a quick learner, my boy." He gazed down at Nancy.

"We need to get out of here. Like right now," said Ethan, his stomach queasy just looking at Leonard's face. "She said she talked to the cops, and who knows when somebody might show up." He glanced towards the door. "So let's go."

"Yeah," Leonard nodded, too slowly. "In a minute."

"Come on, Leonard. Now. We don't know if anybody else saw us."

"Nobody saw us."

The older man traced his foot down the length of the woman's torso. With the top of his shoe he slid her shirt up above her waist. All the while, blood sluiced out in an ever-widening crimson halo from her face.

Ethan's sweat covered his face. "This is crap, Leonard. She wasn't supposed to be part of this. We need to find Garrahan and the Donahues." He didn't like the idea of getting caught in this apartment. He also didn't like the idea of what Leonard was doing.

Leonard barely looked at him from the corner of his glinting eyes. "Don't fuck with me right now, Ethan." His foot rubbed up against the dead woman's bra as he unzipped his pants. "Got it?"

·

·

CHAPTER 34
MAY 7
TUESDAY, 9:45 AM

"Why are you helping us?"

Garrahan didn't have an answer to Elizabeth's question.

"Sometimes things happen," was the response that his gut shoved into his brain, although not to his mouth. Somebody had to help. That unlucky somebody was him.

"It seems like the right thing to do."

This did not feel real. It was a twisted version of a big drunken road trip, no plans and no directions. A lost weekend that would peter out when everybody was sober—and ready to go home. The things he was doing right now couldn't be real. Not when they included talking about a monster.

He closed his eyes tightly, then snapped them open. Unfortunately, it was all real. He and Elizabeth were in a very bad thing together. Her husband was dead, and people in Morris were hiding something. Something they would hurt a girl and her mother over.

"Have you ever seen the creature?" he asked.

"I have," Elizabeth said. "Nearly everyone in town has, at one time or another. Usually as a kid sneaking a glimpse through the shutters or an attic vent." She seemed to be remembering something. "One look was enough to convince us not to do it again."

"Have you seen it as an adult?"

"No. We don't tempt fate as adults. We don't want it to see us."

She'd only seen it as a child? Garrahan noted that.

"What does it look like?"

Elizabeth took a deep breath. "It's indescribable," she said, her words a soft stream of air. "Majestic. Gigantic. It can look into second story windows. Glittering skin. Huge eyes that glow. The teeth . . . the claws . . ." She trailed off.

Garrahan looked at her through squinting eyes. "It sounds like a huge bear."

She made a mocking "*puh*" sound with her lips. Her demeanor changed dramatically. "I know what a bear looks like."

"Maybe something else." Her description also reminded him of the huge dragons he'd seen in Chinatown parades. Monstrous figures wielded in the strobing light of fireworks by men in costume.

He remembered a paper he'd read years ago called the Martinson Paradox. In it, people believed their nightmares happened in real life—they were actual events occurring elsewhere in the world. The people in Morris certainly talked as if they believed their nightmare monster walked amongst them while they slept.

Another idea crept out of his mouth. "Perhaps it's something we think is extinct, but isn't, like a dino . . ."

She squinted at him in the mirror. "I don't mean to be rude, but I know what the Behemoth is. It's not a creature you find in the Encyclopedia Britannica or National Geographic's Guide to Animals. The Behemoth is in the Bible, and is like no animal—I should say, no other being—on Earth." Her eyes bore into his. "And just because we keep to ourselves and don't go to the same church as you doesn't mean we're idiots. We have the internet in Morris, we have video games. Okay?"

He wanted to reply with a defense of his idea—lost species were being discovered all the time—then decided this wasn't a fight he wanted to start.

"Okay," he replied. "I thought that there might . . ."

"Don't treat me, or my family, as if we're crazy or ignorant," she half-spat. "Like we're claiming to see UFOs."

Her stridency made him uncomfortable. She had the confidence and conviction of a preacher proclaiming that the end of the world was imminent. Bruce and Elizabeth both sounded like that. Hellfire preachers. Even Abby had gotten belligerent when she told Garrahan the story.

He'd heard the gossip about Morris, its near-Amish affinity for keeping to itself and spurning outsiders. Yet he'd never heard any tales of any monster. The chats he'd had with the ladies at the grocery, who qualified as professional gadflies, never once alluded to a ritual or a monster.

The only people telling him this story were the Donahues. And they had obviously run afoul of some unpleasant people.

So what the fuck were they really hiding up in Morris?

"Have you ever seen the ritual?" he asked.

She shook her head. "No. It's at night. People stay in their homes when it takes place."

"If you've never seen the ritual, and you haven't seen the Behemoth since you were a child, why won't you consider there might be something else that . . ."

"I told you it is real," she said, her voice rising. "As real as this car."

Her stern words woke Abby. The girl sat up groggily.

"Hey, we're back in New York," Abby exclaimed. "I can see the Empire State Building." She pointed out the window, and Elizabeth's gaze followed her daughter's finger.

Garrahan took the opportunity to change the subject.

"If I wasn't here, what would you do?" he asked her.

"If you weren't here, we wouldn't be here." Elizabeth's voice softened.

"That's not what I mean. If you were on your own."

"We would go far away. Maybe California. Or Oregon."

"Is there a reason for that?"

"There's no reason for anything right now. Except to get as far from Morris as we can. Keep Abby safe."

"Will people from Morris come after you?"

"Most people in Morris are decent. You don't bother them; they don't bother you. But they like their way of life; they believe in it. They'll support Edward Malden and the council. They trust him to keep Morris the way it's always been." She sighed. "He'll send someone after us."

"Who is Edward Malden?" Garrahan asked.

"He is the man entrusted with protecting the Behemoth. He's also the town councilor—like a mayor. He oversees the town's business with outsiders. If there were state troopers at your office this morning, it was his idea to alert them."

"Is he the police chief as well?"

"No, that's Earl Pittsley. Like everyone else employed by the town, Pittsley answers to Edward Malden. What Malden says, goes."

"Why does Malden get to be in charge?"

"His family has been in Morris almost since the beginning. They go back to the second colonial settlement, the one that established the town as it is now. He has duties he inherited when his father died." Elizabeth watched the buildings get taller and thicker as they drove across the Third Avenue Bridge into Manhattan. "It was Malden's idea to take the girls back out to the forest. To lure the Behemoth back."

"Why didn't anybody stand up to him?"

"Why should they?"

"To stop their daughters from dying."

Elizabeth shook her head and smiled. "You still don't get it," she said, her eyes gazing into his. "Since the Behemoth escaped after the car crash, people think it's worth it if their daughters are offered up." She leaned her head back. "They think it's the right way. God's way."

"But you don't."

"I do," she sighed. "But not when it's my daughter."

CHAPTER 35
MAY 7
TUESDAY, 10:00 AM

Garrahan parked in front of a fire hydrant half a block from his apartment. He left the engine on.

"Can you drive this if a cop comes by? So we don't get ticketed or towed?" he asked Elizabeth.

"As long as I don't have to drive around the city."

"Just long enough for me to get a few things. If a cop comes, honk a few times and drive to the end of the block. I'll come right out."

"I can handle that," she grimaced.

"I imagine you can." Garrahan headed up the building stairs.

Elizabeth watched him disappear through the glass doors. She sat rigidly in the driver's seat, hands clenched around the steering wheel. She hadn't driven in over a decade.

As he bounded up the stairs, Garrahan realized he hadn't been to sleep since the night before last. His head was getting light, and his balance was skewing.

He walked down the hall, almost on tiptoe. It felt silly, but he didn't want anyone to hear him. He held his keychain tightly so it wouldn't jingle in his fingers.

If Elizabeth Donahue and Dave Vanukoff were right, somebody was certain to come looking for him. The apartment wouldn't be a safe haven.

His doorknob clicked when he slid the key in, but the bolt wasn't locked. Maybe Nancy was inside. He should have tried calling her again.

Outside, Elizabeth swiveled her head, looking for anything that didn't seem right. Then again, nothing seemed right to her. Not in the city. She didn't know what passed for normal here. There were too many people walking on the sidewalks and cars whizzing by on the crowded street, all barely brushing past the car door. She noted the small stores on the corner behind her—a delicatessen, a laundry, a nail salon, a Chinese restaurant.

There was more activity around the car right this now than there was in Morris during an entire year.

* * *

Garrahan opened the door and slipped into the apartment. Nancy was inside. On the floor.

It took his mind a moment to register what he was seeing.

A misshapen, blood-spattered Nancy, but still Nancy.

Garrahan felt his eyes unfocus, and his legs quivered. He took a half step forward. A half cry, half-strangled scream came out of his mouth. He dropped to his knees. He put his hands on her face.

The sound turned into words. Whispered over and over. "No, no, no, no, no . . ."

* * *

A silver truck squeezed past Garrahan's car, slowing to a stop in front of Elizabeth. It was hard to see clearly through the darkened back window. The driver's bullet-shaped head, rising, seen in silhouette, made her think of Leonard Smeak.

She reached across the seat, frantically grabbed her daughter. "Abby! Wake up! Now!"

* * *

Ethan craned his neck to look out the back window. "That's got to be her. It looks like Elizabeth."

Leonard adjusted his rearview mirror, trying to see. "Are you sure? Can you see the kid?"

Ethan shook his head. "No. I don't see Garrahan, either."

"Maybe he's getting a big surprise upstairs," Leonard smirked. "We'll see how long it takes him to get his ass back down here."

* * *

Garrahan felt like he should retch or throw up or something. That was what a sight like this was supposed to provoke. At least it did in the movies. But he didn't feel sick to his stomach. He felt . . . detached.

Removed. Somewhere else. Drifting.

He was watching his world from a long way away. On a big video screen across a stadium.

He looked at Nancy—without blinking—for a long time.

She was dead. Violated. Gone.

* * *

A taxi pulled up behind the silver truck just as the passenger door was opening. The cabbie leaned on his horn, blasting the man back inside the vehicle. The taxi was joined by a blast from another car, and another. Their horns fused into a deafening cacophony.

The sheer persistence of the noise forced the truck forward, pushing it slowly down the street. The man in the passenger seat got out at the corner.

Elizabeth's head filled with the angry squawking sounds.

"Stop shaking me, Mom. I'm awake," Abby moaned.

"Get out of the car," Elizabeth hissed. "Go to the corner. Run!"

CHAPTER 36
MAY 7
TUESDAY, 10:07 AM

The blood was still wet. It had soaked up into Nancy's clothes, climbing off the floor in defiance of gravity.

Garrahan wanted to pick her up off the ground, to see if she would respond.

He stared at her face and wondered what he was supposed to do. Supposed to feel. Anger, sorrow, loss, fear, pain. Anything.

All he felt was empty. Vacant, like a gutted building.

Outside, a horn started blaring. Then another. And another.

Garrahan stood with a jolt. He moved to the door, eyes still on Nancy. Maybe he should kiss her goodbye. The thought made him feel silly.

She was gone. Gone in a bad way.

He would come back. He had to go now. Quickly. He couldn't stay.

As he squeezed through the door, he wanted to tell Nancy he was sorry. Sorry for everything. Sorry for anything. Whatever she thought Garrahan should be sorry for, he would be sorry for that. She could not tell him what those things were.

Bleating horns propelled him into the hall and down the stairs.

Once outside, he looked down the street. The honking was from a cab tailgating a silver truck inching down the street. Other horns brayed behind it, revelers in an angry parade.

His car was empty.

Abby and Elizabeth were gone. The side door was ajar.

Garrahan whirled madly on the sidewalk, like a merry-go-round. He felt like he had blood on him, on his clothes, on his hands. Could everyone see it?

The honking dissipated as traffic sped up. Garrahan ran to his car, then turned and burst into the deli, a place where he had bought countless cups of morning coffee. He hurried down the tiny crowded aisles.

Abby and Elizabeth stood mute at the back of the store, backs pressed against the misted glass door of the soda refrigerator. Elizabeth's hand was over Abby's mouth.

"They're here," Elizabeth whispered, her eyes wide.

"Where?" asked Garrahan, afraid to turn around.

"They drove by. Leonard and Ethan. They drove down the street."

"Did they see you?"

Elizabeth nodded almost imperceptibly, afraid to admit it. "I think so."

"Shit," Garrahan said, his blood racing. "They're probably coming back around the block. That gives us two minutes—if we're lucky."

He grabbed Abby. "Let's go." They dashed to the car and pulled into the street.

The traffic light was red. They were stuck behind two cars. Garrahan drummed nervously on the steering wheel. "Come on, come on, come on . . ."

He glanced out the rearview, hoping he didn't see anyone speeding towards them. "Keep watch out the back. See if they drive around," he demanded. His heart was pounding so hard he could barely breathe.

Abby and Elizabeth turned, like clockwork dolls, to the rear window.

A young man walked towards their car. He looked like a boy, really. Garrahan barely noticed him.

The light changed. Garrahan tapped the accelerator.

The boy stepped in front of Garrahan's car.

CHAPTER 37
MAY 7
TUESDAY, 10:09 AM

Garrahan barreled past him. He sideswiped the man's hip with the sideview mirror.

"That's Ethan!" yelled Abby.

Ethan didn't know whether to shake his fist or wave.

Garrahan glanced over his shoulder. "Are you sure?"

"Of course!"

He was waiting for us, thought Garrahan. *Trying to block the car. Christ*. They had to get away before the other one came around.

They continued headed uptown, away from the thickest traffic. Garrahan wanted to get out of Manhattan without being followed. He ducked into side streets and glided over the Willis Avenue Bridge into the heart of the Bronx. Unless his pursuers knew the city better than he did, they'd never be able to follow his path. For a half hour, he worked his way north toward Connecticut on the Old Post Road.

Abby and Elizabeth were still looking out the back window.

"We're okay for now," Garrahan said. "You can stop watching."

.

CHAPTER 38
MAY 7
TUESDAY, 11:15 AM

Garrahan drove without speaking, his teeth grinding in the set of his jaw. He stopped in the town of Fairfield long enough to call Dave Vanukoff.

"One of the detectives came back looking for you," said Vanukoff.

"Too bad. I'm not coming in today."

"People are grumbling about what's going on."

"Let them grumble." Garrahan was more worried about what people might find rather than what they might say.

"Is Nancy with you, Robert?" Vanukoff asked.

"No, she's not. Why?" he asked, keeping his voice flat. It physically pained him to deny her death.

"Curious. She hasn't been around all day. We figured she was with you."

"She's not." Garrahan said testily. The lump in his throat broke up. "I haven't had a chance to call her."

"It might be worth . . . hold on. Michelle wants to talk to you."

Vanukoff handed the phone to Garrahan's intern.

"Hi, boss. How's it going?" she asked in her perkiest voice.

"I've been better." He didn't want to think about work. He wanted to get on the road. "What's up?"

"You got a call from a guy who wanted to talk to you. But he wouldn't leave his number."

"It can't be important if he didn't leave his number," Garrahan replied, agitated.

"It's strange. He didn't want you to return his call. He said it was important he initiate the call; he wanted your cell number. I told him I wouldn't give it until I cleared it with you. He said he'd call back to get it."

Someone being a pain in the ass. "Did he leave his name?"

"Yes. Edward Malden."

Garrahan almost bit through his phone.

"If he calls back, give him the number."
"You got it. Have a great day, boss."
That was no longer possible.

CHAPTER 39
MAY 7
TUESDAY, 11:35 AM

The phone rang twenty minutes later. Garrahan pulled to the side of the road. He didn't know what he expected to hear, but he didn't want to drive while he was hearing it.

"Hello?"

"Mr. Garrahan?"

"Yes?"

"My name is Edward Malden. I'd like to speak to you if I may."

"What do you want?"

"I want you to bring the Donahues home."

"They're not interested in 'coming home'," Garrahan replied.

"Nonetheless, we are interested in having them return," Malden said dryly.

Garrahan shook his head. He was speaking politely to a man who might have overseen Nancy's death. Anger worked into his chest. Fuck being nice. He found himself suddenly wanting to hurt this man.

"Listen, Ed—may I call you Ed?—I know what you want. But you need to leave me alone." Garrahan caught Elizabeth's eye. "Leave the Donahues alone, too." Garrahan heard the strange sound of his voice cracking.

"I'll do that," said Malden. "Bring the Donahues back. We'll be done."

"I don't believe you."

"Bring them back," Malden repeated.

"No," said Garrahan hoarsely.

Malden clucked his tongue. "I hoped we could work this out without resorting to any ugliness. But if you . . ."

"Don't threaten me," Garrahan blurted out. "I know you and your people killed my girlfriend."

"Your girlfriend is dead? I'm sorry to hear that." Malden betrayed no surprise.

"You murdered her!"

"I don't know what you're talking about." A pause. "If it's something you want to discuss, though, I'd prefer to do it in person," said Malden.

Garrahan pushed the car door open and walked to the side of the road. Out of hearing distance from Elizabeth and Abby. "That is never going to happen."

Garrahan heard Malden sigh. "Mr. Garrahan, we have one of your home furnishings in our possession. It's a rolled-up carpet, very heavy. It appears to have been recently stained." Malden let the words hang. "It's not something we would normally keep, but you wouldn't want anyone else to take possession of it. I'm sure it has sentimental value."

Garrahan's throat tightened. "I haven't done anything to you," he said, his words faltering. "I've never hurt you or anyone in your town . . ."

"I appreciate the sentiment, but this is bigger than you. Or me, for that matter." Malden cleared his throat. "Right now, you are to Morris what the infidels were to the early Church. You are dangerous. That said, I think we can effect a compromise. One that allows me to protect my community. And allows you to keep your life."

"Forget it. I'm going to the police. First Bruce, now Nancy. The cops will love hearing about you."

"Pardon me, but you're wrong. We've contacted the authorities. They've been to your office. The only reason they haven't been to your apartment is because I haven't called them again. And you know what they'd find there."

"They'd find a woman that you killed," Garrahan spat.

"No, they wouldn't. They'd find a great deal of blood spatter on your wood floors, but that is all. The carpet is gone, as I mentioned. One can only imagine what might be rolled up in it. The blood that remains in your apartment would make you a likely suspect in foul play, what with all this depravity you're engaged in—hit and run accidents, kidnapping a mother and daughter . . ."

"You fucking bastard!" shouted Garrahan, no longer able to control himself. "I can't believe you would . . ."

"Mr. Garrahan, calm down. If you help me, I will help you."

"I'm not helping you with anything."

"If you help me, I give you my word you'll be safe. So will the Donahues."

That stopped Garrahan. Now he was confused.

"Help you how?"

"I won't talk about it on the phone. Only in person."

Garrahan sneered. "I'm not coming to you in Morris. I'm not stupid."

"I don't think you are. Neither am I. Shall we meet in Ashford? Tomorrow, perhaps?"

"What exactly do you want?"

"We can talk via phone all day, Mr. Garrahan. We won't be any closer to achieving our goals. Let's meet at the diner in Ashford, the one on Main Street. At 11 AM."

"Fine. I'm bringing the Donahues."

"I was hoping you would. See you then."

CHAPTER 40

MAY 7
TUESDAY, 11:45 AM

Wandering away from the car, Garrahan thought over what he had just heard.

He pieced together how a conversation with the police would go.

"So, you're reporting what exactly, Mr. Garrahan?"

"The murder of my girlfriend."

"And this took place where?"

"My apartment."

"And how was she killed?"

"She was shot."

"Do you know who did it?"

"People from a village a few hours north. Morris."

"And is there a motive for this killing?"

"Yes. They were trying to find me. They killed her when they came to my apartment."

"You can identify these people?"

"No, I can't."

"But you know who they are?"

"Not by name."

"Why do they want to kill you?"

"Because I talked to a man who had information about illegal activities the Morris townspeople are involved in."

"Who is this man?"

"Bruce Donahue."

"And where is he now?"

"Dead. He was killed here in New York yesterday."

"By whom?"

"A hit and run driver."

"Do you know who the driver was?"

"No."

"And where were you at the time?"

"I was with Bruce."

"Did you report the hit-and-run?"
"No."
"Why not?"
"Because I had to go protect his wife and daughter."
"Did Mr. Donahue ask you to protect them?"
"Not exactly."
"So the wife and daughter came to you?"
"No, I rescued them from their house."
"In Morris?"
"Yes."
"And what illegal activities are taking place up in Morris?"
"I'm not sure how to describe them."
"Try."
"Okay. They're killing children, specifically girls. One a year."
"How do you know this?"
"Bruce Donahue and his wife told me."
"Did the Donahues tell you why they were killing kids?"
"Yes."
"Why are they doing it?"
"As part of a ritual."
"Meaning they are killing girls in a ritualistic fashion?"
"Not exactly."
"Then what is this ritual?"
"I'd rather not say."
"Why not?"
"Because it's absurd."
"Try me."
"They told me the girls are killed by a beast from the Bible."
"The Bible?"
"Yes."
"You've seen this beast?"
"No."
"But you think it's killing kids?"
"No."
"What do you think?"
"I'm not sure."
"Hmmm. Just to be clear: Bruce Donahue told you about a religion that worships a kid-killing monster, correct?"

"Correct."

"And because he talked to you about this religion, people are now trying to kill you?"

"Yes."

"But they killed your girlfriend instead?"

"Yes."

"Over a monster?"

"No. She was in the wrong place at the wrong time."

"But the monster does kill people?"

"From what they say, yes."

"But it didn't kill your girlfriend?"

"No."

"Where is your girlfriend, or her body, right now?"

"I don't know."

At this point, Garrahan couldn't go any further. He cursed into the air—"Fuck, fuck, fuck!"—and hoped the Donahues couldn't hear him inside the car.

It was ludicrous. A basic question-and-answer session wouldn't pass a credibility test. He imagined the cops laughing uproariously at every word he said.

Malden had him in a very small box, locked tight. He had to think his way out of this.

CHAPTER 41
MAY 7
TUESDAY, 4:12 PM

Garrahan couldn't go to Manhattan with the Donahues tonight. He didn't dare go to the Ashford house. People were certain to be waiting for him there.

The three of them checked into a motel near Springfield.

Abby and Elizabeth were nervous about being in a motel. Except for Abby's brief stay in the Lowell Hotel in New York, they had never stayed in a hotel, motel, or inn. They didn't like the idea. As far as Garrahan was concerned, they had no choice. He got a room with two double beds; one for him, the other for the Donahues.

They spent the evening in the room, leaving only to get takeout food next door. The next few hours were spent silently watching the news on TV. At bedtime, they had no toiletries or change of clothes, so they all laid down on top of their beds, staring at the ceiling.

They looked like cadavers in coffins.

Garrahan's body was on autopilot. He'd crisscrossed New England three times in the last twenty-four hours. Manhattan to Morris with Abby last night. Morris back to Manhattan with Abby and her mom a few hours later. Heading back towards Morris now. His head was reeling.

"What do you think Malden wants?" Elizabeth asked in the quiet room.

"I was going to ask you," Garrahan replied, noting a large water stain on the ceiling. "He said we could help each other."

"He's not an evil man," said Elizabeth, propping herself up on one elbow "Even after what has happened. He's doing it because he wants to save his church. He is a man of God."

Garrahan tried not to sound disparaging. "With all due respect, that's bullshit. You've lost a husband and I've lost a girlfriend because of this religion. I'm not a believer. I don't think it's worth dying for."

"True believers argue that their religion is worth dying for."

"I don't want to hear this," Garrahan said, closing his eyes. "Malden is bad, and I expect him to behave badly. I don't trust him. Maybe I can get him to leave us alone. Then everybody can go back to doing what they've always done. Everything will be wonderfully fine after that," he said sarcastically.

"Except it won't," Elizabeth whispered. "Not until he can perform the ritual again."

Garrahan was fed up with that line of discourse. He didn't bother to respond.

The room was saturated with their silence. A few minutes later, the soft breathing of Elizabeth and Abby as they fell into sleep signaled the end of their day.

Garrahan stared at the ceiling, replaying the events of the last two days. He thought about Bruce, Mrs. Bower, the Donahues, and Nancy. Mostly about Nancy.

The reality overwhelmed him. Nancy was dead. Killed because she happened to be his girlfriend. And he had left her on the floor of his apartment.

In the dark, he got up from the bed and walked into the bathroom. He turned on the shower so the Donahues wouldn't hear him.

Then he knelt next to the bathtub, crammed his face into a threadbare white towel, and sobbed from deep within his soul.

.

CHAPTER 42
MAY 8
WEDNESDAY, 10:58 AM

Garrahan, Elizabeth, and Abby walked into the Ashford Diner at two minutes to eleven. At a table next to the front window sat Edward Malden, in a dark suit and darker tie. *He looked like an actor*, Garrahan thought. Malden held himself stiffly and regally at the same time. Waiting for his next casting call.

As they approached, Malden stood and smiled. He extended his hand to Garrahan, who ignored it. He nodded to the Donahues. "Abby, nice to see you," he grinned. "And Elizabeth . . . well it was only yesterday morning you left us."

That was a gut punch. Yesterday? All this had happened since yesterday? He had met with Bruce Donahue two days ago. It seemed impossible.

They sat down.

"Should we order?" asked Malden, picking up a menu.

"We're not hungry," said Garrahan evenly.

"I see," said Malden, dropping the menu. "Abby, would you like some ice cream?"

There was unmistakable fear in her eyes. "No, sir," she replied to Malden.

"We're all hoping you come home to Morris and . . ." Malden began, talking directly to Abby, avoiding Elizabeth's stare.

"We're not here to talk about returning," interrupted Garrahan. "We're here to talk about a way out."

"I'd prefer to talk to you about that aspect of this privately," said Malden, turning to face Garrahan. "Would you care to come outside with me for a moment?"

"And get hit by a car? I don't think so," sneered Garrahan.

"You'll be safe. I promise," said Malden.

"I doubt it. Talk right here."

Malden shook his head. "What I have to say is between you and me."

"Forget it."

"Fine," said Malden, standing up. "I will forget it. And you would be wise to get yourself a carpet cleaning service in Manhattan."

Garrahan grabbed Malden by his shirt. He'd never grabbed anyone like that in his life.

"I've got a better idea," Garrahan said, his fist clenching tight around Malden's bunched up collar. "You want privacy, I'll find us privacy."

He dragged Malden across the diner to the men's room. He barged through the swinging door into a dimly lit bathroom with a urinal, toilet stall, and a steadily dripping faucet.

Malden's eyes were wide, not expecting this turn of events. Their faces were inches apart in the cramped bathroom.

"We've got privacy," hissed Garrahan. "Talk to me."

Malden pried Robert's hand off his shirt. "I want you to assist me." Malden did not use the words "help me."

"I know. Why?"

Malden cleared his throat. The scent of minty-lemon antiseptic was seeping into his nostrils. The smell of faked cleanliness.

"I need you to do research."

"What kind of research?"

"Historical research," Malden said. He was clearly having a difficult time with this. "I need information on events that occurred in Morris many years ago."

"It's your town. Why do you need me?"

"Because our records were destroyed. In a fire. And I can't go around asking for historical documents. It would create suspicion, here and in other towns."

"What events?"

"The death of five priests. Decades ago."

"What about them?"

"They are the key to restoring order in Morris."

"I thought you were going to sacrifice more little girls to do that."

Malden looked away. "That's one of many things I am considering."

"You're not sure which plan will work, are you?" Garrahan asked.

"I'm prepared to take any measure I believe will achieve our goal."

"You don't know what to do. So you're going to slaughter a bunch of . . ."

Malden's head snapped around, eyes blazing. "Sacrifice. Not slaughter. Don't make light of something you don't understand. That's stupidity."

"Apparently you're too stupid to fix your own mess."

"That's inaccurate," Malden said with a growl. "I am, however, looking for alternatives. That's why I need your . . . assistance." He cleared his throat again, and his voice got steely. "If you assist me, I promise your safety and that of the Donahues."

"How do I earn this safe passage?" Garrahan snickered.

"Find information. There were accounts of the priest's deaths in the newspapers in surrounding towns. Police reports were filed. I need the details."

"Why?"

"They'll help us understand why the priests killed themselves the way they did. How they got the Behemoth to return to Morris."

"You're losing me," Garrahan said, shaking his head. "Hasn't the Behemoth always been in Morris?" He caught himself and laughed. "I can't believe I am talking to you about a fucking monster."

Malden shifted his weight. "Let's continue this in my office, shall we? It would be more comfortable. I can show you what we need."

Garrahan pondered that. "We'll do it this way. I'll meet you there. I want to get some things taken care of first."

"Fine. If you agree to assist me, I will meet you in my office." His nose crinkled and he glanced at the toilet. "Anywhere is better than here."

"I'll meet you in Morris this afternoon."

"When?" Malden asked pointedly.

"When I show up," Garrahan shot back.

"All right. Your way. This time. Not a word to the Donahues about this. I'm asking nicely. This time." Malden had regained some of his authority.

"After we talk, I'll let you know if I'll keep it a secret."

"It is in both our best interests for you to do so," said Malden. Garrahan saw a grimace flicker past the older man's lips.

They walked back into the fresh air of the diner.

CHAPTER 43
MAY 8
WEDNESDAY, 11:25 AM

Garrahan and the Donahues waited until Malden drove away before leaving the diner.

"Where are we going?" asked Abby. "To New York?"

That had been Garrahan's initial thought—drive towards the city. Now that she mentioned it, he realized that was what Malden would expect. He made a U-turn in the middle of the road.

"No, not to New York," he said, wrenching the steering wheel.

"Then where?" asked Elizabeth.

"I'm meeting Malden this afternoon. You need to be someplace safe. I'm figuring out where that might be."

South was out; that led to New York. Too obvious for him to head that way, too easy for people to track him. East led to Boston. Garrahan's sister lived that way, and he didn't want Malden anywhere near them. West was barren, farms for a few hundred miles. That left north. There were plenty of medium-sized towns between here and the Canadian border. A tiny hotel to hide out in for a day or two was what he wanted.

"We're going north," he announced, like the dad on a family trip.

Elizabeth shuddered. "How safe is that?" she asked.

"Safer than you'd be in Morris," he replied. "If we outrun Leonard and Ethan for a while, we'll be all right. It'll buy us time while I talk to Malden."

"Did Malden say what he wants?" she asked.

Garrahan wasn't certain how to answer. "He wants to make a deal. I told him you had to be guaranteed safety, which he agreed to . . ."

"He's lying," Elizabeth scoffed. "No matter what happens, he won't let us go."

Garrahan shrugged. "Maybe not. I need to talk to him just the same." His hand tightened. "He has Nancy's body somewhere. He'll use that against me. I'm sure of it."

"How?" asked Elizabeth.

"I don't know," he replied, angry that Malden could make him look like the guilty party. "Maybe your goddamn monster will help him."

Elizabeth didn't answer. It was a stupid thing to say, but he wasn't taking it back.

They drove in silence for an hour. The drive was beautiful. Under other circumstances, Garrahan would have enjoyed it. Trees hung in green canopies over the backroads, obscuring the sky while letting sparkling fragments of sunlight in.

In a town called Roseville, near the junction of Interstate 95 and 25, he found The Shady Farms motel. He parked and walked into the lobby. Five minutes later, he got back into the car and onto the highway, heading west.

"What happened?" asked Abby from the quiet of the backseat. "Aren't we staying there?"

Garrahan shook his head. He felt like an asshole for not letting them in on everything. "No," he said. "I decided we should check in at a few different places. We're in that one under my real name. We'll find another one and sign in under a fake name. That way," he said, looking in his mirror "if they come for us, they'll have to do some hunting. If they find that place first, we get extra time."

Out of the corner of his eye, he saw Elizabeth smile. "Are you sure you haven't done this before?" she asked.

They both laughed. It sounded good.

CHAPTER 44

MAY 8
WEDNESDAY, 12:15 PM

At a Courtyard Inn, Garrahan used a fake name and registered as one person. Elizabeth and Abby snuck in with him, hoping no one would notice. People rarely did.

"You'll have to wait here until I'm done with Malden. After that, we'll figure out what to do." He looked at them, Abby sprawled out on the bed and Elizabeth in a chair by the desk. They looked like they were relaxing from a day of vacation.

"I hate to bring this up, but we're going to need clothes," said Elizabeth. "We can't live in these. They'll begin to grow on us."

Garrahan hadn't thought of that. "Um, okay," he stammered. "What do you want me to do? Pick up clothes from the house?" It seemed like the easiest thing to do.

"If they'll let you," Elizabeth nodded. "Or maybe have someone pack a suitcase."

"And if they don't?" Garrahan asked. He was out of his league when it came to women and clothes.

"We'll have to buy new ones," Elizabeth shrugged.

"Cool!" said Abby, involuntarily. "I mean, yeah . . . if we need new clothes, that'll be okay."

Her mother shook her head. "Your clothes are fine, young lady." She turned to Garrahan. "Get some jeans, a few shirts, shoes out of our closet, some underwear . . ."

Garrahan could see Abby's face go red when her mother finished the list.

"If that's too much, we can just wait and shop when you get back." Elizabeth stood up and stretched. "Unless we all go to Morris soon."

"You're not going anytime soon. Not until we determine what's going on. Even then, who knows what's going to happen? I still have to take care of . . ." He almost said Nancy's name. "I've got to straighten thingsptus out in New York. We'll know more tonight."

He checked his watch and got up to leave. "Don't go anywhere. Don't answer the phone. I'll be back before it gets late. Hopefully by six or seven at the latest."

"What if something happens to you?" asked Abby, bolting up from the bed. "How will we know?"

Memories of running to Abby's hotel room zipped through Garrahan's head. He had gone there to tell her about her dad. If anything happened to Garrahan now, the only person to tell Abby anything would be Malden. That couldn't happen.

He paced for a minute. "I'll call you at six o'clock to let you know what happened. I'll let the phone ring twice, then hang up. I'll call again, let it ring twice and hang up again. That's two sets of rings. After that, go ahead and pick it up when I call the third time. That should be safe enough."

"What if you don't call?" asked Elizabeth. She shuddered.

"If I don't call, then something happened to me. That means you'll be on your own, because I won't be around to help." He shrugged.

Abby jumped off the bed. She wanted to hug Garrahan but stopped herself.

"Be safe," she said.

"I will," he answered. He reached down and touched Elizabeth on the shoulder.

"For what it's worth," she said, "Thank you. Again."

By the time he thought up a good reply, he was driving to Morris.

CHAPTER 45

MAY 8
WEDNESDAY, 1:11 PM

Edward Malden stomped across his office, muttering to himself. Shouting at the walls. Curses blasted out of his mouth as if he had Tourette's.

Malden's meeting with the town council had gone badly. All the members had expressed their dismay that the marker was still down. Since the night of the car crash, people in surrounding towns had gone missing. Rumor was making its way through the region. If rumor turned to suspicion, that would be bad for Morris. Very bad indeed.

Malden hadn't done anything to fix it, a council member had shouted accusingly.

The village council had final approval in all matters affecting the way Morris was run. But they always deferred to Malden. Always.

Until this morning.

It was the first time in his life that his sway over the town had slipped.

It was because they were afraid; he knew that. Afraid of prying eyes from other towns. Afraid they might be forced to stop.

Restoring the ruined marker was something he had to put off for a few more days. Putting a stop to Garrahan and Elizabeth Donahue was something he needed to do right now.

Garrahan was toxic because he was in the news business. It was doubtful that the surrounding towns could make a link between Morris and a few missing persons. But someone like Garrahan could make that connection—and make it known to the outside world.

The solution was to have Garrahan disappear forever. Before he could talk about what he found.

That did not solve the problem that Malden was facing: details of the deaths. The reason for the markers.

Garrahan would have to be dispensed with, but perhaps he could be used first. Used to solve the problem. He was a man with many resources. A journalist, probably a trained researcher of documents and news. Skills that could be useful in finding the missing pieces of the town's history, pieces that could fix Malden's problem.

Garrahan had to be convinced the best way to "make everything right" was to assist Malden. Help Malden, save the Donahues. Because Malden himself was running out of options. He had planned a sacrifice. That failed. Abby Donahue had run away. Her disappearance made everyone in town edgy and nervous. Another girl had to be selected for sacrifice.

If he was being honest, Malden would admit that he didn't know how to restore order.

The five priests who had died decades ago had known what to do. Their grave markers became the boundary within which the ritual could be carried out. The markers protected the town and its secrets. The rest of the world was none the wiser.

Malden had a simple problem. He didn't know why the priests had died. The priests had written a document describing how their deaths would protect Morris. A document essential to protecting the Behemoth. All the answers were there in pen and paper.

That document had been reduced to ash in the fire that destroyed the village church.

Malden had never read it. Nor had his father. They didn't think they would ever need it. No one could have anticipated the chaos resulting from a car full of drunk boys smashing into a gravestone.

As the town's minister, Malden needed to make things right. To make it all normal again. If that didn't happen, he would be in trouble. And the whole town would suffer.

CHAPTER 46

MAY 8
WEDNESDAY, 1:30 PM

Driving into Morris, Garrahan called Dave Vanukoff. Vanukoff said people were looking for him. And Nancy. Tongues were wagging.

"It'll get cleared up in the next few days. First, I've got to get through a meeting in Morris. The man in that meeting needs to know you and I are in contact."

"What, are they gonna kill you or something?"

"I don't know," Garrahan said earnestly.

"You're fucking kidding me."

"No, I'm not. I don't trust the guy I'm seeing to tell me the color of the sky without lying. So I'm going to walk in, show him that you're on the phone, and then let you off."

"Can't I listen to the whole thing? I can help you."

"No, you can't. As it is, even I don't believe the shit they're telling me."

"Telling you about what?"

"Those deaths I asked you to look into."

"Jesus. I told you. Those were . . ."

"Accidents, coyotes, wolves, whatever. As absurd as it sounds, they are all connected to the hit and run in New York."

He drove to the town hall entrance. A small sign said, "Village of Morris: Clerks, Selectman, Office."

"Okay. I'm here. Stay on the line so they'll know you're on."

"No problem. I wouldn't miss this for anything."

Across the street, people were tending their yards. Others loitered outside a small market. Somewhere—he couldn't see where—groups of children were laughing and playing. Regular people going about a regular day. A small New England town, like hundreds of others.

Or not, he mused.

He walked up to the front door of the village hall and rang the doorbell. Something clanged deep inside the building. A moment later, a young woman appeared. She seemed surprised to see him.

"Can I help you?" she asked.

"Yes," Garrahan answered. "I'm here to see Edward Malden."

"Oh, yes. My, of course," the woman said, as if she had forgotten something important she wasn't supposed to forget. "Come right in."

The woman glided up a long wooden staircase that led to offices on the second floor. She stopped outside a door, knocked twice. Malden's voice filtered through. "Bring him in, Amelia."

She opened the door. Malden was looking out the arched window, staring at something down on the street. "That'll be all, Amelia. Please close the door behind you."

As Malden turned, Garrahan held up his cell phone. "Before you get started, I've got one of my reporters on the other end. He knows where I am. If anything happens to . . ."

Malden waved him off dismissively. "Put that away, Mr. Garrahan. No one's going to hurt you. I'm not stupid—this is a business meeting. No need for theatrics." Again, he waved at the phone. "Shut it off."

Garrahan put it to his ear. "Hear everything, Dave?"

"Loud and clear. What now?"

"I call you back within three hours. If you don't hear from me, get somebody up here. You know what I mean."

"Like cops?"

"Exactly." The phone beeped off. Garrahan slid it into his pocket. He glared at Malden."

"Well?" asked Malden.

That one word set Garrahan off. Angrily.

"Well? Is that all you can ask is 'well'? When I leave here, I am going to have you charged for every fucking thing you've ever done. Murder. Kidnapping. Abuse. Everything." Garrahan felt his face flaring red with anger. Spittle flew from his lips. His rage was finally set free. "Beyond that, I really should kill you myself . . ." He bared his teeth.

Malden had prepared himself for just such an outburst. He reached into his desk and retrieved a pistol.

"Don't get stupid on me, Mr. Garrahan," he retorted, his own voice rising. "You've interfered in my town's business, in my religion. You've caused chaos in my church." He gestured violently with the gun. "In any other part of the world, people in my position would have you killed, and the faithful would thank me. They would dance on your corpse. You are an infidel. In the name of my God, I could butcher you six ways from Sunday and know that I am right in doing so."

Garrahan refused to move or lower his voice. "Killing people? For no reason? How are you right in doing that?"

"Every person who has died over this has died for a good reason." Malden said it with clenched teeth and jaw.

"Including my . . ." Garrahan couldn't bring himself to say the word girlfriend. "Including the woman in my apartment?" His eyes bulged from the fury in his head.

"God does not discriminate. Some must die so the faith of others can be protected." Malden pointed with the gun. "Why don't you and I sit down, Mr. Garrahan? It will help calm us."

Garrahan glared at Malden, not looking at the gun. He sat down on a sofa beneath the window.

"Mr. Garrahan, I am in a difficult position. You can be of service to me. If we reach an agreement, I will let you and the Donahues go.

"I doubt that."

Malden sighed. "Should I shoot you now, then? Should I take my church's revenge on you without further discussion?"

"I haven't done anything to your alleged church."

"No? You were ready to provide haven to a man who sought to ruin us, who tried to destroy our way of life."

"Bruce Donahue came to me. I didn't ask to get involved."

"No? You didn't drive here and spirit Elizabeth Donahue away in the middle of the night, threatening to kill Loretta Bower in the process? You weren't involved in that?"

"I helped people who needed. . ."

"You're helping people who wish to bring an end to this community. That makes you a threat to me and every person who lives here."

Garrahan stood up. "Then I'll go away. Never come back. Let me take Elizabeth and Abby. You'll never hear from us again."

"It's not that simple," Malden snickered. "It never is. But there is a way out for you. One that allows you to live—although everyone in this town would like to see you die—and one that serves my purpose."

He held the gun up again, as if showing it to Garrahan for the first time. "Your choice."

"What do I have to do to earn this honor?"

"You deign to make light of this, Mr. Garrahan. It is not a wry or humorous situation."

"Then what is it?" Garrahan felt sweat on his hairline.

Malden put the gun in his pocket. "I'll start at the beginning. I presume you're amenable to that."

"I am."

Malden sighed. "Then sit back down. This will take some time."

CHAPTER 47
MAY 8
WEDNESDAY, 2:00 PM

"What religion are you, Mr. Garrahan?"
"Catholic. Lapsed."
"Have you read the Bible?"
"Parts of it. In high school and college."

"Most people have never read any of the Bible—even though they swear they believe in it," Malden said. "Do you know the Old Testament story of Behemoth?"

Garrahan thought. He looked at the ceiling, as if the answer was there. Then back at Malden. "A creature that God let loose on the land or something. Like Leviathan."

"A passable guess for someone not tutored in the Bible." Malden grinned with tight lips. "Behemoth is God's greatest creature. One of His most terrifying. According to Job, Chapter 40, Verses 15 to 18, Behemoth was made at the same time as man. It was monstrously large and extremely powerful. Bones of bronze and limbs of iron. According to Deuteronomy 32, Verses 23 through 25, it had fangs. It was big enough to drink down rivers. As far as the Bible is concerned, Behemoth is the most incredible creature that God put on this planet. And God put that beast here specifically to remind us there are creatures more powerful than man." Malden paused to sip water from a crystal glass.

Garrahan clucked his tongue. "Thanks for the quick Bible study lesson. Anything else?"

"That's the beginning. The next part requires more open-mindedness on your part."

Garrahan had an idea what was coming.

"When Morris was first settled, the earliest inhabitants found it overrun by wolves and coyotes, even bears. But they found something more. They found the Behemoth."

Garrahan opened his mouth to speak. Malden held up a hand. "Long before the Europeans came, local native Americans had built a legend around this creature. They believed it was the beast that carried God—or their version of God—over the land while he created hills, valleys, rivers, mountains, trees, flowers, everything. When God was finished, he left the beast here to live out its days, to feast and graze as it needed."

Garrahan opened his mouth to stop the bullshit. Again, Malden waved him off. "The Scandinavians, who frequented the area before Columbus arrived, had a legend about the creature. They believed that a malevolent God shaped this world with his bare hands. He dug out the lakes, molded the mountains, and traced the rivers with his fingers. In their telling, this God was horrific and terrible. His hands and fingers were claws and talons. The world was smooth and round, and this God tore into it greedily. As he did, one of his claws broke off deep in the Earth. And that claw—that part of God—grew until it became a creature that was part animal, part God. It came to be known as the "claw of God."

Malden poured himself another glass of water. He didn't offer any to Garrahan.

"When my ancestors, and the ancestors of most people in Morris, first came here from Europe, they encountered the creature. It wasn't pleasant. The creature fed on their livestock. At first. In time, it came to feed on the people themselves.

"The earliest settlement was wiped out. People died or escaped. Only one settler, Clifford Morris, saw the beast for what it truly was: the creature described in the Bible as Behemoth. Instead of fearing it, he told his settlers it must be appeased, that it must be given sacrifice. He based his belief on the verse from Psalm 34:11. "Come, you children, listen to me; I will teach you the fear of the Lord."

"Clifford Morris was right. After offering sacrifice, the creature stopped feeding on the townspeople. It had been shown deference, adoration, and respect. It gave us respect in return."

Garrahan couldn't restrain himself. "You believe this nonsense? Hundreds of years later?"

"It is precisely because it has been going on for hundreds of years that I do believe, Mr. Garrahan."

"You think this, this . . . thing has been around that long?"

"I know it has."

"The same monster?"

"The same beast. Yes."

"Have you ever seen it?"

"As the minister of this town, this congregation, I have seen it during rituals."

"Ah, yes, the famous ritual. What is that, really? What is it that's so awful you've created a monster story to cover for it?"

Malden frowned for an instant, then shook it off. "In due time." He motioned with his hand towards Garrahan's shirt pocket. "You can call someone as we stroll if you think it's necessary."

Garrahan ignored it. "Where are we going?"

"To the church."

CHAPTER 48
MAY 8
WEDNESDAY, 2:20 PM

They walked into clear sunlight. Malden waved to a woman who was planting marigolds. She smiled and waved back. "Beautiful day, isn't it, Edward?"

"Indeed it is, Linda."

So very normal, Garrahan thought.

Garrahan and Malden walked to the front of the new church. Its design matched the town hall. Bland modern New England architecture masquerading as old New England architecture.

"How come you don't use that church?" asked Garrahan, tilting his head in the direction of the boarded-up Gothic structure. He noted the thick chains on the church doors.

"That's a part of the story I'll get to," Malden replied.

Entering the church, Garrahan was struck by its ordinariness. It could have been a Baptist congregation hall in the South, or a Lutheran hall in the Midwest. It had the look, feel, and smell of a small-town church waiting for its worshippers to build a bigger, real church.

"This way," motioned Malden. They headed into a room off of the main hall.

It was the daycare center, or whatever passed for that in Morris. Kids' toys were piled up in corners of the room, complete with Legos, bean bag chairs, a small slide and a miniature kitchen for pretending to make cakes and cookies. A playroom found in every town in America.

The children's drawings on the walls showed this wasn't like any other town in America. Dozens of pictures covered every inch of space. Kids had all signed their pictures: there was Wyatt, Clinton, Ashley, Alex, Ryan . . .

The crayon images on white paper were done with quick and crude lines, swirls, and stick figures.

Each picture was of a monster. The same monster.

It was reared up on two legs. Some pictures showed it with blood in its mouth, always towering high above the trees.

Animals were clenched in its claws. Cows, dogs, horses, birds.

In three of the pictures, the creature held a little girl.

And the little girl wasn't always in one piece.

"What the Hell is this?" Garrahan whispered.

"This is our children's center. Kids come to play. To get their religious instruction."

"No. These pictures. Why did they all draw that thing?"

"Because that thing is the core of our faith. I'm sure you drew pictures of Christ's birth or his death during your Sunday school lessons. Jewish children draw pictures of the menorah, or Moses parting the Red Sea. Our children are no different. They draw the Behemoth."

Garrahan walked around the room. He bent down to each drawing. He contemplated them like paintings in a museum, as if there was something hidden within the colors.

There were so many. Even though they were childish scrawls, every one was truly frightening.

None more frightening than Abby Donahue's drawing.

It depicted the monster with a girl in its hands. Blood ran from its mouth, from her body. The picture was splashed in vivid red from how much blood Abby had included. It dripped from the beast's mouth and claws to the ground, where it puddled.

The girl in the picture had her mouth open in a scream.

Garrahan tapped the picture with his forefinger.

"Why . . .?" he began.

"That's Abby's picture from last year." Malden said it almost sadly. "It was difficult for her. The girl chosen last year, Devin Folger, was Abby's best friend. I don't think Abby had quite gotten over it. But they all do. We all do. In time."

"What do you mean by 'chosen?'"

"Hold on. I want you to see how important the Behemoth is to us. We fear it but live in awe of its relationship to God."

"What relationship?"

"The fact that God put the Behemoth here to remind us of his own power and majesty. As a reminder that we are here but for his grace, and to serve him."

"Yeah, okay. I've got that part. You're worshipping this thing that eats your kids . . ." Garrahan said, sarcasm oozing. This was becoming a bigger freak show than he'd expected.

Malden sighed. "You're a sometime resident in Ashford, Mr. Garrahan. You heard about the boys who died in the car accident a while back?"

"Yes. Eaten by coyotes, according to the police."

"Wrong. That's what our doctor told the authorities. You might have heard that the bodies were not shown to the parents. That wasn't quite true; we let one parent in to identify the boys. One of the fathers. He saw his son, what was left of him, and fainted dead away. That's how we persuaded the mothers to avoid the remains." Malden wrinkled his brow, remembering something. "Actually, the father did the persuading on his own.

"What was left of the boys was little more than bone meal. Not even a hundred coyotes could have done that. The Behemoth got to them and devoured them." He said it as if discussing the weather. "I daresay the creature is responsible for other disappearances over the last few weeks."

Garrahan tilted his head. "I'll humor you and say a monster ate those kids. What does that have to do with you, your town, your religion or anything else? And if it's a menace, why doesn't someone go and hunt it?"

Malden's body stiffened, his skin tone fading. "The point of all this, Mr. Garrahan, is that the Behemoth needs to be protected. Not hunted. For the first time in memory, it has left the sanctuary of our village and of the surrounding forests. It is feasting on people in other places. I fear it may attract attention that could result in what you describe—someone going out and hunting it."

"That would be bad for your religion—if the Behemoth was to get hurt or killed. Correct?"

"We have been entrusted with protecting it, with providing for it. That's the way it has been for many, many decades. We cannot fail in this."

Garrahan rubbed the bridge of his nose with his fingers. He was getting a headache. "Don't people in other towns suspect this creature of yours?"

"Older ones might. Like you, they would be inclined to dismiss it. An old legend, as it were. Silly local lore."

"Why are you the only ones who know about it? Is it like magic—only you can see it?" Garrahan meant it to sound condescending.

Malden took no offense. "No, any human can see it. We've managed to keep it out of view, so to speak." He cleared his throat. "That's where you enter the story."

Not bloody likely, Garrahan thought. "Okay," he said, nonetheless. "That entails what?"

"You'll see."

CHAPTER 49
MAY 8
WEDNESDAY, 2:30 PM

In nearby Woodcrest Acres, Ginnie Pierce sat in her kitchen and finished reading the news on her tablet. She was tempted to print out an article about a small boy who had been kidnapped from his bedroom. She decided to bookmark it instead. Printing it would add more clutter to the files she had in the attic. She was getting too old to keep up with those.

At this stage of her life, six years past seventy, she didn't care much about disappearances in and around Morris anymore. No one had vanished in decades, until now. Adding new stories to her files wasn't proof of anything.

Most locals were too young to have heard the stories about the creature in the Morris woods.

Her grand uncle had come close to unraveling the secret behind the Morris monster. He'd spent years trying to find out what it was. Then he disappeared. One day, gone. Never heard from again.

He disappeared on the same morning that five other priests killed themselves. In the ensuing cover-up of their deaths, no one noticed that her uncle was gone. No one missed Father Albert Pierce.

His musings about Morris lived on in the tattered journals Ginnie kept. When she was dead and gone—that couldn't be too many years from now—there'd be no one to read them. Father Albert's writing would be thrown away with her other boxes of decaying keepsakes.

Hell, maybe she should start spring cleaning and toss the papers right now. What did they matter? No one remembered Father Pierce . . . or what he made those other priests do.

CHAPTER 50
MAY 8
WEDNESDAY, 2:45 PM

Garrahan insisted on taking his car. They rolled the windows down, the breeze cooling the interior.

"Drive to the state road," said Malden. "You know the way."

In five minutes they were outside the confines of the village. The road was not well traveled. Dry grass and weeds grew high along the fading blacktop. They came to a turn leading to the highway access road.

"Stop here," Malden told him.

Garrahan was struck by the sound of crickets and cicadas. The noise was an electric hum, like a vast vibrating wire churning electricity through the air. It was deafening. It made the afternoon heat more oppressive.

This feels like a movie scene where I'm supposed to get shot and dragged into the woods, he thought.

Malden came around the front of the car. "We start in there," he said, nodding towards the field that lay past the shoulder of the road. "Watch your step."

Malden marched down the sloping shoulder into grass that reached up to his shoulders. Garrahan followed, fighting the urge to slash at the weeds that swished in front of him. Malden never lost sight of where he was headed, despite the fact there was nothing to see. Just acres and acres of wild grass and trees. For miles.

Suddenly, Malden stopped.

"Here," he said.

Garrahan looked down. The grass was cleared away in a small circle about fifteen feet across. In the center was a marker. No different than historical markers that trumpeted the passing of the Minutemen or a sleepover of the Continental Congress.

The marker had been knocked to the ground. It was three feet high, in the shape of an obelisk. The stone was chipped and gouged. Freshly.

Garrahan read the engraving. "Father Timothy Moynihan," he said aloud. The words below: "One Of Five."

He traced a finger across the etched letters. "What is this?"

Malden scanned the horizon, keeping watch.

"It's a burial marker."

"Like a gravestone?"

"Not 'like.' It is a gravestone. It's the grave of Father Timothy Moynihan."

"Why does it say 'One Of Five'?"

"Because there are five graves in total. They're spread through the forest for a few miles."

"Why are there five?"

Malden kept scanning the field. "There were five priests. Priests who died at the same moment on the same day."

"How did that happen?"

"They all committed suicide. All at the stroke of six o'clock in the morning. Dawn. Each with a single bullet to his brain. Each was buried where he fell."

Malden toed the ground next to the stone. "This was the spot given to Father Moynihan to kill himself."

The high wire buzz of the cicadas were loud inside Garrahan's skull.

"I'll need more background than that. You need to produce some evidence before I believe any more of your stories," he said, staring down at the marker.

"Unfortunately, I know little of the history. That is why I brought you here," Malden said. His gaze never left the horizon.

Most of what he had learned, he told Garrahan, he had been told as a boy. "What I do know is this . . ."

On a grim and gray autumn dawn more than seventy years ago, five priests from towns surrounding Morris appeared on the outskirts of the village. Each went to one of five different points that had been indicated on a map. Each had a small pistol with a full chamber of six bullets.

The priests were not from a single parish, or even a single faith. Father Timothy Moynihan and Father Albert Giordano were Catholic, one from Ashford, the other from Roseville.

Father Vernon Lindt was a Methodist from Woodcrest Acres. Father Marcus Kohler was a Lutheran from Dunstam. Jared Linik was an Episcopalian minister from Longhaven.

They ranged in age from twenty-eight to sixty-two. The only thing they had in common was that they were ordained men who served their respective faiths.

"You with me so far?" Malden asked.

Garrahan nodded.

The postwar years brought rapid growth to the small towns around Morris. Highways and paved roads were laid down with lightning speed and efficiency. The population more than doubled in five years.

For two centuries, the Behemoth had limited its feeding to the sacrifices offered by Clifford Morris and his kinsmen. Encroaching development crowded the creature. It ventured from hallowed ground. People in surrounding villages went missing.

Residents who lived on the edges of the growing towns reported hearing sounds at night. Screams like a pack of wolves, rampaging through the forest. Whispering of evil things in the woods began to spread.

The people of Morris feared, then as now, for the safety of the Behemoth. They could not allow it to fall into the crosshairs of scared and armed citizens. They needed to keep it close to themselves to keep it safe.

Samuel Malden, Edward's grandfather, was leader of the village then. He agonized over how protect the Behemoth. He read everything he could find that might help him. He studied the Bible, native American legends, Scandinavian myths, all the texts written by Clifford Morris.

A theme ran through the stories: the idea that blood could delineate the sacred area of the creature's world. Surrounded by blood, the Behemoth would be protected from assailants. By an invisible wall. Conversely, blood would keep the creature in a confined space. A place of refuge.

Malden's grandfather knew it was dangerous to encircle the Behemoth. Perhaps sacrilegious. That did not matter. Protecting the creature was of paramount importance, he decreed. Even if that meant restricting it, forcing it to remain hidden.

Convinced of what to do, Samuel Malden went looking for holy blood.

To his mind, that meant finding men of God to aid him. Priests.

CHAPTER 51
MAY 8
WEDNESDAY, 3:00 PM

Edward Malden's history broke down and evaporated right there. By his own admission. There was no longer any written record of what transpired.

Anecdotal stories suggested Malden's grandfather had approached many priests with his idea. He was roundly rejected. Yet so persuasive was his story, his faith, and his understanding of scripture, that he ultimately persevered. Through an intermediary, he found five priests who agreed to help him. These five would protect a beast—which they came to believe was the Behemoth of the Old Testament—with their own blood.

To a man, they consented to give their lives in service of the Behemoth. It would be protected, reined in. They would create a line which it could not cross.

They lured the Behemoth into the village. They prevented it from leaving by splashing their blood on the ground.

That was all Malden knew about the priests and the events leading up to that day. The rest, including what happened to the intermediary, was lost to time.

Everything else was just guessing.

When the bell in the church steeple chimed six o'clock on that long-ago morning, the beast lumbered into town. Each of the priests placed a gun to his own head. At the last toll, each fired a single bullet into his skull.

They died instantly. Each man was found crumpled in the dirt with a vial of holy water in his pocket.

Later measurements determined that the priests were positioned equidistant from each other. Each priest occupied a single point. Their five positions formed a perfectly symmetrical pentagon. The pentagon wrapped for miles around Morris.

The pentagon was the boundary of the Behemoth's world.

The plan worked perfectly.

The details of the plan did not survive.

Written on sheets of paper and locked inside the church, the documents were destroyed when a fire swept through the building.

The fire occurred when Malden was four years old. His grandfather had died the previous year. Malden's own father, George, had never read the papers about the five priests. The pages were in a church vault—should they ever be needed. In case of emergency.

The fire eviscerated that option. It started in the middle of a night storm, an ironic act of God. Multiple lightning strikes hit the steeple, igniting ceiling beams and spreading flames down the wooden supports.

By the time the town realized there was a fire, an entire buttress had fallen in on itself. Under tons of rubble were buried the lushly paneled offices of the Malden family.

Nothing of the offices remained after the fire was extinguished. No furniture, not a shred of paper. Part of the outer structure still stood, a blackened and scarred shadow of its original majesty.

The destruction of the papers did not concern George Malden. He didn't think the Behemoth would escape into surrounding towns again. Another plan would never be needed. That was what Malden's father believed.

His father's short-sightedness left Edward Malden with third-hand information about the priests and their scheme. It amounted to nothing.

Malden desperately needed to know what the priests had done. How they brought the Behemoth back. How they concocted their plan.

Because he needed to do it now.

CHAPTER 52

MAY 8
WEDNESDAY, 3:20 PM

"No one knows what happened that morning?" Garrahan asked, pointing to the marker.

Malden shook his head.

"How can there be no record? There must have been news reports about the suicides."

Malden continued shaking his head. "It was before the Internet. These were little towns, each with its own paper or monthly bulletin. Besides that, the dead men were priests. Priests who had committed suicide. A mortal sin in every one of their faiths. None of their superiors or supervisors or bishops wanted to publicize those deaths. As much as possible, the hierarchy hushed it up." Malden shrugged, with a hint of a smile. "We've learned in recent years how thorough churches can be when it comes to covering up unsavory episodes. "

Garrahan walked around the marker, wondering where the next one was. "With no information, you expect me to figure out what happened?" He harrumphed.

"There is information. The shreds that made it to the news has been catalogued in our library. Scans of old newspapers." Malden waved his fingers contemptuously. "More useful would be a trip to the parishes, to the priests' families. Find what is hidden."

"You haven't thought that through. They were priests. They don't have grandchildren or family albums or . . .

"IT'S ALL WE HAVE!" Malden screamed, whirling on Garrahan. "I can't go door to door looking for answers. You can! And I expect you to!" His face had turned a livid shade of scarlet. His body leaned in over Garrahan.

For the first time, Garrahan could see unbridled menace in Edward Malden. He stepped backward.

Malden took a handkerchief out of his suit pocket, dabbing his forehead and corners of his mouth. Garrahan hadn't seen a handkerchief in forever.

The act of wiping his brow and lips released something pent up in Malden. He calmed down and cleared his throat. "The issue is to determine why my grandfather's plan worked," he said, his voice even and low. "They must have discovered a way to control the Behemoth. Or something it responded to. You're a journalist. I want you to find out what they did."

"You'll have to tell me more about . . ."

"I've told you everything I know. Everything." Malden gestured towards the town. "The one person who knows more about this than I do is Joel, our librarian. He will give you what you need."

Malden walked away.

"I want to see the other markers," Garrahan said. He was out of ideas and unexpectedly alone. The sensation of being defeated.

"Joel will show you."

CHAPTER 53

MAY 8
WEDNESDAY, 3:30 PM

Garrahan followed Malden to the town hall. In addition to offices, it housed a surprisingly modern and bright library. Shelves were stocked from ceiling to floor with books. Desks with computers and tablets lined the walls. Garrahan was impressed.

"We aren't heathens," Malden said, noting Garrahan's look. "Our beliefs do not trap us in the past."

Garrahan kept his reply to himself.

Sitting at the reception desk was a skinny young man with horned rim glasses. Twenty-one or twenty-two years old, Garrahan guessed. A boy.

Malden walked to the desk. "Mr. Garrahan, this is Joel Emerson. Joel, say hello to Mr. Garrahan."

The boy stood up, arms and legs gangling. "Hello, sir," Joel said.

Garrahan shook his hand. "You're the librarian."

The boy nodded eagerly, but nervously. "Yes, sir. And town historian. And someday, hopefully, a minister."

"I'll leave you to chat," Malden said to Garrahan. "Come see me when you're done."

Once Malden was out the door, Joel walked out from the desk. In a stage whisper, he said "Mr. Malden says you're assisting us with . . . the problem." He grinned as if they were new friends.

Garrahan shuddered. "I'm trying to help people get away from this town."

Joel straightened, stiffly. "But it's not the town that is a problem. It's the . . ."

Garrahan made a face. "I know. It's the Behemoth. The monster. Everything is because of the monster." His voice curdled.

"It's not a monster," said Joel, defensive and meek.

Sure, Garrahan thought. "Tell me what you know about the five priests."

Joel closed the door to the library and went to the computer. He motioned Garrahan to a chair next to him.

"I have scans of all the papers that reported on the deaths. There weren't many." He flicked through newspaper images that appeared on the screen.

Garrahan shook his head at the paucity of data. Reporting on the deaths was nearly nonexistent. It reinforced his feeling that the monster and the priests were part of a ruse or some bullshit story.

What Joel did have, surprisingly, were the names and addresses of living relatives of the five priests. "The Internet is a wondrous thing," he said aloud.

Joel had also created a written history of the town. Part of that history included what people had heard—in most cases, been told—about the grim morning when the priests died. Again, there wasn't much there.

After an hour of sitting with Joel, Garrahan was fidgety. He felt like a prisoner. "Were any documents discovered in the church after the fire?" he asked, standing up from the computer.

"Nothing," Joel said. "The ruins are there like it happened yesterday. There's nothing to see."

"We should take a look," Garrahan said, daring Joel to say "no."

"Sure. A waste of time, but I'll take you. Whatever you want, I'll do. Mr. Malden's orders." He grinned.

They walked into the day, now bright and cloudless. The hulking church was directly across the village green, a stone's throw. Windows and doors boarded with thick slabs of wood. From this angle, the church was beautiful and gothic. The spire stood proudly, more than a hundred feet into the air.

Not until they walked around the far side, which faced the forest, did Garrahan see the extent of the damage. Jet black scorches marked the entire side of the building. The roof was caved in, as if some giant hand had pummeled it down to the ground.

Prior to the fire, the church had been stunning. It had the kind of jaw-dropping beauty Garrahan had seen in cathedrals in France and Italy. Light streamed to the ruined interior through a few uncovered stained-glass windows. The sculpted detail was marvelous. He couldn't think of an American church he'd seen that was so exquisite.

The longer he looked, the more the damage came into focus. It morphed into a scene reminiscent of a World War II photo; a work of art bombed until the rubble overwhelmed the architecture.

"Why wasn't it rebuilt?" Garrahan asked, looking at the towering piles of broken stone and splintered beams.

"Same reason as anywhere else," answered Joel, pushing his glasses up on his nose. "Lack of money, resources, time. Construction on this church started in the late 1600s and finished in 1710. To restore it to original condition would have bankrupted the town. It was easier to build a meeting house and keep updating it. The newest version was built fifteen years ago."

"So what's inside?"

"Church stuff. Altars, pews, lecterns. Lots of broken stained glass."

"Anyone try to salvage that stuff?"

"A surveying team went in right after the fire. One of the workers died when a chunk of marble fell on him. Others were hurt pretty bad. After that, Elder Samuel Malden—Mr. Malden's grandfather—forbade anyone from going in. That edict has never been lifted. Too dangerous. Nothing's been touched since. Not even the coffins, and they were far enough away from the collapse that they barely got scratched."

Garrahan stopped. "What coffins?"

"Mr. Malden didn't tell you about the coffins?"

"No, he didn't."

Joel wiped his hair away from his face. "I can show them to you."

"How safe is it?"

"They're in the old chapel area. Nothing's fallen there in fifteen years. Although I'm not promising anything."

"Let's look."

Joel unlocked the wrought iron gate that surrounded the church. He guided them through a crumbling archway that led into a side chapel off the main building. The rubble was more gargantuan here. Huge chunks of fallen building wedged on top of each other like discarded building blocks.

Garrahan looked around. Most of the chapel roof had disintegrated; he could see straight to the blue sky above. Parts of the roof angled crazily upwards, casting long shadows across the chapel. Some of those shadows draped a row of coffins.

They stepped over cracked timber and crushed stone. Garrahan put his hand on the first coffin.

"Who's in them?" he asked.

"No one," Joel replied.

"Why are they here?"

"They were supposed to be for the priests."

The story, as Joel understood it, was that the priests would to be buried in the ground where they died. Out in the fields, in hastily dug holes, with the markers. The priests knew that. However, they had struck a deal with Grandfather Malden. Morris would provide the priests' families with coffins that could be buried symbolically. In family plots or local cemeteries.

That plan didn't work out.

The priests committed suicide. That was a mortal sin. Their parishes wouldn't even allow symbolic coffins to be buried in the church graveyards. It would despoil the holiness of hallowed ground. The churches—and the priests' families—told Morris to keep the coffins.

The coffins had been stored inside the chapel, and there they had remained. They survived the fire and cave-in; they survived ravages of weather and time. Here they were, untouched, decades later. Never used.

Garrahan walked around them, absent-mindedly wiping dirt off their curved tops.

He stopped and pointed. "There are six here." He counted again. "Six."

He turned quizzically to Joel. "You and Malden said there were five priests. Five markers."

Joel rubbed his temples. "Yeah. This is where it gets kind of weird."

.

CHAPTER 54
MAY 8
WEDNESDAY, 4:15 PM

"Five priests were found dead," said Joel. "We know their names; we know where they were from. And their deaths made a nice, tidy, geographic pentagon around the town. Part of the mystery is we don't think Grandfather Malden actually met those five priests in person.

"He met another priest, named Pierce. Pierce handled the discussions between the town and the priests. The intermediary. We're guessing he was priest number six. I don't know how he fit in beyond that—none of us do. The people here made a coffin for him, like they expected he was going to die with the other five. But no one ever found him. He vanished off the face of the Earth."

"How do you know that?"

"The others died by their own hands . . . and were shunned by their families and faithful. In helping Morris, they brought shame to their parishes. Their churches kept it hushed up. We know that. You saw the lack of news about their deaths.

"With Pierce, though, there were a handful of articles about his family claiming he was missing. No one ever found him. He apparently wasn't one of the suicides, either."

"With so little information to go on, how do you know about Pierce?"

"Grandfather Malden rarely told stories about what happened that day, but he did talk about Father Pierce. Pierce was an outsider who helped the Morris congregation. Grandfather Malden wanted the town to know that Pierce was a good man. He praised him publicly."

"Anything else?"

Joel pursed his lips. "We have old documents that mention a Pierce family selling tractors to Morris farmers, but that's it.

Nothing about a priest." He raised his palms; that was all he had.

"I've searched genealogy records. He's got distant relatives a few towns away. They're too young to know much about him."

Garrahan stared at the coffins. Five priests died. Six priests were supposed to. What happened to the sixth one?

"What do you think happened to Father Pierce?"

Joel gave a nervous shrug. "I can't presume anything. It's not my place to guess."

"I'm not asking for your professional opinion. I'm asking for a theory."

The young man let out a perceptible sigh. "Pierce probably got cold feet and didn't go through with it." He shrugged again. "That's one possible theory."

"Not exactly a stretch of the imagination there," Garrahan said. "So he takes off in shame, never to be seen again?"

Joel nodded.

Bullshit, Garrahan thought. *Another loose end.*

Garrahan and Joel walked the length of the chapel. Garrahan walked across the rubble to the large doorway that connected the chapel to the main room of the church. He peered into the church as far as he dared without actually going in. It was too dark to see much.

"Anything left in the main church?"

Joel shrugged. "Like I said, pews and stuff. I've never gone all the way in. I've seen a bit from out here with a flashlight, plus what the stained-glass lights up. I can't imagine how they lit this thing back in the day . . ."

Garrahan didn't want to hear any more. "We're done for now," he said, interrupting. He turned without a word and headed out through the ruined chapel.

They went to the library. Garrahan saw more kids' drawings, like the ones in the playroom. All the same subject. Like an art show.

He pointed to a large picture. It showed a child crouching in front of the Behemoth.

The child was tied to a stake.

"Where is that?" He pointed to the stake.

"In the woods. It's the altar."

"Can I go out there?"

Joel rummaged in his desk. "It's a couple miles away. I'll drive."

A dirt road from town led to the forest. The trees formed a giant wall alongside the road, obscuring the sunlight.

"Does your monster live out here?" Garrahan asked.

Joel drummed his fingers on the steering wheel. "No one knows where it lives. In the woods, we think. The Vikings thought it lived in tunnels under the ground. The native people believed it dug itself a new lair every night." He glanced at Garrahan. "It doesn't take much space to hide out here."

The road dead-ended into what appeared to be impenetrable jungle. Garrahan could barely make out a path cut into a space between trees. It led into blackness.

He was surprised at how secluded this was. They had driven barely five minutes and it was like they were in a different world.

An eeriness suffused the forest here. It gave Garrahan a chill.

There were no sounds. No insects, birds, people, or faraway cars. As if the trees were smothering sound in their branches.

"Want to walk in?" Joel asked. "It's not far."

Suddenly, Garrahan didn't want to. He had a feeling that if he went in, he might not come out.

"What's the altar made of?" he asked, stalling.

"A stone pillar. It's been there for hundreds of years." Joel paused. "It does what it's intended to."

"I don't want to hear about that right now," Garrahan replied.

He was surprised to feel his heart beating hard against his ribs.

CHAPTER 55
MAY 8
WEDNESDAY, 4:50 PM

When they walked back into the town hall, people were in the lobby. Four men and two women, all middle-aged, all gesturing, voices raised.

The instant they saw Garrahan, they stopped talking—as if they'd been punched. He had walked in on something he wasn't supposed to know about.

Joel cleared his throat and looked from the group to Garrahan. His face went scarlet.

"Ladies, gentlemen," Joel said, voice cracking. "I wasn't expecting you." He looked at his watch. "The council meeting isn't till quarter after."

"We have things to discuss before the meeting," said one of the men. He eyed Garrahan and asked, "Who are you?"

Joel jumped in. "This is Robert Garrahan, who is assisting Mr. Malden right now." A couple people nodded knowingly. "Mr. Garrahan, this is the town council." He started pointing to them, one by one. "Lisa Matali, Dennis Janlov . . ."

Dennis Janlov held up his hand to stop Joel. "No need for introductions, Joel. We need to be moving along. Excuse us." They disappeared through double doors without another word.

Garrahan didn't ask what had just happened, but Joel—still blushing—offered anyway. "Weekly board meeting." He looked at his watch again. "But they're early. Can you wait a minute? I need to make sure they're settled in." Joel hurried out of the lobby.

Garrahan looked at the visitor's log on the lobby reception desk. Making sure that Joel was out of sight, he ripped the top page out of the book and jammed it into his pocket.

Joel was back seconds later, thumbs up.

"All's good," he said, his face still red.

They walked into the empty library.

Garrahan turned to Joel. "How come you know so much about the creature and about what happened to the priests?"

Joel smiled, allowing himself a measure of pride. "No one else was as good at gathering the information, I guess."

"How did you get it?"

"Mostly Internet," Joel beamed. "A lot from libraries in other towns. I scanned old newspapers and circulars. You don't attract a lot of attention as a kid in libraries. Mr. Malden, on the other hand, could never . . ."

"Could never look for information without creating suspicion. I've heard."

Joel picked up a folder from the reception desk. It contained everything he had compiled on the priests' deaths. He included a flash drive that had all the information on it—should Garrahan want to view it on his computer.

Garrahan looked quickly at the paper files while twirling the drive between his thumb and finger.

Joel watched Garrahan play with the drive. "And, um, in case you think you can take this to the police or anybody else. . ." he pointed to the drive. "The outline is authored by one Kenny Theorbo, age 11. He wrote it for a fantasy storytelling class in fifth grade. That's the story I would tell."

He made an odd, not quite grim, smile. "There actually is a Kenny Theorbo here, and he will say he wrote it." Joel folded his skinny arms across his chest. "That is, if you were thinking of using that for something other than helping Mr. Malden."

Garrahan shook his head. It was amusing watching Joel try to be a hard ass. "Save the overacting for when Malden's around," he said. "Because no matter how much bullshit you put in here," he waved the folder, "I'm not swallowing it."

Joel looked at him, wounded. "I guess you either believe or you don't. That's up to you." His voice sounded sad, as if addressing a lost soul.

"There are certain objective truths," Garrahan replied. He looked at the kids' drawings of the Behemoth. "Things are either true or not true, no matter what you're taught, or what's drilled into you. Or what you tell the outside world. No amount of telling makes it truer."

Joel kept his ground by not answering.

Garrahan's eyes fixed on the drawings. The kids, the monster, the blood.

"When was the first time you saw it?" he asked Joel, offhandedly.

Joel pursed his lips. "I've never seen it."

That startled Garrahan. "Pardon me?"

"I've never seen it," Joel replied, his shoulders hunching up.

"Malden told me everyone sees it once."

"Not everybody sees it. Most everybody does. Usually when they're little." He gulped.

A chink in the solid armor of the story, Garrahan thought. "How is it that the guy entrusted with knowing about the Behemoth has never seen it?" He eyed Joel. "That doesn't seem right, does it?"

"I'm not as adventurous as most. I never snuck a look as a kid."

"You still could," Garrahan offered.

"That's not a good idea," Joel said, forcefully. "No matter how old you are."

Garrahan mulled that over. Someone who believes but has never seen. An interesting twist. Something to think about later.

"I'm leaving," Garrahan said. "I'll be in touch tomorrow. What's your number?"

Joel gave it to him, and Garrahan tapped it into his phone. "Tell Malden I'll be back in a day or so."

Garrahan walked swiftly out of the library.

Joel followed, holding out his phone. "You should tell Mr. Malden you're leaving."

Without looking back, Garrahan said, "You should tell Mr. Malden to show you his monster."

.

CHAPTER 56
MAY 8
WEDNESDAY, 5:05 PM

As he pushed the ignition, Garrahan speed dialed Vanukoff, urging him to pick up.

"I'm still alive," he said when the call clicked through.

"You going to tell me what's going on, or do I have to guess?" Vanukoff asked.

"I'm not sure yet. It starts with a mass suicide about seventy years ago. Five priests killed themselves, all on the same day."

Vanukoff interrupted with a whistle. "That's a story. If you'd had me check into . . ."

"There's more," said Garrahan, impatiently. "It's been covered up for years. Whatever is going on in Morris is related to those priests. Or what they discovered."

Without being specific, he told Vanukoff he had to stay in Morris to sort out problems for the family of Bruce Donahue. A harmless lie.

"You're not telling me everything, are you?" Vanukoff mused. He could smell the lie.

"It's all I can say." Garrahan retrieved the paper he'd torn out of the register. "I need you to look up some names. Get everything you can on them." Garrahan read the names of the eighteen people who had signed into the town hall that day.

"Anything else? Vanukoff asked.

"Last thing," Garrahan replied. "As far as you know, and everyone at work knows, I'm tending to a family emergency." The best excuse he could come up with.

They finished, and Garrahan checked his rearview to see if any other vehicles were nearby. Nothing looked out of the ordinary. He drove to the outskirts of town, continually glancing at the mirror.

He didn't see a single car driving out of Morris. Garrahan blew out a heavy sigh as he accelerated up the highway ramp.

He also didn't see the tracking locator Malden had shoved under the passenger seat.

CHAPTER 57
MAY 8
WEDNESDAY, 6:20 PM

When he got to the motel, Garrahan found Elizabeth and Abby watching TV. The drapes were closed. They were both on the bed, huddled under the covers.

Their eyes grew wide as Garrahan opened the door and entered. They were still spooked at being in a motel room.

He sat down and explained what Malden wanted. He saw no alternative except to help Malden.

Instead of arguing, they nodded their heads. They knew what kind of man Malden was.

"Tell me about Joel," Garrahan said, after filling them in on his day.

"Not much to tell," Elizabeth said. "One of Malden's assistants. He runs the town library and schedules things like Sunday camp and kids' programs."

"And he's kind of cute," Abby giggled.

"Hey! I didn't know you thought that!" her mother said, in mock disbelief.

"Well, he is," said Abby, snuggling into the crook of Elizabeth's shoulder.

"I guess so," Elizabeth acknowledged.

"Why does he get to travel outside of Morris?"

Elizabeth shrugged. "Everyone can travel outside of Morris, for short distances. It's discouraged. The town leaders want people to feel safe in Morris, and uncomfortable anywhere else."

She explained that people took the occasional supervised shopping trip to Ashford or Longhaven to buy a necessity like a truck (Morris had no dealership) or a special-order item. Like the rest of the world, though, people in Morris could get almost anything they needed online. UPS made drop-offs at the village hall.

"There really isn't a lot of reason to leave. Joel goes more than others because he's always hoping to fill the gaps in our history. He visits libraries and courthouses to look for records."

As they talked, Garrahan saw anxiousness on the Donahues' faces. They were shell shocked. They needed a break from running and hiding.

"Let's get some dinner," said Garrahan, standing up. "Maybe find a place to see a movie or listen to music."

Abby jumped up so fast she almost tossed her mother off the bed. "That sounds amazing!" she squealed excitedly.

Half an hour later, they were sitting in a small diner having buffalo wings and root beer. Garrahan thought Abby looked to be having the time of her life. It would have been immensely enjoyable . . . if she wasn't in danger. For now, for part of an evening, that was forgotten.

CHAPTER 58
MAY 8
WEDNESDAY, 6:30 PM

No other attacks had been reported outside of Morris. Malden confirmed it.

The sleeping boy taken from the house had been the most recent.

Malden wanted to tell the council that there would be no more. But he couldn't—yet. They were not happy.

There was no guarantee Garrahan would be of any help. For the time being, though, he wouldn't be of any harm. Not if he kept to his mission.

Malden needed to do one more thing to ensure that Garrahan stayed focused.

Leonard sat across the room, his hand curled around a warm glass of scotch. Malden hadn't offered to add more ice to it.

"We have to resolve the unfortunate incident that took place in his apartment."

"I told you that it was an accident," Leonard said, shifting slightly in his chair.

"Call it what you will. I consider it a mistake."

Leonard hated having to sit and get lectured by Malden.

Leave me the fuck alone, Leonard thought, *and let me do my job.*

"As it turns out, the girlfriend is leverage," Malden offered. "Garrahan doesn't know what we'll do with her body. He can't afford to let anyone know what happened."

Leonard wanted to smirk. Things might not always go according to Malden's grand plans, but Leonard always made sure they worked out for the best. He didn't need a sermon every time Malden failed to see the big picture.

"What do you want to do with Garrahan in the meantime?" Leonard asked.

"He's got things to keep him busy," Malden said, dismissively. "That said, I have something I need you to do tonight. Something to keep you busy."

Music to my ears, thought Leonard, listening to Malden's directive.

"You need to be careful, Leonard. No mistakes this time. No accidents."

Leonard nodded, ready to leave and get started. He placed his glass on Malden's desk.

"I'm serious, Leonard," Malden said, leaning in slightly. "You think you're doing an impeccable job, that you're bulletproof." He waited until he saw Leonard's controlled smugness waver, then opened the door to his office. "If you mess this up, you will have no future in this town. And if you have no future in this town, then you have no future. Period."

Walking across the town square, Leonard cursed under his breath. When Malden got all high and mighty, Leonard wanted to punch someone in the mouth. Secretly, he wished it could be Malden.

He stopped at Ethan's house, knocking heavily on the door. Ethan was genuinely surprised to see him. The two hadn't spoken since returning from Manhattan.

Ethan was still creeped out by everything Leonard did in the city. He wasn't anxious to spend any more time with Leonard.

"I've got to go for a drive tonight," Leonard said, toothy smile wide on his face. "Malden's orders. Thought you might like to join me. Get out of town for a few hours." He leaned himself into Ethan's doorway.

The last thing Ethan wanted was to go for a drive with Leonard. "Oh, man. I really can't. I promised Joel I'd help him memorize his lines for the ordination. Mr. Malden told him he's got a lot of work to do." Ethan didn't know the first thing about what went into Joel's studies, but he was making up the most plausible lie he could.

Leonard scoffed. "Are you serious?" he snickered. "You can do that anytime. There's no rush."

Ethan trembled slightly, hoping it didn't show. "Joel's got to have someone listen to him so he can get it right."

Leonard shook his head.

"Ethan, Ethan, Ethan," he lamented. "Joel will only get to be deacon here after Malden's kicked the bucket. And that ain't going to be for thirty years or more. Both you and Joel will be grandfathers by then." He clucked his tongue. "Tonight, you're still young."

Ethan tried to show some spine. "Look, Joel's asking me to help him. He wants Mr. Malden to have confidence in him." Seeing a way to turn it around, Ethan lobbed it back at Leonard. "Just like Mr. Malden's confident in you."

The kid had a point, Leonard thought. Leonard wanted company, but obviously Ethan didn't have the balls to come out and play.

"Alright. Don't say I didn't offer. Who knows when the next opportunity might come along?"

Grin still on his face, Leonard turned, knocked a couple of times on the porch railing to signal the end of the conversation, and walked into the darkness.

Ethan closed the door. He leaned against the wall, his body slumping. He stayed that way for ten minutes, until he was sure Leonard wasn't coming back.

Then he went upstairs and turned off the lights before climbing into bed.

CHAPTER 59
MAY 8
WEDNESDAY, 10:30 PM

Garrahan sat up all night reading Joel's research. He kept the light low. Next to him, Abby and Elizabeth slept, wrapped around each other in the double bed. It was the quietest and most peaceful time they'd had together.

Joel's notes were good. In another world, another life, Joel would be an exceptional journalist. Everything was well laid-out, explained in detail. Good reporting of the facts.

He had included satellite images from the Internet. On those images, he noted each point where the priests killed themselves. Red lines connected the five points. It outlined a perfect pentagon.

Each red line was one mile long. They encompassed woods and a swath of the Butternut River, forming a boundary around Morris.

It was a pentagon. But there were six priests involved. Why not six points? A hexagon? Or a circle?

Another question. Who—or what—picked those five points?

Garrahan doodled on the map with his pen. He crisscrossed lines between the points and angles. He drew a five-pointed star inside the pentagon. That didn't make any sense. He scratched it out.

He got nowhere pondering maps. He needed data, history, information.

He thumbed through the pages. Joel's dossier had no personal interviews. No one-on-one telling of tales. That was understandable: it would have been suspicious for a kid from Morris to go sniffing around about hushed-up deaths.

Joel compensated for that shortcoming by compiling a list of relatives. He also came up with addresses of the churches that the priests had belonged to.

Garrahan read through the lists. He was going to have to do the personal interviews himself.

CHAPTER 60
MAY 9
THURSDAY, 9:00 AM

It was light when he woke up. Abby was sitting up in bed, reading a magazine from the motel lobby. Elizabeth was still asleep.

Garrahan waved silently to Abby. She waved back.

Garrahan made his way to the bathroom. Ten minutes later, he was ready to leave. He had to talk to Elizabeth first.

Abby patted her back. Elizabeth rolled over slowly, opening her eyes.

Telling his plans for the day, Garrahan said he'd be gone until late afternoon. Maybe later. He didn't want to leave the Donahues in the motel all day. He didn't want to drag them around, either.

Elizabeth and Abby wanted to stay near the motel. They would walk around the little town on their own. It would be an adventure. They would check out stores and shops. Be free for a while.

They needed some clothes, since Garrahan had completely forgotten about that during his meeting with Malden. He was embarrassed by the oversight.

The Donahues also needed a disposable cell phone. He looked at the time on his own phone. It was nearing ten.

Abby and Elizabeth washed up quickly and hurried out to the car. There was a mobile phone store two miles away. They were in and out in fifteen minutes.

A barely surviving department store sat across the road from the motel. Garrahan dropped them off and promised to call in a few hours.

He watched them walk into the store through revolving doors. Elizabeth tripped trying to navigate her way in.

Garrahan felt guilty leaving them alone. But he couldn't help them if he couldn't get Malden off their backs.

His first stop was Woodcrest Acres. He searched for information pertaining to Father Vernon Lindt. It didn't take long to realize there was nothing to be found.

The building that had been the Methodist church was now a woman's shelter. It was converted by the town eight years ago. The Methodist congregation had dwindled so much that it held services in the local high school. None of the church's records had been preserved, not that anyone knew of. The current pastor knew nothing of the parish's history—he'd transferred in from Wisconsin a few months ago.

It was indicative of how Garrahan's day was to go.

In Dunstam, the Lutheran church had a journal containing entries for every single day going back almost a century. The kind of data Garrahan was looking for. A beautiful piece of captured history. And ultimately disappointing.

On the date of the suicides, it simply read: "Fr. Marcus Kohler: Left on sabbatical to take care of sick mother." That was the last mention of Father Kohler. Anywhere.

The Catholic Church in Roseville was just as succinct regarding Father Moynihan.

"Fr. Timothy Moynihan's request for transfer granted immediately. Farewell."

Nothing more. No mention of suicide. No death notice.

Garrahan's search for Father Linik in Longhaven elicited a shrug from the woman at the front desk of the parish house. She'd worked here for thirty years and never heard of a Father Jared Linik.

The church wasn't good about keeping records in the old days, the woman lamented. "Today, everything is on computer"—she caressed it with a flourish of her manicured nails—but she didn't know where to find older paper documents.

The basement, maybe?

The woman led Garrahan to the clammy recesses of the cellar. Lit by yellowing fluorescents, she pointed to stacks of office boxes.

"Could be in there. I wouldn't know," she said laconically.

Garrahan made his way to the first stack. He opened the topmost box. Inside, the skeletal remains of a mouse lay on curling papers. It crumbled at his touch.

Ignoring the rodent, he grabbed the box. It sagged as he moved it.

"That's probably damaged from the flooding a couple years back." The woman paused. "Or maybe the flood fifteen years ago. That one reached all the way to the ceiling," she said, raising her hand above her. Another flourish.

"You've had two floods down here?"

"In the last fifteen years," she nodded. "Many more before that."

Garrahan tried other boxes. Each one disintegrated when he opened it. Nothing was left of the documents except dank pulp.

He wiped dampness off his hands. A waste of his time.

And so it went.

His last stop was Ashford. He knew before he started that it was a lost cause. He had driven by the Ashford Catholic Church in the past and never gave it a thought. Still, he had to stop in.

The woman in the rectory was nice enough. She told Garrahan the current church had been built on the site of the old church, which the parish had outgrown in the early 1990s. This newer church, with state-of-the-art audio and video system for use during Mass, had been built in its place.

When he asked where old records and documents had gone, she shrugged. The only things on file were databases that kept track of parish employees, schedules, and the budget. "Anything else was probably shredded or ended up with the bishop. Or at the bishop's lawyer's office."

Garrahan thanked her. He went outside and stood on the sidewalk, staring at the sky. He'd come up with nothing.

All five priests a dead end.

All forgotten.

The priests were victims of faded history, lost files, a pre-Internet age where a paper trail was the only trail. And, in all probability, victims of a conscious effort to make sure they were erased as people.

One piece of evidence that Garrahan got for his trouble was that two of the priests had been written off on the same day, never to be heard from again. Kohler and Moynihan. Gone. That confirmed part of the Morris story.

He looked at his notes. He didn't think he'd missed anything on the five men. Maybe a full team of investigators and months of free time would have turned up more.

Neither of which he had.

That left Father Pierce.

Albert Pierce was the only one of the priests who had an obituary. Not technically an obituary; a report in a local paper that he had gone missing.

The people of Morris expected Pierce to be a dead priest—they made him a coffin. He never showed up for the suicide party. What happened?

Joel identified a possible relative of Pierce's living outside of Ashford. Ginnie Pierce.

Father Pierce had no direct descendants, so she might be related in name only. Her side of the family might not even have known Father Albert Pierce.

Garrahan checked her address and his notes. She was the end of the line.

CHAPTER 61

MAY 9
THURSDAY, 1:00 PM

Mary McNeeney peered out of the grocery store as a car pulled from the curb.

"Isn't that Robert Garrahan's car?" she asked Ruth Bihlman.

Ruth twisted in her seat by the door. "Sure is," she muttered.

"Not like him not to stop in," Mary said.

"Must be busy," Ruth shrugged. Mary opened a roll of quarters into the cash register.

A moment of quiet. Mary turned to Ruth. "Weren't we talking to him about the disappearances last time he was in?"

Ruth nodded.

"We said bad things come in threes. That boy in Roseville disappeared a few days later. That made four. At least," said Mary.

"The disappearances have slowed," Ruth said, not looking up from her paper. "Nothing bad since summer's here. Maybe the badness is gone."

"Badness never goes away," Mary sniffed. She broke a roll of dimes into the tray.

"It just goes to sleep, or it moves on."

CHAPTER 62
MAY 9
THURSDAY, 1:16 PM

Ginnie Pierce was digging deep in her garden when Robert Garrahan rolled into her driveway. Her house was a few hundred yards from the nearest neighbor. To Garrahan, it was the middle of nowhere.

Ginnie stood as Garrahan strolled over.

A good-looking young man, she thought. *With pain on his face.*

They exchanged pleasantries. Garrahan mentioned he was from Ashford. Then he got to the crux of his visit.

"I'm a writer for a news company in Manhattan. I'm researching the disappearance of some priests a few decades back. I believe one of them was related to you."

Ginnie did not hide her surprise. Not by a long shot. Her body flinched.

"You know about that?" she choked out.

It wasn't the question that jolted her. It was shock that someone else knew.

Garrahan was as surprised by her reaction as she was of the question.

"There were five priests who died in Morris. Father Albert Pierce disappeared the same day they did," he replied. "He wasn't listed among the dead."

Ginnie laughed. It was a hearty laugh for an old woman.

"He was my great uncle. I never met him. I didn't think anybody outside my family knew about him."

"I don't think many people do," he replied. "People in Morris, though, are inter . . ."

She laughed again. "Ah, yes. Morris. Where his story begins and ends."

"What do you mean?" he asked.

"You know. The gossip that people in small towns make about people in other small towns. The things I've read in Uncle Albert's papers."

Garrahan's turn to gasp. "Your uncle kept papers?"

"I wouldn't call them papers, as such. He kept a diary and a notebook, along with a few maps. Most of them are about Morris." She smiled. "I was getting ready to toss his things. I never thought anyone would care."

"Can we talk about him?" Garrahan urged.

"Sure. How about something to drink? Water? Iced tea? Beer?" They walked into the house.

She poured cold water from the tap. Sitting at a dining room table, she listened to Garrahan's story.

"People in Morris want to know what happened all those years ago. They think it has to do with this creature." He left out the gory and garish elements, including Nancy and the Donahues. "I think it's a cover for something else."

"My uncle believed in that creature," she said.

Garrahan shouldn't have been surprised. He was. He asked the next question softly.

"Do you believe in it?"

She shrugged. "Not inclined to." She got two beers from the refrigerator. "I spent thirty years in the Army medical corps. Two tours overseas, then traveling in military helicopters all over the States. I did preparedness training for medical teams." She fingered the glass, remembering something long gone, still memorable.

"I saw a lot of the world. Most of it from flying less than a mile above the ground. There's a lot of strange things out there. A lot of places nobody's ever explored. There are more places in the world where people aren't than where they are.

"That's a way of saying it could be true." Ginnie smiled. "I'm not saying it is, but plenty of animals—creatures, beasts, call them what you want—are hiding out there. Hell, huge snakes and giant squids are all over the world and they hide out just fine."

"But this is a monster people think lives in the forests near their . . ."

"Have you been in the woods around here?" she asked, cocking an eyebrow. "I mean, deep in the woods? They go on for miles and miles. As far as thirty miles in a stretch. You could hide a stack of Sherman tanks in there and never find them if you looked your whole life." She sipped her beer. "There are homes—big homes—in those woods. Nobody knows about them except the people living in them. I've stumbled on a few."

Ginnie was right. The world was a big place. Lots of things stayed hidden forever. Planes that disappeared in the ocean, never to be found. Villagers kidnapped in wartime and taken away, never to be found. Who knew what else the world kept hidden, never to be found . . . but a Behemoth?

"I'm trying to find out why your great uncle's name is associated with the Morris deaths." Regardless of the monster story, he wanted to add.

Ginnie didn't have regular visitors. With Garrahan as an audience she warmed to her topic. "Uncle Albert was an enigma. A person who believed in hidden things and supernatural mysteries. I imagine that's why he became a priest." She twisted the top off another beer. "Even as a Catholic priest, he believed in the Behemoth."

"Why should he believe? Did he ever live in Morris?"

"No, he didn't. But he saw it once," she said, sipping more beer.

"When it killed one of his friends."

CHAPTER 63
MAY 9
THURSDAY, 2:00 PM

Albert Pierce's father was a tractor salesman who lived in Woodcrest Acres. Tractors were a novelty; a lot of farmers weren't convinced they would replace cattle for plowing fields.

Albert's father had a territory that spread eighty miles in every direction. Morris was one of the towns on his route. He went there every six weeks. He liked going to Morris because he could make his calls and get home by dinnertime.

There wasn't much business, maybe a tractor every year or so. In any event, there was always maintenance to be done. Albert's father would check on his customers to make sure the machines were performing as promised. If need be, he'd get his hands greased up, climb under the tractors, and help with repairs.

On occasion, he drove into Morris just to say hello and see if there was anything he could sell to the locals. On those trips, Albert's father brought Albert along. Partly for company, partly out of a perceived fatherly obligation to spend a modicum of time with his son. Mostly to have someone to practice his sales pitches on.

Albert enjoyed the trips, despite nothing much ever happening. It was fun to ride with his dad. He didn't mind that he had to sit in the car when his father went in a store to talk business.

That changed on one trip. Albert's dad got corralled into helping pull a tractor out of a ditch. It was going to be a long day, so Albert was allowed outside the car—and told not to wander far away.

He saw his father across a field with men rigging chains to a beat-up pickup and the tractor. The tractor lay on its side like a dead animal in rigor mortis, limbs stretched out.

A young boy walked up to Albert. He moved so quietly that Albert didn't see him until he said "Hey."

Albert jumped. The boy was about his age, maybe eight or nine. He carried a tackle box.

"Whatcha doin'?" the boy asked.

Albert pointed to the tractor. "Waiting for my dad."

"Uh huh," the boy muttered, looking at the phalanx of humans swarming into the ditch.

Staring at the tractor, they didn't say anything for a few minutes. The boy broke the silence. "That ditch leads to Willowick Creek. Good fishing this time of year. You want to go?" The boy tapped his tackle box.

Albert wanted to. It was hot and boring sitting here watching the men. They didn't seem to be making progress. Plus, it had been a year since he'd last gone fishing with his father.

"I can't. I have to wait for my dad."

"We're not going far."

Albert played the scenario out in his mind. He'd go over and ask his dad if he could go. His dad would be sweaty and angry at how long everything was taking. He'd yell at Albert to go sit in the car and wait. "I better not. Maybe next time."

"Okay," the boy answered. Shuffling off, he turned around. "It's great fishing. The best ever. I've got an extra rod, too." He walked into the woods.

Albert looked wistfully after the boy. He went to sit in the car.

Three hours later, Albert's father slid into the front seat. He was drenched in sweat and in a foul mood. He threw the stick shift into gear and hurtled home.

Over dinner, his father relaxed. He reveled in the story, telling his wife about the derring-do that had freed the tractor from the thick and dangerous muck.

When his mother asked what Albert had done during all this, he mentioned that "I met a boy from Morris. He asked me to go fishing."

That simple utterance deflated his father's dinner-time ebullience. "Listen here, Albert," he said, leaning in and pointing at Albert's face with his knife, "You are never to go and do anything in the town of Morris. With anyone, ever. Do you understand me?"

"But we were just going to go fishing down at . . ."

"I don't care what you were going to do," his father glowered, knife still pointing. "Morris is not a place to go running around. You sit in the car when we go visit. You talk to your little friend there. But nowhere else."

That was that. No discussion, no backtalk, no reasons given.

The next time Albert was back in Morris, his father made an actual sale. There was some celebrating and backslapping. Albert waited in silence.

The local boy stopped by the car again. His name was Randall. His family lived in Morris. Near the church.

"You want to go fishin'?" Randall asked.

"Can't," was Albert's answer. He hung his head. "My dad doesn't want me hanging out here, except to ride with him."

"We'd just be fishing."

"I told him that," Albert protested. "He says I can't leave the car."

"Well, come sometime without him. There's a shortcut through the forest to Woodcrest Acres. You could ride a bike here in less than an hour."

"Nah. He'd know if I was gone all day."

"Come at night, then," said Randall. "I got glowworms for fishing in the dark. It's cool to watch."

Albert liked that idea. He could leave one evening when his dad was on a road trip. His mom always went to bed early. He could sneak out of the house and go night fishing.

Albert and Randall made a plan.

Two weeks later, his father was on an overnight sales trip in the Berkshires. His Mom went to bed right after dinner. It was 8 PM. Albert strapped a tackle box to his handlebars. For the next hour, he rode his bike through the fields and woods. He found Randall under a large tree outside the village, where the creek cut a wide gash into the ground. The moon lit up the water and the surrounding fields. It looked as bright as day, with dark blue shadows.

They fished wordlessly. The only sound was the weights on their lines hitting the surface of the water.

An hour passed. Neither boy had gotten a tug on his line. "We can move a little farther up the creek," said Randall. "There's a bend where fish hang out."

They walked half a mile in the moonlight, careful not to trip over tree roots and ground vines. The night got blacker as the canopy of branches got thicker.

Another hour. Still nothing tugged at their lines. Nonetheless, Albert loved being out under the stars. He enjoyed the silence and company of someone who might become a new friend.

"I should go. It's been a few hours," he said to Randall.

"Yeah, me too. I'm not supposed to be out this late. Not when it's this dark," Randall said as he reeled in his line. "But I'm not a scaredy cat. I'll go out when I want to. Nobody can stop me." It was an odd thing for Randall to say.

They walked towards the tree where Albert had left his bike. "I'll see you when I come back with my dad. Another month or so."

"Great. See ya then." Randall gave Albert a light punch on the shoulder. He walked back toward town through the field.

Albert tried attaching his tacklebox to the handlebars. Even with a bright moon, it was not working. He dropped the box a couple of times before finally getting it tied on tight. He climbed on the bike and watched Randall, maybe a hundred feet away, wave goodbye.

Waving back, Albert saw something—or a shadow of something. It raced across the field towards Randall.

The shadow moved oddly, like a flock of birds or a swarm of bees. It was slithering and flying at the same time.

Dark and fast, parts of it glinted in the moonlight.

Albert saw Randall stop. The boy dropped his tacklebox.

Randall threw his hands up. Trying to prevent something from happening.

The beginnings of a scream came out of Randall's mouth.

The black shape was on him.

Albert forced his eyes to stay open.

The black thing didn't stop moving.

Randall was gone.

He had become part of the black object. Or swallowed whole.

The thing left a trampled swath of matted grass as it made its way into the woods.

Where Randall had been, there was nothing.

Albert's first instinct was to go to where Randall had been standing. Then fear kicked in.

Before he knew it, he was pedaling his bike as fast and far away as he could. Away from Morris. Away from the monster or monsters in the field.

He had no memory of getting back into his room. He was only aware of waking up in his own bed, wearing all his clothes. His sneakers were on, still wet from walking along the creek. His eyes were burning, as if he'd been crying for hours.

Albert thought he'd been dreaming. His wet socks and shoes proved that was not the case.

Something had taken Randall. Maybe eaten him.

Thinking about it made Albert want to throw up. Running to the bathroom, he did.

He couldn't say anything to his parents, because he wasn't supposed to be sneaking out in the middle of the night. Let alone going to Morris.

All he could do was wait until his father's next trip. That was an entire month of waking up in the middle of the night, ready to scream out when he dreamed the dark thing was on top of him.

They visited Morris four weeks later. Albert asked a man working underneath a tractor if he knew a boy named Randall. The man—who seemed surprised to be asked that question—shrugged and said, nope, he'd never heard of a kid named Randall. And he knew everybody in town. No boys named Randall.

That was a lie. Albert knew it. He also knew there was nothing he could say.

He was eight years old. His new friend had been ripped away in a scene from a nightmare. This man claimed there had never been a Randall.

Randall was very probably dead.

Dead in a way that no one wanted to talk about.

Hiding under his covers that night, Albert decided to spend his life finding out what happened to Randall.

CHAPTER 64

MAY 9
THURSDAY, 3:30 PM

"Your great uncle wrote all this down?"

Ginnie shook her head. "Not that part. That was the story passed down amongst the relatives. The shaggy dog tale we heard at family gatherings." She got a distant look in her eyes. "Of course, those family gatherings stopped happening years ago. Aren't too many Pierces left up in this part of the state." For the first time, her voice was sad.

"May I look at what he wrote?"

She hesitated. "No one has seen those pages outside of our family," Ginnie said. "It's strange to consider sharing them." She tapped the table. There were now four empty beer bottles on it. "Give me a second and I'll get them from downstairs."

Ginnie returned with an old wooden crate. It looked like it had been used for storing milk bottles or wine. It was partially full of paper. *Not much paper*, Garrahan thought at first glance.

The box contained a thick diary and a stack of papers with doodles. Looking closer, he saw that the doodles were mostly maps. They were tucked in with drawings like those Garrahan had seen too much of in the Morris daycare center: a monster crashing through trees and farm fields.

They were pictures that Father Albert had drawn over the course of his life. Garrahan thumbed through them. They became more detailed—and more horrific—as the priest got older.

"Can I take these?" Garrahan asked, looking up from the table.

"Afraid not," Ginnie said. "You can stay and read them for as long as you like. You can take pictures of them, if you want. But I don't feel right letting them go."

She pulled the priest's diary out of the box. "Maybe if you can tell me what happened to him, I'll give it up. Till then, I should probably keep an eye on it." She made a half smile. "Family history, and all."

"I understand," Garrahan said. Ginnie went to her garden while he spent two hours photographing each page with his phone.

He finished just as the sun was sinking into the trees. He shook his head at what he'd read. Father Pierce was as deep into believing in the creature as Malden and the Morris townspeople.

"Do you mind if I come back in the next day or so to follow up?" Garrahan asked.

"I'd enjoy that," Ginnie replied.

He thanked her and left, suddenly concerned about how late it had gotten. He hoped the Donahues weren't worried.

He dug out his phone and called Elizabeth's new number.

It rang once and immediately picked up. She must have been waiting for his call.

It wasn't her voice.

"So good to hear from you, Mr. Garrahan," said Edward Malden. "I trust you've been busy."

CHAPTER 65
MAY 9
THURSDAY, 7:45 PM

The locator served as a shining beacon in the countryside.

Elizabeth and Abby had returned to the motel from a day at the mall. Leonard was sitting on their bed.

There was no discussion. No arguing, no fighting. They went quietly to their house in Morris. Edward Malden was waiting.

There were tears and protestations in the living room. It didn't last long. Malden assured them he wouldn't hurt them. They had to remain in their house—under guard—until Garrahan did everything that was asked of him. Once he did, everything would be normal again. Malden promised.

Just like old times.

Garrahan had not thought Malden capable of putting a high-tech tracking system in his car. He still thought of Morris as populated by backwoods Quakers with no access to technology. He needed to change that thinking. Change it fast.

He drove into Morris, not sure what to do. He felt like this venture had occupied him for months. It was a mere four nights ago that he whisked Elizabeth out of this same house.

That had been for naught. He was back where he started. Worse than when he started. Four days ago, no one he knew was dead.

He walked through the Donahue's front door. He'd been in this house only once, in the middle of the night, to retrieve Elizabeth. It was spacious and warm in the early evening light.

Elizabeth and Abby were next to each other on a couch. Not comfortable, yet not afraid.

Malden sat across away from the window, sinking into darkness. A man Garrahan didn't recognize—Leonard—paced the hallway. In the kitchen, Mrs. Bower puttered at the stove.

"You know everyone, I believe," Malden said, pressing his fingertips together. "Oh, but you've not met Leonard in person." He nodded toward Leonard, who didn't stop his pacing or acknowledge Garrahan.

"I've heard his name," Garrahan said through clenched teeth.

Malden smiled thinly. "Everything's in order then," he said, standing up. He walked over to Garrahan and leaned his face in close.

"This is how it goes from here on in. The Donahues are home. They will remain here. They will not be leaving." He looked over at Abby, who flinched. "You, Mr. Garrahan, will stay here, too. You will work here when you're not out investigating."

He lifted his hand towards Leonard. "You'll have people here round the clock to help you out."

Garrahan heard Elizabeth wince.

"Let's go have a chat." Malden commanded, motioning Garrahan outside.

Garrahan paused. "Are you okay?" he asked Elizabeth and Abby. They nodded, shakily.

Standing by the gas pumps, Garrahan told Malden what he'd found. He had photos of maps and diary entries from Father Albert Pierce by way of his grand-niece. He hadn't had time to review them. He would do it over the course of the night.

"This is good news," Malden said, betraying something akin to joy.

"What are you going to do with the Donahues?" Garrahan asked, his voice tight.

"They're staying here. I told you that."

Garrahan shook his head. "They don't want to stay here."

"Oh, I think they do. They had to return here to realize they missed it."

Malden turned to walk back into the house. Garrahan grabbed his sleeve.

"Have you considered what's going to happen with Bruce Donahue's body? He's still lying in a morgue in Manhattan. His family hasn't been able to claim him. The police will start . . .

Malden pulled his arm away. "Do you think we're that stupid? Bruce's body was retrieved in New York by Ethan yesterday. 'On behalf of the family.' He is currently being prepared for burial in our cemetery."

Garrahan was too stunned to respond. Malden had covered every base.

Malden's grin set hard in his face. "Don't take me for a rube, Mr. Garrahan. As you oh-so-worldly New Yorkers are fond of saying, this isn't my first rodeo."

He walked a step closer to Garrahan. "I've been to a great number of rodeos, and I've won them all." An inch closer. "I'm very good at my job. So were my predecessors. That is why we've kept Morris under the radar for more than a century. Very few, if any, people outside of this village know anything about what we do here. That's the way it's always been. That's the way it needs to stay."

Garrahan tried not to let his blood boil. He had seen the nastiness of which Malden was capable.

"You need me," he said defiantly. "I'm the only hope you've got to fix whatever it is you're trying to fix."

"No, you're not our only hope. In fact, there are several plans in place right now. You're a part of one of them. If the plan involving you doesn't work, we have other paths to pursue."

Garrahan was sure Malden was lying. Just as he knew Malden was lying about the town's beliefs and the real reason for the deaths of the priests.

"Then I should just leave," Garrahan stated, flatly.

Malden shrugged. "You're certainly free to leave. Of course, then you'd have no idea where your girlfriend's body might turn up. Or what might become of the Donahues, whom you kidnapped from this very house."

He and Malden stared eye to eye for a moment, the sun sinking behind them. A deadlock, with neither man ready to give what little ground he had established.

Malden closed the gap between them. They were nose to nose.

He lowered his voice. "Don't make the mistake of thinking you understand what you're up against. I told you I've never lost a rodeo. You're not even in the ring."

CHAPTER 66
MAY 9
THURSDAY, 8:00 PM

Malden marched into the Donahue house, feet pounding loudly on the floor. He did not wait for Garrahan to follow.

If no one had been around, Malden would have cursed at the sky. That, or smashed something against the wall. Garrahan was his best hope. Garrahan could not know that.

Garrahan had made an impressive first step by getting the notes of Father Albert Pierce. There was no guarantee it would bear fruit. Or when. A day? A month? Malden had to show he was still in charge and making things happen.

This was as good a place as any to make a pronouncement, he thought.

"After much thought, I have decided we will have a feeding. Beginning tonight."

Mrs. Bower dropped the pan she was using to the floor. She rushed into the living room. Leonard scrunched his face and let out a half whistle. The Donahues cast their gazes at the floor.

Bower wiped her hands on the side of her apron. Her eyes were wide, bulging with fear.

"You can't! Not tonight! There's no time to get ready!" Her tone was beseeching.

"I can. I am going to. Leonard, have Joel ring the bells. Get one of the farmers to provide the cattle."

Leonard flashed a thumbs up and hurried out the door. He winked at Garrahan, who was still by the gas pumps.

This was the part of his job Leonard hated. He had to get the nervous nellies in town ready for the feeding—a ritual none of them liked—and he had to get it done before dark.

He'd start by going out to Tom Rossberg's farm. Tom had sliced up plenty of bulls in his day.

The rest of the town would be up in arms about having to double barricade their homes.

Back in the dimming light of the living room, Malden continued. "You and Leonard will stay here tonight, Loretta. So will Mr. Garrahan. Make sure everything gets locked up. If you need to take care of your own house, go do it now."

Mrs. Bower ran out the front door, hands frantically scrabbling over her clothes.

"You should make sure Mr. Garrahan doesn't do anything stupid tonight," he said to Elizabeth. "Perhaps you could lock him in his room."

Malden walked out as Garrahan walked back in.

By the time Elizabeth explained to Garrahan what was going to happen tonight, Abby was crying. The bells in the church had begun to ring.

CHAPTER 67
MAY 9
THURSDAY, 8:10 PM

For Garrahan, this was a new twist. Panic infected everyone. A frenzy he'd not previously seen.

The ritual he'd heard about since Bruce Donahue darkened his door involved taking a young girl out to the altar. Chaining her in the middle of the forest. Leaving her there.

"Feeding" was significantly different.

It was the offering that took place once a season. It "provided sustenance to Behemoth in time when sacrifice was not proffered," to quote Elizabeth. Feeding the beast with something other than a small child.

Large animal carcasses were involved. No humans.

"Why is everyone so worked up?" Garrahan asked. Wasn't this better than taking a girl into the woods to face whatever lurked out there?

Not according to Elizabeth. The annual ritual was done privately. It involved only the town council and the family of the girl who was selected by lottery. Everyone else went about their business. The ritual didn't touch their personal lives. Or their houses.

The feeding was a different story. During spring, summer, autumn, and winter, the creature was given an offering of raw flesh to keep it fed and sustained. Always on the last day of the season. Townspeople had time and opportunity to safeguard their families and homes well in advance.

That process always began three days before the feeding. Residents turned off lights and bolted doors. They sat quietly in their homes. Waiting for the creature to make its rounds.

Feedings were scarier to residents than the annual sacrifice. The feeding endangered everyone, young and old. It lured the Behemoth into town as they slept.

With the annual sacrifice of a child, the beast was given its offering deep in the woods. Miles away. Out of sight and almost out of mind.

With the feeding, the creature came to their doorsteps.

CHAPTER 68

MAY 9
THURSDAY, 9:00 PM

It was dark when Ginnie Pierce finally called it a day and sat down on the porch.

Robert Garrahan had left a few hours ago. She'd gone back to her gardening, digging dirt until nightfall.

She sat on a lounge chair with legs outstretched, back aching. The air was moist. Moths and mosquitoes flew around the bulb that hung over her chair.

With an icy beer in one hand, she reread her great-uncle's notes. She hadn't read them carefully in many years, although she knew the story by heart. The tales always came to mind when an "Uncle Albert story" was in the news. Like those kids getting killed. The old lady. The sleeping kid. Uncle Albert stories.

Then again, maybe any mysterious disappearance was an Uncle Albert story.

She laughed as she read his words. Kids and old people disappeared all the time, she mused. Sometimes no one ever found out why. Maybe those left behind when people disappeared fabricated weird stories to explain what happened.

By the time Ginnie finished reading pages she hadn't read in years, she was convinced of one thing. What she'd grown up hearing about Uncle Albert and the priests was horseshit.

She would have been pleased that Garrahan thought so, too.

CHAPTER 69
MAY 9
THURSDAY, 9:00 PM

The bells pealed until the last trace of sunlight disappeared below the tree line. Lavender glowed in the far western sky. In Morris it was as dark as midnight. The forest surrounding the village made everything blacker.

Garrahan sat in the Donahues' kitchen. All lights were out. Windows were closed and shutters barred. He read Father Pierce's notes by the light of his phone.

"Barred" was a literal term. The shutters were reinforced with steel rods that gave the appearance of cellblock bars. They were latched to the house with metal locks.

The doors, made of iron, were secured in place with five sliding bolts, two of which were pushed into the concrete foundation of the house.

The Donahues—and every denizen of Morris—were in lockdown for their own protection.

Elizabeth and Abby went about closing windows methodically in a ritual with which they were all too familiar. Garrahan looked out at the neighborhood with amazement. The moment the bells tolled, people appeared outside their houses like bats flushed out of caves. They performed the same tasks: closing windows, hammering shutters in place, clamping locks down on iron chains.

Within minutes, every house was battened down as if expecting an onslaught of artillery fire. Windows, doors, and garages were shielded by sheets of metal and steel bars.

The houses became fortresses, their lights disappeared. No porch or table lights, no flickering of TVs or candles. The barest of illumination from streetlights.

"Why are the streetlights on?" Garrahan asked.

"To guide Behemoth to its offerings," Abby replied, not looking up from her book.

"And so there's light for the truck with the flesh," her mother added.

When it was time to lock the Donahue's front door, Garrahan protested.

"I want to see what goes on," he demanded. "How else am I supposed to believe this?"

Elizabeth pushed him away from the door. "Not from here," she said, firmly. She knelt and bolted the door, leaning her weight into it.

She led him to the attic stairs. "If you're intent on seeing what's going on, go to the attic. On the side facing the town green, there's an air vent. It's small, and the space is cramped, but you can see to the street." She looked at him without blinking. "It's not a good idea."

His first impulse was to get mad. The absurdity of this made his brain buzz.

"I'm here against my will, and so are you," he replied. "I never wanted any part of this, yet here I am. If I can see what's at the root of this, then I want to see it. Okay?" He felt petulant.

Elizabeth shrugged defeatedly. "Okay, okay. But don't make a sound. Not a breath, not a whisper, not a cough, not a sneeze. Our house needs to be mute in order to have the Behemoth pass by."

Garrahan kept from rolling his eyes. He ascended the stairs and eased his way into the attic. Cramming into a space between the roof rafters, he pressed against the vent and peered out.

He heard a truck rumbling down the street. It was moving slowly and making stops up the road.

After several minutes, the truck came into view. A flatbed, slightly bigger than a pickup. It pulled up to one of the large bowls that Garrahan had once thought might be for displaying flowers or plants—civic beauty bowls.

Elizabeth, in her description of what was going to happen, had indicated that he was far off the mark.

They were the bowls for feeding.

Two men got out of the flatbed, circling around to the back. There was a mound of something on the truck. Elizabeth told him they were the freshly carved carcasses of several bulls. "Freshly carved" meant the bulls had been slaughtered, hacked, and thrown on the flatbed in the space of less than two hours.

He heard chains clanking and men grunting as they hauled huge slabs of flesh into the bowl.

The two men were shadows and outlines in the streetlight. They dumped the flesh and climbed back in, like garbage men finished with a stop. The truck motored down the street and out of Garrahan's field of vision.

He sat on his haunches and listened. The truck made several more stops before its existence was no more.

This then, was the feeding. The town sacrificed a child to the creature in an annual ceremony, part of paying penance for the town's collective sins, paying homage to God's greatest creation. The feeding made sure the Behemoth stayed alive. Not that the creature couldn't take care of itself, as the village elders had always maintained. The offering of raw flesh was a way to keep the beast sated and keep it from hunting the streets at night.

It had worked without fail for the better part of a century.

The townspeople believed the feeding essential in appeasing the Behemoth, although many of them objected to it. The meat began to smell the day after it was placed on the concrete bowls, attracting flies and ravens. If there was meat after three days, its stench pervaded the neighborhoods. Some villagers advocated for putting the bowls in a different part of town. The Behemoth would surely still find the offering.

Malden always reminded them, in world-weary tones, that the point of paying homage to the Behemoth was to acknowledge its sovereignty over man—and to be reminded of its fearsomeness. Keeping the offerings in plain sight reminded the townspeople of God's power—and the power of his creations. Shunting the bowls off to the forest would be an insult to God, an attempt to diminish his creature's presence.

That was as far as the discussions got. Malden made sure the malcontents were sufficiently chastened.

Garrahan went downstairs after the truck's engine could no longer be heard. Elizabeth assured him that when the Behemoth came to the bowl near their house, he would hear it. He could stay in the attic and keep watch, she suggested.

The night began.

Loretta Bower fidgeted in a chair, looking nervously at the door. Leonard, who had come in before the truck started its journey, sat with a small tablet, watching a reality show involving teenaged moms.

Elizabeth and Abby fell asleep on the couch. It reminded Garrahan of how they'd looked in the backseat of his car.

Garrahan sat on the stairs, elbows on his knees, alert. He stared at the front door, hoping for anything—a noise, a scratch, a scream—to occur outside.

He was able to stay awake for hours. Long past the others.

At 3 AM, he fell asleep.

CHAPTER 70
MAY 10
FRIDAY, 6:16 AM

Robert Garrahan woke with a start.

Something made a sound outside.

He stood up quickly, finding his balance on the stairs. For a moment, he wasn't sure where he was.

The shuttered windows blocked out all light. He had no idea what time it was.

He checked the clock. 6:16 AM. Daytime.

Garrahan ran into the attic. Sunshine seeped in through the vent. Dust motes were caught in diagonal streams of light. He pressed his face to the vent and gazed out. People were unlocking doors and opening shutters. Some were walking around the neighborhood.

The concrete bowl near the gas station glistened in the morning sun. It was piled high with dripping red slabs of meat.

The Behemoth had not come.

Garrahan leaped down the stairs, waking the Donahues. As they sleepily opened their house, Garrahan tried not to jump for joy. Their monster had not appeared.

It had been a ruse. A show.

Abby pursed her lips, as if explaining something to a small dog.

"It doesn't always come on the first night. It sometimes doesn't come at all." She shrugged. "It doesn't always need to feed. Besides, since it escaped, we don't know if it will come back for the offering."

Garrahan's victory deflated. Precisely when he had thought he understood how it worked in Morris, they had disarmed him.

Leonard walked out the front door without saying a word. Loretta hurried off in the direction of her home. Elizabeth turned on the stove and started making eggs for breakfast. She didn't ask anyone if they wanted anything; she just began cooking.

Garrahan moved as in a dream. He was under house arrest, threatened with bodily harm, yet the scene around him resembled a family in a rural town heading off to work.

Half an hour later, Edward Malden strode through the door unannounced and without knocking. "What did you learn from reading Father Pierce's notes last night?" he asked.

Garrahan had forgotten about them. He looked groggily at Malden. "I learned that the Behemoth didn't follow your plan."

Malden's body tensed. Clenching his fists behind his back, he smiled at Garrahan. "Are you saying you didn't find anything?"

Garrahan walked past Malden. "I'm saying I didn't get to it. Your offering of the flesh put me to sleep." He yawned. "I woke up a little while ago."

Enticed by the aroma, Garrahan walked into the kitchen. Malden hesitated, then followed. "You'll continue today."

"Right after breakfast. If it's a little later than that, you know where to find me."

Malden ground his teeth together loud enough that Garrahan and the Donahues could hear it.

"Don't waste time," Malden hissed. "Mine or yours."

He spun on his heel and stormed out.

"You know he will hurt you, don't you?" Elizabeth said over her shoulder to Garrahan.

"I don't care all that much right now," he said curtly. "I'm very tired. And tired of all this."

He looked longingly at the eggs and decided against eating. "I'm going to lie down upstairs. Get some proper sleep. I'll set my alarm."

Elizabeth and Abby watched him go. They ate breakfast in silence, waiting for Mrs. Bower and Leonard to come back.

CHAPTER 71
MAY 10
FRIDAY, 7:30 AM

Garrahan opened the windows and paced the bedroom. One question poked hard at his brain: what were these people hiding?

Locking up houses and dragging out animal carcasses was too elaborate a process for a simple deception. It was a lot of staging to get him to believe nonsense.

What, then?

The strangeness around him boiled down to three different scenarios.

The first was that the Behemoth was a cover for something illicit in the village. He thought of places in Central America where entire towns were in the employ of drug cartels. Everyone from the local sheriff to the school bus driver acted as if nothing untoward went on, yet they all knew that people were being killed, drugs were being trafficked, and lots of money was being made in the process of cultivating and distributing drugs.

That seemed a reasonable scenario. Yet Garrahan couldn't figure out what Morris might be engaged in. With girls involved, it could be international slavery, sex trade, pedophilia.

The second notion was that Malden was pulling the wool over the collective eyes of the villagers. Residents believed the bullshit behind the Malden family's longstanding religious mythology and tradition. They'd grown up with it and were taught to believe. Malden was profiting from that blind faith, hiding something behind it. Given Malden's behavior, and his ability to control the townspeople, there was merit in this.

The last scenario was the one Garrahan had the hardest time accepting. It was that the Behemoth, whatever its origin, was a real creature that came out of the woods and scared the shit out of these people. If this was true, there had to be some way to verify it. He doubted the creature could live up to the Biblical qualities ascribed to it.

A large creature up here might be a bear or a mutant wolf. But that wouldn't scare a whole town for decades on end. Unless—like the people in Scotland who live near Loch Ness—they wanted desperately to believe in a monster. Any kind of monster.

Garrahan dropped on the bed. None of the three ideas were wholly believable. The most likely was Scenario Two, that Malden and cronies like Leonard and Ethan were hiding something very bad. It made sense given that they had resorted to murder.

Too many questions, Garrahan thought.

He closed his eyes and was asleep in moments.

CHAPTER 72
MAY 10
FRIDAY, 10:40 AM

A call woke him. Dave Vanukoff started in immediately, ignoring the sleepiness in Garrahan's voice.

"As much as I was hoping there was still a slave trade in your corner of the world, I couldn't find anything salacious. I found nothing in Morris."

Garrahan closed his eyes. Partly out of fatigue. Partly from disappointment.

"However," Vanukoff continued, "one of the people on your list—Leonard Smeak—did come up in my search."

"Five years ago, there was a large meth lab near you. Hidden in the woods, in a remote part of Longhaven. A big deal. Several million dollars in drugs funneling through every year. A man named George Smeak was arrested for running the lab. His distant cousin—Leonard, a name on your list—posted a hundred grand in bail for George. He then skipped bail. He's been a phantom ever since."

Fucking Leonard, Garrahan thought. *He had money to help his cousin. A cousin who ran a meth lab in the forest outside of Morris.*

"Is that it?" Garrahan asked, rubbing his forehead.

"Isn't that enough?" replied Vanukoff, exasperated. "None of the other people on your list came up except in genealogy records or business filings. Not a single thing in the courts. It's like they don't even issue fucking parking tickets in Morris. Everyone's clean. Leonard Smeak showing up means he's different from everyone else there. He's on the radar."

Leonard was the town goon. He did the dirty work. Maybe that involved working with Cousin George's meth business.

"This is good," Garrahan said. "I don't know how to use it, but it's better than anything I've gotten." He thanked Vanukoff and signed off.

Wide awake, Garrahan plowed through more of Father Albert's journals.

After an hour of reading, he went downstairs.

The front door was open. Mrs. Bower was sitting in her chair, picking at her thumbnail. Leonard was walking around the gas pumps, phone pressed to his bald head. Elizabeth and Abby were reading.

Compounding the dreamlike quality of his captivity, no one paid Garrahan any attention. He was a ghost floating past them, barely stirring the air.

"I need to spread out my papers," he said to no one in particular. "Is the kitchen table okay?"

Elizabeth smiled wanly. "Sure. Let me clear it off."

She moved napkins and magazines off the table, placing them on the counter.

"Everything okay?" he asked, voice low.

"As okay as it can be," she answered. "Abby's scared. So am I. Having Leonard around is not a good sign."

"Is it bad the Behemoth didn't come last night?"

"Not sure. I walked to the market with Mrs. Bower this morning. We heard people grumbling. They're more concerned about how Malden's handling this than whether the Behemoth accepted the offerings."

Garrahan didn't understand what that meant. If Malden was in danger of losing his job, though, all the better.

He shuffled through Father Pierce's papers and maps, laying them on the table.

The largest map was hand-drawn with a thick pencil. It was stained and torn, edges frayed from decades of being stuffed in a box.

Garrahan compared it to the maps Joel had given him. The town boundaries were the same in Pierce's day as they were now.

The notable thing on Pierce's map was the huge pentagon that surrounded Morris. Pierce had drawn it as the inside of a five-pointed star. The points radiated far beyond the boundary of Morris. The tip of each star point landed on a different town: Ashford, Roseville, Woodcrest Acres, Dunstam, and Longhaven.

The towns where each of the dead priests lived.

Turning the map so that north was up top, south at the bottom, the star appeared upside down. A pentagram.

In the center of the pentagram—the center of the star—was Morris, encased in a perfect five-sided gem. The exact center of that gem was the village church.

Garrahan had seen enough horror movies to know about the inverted pentagram. A symbol of evil for centuries. Two points up, one point down, the star appeared in books on witchcraft. It was beloved by Satanists.

He grinned at the absurdity. Like the story of the Behemoth, pentagrams and Satanic rituals fell under the category of pop culture bullshit.

Nonetheless, it was weird to see it on a map created by a Catholic priest. The points of the pentagram seemed to be how Father Pierce had selected those towns—and their priests.

Why a pentagram?

Garrahan looked at other towns on the map, like Prown's Valley and Hollistown. They were about the same distance from Morris. Pierce could have selected them. He had not. Instead, he chose only the towns that perfectly fit the points of the classic inverted pentagram of evil.

Yet again, he wondered. Why?

CHAPTER 73
MAY 10
FRIDAY, 11:21 AM

Father Albert Pierce committed to his journal in earnest when he was forty. By that time, he had been a priest for twenty years.

His writing did not explore his ideals, his desires, or his goals. Rather, it was the minutiae of his life. He wrote at great length about things as trivial as the quality of his soup ("The cook once again failed to chop the carrots into small enough pieces for the broth") or his annoyance with the mailman ("Why does he act like I have nothing better to do than listen to how many parcels he delivered this morning?"). Conversely, he would give a meeting with his superior nothing more than a cursory line ("Met with Bishop Scherwenka at 11 AM. Pleasant enough.").

Buried in this were scattered references to his friend Randall, and his musings about the origin of the Behemoth. Garrahan read each and every entry to see if anything of value was tucked into the scribbling. Needles in a haystack.

Eventually, a narrative emerged from an ominous entry. "Two children disappeared near Morris last night. No clues, no suspects. Near where Randall got taken."

Months later: "An old man gone. Family thinks he was kidnapped, but no ransom. Close to Morris. Who takes these people?"

A single line below: "How long has it been going on?"

Then something physical in Pierce's scribbling.

"Two books! Proof I am not the first to question this. *The Discoverie of Vinland and Regions South and North* and *Landscapes, Legends & Lore of The New Americas*. Pierce emphasized his enthusiasm with a line of exclamation points.

Garrahan typed the name of the books into his computer. The search results were immediate. The first book was written in 1658 by a Swede named Ranulf Nordenskjold. It was a history of the Viking exploration of the "world across the ice"—North America.

The second was written in 1818 by Charles Sauvion, a French-Canadian. The book described the belief system of native American tribes in the Northeast, including the Iroquois, Mohegan, and Nanshaquot.

Garrahan looked for online copies of the books. He came up empty. He called Ginnie Pierce.

"Did Father Pierce leave any books behind?"

"I have a few boxes. Never really looked through them," she replied, trying to remember where they were. "If you want to come look, I'll be here for a couple hours."

Garrahan went downstairs. He told Leonard he had to pick up some books.

"What kind of books?" Leonard asked.

"History books."

Leonard shrugged. "I'll drive you." He gave Garrahan a twisted sneer. "Least I can do."

There was no way around that. They drove to Woodcrest Acres without speaking.

Leonard waited in the car while Garrahan talked to Ginnie. She was sitting in her kitchen, thumbing through Pierce's diary and drinking beer. She had retrieved five boxes of books from her spare bedroom.

"I'll know the books if I see them," Garrahan said, kneeling down. He pulled out musty-smelling texts with both hands. Dust drifted up around him.

He found the Viking book in the first box. Two boxes later, he found the book on native Americans. They weren't original editions. Both had been reprinted in the early 1900s.

Father Albert had dog-eared pages and marked passages with arrows and underlines.

"Are you okay with me borrowing these?" he asked, looking at Ginnie. She hadn't wanted to part with the original journal, but these were just books. "I'll bring them back."

She nodded. They were, after all, just old books.

He put them on the table and sat down. She pushed a beer towards him.

"I stayed up and read the original diaries," Ginnie said nonchalantly. "I was bored. And buzzed." She smiled, in an endearing way that only ladies comfortable with their station in life can do. "A long time since I'd looked at them."

Garrahan smiled back. "Anything interesting?"

She laughed. "Depends on who's listening. How far have you read?"

"Maybe half. Kind of tough reading it on my phone." He made a tiny grimacing sound, indicating a minor burden.

She laughed again. "You can take the original." She handed the journal to him across the table. "I don't need it here. You're doing more with it than anybody has in nearly a hundred years."

He thanked her. "Anything catch your eye?"

"Other than thinking that my great uncle might have been traumatized by something he saw as a kid, there isn't much that makes sense. Not in this world."

Garrahan nodded in agreement.

"One thing I did notice," Ginnie mentioned, as if reluctantly letting the information go. "I don't think those priests were alone when they committed suicide. Someone was with them. It might not even have been suicide."

"Why do you think that?"

She shook her head. "I don't want to influence you. Spend some time towards the end of the book. There are pages where every word runs together—almost impossible to read. On one of them, Father Albert uses the term "target practice." Read it carefully and see what you think."

"I will," he nodded.

"Seriously. Go over it closely. When you're done, let's talk.

"It's a deal."

Garrahan thanked her again and apologized for bothering her.

"Are you kidding?" she replied, smiling wide. "My pleasure. I haven't talked to anyone about my family in ages. It's nice getting the chance to remember some of this. Thank you," she said.

He shook her hand and got back into Leonard's car. It was as icy in the car as it had been warm in Ginnie's house.

During the drive, Garrahan was tempted to make mention of the meth lab. On second thought, he wasn't ready to let Leonard or anyone in Morris know what he'd discovered.

Leonard broke the silence. "You and your books aren't going to change anything around here." He said it in a flat, disinterested voice.

Garrahan hated every sound that came out of Leonard's mouth. "And why is that?"

Leonard clucked his tongue. "Because we like our history to stay the way it is."

He barked out a laugh and turned on the radio. Music blared all the way to Morris.

CHAPTER 74

MAY 10
FRIDAY, 5:05 PM

It was late afternoon. The family would soon lock up the windows and doors for the second night of the feeding. Garrahan squirreled himself away in the bedroom.

He opened Ranulf Nordenskjold's *The Discoverie of Vinland and Regions South and North.* He flipped directly to the bent-over pages. He was already worried about how long it would take to get through all the things he needed to read. Time was a luxury he did not have.

The dog-eared chapter was titled "*The Beast to Be Found.*" There were archaic descriptions of wolves, deer, mountain lions, raccoons, bears, and other animals the Vikings had encountered on their voyages to the "*newfound land.*" Many of them were common animals. Ranulf Nordenskjold described them as mundane local fauna.

Two animals in the chapter were given special sections. Father Pierce had circled these with thick pencil lines.

The first was a giant bird. Nordenskjold had described it as "*large enough to carry away the carcass of a deer.*" One story claimed it had grabbed a man by the arm, "*lifting him above the shoulders of the other men, until his feet were grabbed by his confederates, who were able through their great strength and persistence to pull him back to earth and away from the raptor.*"

The second creature had been of more interest to Pierce.

"*Therein lived the most deadly of the new land creatures, a single one, so far as the warriors would tell. The creature emerged at night. It was the size of a bear standing on two stags. There were men who proclaimed it floated above the ground. Others swore an oath on their shields that it galloped like a tremendous cat on gigantic clawed feet. Others still claimed it was a black shadow, yet hard as oak, that pushed through thickets and trees like dry straw.*"

"It was given the name Skuldrir, as if born of a giant wolf and the goddess of Fate. The tales do not state the precise number of occasions it was met. It was not less than thirty times in half as many years.

"Some said its skin shone like mirrored ice on a black sea. Others that it was darker than the blackness in nighttime blood, darker than volcano rock, darker than beyond the moon. Its outstanding feature was its head, with teeth and eyes that could put fear to a whale. Its hands—if they were to be called that—slashed at living things with the strength of more than a dozen axes."

"The creature devoured men while they slept in the dark. So silent was the beast that a man next to a taken man never heard noise or cry when the Skuldrir crept away. Its silence and murderousness was proof that the beast was a god of the House of Loki, the most infernal of the Lords of Asgard. It had been sent from Náströnd, the shore of corpses, and it had ripped the land with its monstrous claws and created rivers and valleys."

Nordenskjold's recounting fit with Malden's claim of Scandinavian legends about Morris and its forests.

"Of all beasts encountered in the new lands, Skuldrir was feared most. Those who gazed upon the monster, for even the barest moment, never forgot. Many more were there who never saw the beast, and loathe they were to afford credence to stories of such an abomination."

"Many men—mayhaps the number of an entire seafaring crew—were taken by the Skuldrir. Those who saw it swore upon their honor it occurred before their own eyes. Yet they could not prove the wickedry of the Skuldrir. In all their time in the new lands, not a single warrior was able to bring forth an object to prove that the Skuldrir lived."

"Indeed, those who returned home with stories of the Skuldrir were accused of the deaths of their brothers in the new land. So abhorrent were their tales that no one of sane thought believed them. It was insanity to claim such a beast had appeared out of empty darkness to slaughter the bravest and strongest amongst them, and then disappear without engaging in battle."

The author attempted to describe the Skuldrir in his own words, building on the centuries-old tales he was recounting. *"Aggregating all of these (tales) creates a novel portrait of a beast of near-Biblical grandeur."* Pierce had underlined this last phrase twice. *"As large perhaps as the legendary mammoth but graced with the speed of a cat from Asia's jungles. Fitted with the teeth and claws of an overgrown lion."*

Nordenskjold did not accept the stories outright. *"This does not address, nor can it, the actual appearance of the animal. Reports are universally confused, as if watchers had seen the animal through a fog or haze. Its skin is by turns sleek and shiny, dark and obsidian-like. Reports tell of wings that line the outer edge of the forelegs, and the creature could stand upright on its rear legs. Its strength was greater than any group of Vikings could muster against it. It moved faster than any man, be he armed or not."*

"There is no doubting its strength, nor its size. Carrying away a man is something not even the largest of beasts, apart from the fabled elephants of Africa, could possibly do. The elephant is a tranquil creature, not something that feeds on the flesh of grown men. Such predation is in the nature of the Skuldrir."

In his conclusion, Nordenskjold let disappointment get the better of him. *"It seems to this writer,"* he noted, *"that the men of these expeditions did indeed discover something monumental. It is not known if the Skuldrir has survived the years. The most recent Viking raid was in 1358—some three hundred years ago! There are no reports from the recent colonies established by the sailors of Europe or the British Isles. Possibly the Skuldrir was hunted to extinction. Possibly it was the last of its kind."*

Pierce had written comments in the margins. *"Section reads like 'Book of Job' here,"* he wrote, and *"Author obviously familiar with Deuteronomy."*

Near Nordenskjold's description of the size of the Skuldrir, Pierce scrawled, *"Could this truly be the Behemoth of the Old Testament?"*

CHAPTER 75
MAY 10
FRIDAY, 9:00 PM

Garrahan looked up from the book and checked his phone. 9 PM. He didn't hear anyone downstairs and continued reading.

The house was sealed shut.

A piece of paper was tucked into the last page of the Skuldrir chapter. It was a sheet torn out of an old magazine. The page was a review of the book Garrahan held in his hands, or at least one version of this book. The article was called "'*The Discoverie of Vinland and Regions South and North': Commentary on the Revised Translation.*"

It was a scholarly criticism, with one paragraph circled by Pierce. It read: "*The newest version of Ranulf Nordenskjold's book continues past failures in that it suffers from a lack of updating and revision. The most glaring example is the continued inclusion of stories related to the existence of something Nordenskjold refers to as the "Skuldrir." Research by subsequent editors of this tome should have uncovered the probability—nay, the likelihood—that the existence of the beast was a hoax perpetrated on the invading Norsemen by the local Indians. Known for stealthy night hunting, these Indians most certainly utilized their parlor trick of banding together to appear as one creature in order to create fear among the Vikings. Tired and far from home, the Vikings can be excused for regarding this beast as the very Devil itself. The editors of this current revision, however, cannot. Extensive annotations would remedy this literary disservice.*"

That was an unexpected perspective. This critic wasn't buying the standard version of the legend.

Garrahan turned to the second book, *Landscapes, Legends & Lore of The New Americas* by Charles Sauvion. He turned directly to the pages Pierce had folded over.

They began with a description of the Nanshaquot people, who were spread throughout much of what would become New

England and upstate New York. Their land was used for farming and hunting, and they did not often migrate.

A light tapping on the door interrupted Garrahan's reading. "Come in," he said, not getting up.

Elizabeth stuck her head in the room. "We're going to bed, Abby and I. Wanted to let you know."

"Okay," Garrahan replied, nodding.

"Be quiet and keep the windows closed tonight. Again."

"I figured."

She looked at the book he was holding. "Getting anywhere?" she asked, trying to smile.

"Not sure. Maybe. Your Behemoth has a history, at least according to the Vikings." He pointed to the book on the bed.

"It's been here for centuries," Elizabeth mused.

"Not everyone thinks so," he replied.

Her lips tightened. "See you tomorrow, then."

Elizabeth closed the door behind her.

He read about the Nanshaquot. The writer treated them fancifully, almost dismissively, as if reporting on quaint traditions. "The Nanshaquot are a practical people but differ from their native brethren in their belief of a physical Powerful Being in their midst. Native peoples in general are wont to attach beliefs to inanimate elements of nature or specific ancestors. These take the form of revered animals of the forest and vales. Oddly, the Nanshaquot have singled out one spectacular creature as a form of deity."

"Their belief is that the spirit God of all creation surveyed his Earth by riding over it on a beast that was equal parts dragon, wolf, deer, and bear. When the spirit God was finished viewing all he had created, he released the creature and allowed it to run free to hold dominion over any lands it chose. The Nanshaquot believe it chose their land and roams there still. There are seasonal rites to the beast, which has no name, and these rites serve to appease and pay tribute to the animal. Frequent suggestion has been made that there were human sacrifices, but no witness to this effect has been cited."

"The spread of colonization dislodged the Nanshaquot from their original lands. With evident despair, those few who survive claim the beast did not follow them to their new locales. Their legend has been perpetuated by European and British settlers in the region, who claim that the monster is a real beast. These colonists appear to have been so frightened by the Nanshaquot that they believe the tales. Or, perhaps, the stories are the colonists' nefarious way of keeping new settlers away from the lands they have taken. Stories of evil beasts hold sway over those simple-minded enough to believe them."

Garrahan laughed. Finally, a plausible explanation.

However, scaring off "new settlers" wasn't a strong rationale centuries later for propagating a silly religious story. Morris could maintain its insularity in modern times simply by not selling property to outsiders.

Garrahan closed the cover and looked at the two books. They were several hundred years apart in their telling. They both had a monster that rampaged through their lands. They were from two entirely different cultures yet described the creature in the same way Malden had.

Notably, each story had its detractors. Historians who scoffed at the possibility such a beast could have run about unfettered and unidentified in an inhabited region of North America.

The books didn't tell Garrahan anything more than he had gotten during Malden's impromptu history lesson. Malden could have read the same books and come up with the same stories.

The catch was that these books were Pierce's, not Malden's. And it was Pierce who was involved in the scheme that led to confining the Behemoth—or whatever was disguised as the Behemoth—inside Morris.

In short, a number of historians had dismissed the creature as a fantasy. A myth concocted by native Americans, and later by settlers, to keep intruders at bay. If that was true, Malden might be the latest in a long line of charlatans.

CHAPTER 76
MAY 10
FRIDAY, 11:00 PM

The later entries in Albert Pierce's journal reflected a growing belief that the monster had existed in and around his home for hundreds of years. Like a Jersey Devil or a Sasquatch, it was a creature that lived deep within the dense woods, venturing out only for food.

Pierce heard rumors from his parishioners about people in Morris being God-fearing Christians—with an unhealthy dose of Biblical orthodoxy thrown in. "They take Old Testament writing serious, with every word being true," one woman confided to him in the confessional. "They don't handle snakes and such, but I've heard they say prayers to the Old Testament fallen angels and creatures like Leviathan."

She was close. Leviathan was the Bible's water monster.

"It isn't right," the woman continued, "None of it. This is the twentieth century, and people are too smart to think things like Noah's Ark or Samson and his hair are real."

The native Americans, the Vikings, even the people in Morris all thought this beast was a God. Pierce believed it must be an abomination.

Nothing in the things he read, or the rumors he heard, conveyed anything good about the creature.

It elicited fear. And it killed.

That was not a gift from God. That was the work of Satan.

Pierce's journal entries turned peculiar two years into his research. He began writing about "the presence of the demon."

He had gone to visit Morris. It was his first trip there since Randall was taken thirty years earlier. According to his journal, Pierce arranged a meeting with Samuel Malden. He was the head of the Morris congregation "or whatever they consider themselves," he wrote. Samuel would one day be Edward's grandfather.

After the meeting, Pierce's entry read:

"Malden is to outward appearances a smart and honorable man. He admits his church is not aligned with traditional Christian denominations. It has a more literal interpretation of the Old Testament than most New Testament Christians."

Malden read Father Albert the central tenets of their religion. These were based on two hundred years of worship as established by Clifford Morris after the village was settled. Those tenets were taken directly from the Old Testament.

First was The Book of Job, 40:15. "Behold now the Behemoth that I have made along with Man . . . Nothing on earth is its equal."

Second was Deuteronomy 32:24. "The people shall be wasted with hunger, and the teeth of beasts will I send upon them."

There was also a passage from Ecclesiasticus. "There be creatures that are created for vengeance; in the time of destruction they pour out their force and appease the wrath of Him that made them."

Three passages formed the core of the ceremonies and the structure of worship in Morris.

"Is there a Behemoth?" Pierce asked Samuel Malden.

Malden shrugged. "There is a creature the Bible tells us is more important than man," he replied. "And we revere that creature, because the Bible tells us we must."

"But is it alive?" Pierce asked, pleading.

"As much as any element of the Bible is alive for us," responded Malden cryptically, with no emotion.

Pierce bit his tongue in frustration. Those were not answers.

He took his leave from Morris.

The two men did not see each other for another eleven years.

CHAPTER 77
MAY 10
FRIDAY, 11:50 PM

The next ten years of the diary were mundane explorations of Pierce's daily life. His only additional reference to "the demon" or "the Behemoth" was an occasional question: "Is the Behemoth a beast created by Satan?" or "Would a just God, a New Testament God, allow such a creature to run free among his people?"

Out of nowhere, memories of Randall came back to Albert. They haunted him in his dreams. He couldn't sleep through the night.

The priest took to noting disappearances in surrounding towns. Mostly children, occasionally older people. He transcribed reports from local newspapers into his journal.

Those newspapers were from towns radiating out over more than forty miles. The stories of missing people almost never appeared in more than one paper; there was little to link news from one small town to the next. The only thing linking them was they all bordered Morris.

Increasingly, his dreams featured a black monster, silent and huge, snatching everyone he'd read about in the newspapers. He imagined the thing clutching children by their throats and disappearing into the dark. It built a stockpile of bones and crumbling remains near the river where Randall had been taken.

Every morning, Pierce woke up feeling ill. Some days, he would run to the bathroom, vomiting from the horrific visions he saw in his dreams.

Pierce's housekeeper told him she heard him screaming in his sleep.

He prayed to God for relief, as many hours a day as he could. The nightmares continued, and he sank into a nonstop swamp of lurid thoughts. His brain was delirious with dreams of the monster. They were so real it was as if the creature was pushing through the front of his skull.

On the verge of physical and mental collapse, Pierce paid a visit to Malden. Eleven years ago, he had been polite. This time, there was no dancing around his concern.

"I know there is a creature," he said to Malden, who sat placidly behind his desk. "It's hurting people. No one understands it. Not in the towns. I do. I've seen it. I want to stop it."

He saw Malden flinch slightly.

"I'd like your help," Pierce said. "I'll do it without you, if I have to."

Things had changed in Morris over the past decade. Construction was booming in the post-War years. The state had paved a highway through the region. New surface streets and bridges accompanied the highway. The sleepy towns of Ashford, Woodcrest Acres, Longhaven, and their ilk were growing. People from Boston and New York were looking for places to vacation. The beautiful remoteness of the valley became a lure for summer homes and winter retreats. The solace, solitude, and secrecy of the villages started to fade like an old man's nostalgia.

Malden had a dilemma—one his grandson would face more than half a century later. The Behemoth had started roaming the countryside. It was a danger to those who didn't worship it, and thus a danger to itself. If it should be seen, captured, or killed, there would be no redemption for Samuel Malden or any of his congregation. Their sacrifices and their obedience would be for naught. As prophesied in the Bible, they would suffer the consequences in the afterlife.

Malden admitted this to Father Pierce.

Yes. There was a creature. It was roaming.

The Behemoth was spreading its dominion over wider stretches of land.

Malden did not know how to rein it in.

Head in hands, Malden displayed a rare moment of humility. He was open to accepting help.

Pierce listened to Malden's history of the Behemoth. He believed he had seen the same beast take Randall. He wasn't, however, prepared to believe Malden's religious stories. This was, after all, a Christian congregation. Belief in a creature was idolatrous. Was Malden toying with him?

No matter what Malden claimed, something was out there. At the very least, an animal on a rampage. Whatever it was, it had to be stopped.

The priest's journal entries began to devolve after the meeting with Samuel Malden. His sentences ran on for pages at a time with no punctuation. There were frequent references to blood and bleeding and needing help from other priests.

In the margins of every page, he drew five-pointed stars. The pentacles and pentagrams of myth. They were scribbled hurriedly, like schoolboy drawings in the pages of a textbook.

Over and over, Father Pierce referenced the huge church in Morris. Malden allowed him to visit it whenever he wanted. Pierce went daily, looking at paintings, carvings, and stained glass. "The cathedral is in the middle of the map," he wrote. "It is at the locus of every disappearance," he stated. "If there were roads, they would all lead to the cathedral."

In the dead center of his scrawled pentagrams, he always printed the word "cathedral."

Garrahan looked up from the book. Reading page after page made his head ache. He rubbed his eyes then looked at his phone.

4 AM.

He listened.

No sound from outside.

No horrific rumblings near the offering bowl.

Nothing.

CHAPTER 78
MAY 11
SATURDAY, 5:00 AM

In the second half of his journal, Father Albert Pierce went off the rails.

Every word was printed in capital letters. Exclamation points littered the text like slashes raining across the paper.

Pierce had made a discovery. One that changed him.

He'd been scouring through books, the church, and the countryside. He'd looked for signs of the creature's whereabouts and its origin. He searched in caves and along riverbeds and in creeks. The pursuit was all-consuming.

Then he stumbled upon something. Or saw something.

Pierce didn't write down where he found it. Nor did he say exactly what it was.

He simply called it "the device."

His thoughts spewed out in a continuous jumble of words, splattering page after page.

"Those who built the church! They knew it! They knew it! They always knew it! It was there under Morris' feet, all along they knew it!"

"A perfect device! Hidden from the townspeople! They control everything. Make it come and go as they please!"

What the fuck is he talking about? Garrahan wondered. A scheme, like a plot device? Or is he talking about a machine, an object?

Pierce's writing didn't make that clear. Because from that point forward, all he wrote about was blood.

Blood sacrifice. Blood rituals. And mostly, blood boundaries.

Exodus 12:23. Written over and over, filling a dozen pages. *"When he seeth the blood on the ground, the Lord will protect you and will not suffer the destroyer to come in unto your houses to smite you."*

Numbers 35: 33. *"Atonement cannot be made for the land on which blood has been poured."*

Ezekiel 45:19. *"The priest is to take blood as an offering and put it at the corners of the sacred place."*

Blood as boundary.

Blood could protect the people outside of Morris. Blood would protect them from the destroyer. From the creature.

He wrote about barrels. Barrels of lamb's blood.

Seemingly out of nowhere, Pierce one day decided to physically mark the map line of the pentagon around Morris. He took a map and a compass and walked the path from point to point. He noted nearby homes and farms, and whether the path could be accessed via roads or trails. It was a long trek; each of the five sides was a mile long. He chopped weeds and brush, and left bits of red cloth tied to trees and fences to identify his trail. It took two full days to mark the entire pentagon.

When he finished, Pierce drove to a sheep farm two hundred miles north of Morris. He collected several barrels of lamb's blood from the farm's slaughterhouse. He told the proprietor he needed it "for religious ceremonies." The farmer gave him the barrels for free just to cart the blood off.

He hauled the barrels to where he'd laid out the pentagon. He said a prayer over each barrel, blessing its contents. Dipping a pail into the first barrel, he pulled out a heavy gallon of blood.

Climbing down off the truck, Father Albert began his walk.

With a holy water sprinkler, Pierce walked around Morris. He dipped the sprinkler into his bucket and splattered blood in front of him as he walked.

A continuous spray of dripping crimson spots stained his path.

He stopped regularly to refill his bucket from the barrels. Every quarter of a mile he moved the truck along so the blood supply stayed next to him. Flies swarmed thickly under the hot sun.

Pierce paced step by step for five miles. He sprinkled blood on trees, soil, fences, rocks, and barren ground. All the while, he recited Exodus 12:23 from memory. He also proclaimed the words of Luke 11:20.

"It is by the hand of God that I drive out demons, and so the kingdom of God has come upon you."

This incantation he hissed as a curse, directing his anger at Malden and the people of Morris. They had permitted wanton death, and they did not care.

In the name of the one true God, aided by blood, Pierce would make it right.

There were five spots on his trek where he did not sprinkle blood. These were the five points of the pentagon. Without blood, they served as openings that would let the beast back into the heart of Morris.

They were the points where five priests would stand. As promised, they would be positioned at each opening with a gun. When the priests shed blood, the pentagon would be sealed. The beast would be trapped inside. It could not retreat back over sanctified blood.

After two days of walking, he was done. Pierce found himself covered in blood spray and slick with sweat. His skin was sticky. Blood coated his eyelids.

He was happy. Giddy, according to his writing. "All is in place! It will be by their own device that they bring back the creature! They don't know! The answer was buried there all along! In Morris for centuries! The answer people need and aren't allowed to have! I will shout it from the top of the Devil's own cathedral! The penalty for twisting the Bible to their beliefs will be their ruination!"

The remainder of the journal—the last twenty or thirty pages—was filled with writing that made no sense.

The last three pages contained only exclamation points.

Thousands of them.

Perhaps Pierce had gone insane.

Garrahan put the book down and fell asleep.

He dreamed of an old priest wandering the fields, shooting imaginary bears with a rifle.

CHAPTER 79
MAY 11
SATURDAY, NOON

Garrahan woke up late.

It was Day Three of his imprisonment in Morris.

The Donahues were at the table, reading. As if they never moved. Leonard was trimming his fingernails on the front steps. Mrs. Bower was watching TV.

"Have you ever been in the church?" Garrahan asked Elizabeth.

She looked quizzically at him. "No, never. It's been ruined since before I was born."

"Does anyone go in? Malden says it's abandoned."

"No one." She scratched her arm. "It's only a shell."

"Why wasn't it rebuilt?"

"Money, from what I understand. We don't have the resources to do it. We'd have to bring in outsiders—a lot of them. Cranes, construction crews, work permits. Nobody wants that."

Garrahan poured himself a glass of juice, thinking.

"Why do you ask?" she asked.

"Because Father Pierce was obsessed with it. He spent days sniffing around the church—with the elder Malden's permission. In most of his notes, he called it the Morris Cathedral. But in his last pages, he called it the Devil's Cathedral. That's an extreme jump.

"He found something or saw something. He makes mention of a "device." Then his writing turns psychotic. Monsters, devils, cults, ancient burials. He throws every spooky thing he can into the mix. Clearly, he was upset—and disturbed—by what he was looking into. Unlike the people in Morris, he considered what was happening to be utterly evil."

Elizabeth cocked an eyebrow. "Then why did he help?"

Garrahan sat down. "I don't know. He might have had a religious mission of his own. He rambles a lot about being afraid of the cathedral. And talking about the device." He drank his juice slowly. "It's like he was losing his mind with each passing hour."

She looked at Garrahan in silence. Making sure Leonard wasn't watching from the front doorway, she nodded towards the laundry room. They slipped quietly away from the table.

In the laundry room, Elizabeth whispered. "Malden's afraid. I've never seen him afraid. I don't know what he's going to do. People in town are nervous, too. There's a fear that state troopers or police or something will come in and destroy Morris."

"Why would the police do that?"

"Because of what the Behemoth has done. Because of what we let it do."

"Are you sure it's not more than that?" Garrahan wondered.

"Like what?" she asked.

"I don't know. Like unsolved local murders. Like drug manufacturing. Like people disappearing and never being heard from again." He could not contain his skepticism. "Maybe people taken from their homes as warnings."

"That's not what happens!" she said, trying not to raise her voice.

"I'm not the first person to think so," Garrahan told her, his own voice firm. "You have to admit that worrying about cops coming, or the Behemoth being exposed, sounds like people wanting to cover up a crime and not a . . ."

"Well, well, well. Aren't you two all cozy?" Leonard walked into the laundry room, his chest puffed out and a smile running from ear to ear. He acted like a hallway monitor catching kids smoking in the stairwell. "Can I get in on this?" he asked, leering.

Elizabeth pushed past him, back to the kitchen. Leonard eyed Garrahan. "You trying to get a piece of that?" He jerked his thumb towards Elizabeth.

Garrahan fought the urge to punch the little fuck in the face. "I don't want a piece of anything." He started to walk out.

Leonard stepped in front of him, blocking the way. "Not even a piece of me?"

Garrahan ground his teeth together. Hard enough that it hurt his skull. This was the man who had killed Nancy. "Yeah,

Leonard. I want a piece of you like you want a piece of me. That said, I don't think Malden would like you fucking with me right now. So why don't you take it back outside? Pull some wings off flies or something. We can play cock of the walk another time."

He stepped around Leonard and marched up the stairs.

The thoughts in his head were drowned out by the sound of his heart pounding in his chest. He realized he was deathly afraid of Leonard.

CHAPTER 80

MAY 11
SATURDAY, 12:40

After the suicides, Father Albert Pierce was never seen again.

He appeared to have run away. Or died someplace where no one ever found him.

How did he vanish?

Maybe Malden kept Pierce protected in town. Maybe he was granted sanctuary and lived in the church.

The church burned three years after the priests died. Maybe Pierce died in the fire.

The thing that nagged Garrahan about Pierce was the six coffins that lay inside that ruin. Pierce was supposed to die with the other five priests. Whatever he'd agreed to with Malden, the plan was for him to end up in a wooden box.

That wooden box—those coffins—perplexed Garrahan. Why weren't they disposed of? They were kept for decades. As if they were waiting.

What good were empty coffins?

They're no good empty.

They have value when something is inside them.

He ran downstairs and out the front door. Leonard, startled, chased him. Before Leonard could say anything, Garrahan commanded "Tell Malden to meet me at the church. I want to go inside. I need him to answer questions."

They moved quickly over the village green, Leonard sputtering on his phone. By the time they got to the little church, Malden was there. Ethan and Joel were next to him.

"What's this about?" Malden asked, his face expressionless.

"I'm going into the chapel. To look at the coffins."

"Why?"

"I think Pierce left something in them."

Malden folded his arms across his chest. "Not likely. My father would have found anything in there long ago."

"You're stopping me?" *Please say 'yes,'* he thought.

"Not at all," Malden replied, nonplussed. "You're welcome to do whatever you want in the church. You can open the coffins. You can climb into them if you desire." He squinted in the sun. "You've been told how fragile that building is. It's more dangerous than you know. I would prefer you not die. Just yet."

"If it gets me out of your shitty town, I'm willing to give it a go." Garrahan stared fiercely into Malden's eyes, not blinking.

Surprisingly, Malden didn't blink, either. "Joel, give him the keys to the gate. But don't go with him. If he causes anything to collapse, I don't want to lose you with him."

Joel fished the keys out of his pocket, putting them in Garrahan's outstretched hand. "I could show him around, if . . ."

"I said 'no'." Malden shut Joel down. "There's nothing for him to find. If it helps him with whatever he thinks he might be onto, fine. Ethan, guard the outside of the church. Make sure that Mr. Garrahan doesn't use the opportunity to sneak away. You have a gun?"

Ethan nodded.

"Splendid. Everyone back to work. Enjoy your search, Mr. Garrahan. Make it quick. The Donahues are counting on you."

Garrahan was dumbfounded. He thought Malden would try to conceal the church and the coffins. Instead, Garrahan had free rein to wander around. He wondered if he'd put too much hope in Pierce's obsession.

Ethan asked for the keys once Garrahan unlocked the chains. "In case you don't come back," he laughed.

Wandering into the chapel area, Garrahan was struck again by the building's size and majesty. It was a beautiful structure. It would have taken years to rebuild. *Might have been worth the expense*, he thought.

He crawled over the clumps of rock and gravel that led to the coffins. The sun was high overhead. It scorched the boxes through the decrepit roof.

Garrahan approached the first coffin. His nerves were on edge, as if he expected a jack-in-the-box to leap out once he unlatched the lid.

He tapped it cautiously, then flicked the latches. His fingers dug into the space between the lid and the casket, prying them apart. He pushed upward.

The hinges on the lid creaked angrily.

The inside of the casket exposed itself to the light. There was no red velvet cushioning, no pillow, no . . .

Nothing.

Empty.

Garrahan threw the lid all the way open.

The coffin was barren.

It even lacked dust, having been sealed for so long.

There was nowhere to hide anything in here. Not a "device," not a body. Not a slip of paper.

He turned to the next coffin.

Still wary, he repeated the process. Slowly opening the lid, he found . . . nothing.

He moved on to the third, the fourth, fifth, sixth. All of them were vacant.

"How can this be?" he asked out loud. The coffins were as empty as Malden promised they would be.

He couldn't believe they held no clues. He sat on a chunk of fallen rock, staring at the six long boxes.

CHAPTER 81

MAY 11
SATURDAY, 1:30 PM

The church had ensnared Father Pierce. Seized his mind.
There was something here.
Maybe not in the coffins. Maybe inside.

Malden warned him it was dangerous in there. It was already dangerous out here.

He clambered into the main body of the church.

Luminous haze filled the air. Sunlight lanced through the stained-glass windows like tiny colored spotlights. He flicked on his phone's flashlight.

There was less rubble inside the church than outside. The damage in here had come from stone columns falling down. Two lying on the floor, like huge stone cylinders from a crumbled Roman plaza. A third angled precariously over the pews.

Above, the massive expanse of the ceiling was dim and distant. Cracks running in long lines revealed slivers of blue sky beyond. He wondered what was propping the arched roof up.

The church was gargantuan. Pierce was right to call it a cathedral.

The altar was to Garrahan's right, nearly a hundred feet away. To the far left were the huge doors of the main entrance.

A beam of stained-glass light landed on a large marble structure near the center of the church. It was eight feet high, maybe more.

Garrahan walked across the floor, pausing after each step to let his eyes adjust to the light. He tried not to picture the entire church falling down on top of him.

Walking around the marble structure, hands running over the cold surface, he found carved letters. The name "Clifford Morris" was engraved in the stone.

The centerpiece of the church. A memorial to the town's founder and namesake.

Garrahan thought it likely that Clifford Morris's remains were inside.

But it didn't seem to be a vault. There was no way inside to view a coffin or a body. If Morris's remains were entombed inside, they were sealed in forever.

He spent a half hour investigating the perimeter of the entire church. He avoided debris, broken glass, fractured timbers, and shattered chunks of the marble floor. He shone his light on the walls, the religious paintings, the intricate woodwork that adorned the confessionals.

He found nothing.

Sweat sweltered around his collar. The air was dank and humid. He sat down against the polished stone wall.

Why would this place be ground zero of Father Pierce's plan? It was a church. Seemingly nothing more.

Pierce said the answer to everything was underneath the town. Right under its feet.

An odd turn of a phrase, that. Under Morris's feet.

Like the town was alive. As if it had feet.

"Right there under Morris's feet," Pierce had written.

Not the town's feet.

Clifford Morris's feet.

Garrahan peered at the memorial in the center of the church.

If the town's namesake was buried there, could something be underneath him?

Garrahan got on his hands and knees and crawled like a child around the huge block of marble. He spread his hands out, trying to feel for aberrations in the floor and on the memorial.

On each side of the monument was a large metal disk embedded into the floor. All four were coated with a layer of debris. Beneath the grit, he felt lines in the metal.

Garrahan laid down next to each one. He blew dirt away. Numbers revealed themselves.

On the disk facing the pews was the number 40:15. Garrahan recognized that. Chapter and verse from the Book of Job, the original Behemoth quote.

"Behold now the Behemoth that I have made along with Man. Its limbs are as strong as copper, its bones as a mass of iron. It ranks first among God's works . . . Nothing on earth is its equal—a creature without fear."

At the head disk, pointing towards the altar, was the number 32:24. The Deuteronomy reference.

"The people shall be wasted with hunger, and devoured with burning heat and bitter destruction, and the teeth of beasts will I send upon them."

To the left, 39:28. Ecclesiasticus.

"There be creatures that are created for vengeance, which in their fury lay on deadly strokes. In the time of destruction they pour out their force and appease the wrath of Him that made them."

At the end, facing towards the entrance to the church—near what could be the feet of Clifford Morris—was a disk with 17:8 inscribed on it. That was a chapter and verse combination Garrahan hadn't come across.

He checked it closely. 17:8. He needed to look that up when he got back.

Garrahan ran his fingers over that disk. It was set into the floor like a manhole cover. The building had shifted over the years. It had raised the disk a fraction of an inch from its resting place.

"Right under Morris's feet."

He dug his fingers under the metal circle. Pried at it with fingertips and nails. It ripped his skin raw.

The disk was impossibly heavy. He barely managed to dislodge it a few inches. He needed something more than his hands to lift it.

Looking around the ruins, he saw a shattered pew reduced to shards of wood. He grabbed a long piece and wedged it into the space he'd created around the disk.

Leveraging his body to force it, the cover slid off.

An opening in the floor.

Garrahan peered into the hole.

It was nothingness. Blacker than the darkness in the church.

He held his light over the space.

The blackness went down. On and on.

He couldn't tell how deep the hole was.

But there were stairs.

CHAPTER 82

MAY 11
SATURDAY, 2:12 PM

The stairs spiraled downward.

The opening in the floor was a doorway.

Garrahan held his light into it. Stairs were carved into a stone wall. They went further than the light.

Like steps descending into a dungeon.

He wondered where it could possibly lead—and what he might possibly find.

Without giving it more thought, he swung his legs into the hole. He sat on the precipice. He looked at the black expanse of the church above him. That gave him pause.

What if the roof collapsed while he was in the hole? He had his phone. Would that bring help if he called? Malden and his minions might be happier if he was buried under rubble.

Fuck it. He'd come this far.

He eased into the hole.

One stair at a time. He tested each step with his foot before settling his weight on it.

His hand traced the curve of the wall as he descended. He counted each stair as he wound down and around.

After forty steps, he began to get nervous.

At seventy, he slowed his pace.

At the hundredth step, he felt tightness in his lungs. The confining walls, the stairs, and the darkness squeezed his chest.

He'd never been claustrophobic. Suddenly, he was.

Another fifty steps. Breathing was difficult.

How far did it go?

He was torn between wanting to rush back up and hoping the end would be a few more steps.

The stairway got colder. Sweat streamed down his neck.

Another step.

Another.

He lost count of the stairs.

The air had turned icy. Suffocating.

He needed to go back up.

Maybe another step down.

Two more.

He braced himself against the walls. They were clammy, wet.

The stairs stopped.

His feet stood on a stone floor.

He'd come down nine or ten stories.

Holding the light over his head, Garrahan looked around.

He was in a cavern.

Garrahan breathed deeply, letting the cool air settle in his lungs.

His heartbeat leveled off. He let his eyes adjust.

It wasn't a large cavern. The ceiling, as best he could tell, was about twenty feet high. The room was maybe forty feet wide. Maybe the size of a basketball court.

He took a few steps. The floor sloped down in front of him.

The clearer his vision became, the more off kilter the place was.

The light from his phone was no match for the impenetrable black of the room. There were shadowed objects around him. He couldn't yet make them out.

This was a room, he thought. *It was used for something.*

He kept close to the wall on his left. Out of the corner of his eye, he saw a club sticking out of the rock. He touched it carefully. A small chain fastened it to the wall. A torch.

In the darkness, he gradually saw more torches. He wished he had matches to light the torches. No one carried matches anymore.

The walls were rough cut stone. The floor was well-trampled and flat, as though many feet, many people, or many heavy things had passed over it.

What would anyone be doing this far below the surface of the planet?

He took baby steps and reached the far side of the cavern in less than a minute.

The far side wasn't the end, though. It was a row of metal poles. They formed a barred metal gate, like the entrance to a castle. Beyond the gate was colder darkness. Frigid air drifted through it.

Garrahan warily wrapped his hand around one of the vertical bars. It was thick; he could barely get his fingers around it. A sheen of rust crinkled into his palm.

Instinctively, he shook the bar. It didn't move. Not even a rattle.

The cavern went farther down. This gate, this wall, this door, barred him from going further.

The metal was spaced tighter than the bars on a jail cell. He could barely pass his hand between them. The gate was as high as the ceiling and forty feet wide.

The bars had been drilled into the rock walls and floor of the cavern. Someone, once upon a time, had taken care to make sure they were anchored deep and secure.

Garrahan realized it wasn't a door, or a gate. It wasn't supposed to be opened. The poles of metal meshed together to form a barrier. No way to go beyond.

And no way for anything to come out from the other direction.

He ran his hands across the bars. The grate was sturdy and strong. He felt no give as he tugged at it.

Extending his phone through the bars, he shone the light as far as it would reach. He held it tightly, praying that his shivering fingers wouldn't drop the light inside the barrier.

There was nothing to see save for more emptiness. A chilly breeze made its way out of the dark towards him.

A dead end. He walked along the length of the barrier, testing its bars. There was no explanation for this, so far below the church. There certainly could have been . . .

His right foot kicked something. It skittered along the ground. He whipped his light around.

Garrahan hoped it wasn't a rat or snake.

It slid to a stop.

An arm.

Flat on the ground, fingers splayed open.

A human arm.

CHAPTER 83
MAY 11
SATURDAY, 2:30 PM

Startled, he recoiled against the gate.

The arm didn't move. He expected it to crawl. Or reach out to him.

It didn't.

It was a human arm. Two long skeleton bones attached to a hand and Chiclet pieces of fingers.

Garrahan spun his light around. There were no other bones. No body. A small metal disk lay nearby.

Nothing else that was human.

He knelt down. The arm was bright white in the surrounding black. He touched it lightly with his finger. Dust from the floor rose in tiny swirls as the bones moved.

It was a right arm, severed above the elbow. The break hadn't been clean. The bone was splintered into fragments where it would have been attached to the shoulder.

The arm had left its body violently. The flesh had disappeared long ago.

Garrahan shone his light back into the barrier, along the floor. There were no bones on the other side. No signs of the rest of the body.

Garrahan guessed that the body had gone through the grate. Not easily.

There was a ring on the fourth finger of the skeletal hand. It dangled limply from the bone. Garrahan, inhaling deeply, slipped the ring off. He held it in front of the light, twirling it around.

On the inside of the gold band was the inscription: "Fr. Albert. God Bless."

Pierce's ring. Pierce's hand. Pierce's arm.

The priest had died down here.

Torn apart.

Garrahan shone his light back around the floor. The metal disk shone in the corner.

He grabbed it and brought it close to his face.

It was heavier than it looked, maybe a couple of pounds. The shape was like a large yo-yo or a swollen hockey puck.

It was metal but had no rust. It was pocked with an organic-looking patina. Mold or lichens, perhaps.

Markings were etched across the top in a geometric pattern.

He turned it over. The bottom was similar to the top, but had three tiny protrusions, like little legs. The whole device—the word came to him unbidden—was bisected around the circumference. Two pieces joined together to form one object.

Garrahan took the sides in his hands and tried to pry them apart. He couldn't get his fingers inside. He tried twisting the halves in opposite directions. It moved slightly, the top piece moving forward with several loud clicks.

That was the extent of it. Nothing came apart. He couldn't move it any further.

He took his left hand off to switch sides.

The moment he let go, he heard a faint click.

His heart stopped. He had a moment to think: "grenade."

A moment of perfect quiet.

The device started shrieking.

A horrific screech that assaulted his body.

A battering ram against his head.

The noise was so deafening that he dropped the object and fell onto the floor.

Inside the cavern, it pierced his brain like the siren of an ambulance. Garrahan covered his ears and scooted back against the grate.

In lasted for five interminable seconds.

Then silence.

He put his hands down and looked at the object.

How could it have made that siren sound?

As he went to reach for it, he heard another sound.

A soft sound.

He leaned forward, listening.

It came again.

Not from the disk.

From the other side of the grate.

He froze.

A sound of something being dragged over the ground. He peered into the darkness, thinking he'd be able to see beyond.

A second sound, also from beyond the grate, moved towards him.

Garrahan grabbed his phone off the ground and held it in front of him.

He couldn't see anything.

More noises. Slow, dragging sounds. Getting closer.

Garrahan realized he was holding his breath.

A tentacle reached through the grate.

It slithered forward, pulling itself along. Squeezing through the grate.

He stepped back, light illuminating the metal bars.

Four more tentacles slid through the openings.

They resembled engorged worms, as thick as elephant trunks.

Twitching slowly, they inched forward into the cavern where Garrahan stood.

They moved across the floor like bloated and pointy fingers. Searching for something.

In horror, Garrahan watched more appear in the grate.

One of the tentacles brushed up against the disk. Garrahan instinctively took a step and leaned over, grabbing the disk away before the tentacle could snare the object.

He backed further away. The tentacles were swelling against the metal bars.

He couldn't see what was pushing them. Or what they were attached to.

Three new tentacles worked their way through the grate.

A new sound entered the cavern. Wet and thick, like oil gurgling out of a broken pipe.

Suddenly, a host of thinner and longer tentacles sprouted through the grate. They slithered along the floor faster than their predecessors, flicking like bullwhips. They glided easily through the bars that held back the bigger limbs.

Garrahan watched in stunned silence. One vine-like tendril reached close to his foot. A second one brushed against his leg. It woke him to the reality of what was happening.

If this thing wrapped around him, he would end up like the last person who'd come down here.

Arm ripped off. Clutching the device.

Garrahan turned to the back of the cavern and raced to the stairway.

Moving like he'd never moved before, he leapt up the stairs two at a time. His shoulders banged against the stairway that circled up and over him.

Twice his feet slipped from under him. His forehead smashed against stone. He didn't stop.

At the top he flung himself from the opening onto the marble floor of the church.

Gasping for air, he flipped onto his back. He kicked at the manhole cover till it slid into place. He scrambled back to the outer chapel.

In the broken sunlight, he sprinted for the iron gate.

CHAPTER 84
MAY 11
SATURDAY, 3:03 PM

Ethan was sitting outside the gate with his back up against a tree. Asleep.

Shouting frantically, Garrahan rushed to Ethan. "Wake up! Wake the fuck up! Lock the gate!"

Dazed, Ethan stared at the man screaming at him. His first impulse was to reach for his gun.

Nothing was happening. It was quiet.

It looked like it always did.

"Lock the fucking gate!" Garrahan screamed.

Garrahan was obviously frightened. *Maybe he'd found the Behemoth*, Ethan thought. *With me here as part of it! That would be a huge feather in his cap if . . .*

"I said hurry!!!" Garrahan grabbed Ethan and yanked him off the ground.

Ethan stumbled to the gate. There was still nothing to be seen or heard. He could actually hear birds chirping in a nearby tree. He wound the chain around the bars of the gate and locked them tightly. He took a deep breath.

"What is this?" Garrahan asked Ethan, extending his hand. It was like a small silver Frisbee.

Ethan shook his head. "I dunno. Why?"

"What's down there?" Garrahan yelled, pointing towards the church. "What is that?"

Again, Ethan shook his head. The way Garrahan was talking—fast and spitting his words—was making Ethan nervous. This guy was losing his shit.

"There's nothing in there. It's an old church."

Garrahan asked another question that came out as a stutter. He looked anxiously at the church. Nothing crept along the ground.

He shook his head, trying to clear his thoughts.

"We need to see Malden. Now!" Garrahan ran towards the village hall.

Bursting into Malden's office, Garrahan found Malden at his desk talking to Leonard. He didn't know where to begin. Too much to ask, to tell, to uncover.

"What is this?" he asked loudly, out of breath and words slurring. He thrust the device into Malden's face.

Malden looked at it without touching it. As if appraising an antique.

"I don't know," he said, sitting back.

"You don't know?" Garrahan was incredulous. "You have no fucking idea?"

"I do not. Should I?" Malden asked. He took note of Garrahan's shaken and pale appearance. The man's eyes were bulging. "Perhaps you should sit down."

Garrahan blurted out everything he had seen below the church.

Ethan stood to the side of the room. It sounded like bullshit to him.

Malden wasn't inclined to buy it, either. He'd never—not once—heard about anything trapped below the church. Nothing in Morris's history alluded to it.

Malden thought while Garrahan raved. What year was the church built? 1710. When did Clifford Morris die? 1724. It had been three centuries since that tomb had been placed in the church, along with the circular inlays on the floor. Malden remembered the memorial from his childhood. He hadn't seen it since the fire. No one had.

Malden scoffed. "You found a storm drain. You said it went downward, with no doors opening into it . . ."

"Does sound like a drain," Ethan concurred.

"It wasn't a drain!!!!" Garrahan shouted. "It was room, a cavern!"

"If it was a storm drain," said Malden, "things coming up could be insects—slugs, centipedes, worms, even glow worms—attracted by the noise."

"They weren't worms!" Garrahan protested.

"You said it was dark, you could barely see . . ."

"I saw tentacles coming through the grates!"

"You also said the grates were small."

Ethan chimed in. "Technically, there's a difference between tentacles and arms. Octopuses have arms, but no tentacles, while squids have two tentacles and . . .

"I don't give a shit about its anatomy!!!" Garrahan bellowed, rounding on Ethan. "It was crawling out of the grate! It came up after the device finished howling."

Garrahan was stunned to be on the other side of the argument he'd been having for days. No one believed him.

Malden reached for the device. Garrahan snatched it away. He held it in front of him.

"This is what happened to Father Pierce," he said, shaking the object. "This is why you have six coffins. He went down there while the other five died. He expected to die, but never came out."

"Why would he go there?"

"To lure your beast to the church. He took this thing down there. He must have set it off or triggered it. Whatever was down there killed him."

A smirk crossed Ethan's face. Leonard shook his head. Malden stayed silent, staring at the device.

"I think it's a warning device," Garrahan said, panting. "Or a signal. I've never heard anything that incredible."

"So turn it on," Leonard said. "I want to hear."

Malden waved him off. "If it's as loud as Mr. Garrahan claims, we should take it someplace less confined. Outside."

"Fine by me," Garrahan said, standing up.

The four men trooped out of the office. Joel met them by the door.

The sun had fallen below the treetops. It would be night soon.

Remembering the shock that knocked him over the first time, Garrahan placed the device gingerly on the sidewalk outside the village hall. It was raised slightly on its three tiny protrusions.

The scene resembled men getting ready to launch a toy rocket.

Garrahan looked tentatively at Malden, then back at the device.

He twisted it the halves as far as he could, hearing it click three times.

He let go and jumped back, hoping to get away from the sound.

The four men were silent, holding their breaths.

Leonard waited a few seconds. He shot a glance at Garrahan. "And this is supposed to do what . . .?

Sound erupted from the device with the intensity of a flash bomb.

Shock waves pummeled their bodies, emanating through the ground.

Ethan fell to his knees, cowering on the grass. Leonard raised his hands to his ears. Malden stood, eyes wide, staring at the thing that was emitting so much energy.

How was this possible? he wondered to himself.

If anything, Garrahan realized, it was louder now than it had been underground. It was like an air raid siren, screeching with fury.

The ground shook beneath them.

It vibrated on the sidewalk. Cracks appeared in the concrete.

The sound was the roar of an angry creature slashing at the air.

And, as suddenly as before, it was over.

"Fuckin' incredible," Leonard muttered, dropping his hands.

Garrahan saw people from the village coming towards them. Others were laying down on the green, covering their heads.

It was like a real air raid. The warning had scared the locals.

"What the . . . ?" yelled one woman as she headed towards them.

"Go back to your store, Diana," Malden shouted. "We're doing an experiment. Nothing for you to bother about."

The woman halted, looked curiously at Malden, Ethan, Garrahan, Joel, and Leonard. She spun on her heel. No one else approached.

"It was louder this time," Garrahan said quietly. "It resonated through the ground."

No one replied.

Garrahan watched the locals return to their business. It was as if the sound had never happened. The eerie shriek rang in his ears.

"Well?" Ethan asked, breaking the silence.

"It appears to be what Mr. Garrahan said. A warning device. A siren." Malden smiled, mirthlessly. "The most impressive siren I've ever heard."

Garrahan watched Malden as he thought over his options.

"We need to inspect the church to see what Mr. Garrahan thinks he saw beneath it."

Fear crossed Ethan's face. Joel scuffed his foot against the sidewalk.

Malden noticed. "I don't mean now," he said, looking at the thinning sunlight. "We can talk about it tomorrow."

He turned to Joel.

"What do you think this is?" Malden asked, pointing at the ground.

Joel gave an exaggerated shrug. "I've never come across this in the records. Not even close." He shifted uncomfortably, pushing his glasses up on his nose.

"Pierce had to get it from somewhere. And he figured out what it did," Garrahan interjected.

Malden tapped Joel on the shoulder. "You need to find out what this is. Who made it, what's in it, what those markings mean."

As Joel bent down to pick it up, Garrahan stepped in front of him. "I'll hold it for now." He grabbed the device off the sidewalk."

"What are you gonna do with it?" Leonard asked, leaning in.

"I can find out more than Joel can. In a shorter period of time." He looked at the blushing librarian. "No offense, Joel."

"I agree," said Malden. "Since you've gotten this far, maybe you can provide a resolution." Malden stared hard at Garrahan. "Of course, it's in your best interest to finish this quickly."

An indelicate reminder that Garrahan remained a prisoner.

"You have a busy night of investigating, then, Mr. Garrahan. I suggest you take that disk and retire to the comfort of the Donahue household." He looked at his watch, and at the sky. "We'll start early tomorrow. First thing, at the village hall."

Malden left with Ethan in tow. Joel headed to the library. Garrahan watched them go. It was like watching a neighborhood party break up. Natural and normal.

"You waiting for something in particular?" Leonard asked.

Yes. For your pointy bald head to split open, Garrahan thought.

He didn't answer the question out loud. He walked quickly to the Donahue's house.

CHAPTER 85
MAY 11
SATURDAY, 4:15 PM

Abby and Elizabeth were standing by the pumps in front of the house.

"What was that sound?!?" Abby blurted out as Garrahan crossed the street. "It was a fire alarm and an earthquake all in one!"

"No idea," Garrahan said, "but this made it."

He showed Abby what he held in his hand. "And before you ask, I don't know what this is."

Garrahan noted that Abby had felt the sound as well as heard it. The thing had shaken the ground.

Inside the house, Garrahan recounted his day. Mrs. Bower sat in the living room, pretending not to listen while she flipped through TV channels. Leonard showed up and sat on the steps, toying with his phone.

Elizabeth made sandwiches for dinner, and the three of them ate while talking in whispers. They ignored Mrs. Bower and Leonard.

Neither Abby nor Elizabeth had ever heard any stories about the device, or about any creature under the church.

Garrahan was faced with a laughable irony. He was here looking for a monster he was sure did not exist—the Behemoth. Yet he was convinced he had found a different monster, a real monster . . . and no one believed it existed.

Perhaps he had overthought it. Been spooked. Was it large insects and slithering invertebrates crawling through an ancient drainage system? He didn't think his mind played that trick on him. He had become claustrophobic on the stairway, had trouble breathing. What he saw might have been exaggerated because—this was hard to admit—he had been scared.

He felt close to a breakdown with the shit that had gone down the past few days. Days, hell—he'd been trapped here for months.

The outside world would start wondering about him, where he was.

He should call Dave Vanukoff. For a reality check. For help with the device.

He excused himself from the table and went to his room. Shutting the door, he called Vanukoff.

"About time," Vanukoff said. "I was thinking maybe you'd been taken out and shot."

"Don't joke. That's more of a possibility than you know," replied Garrahan.

"Are you in Morris?" Vanukoff asked.

"I am. I'm not going anywhere for a while . . ."

"Have you seen Nancy?" Vanukoff asked.

"No," Garrahan lied. "I can't worry about her just now."

"You have to be wondering . . ."

"Yes, I am wondering. On the other hand, I'm dealing with the family of a dead guy whose last words were spoken to me. And people in his town are covering something up and trying to rope me into it." He was oddly pleased that his words sounded plausible.

He sighed. "There's a lot of shit going on. You'll hear more when I come back." Whenever that might be. "Once again, I need you to do some digging for me."

Vanukoff let out a loud sigh. "Whatever you say, boss."

"I'm sending you a picture right now of an object I found. I don't know what it is. No idea who made it. It has markings and I need to find out what they mean. Hieroglyphs, decoration, whatever. Maybe someone at the Museum of Natural History can identify them. Hold on."

Garrahan snapped half a dozen pictures of the device from different angles and sent them to Vanukoff.

On his end, Vanukoff looked at the photos. "Is this a metal puck for air hockey?"

Unable to help himself, Garrahan laughed.

"Doesn't look like much," Vanukoff said, "but I'll send out texts and see if I get any response."

"Don't post it anywhere public, okay? Keep it quiet."

"Why? Is it valuable? Top secret?"

"To people up here it might be. Personally, I won't know if it's valuable until I know what it is."

"Got it," Vanukoff responded and signed off.

Garrahan turned the device over in his hand. He couldn't figure out how it had been assembled. No screws, no soldering marks, no welds, no rivets. It appeared to be two halves of perfectly shaped metal.

He looked at the markings, rubbing the tip of his finger over them. They meant nothing to him. They could have been ancient Abyssinian for all he knew. Or maybe an artist's etchings.

He pasted one of the photos he'd just taken into a visual search engine. The "similar items" were enough to make him laugh again. A pipe fitting for a swimming pool valve. A hood ornament from a 1950s sedan. A planter for growing orchids.

In short, nothing.

He heard Abby and Elizabeth locking up the house. Doors banged shut, bolts were thrown. He looked out his window. The sun was down.

Grabbing the shutters, he pulled them closed. His room was dark save for the light from his computer.

He sat on the bed and typed in phrase after phrase. Everything he could think of. Metal siren disk. Flat siren. Metal noise maker. Steel alarm. Disk siren. On and on. Into the night.

It got him nowhere.

He lay down.

This had to end, had to stop.

None of it made sense.

Closing his eyes, he pictured the skeletal arm he'd found. That had happened a few hours ago. Seemed like weeks ago.

He mapped the layout of the cavern in his brain, trying to capture it precisely. He remembered the clicking of the bony fingers and the ring.

The ring. In his pocket.

He fished it out and looked at it closely. "Fr. Albert. God Bless."

Tomorrow he would call Ginnie Pierce and ask her about the ring.

That reminded him. She told him to look for the word "target" in the mishmash of words that concluded Father Pierce's book.

He opened the journal, too tired to read but wanting to be done. With an effort, he thumbed to the back.

The pages were thick with lines of letters. They formed sentences of a sort. With no breaks and no punctuation, it was brain-bending trying to determine where each word began and ended. It made his eyes and head hurt—the after-effects of working on an overly complicated puzzle.

Ginnie had found something she didn't want to talk about. Garrahan had to find it on his own.

CHAPTER 86
MAY 11
SATURDAY, 8:41 PM

In his office, Malden was doing his own searches.

Garrahan had not recognized the fourth numerical inscription—17:8—on the circular disk next to Clifford Morris's memorial.

The first three numbers were part of the community's core beliefs in the Behemoth. They were testaments to the power God had given the creature. The fourth number wasn't immediately obvious, even to Malden. He scanned each book of the Bible to ascertain what 17:8 referred to.

After making his way through the entire Old Testament and the four Gospels of the New Testament, Malden had come up empty. He wondered if the number was even a Biblical passage.

He poured himself a glass of scotch.

His diligence was rewarded when he got to the very end of the Bible. The Book of Revelations. A fantastical book, the one most open to interpretation and symbolism.

In the case of chapter 17, verse 8, no interpretation was needed. Its meaning was as plain as the black letters printed on a white background.

The passage dared Malden not to believe what Garrahan had said.

"The beast that you saw once long ago shall ascend out of the pit and create destruction. Those who dwell on the Earth, and whose names have not been written in the Book of Life, will be struck down when they behold the beast that was, and has now come back out of the abyss again."

Malden read it carefully.

Twice.

There was something far below the town.

The people of Clifford Morris's time knew about it.

They had locked it up.
They built a church on top of it.
And it lived beneath them.

CHAPTER 87
MAY 11
SATURDAY, 11:49 PM

Garrahan had no idea what led Father Pierce to write the way he did for so many pages at the end of his journal. Random spaces, no punctuation. A litany of words that screamed on the page. They must have been screaming in the priest's brain.

ANDREVERENDMALDEN THINKSHISBEINGIS THERE TOBEPROTECTED AND WORSHIPPEDEVENTHOUGHIT ISADESTROYERTHAT DOESNOTDO GODSWILL ANDWILLANYONEUNDERSTAND THE EVIL THAT EXISTS IN THATTOWNBREAKFAST YESTERDAYWASBLAND WONTCOMPLAIN . . .

He read for an hour before he was able to find a sentence where the word "target" made sense.

THE BEAST HAS TO BE A TARGET IT HAS TO DIE WE HAVE TO PUT IT DOWN MALDEN MUST NOT KNOW.

The intent was clear. "The beast has to be a target. It has to die. We have to put it down. Malden must not know."

That was a shock. Kill the Behemoth? That's not what history said. And it certainly wasn't what happened.

Garrahan backtracked, rereading sentences. Phrases jumped out. "Malden convinced I am here to help." "Fellow priests will learn to shoot the beast. And not miss." "I will face wrath in Morris but will rid this place of its scourge."

It was clear to Garrahan that Father Albert did not want to help the people of Morris. He wanted to wreak vengeance on the nightmare of his childhood.

The intention—despite his promise to Malden—was to kill the Behemoth.

None of the priests went into those fields to die. Certainly not to commit suicide.

They were going to shoot the Behemoth. Kill it the moment they saw it. They expected to live as victors over the Behemoth. And Morris.

Two more sentences made it all perfectly clear. "Malden suggests having guides go with priests to help navigate the fields in the early morning dark. I see no problem so long as they do not interfere."

They interfered, all right, thought Garrahan. They took over the plan and turned it back on Pierce. The guides killed the priests—and brought the Behemoth into Morris.

That was one of the stories that Morris was hiding. It had to be. A final sentence emerged in the letters. "With target practice, the priests will rid us of this horror."

Garrahan strained to keep awake. He would take his findings to Malden, first thing. The ring, which he had held in his fingers throughout the evening, slipped to the floor as he fell asleep.

CHAPTER 88

MAY 12
SUNDAY, 2:53 AM

Garrahan lurched awake on his bed. Eyes flickering, he wasn't sure what woke him. It felt like the room had moved.

He was too sleepy to care. He sank back into unconsciousness, eyelids pulling him down.

The bed moved again. He eyes snapped open. He looked around.

There was no sound. He could barely see.

In the dark, something moved. He fumbled for his phone and turned it on, lighting up the room.

Abby was standing next to the bed, looking at him. She was shaking the bed with her hand.

Her eyes were large and protruding.

Garrahan sat up and cleared his throat. "Abby, what the Hell?" He checked the time. It was 2:53 AM. "Why are you in my room?"

Her eyes were unblinking. She looked pale, dead.

She raised her hand, pointing to the door.

"You need to come with me. Now."

"Why?" he asked groggily. "Did something . . .?"

Abby grabbed his arm, tightly, and leaned her face into his.

Her fingers dug into his skin. When she spoke, he felt her soft breath on his face.

Her voice quivered.

"It's outside the house." She could barely get the words out.

"The Behemoth is here."

CHAPTER 89

MAY 12
SUNDAY, 2:55 AM

They walked into the hallway. Garrahan saw Elizabeth standing in the corner, arms folded across her chest.

"You should hurry," Elizabeth whispered to him. "Be as quiet as you've ever been in your life." She nodded towards the attic stairs. "Please."

He stepped past her.

"No light," Elizabeth said, touching the phone. "Turn it off."

Garrahan got an uneasy feeling when she said that. He paused. As if he were walking into a trap.

"Is it safe up there?" he asked.

"If you're quiet."

"Is someone up there?" he asked, warily.

She cocked her head, questioning. "Why would anyone be up there?"

He didn't know. After being in Morris for so long, he was suspicious of everyone. He looked at Elizabeth, with Abby holding her tight, and was suspicious of them both. What was she sending him to?

"Go," she whispered.

Garrahan tiptoed up the stairs. The steps creaked under his feet.

At the top, the gleam of the streetlight seeped into the attic through the vent.

Crouching low, he shuffled across the gritty floor.

Underneath the vent, he cautiously raised his head. He kept his face in the dark, moving as slowly as he could.

He thought he might see the long slithering arms of the thing in the pit. Or its flesh groping over the ground.

There was nothing below him, nothing next to the house.

He moved a few inches to shift his view. He looked up the street towards the bowls. They were full of rotting meat this afternoon.

Now they were empty.

He hiked up higher on his knees, face angling above the vent to look down.

Garrahan heard a sound. A grinding, slavering sound.

Below him. Close to the house.

He pressed his face hard against the vent. Eyes pushed against their sockets.

There were sounds he'd never heard before. Something snarling and choking at the same time.

He saw nothing.

It was perfectly hidden away from his field of vision.

As if it had been planned, so he'd never actually see anything happen.

He'd have to admit he heard it. That would prove they were right.

Malden claimed there was nothing under the church. Garrahan had seen nothing but slugs in a drainage ditch. His imagination had betrayed him. That's what they all said.

But their monster, their Behemoth, was supposed to terrorize the nighttime. He was supposed to be afraid of that.

One story after another. Their stories. Tales of things hidden in the darkness. Tales they wanted him to believe.

Smoke and mirrors.

So much bullshit.

His whispered to himself. "They are fucking with me."

CHAPTER 90
MAY 12
SUNDAY, 3:06 AM

Garrahan leapt down the stairs.

This bullshit was over.

Elizabeth and Abby were in the hallway, waiting for him. He pushed past.

"Wha . . .?!" Elizabeth gasped.

He didn't stop, rounding the next set of stairs. Elizabeth grabbed his shirt sleeve.

"What are you doing?!" she hissed.

He yanked his arm away. They could barely see each other in the dark.

"I'm going to see who's putting on this show," he growled, keeping his voice low. "I'm sick of this."

He continued downstairs.

"Please don't open the front door!" Abby squealed, her rising voice full of fear.

"I'll sneak out the back," he barked.

He let himself out quickly and quietly. The door clicked shut as he stepped into the night. There was the moon, random streetlights, and little else to guide him.

He took stock of his surroundings.

He was at the back of the house. To his right was the neighbor's backyard. It was veiled in blackness; no lights. He heard sounds coming from the neighbor's front yard—the area he glimpsed from the attic.

He had to sneak alongside the Donahue's house to get a look at whatever was going on underneath the attic window.

Garrahan didn't want anyone to hear him coming. The last thing he needed was for the townspeople to find out he had stumbled onto their game.

The Donahue's shed sat next to their house. It was a small concrete block building, the size of a tiny garage. It rested about two feet away from the main house.

He crept into the walkway between the shed and the house.

It was a tight squeeze. Like pushing into a tunnel.

He held his breath as he walked to the front of the shed.

Garrahan saw the feeding bowls, illuminated by the streetlights.

Without revealing himself, he peeked his head around the shed. His eyes strained to see where the gurgling sounds were coming from.

The neighbor's yard was blackness layered on darkness.

The sounds were still there.

He took a half step out of the shadow of the shed.

Something moved underneath the maple tree in front of the house.

Clutching the edge of the building, Garrahan craned his neck further.

He made out a shape.

Something looming against the neighbor's house.

It seemed to be scraping at the house. Making tearing sounds.

He thought about walking towards it. Maybe catching Ethan or Leonard in the act.

The noises stopped.

For a moment, everything froze in time.

They couldn't have heard him. He'd been too quiet.

Something lumbered into the middle of the lawn.

The ground underneath him shuddered.

A figure caught the glow of the streetlight.

Garrahan caught his breath as it stood up.

His lungs stopped.

Because he couldn't believe what he was seeing.

A monster.

The hair on his skin crawled like insects swarming over flesh.

His brain reeled.

A monster.

Grotesque. Gargantuan.

Its body outlined in a yellow halo of streetlight.

All the descriptions he'd heard, all the children's drawings he'd seen, had been inadequate.

None came close to the horror Garrahan saw rising above him.

CHAPTER 91
MAY 12
SUNDAY, 3:14 AM

It moved past the concrete bowl. Remains of partially eaten cattle lay on the ground.

The thing pushed a slab of meat into the blackness that was its mouth.

Garrahan watched in awe. It was like observing an animal in the wild. His jaw gaped.

The creature was nearly twenty feet high.

If he was still in the third-floor attic, it would have looked him right in the eye.

He wasn't in the attic anymore.

He was on the ground.

Outside.

Right next to it.

The thing turned in his direction. It snorted in the night air.

The dinosaurs had been this big. But this was not a dinosaur.

And it was not human.

As much as Garrahan had been expecting to see a gaggle of Morris men hiding inside a costume or propelling a puppet monster, it was none of those things.

This monster was alive. Garrahan saw wings running along its arms.

Its claws—or talons, or whatever they were—were like tentacles at the end of gnarled hands.

The creature moved in a way that he'd never known an animal to move. It flicked its limbs about like a spider, jointed extremities moving in different directions.

It hovered over the meat, enveloping it like a giant lizard, head and mouth darting with incredible speed. A creature moving in a speeded-up film, each move deliberate and gigantic.

He couldn't believe something so big could move so fast.

Light reflected off its skin with a black metallic sheen.

Teeth emerged from its dark mouth as it lowered its head to grab more food. The sides of its skull were sunken, making shadows where Garrahan imagined its eyes must be.

All the while, the spidery hands worked their way over the carcass.

In a moment, the flesh was gone.

The Behemoth was done here. For now.

It stood up on what Garrahan guessed were hind legs. The head swiveled about—so quickly that Garrahan couldn't believe it—and it stepped away from the light.

It appeared to be deciding what to do, or where to go, next.

Garrahan made no sound. He did not breathe. He did not blink.

Yet somehow, the creature knew he was there.

It twisted in his direction.

Without warning, the thing skittered to where Garrahan hid. Startled, he jumped away as a probing talon reached into the space between the shed and the house.

Garrahan retreated into the darkness.

The thing knew he was here.

It wanted him.

His awe turned to mind-crushing fear.

The creature released a horrific shriek that rattled Garrahan's skull.

Long, loud, and drenched with fury.

The sound that came out of the beast made Garrahan more afraid than he'd ever been in his life.

Mouth open, it brought its head down to the shed's roof. It pushed its talons into the narrow space. Grabbing for him.

Its body was too big to get between the house and shed. That didn't stop it.

The creature turned, trying to force its way into the passage.

Garrahan heard shingles rip off the roof. The thing's shrieking convulsed into strained grunts.

It blocked out the light, leaving a silhouette hulking over him.

The creature tilted its skull over the shed looking for a way in. Garrahan saw something gleam inside its face. A green luminescence where its eyes should be. Skin glimmered as if made of liquid chrome. Its hands and talons were sleek and metallic as they stretched closer to him . . .

Fear finally shot through Garrahan's body—assaulting him.

He had to get out.

If he tried to run to the house, the creature would grab him. He couldn't outrun it.

There was no guarantee that he wasn't locked out. The Donahues would be protecting themselves. As they should.

A talon scratched at the concrete next to his face. He backed up, cowering against the wall.

The creature shrieked again.

Garrahan was at the end of the shed. From here to the back door was fifteen very quick steps. Too many. Too uncertain.

The thing tried to push itself further into the space.

There was no protection for him out here.

None.

He fumbled for the shed's door. His hand grabbed the metal knob.

It opened.

The creature heard the click of the lock and reared up. It lunged to the other side of the shed.

Garrahan spun into the door, his body hitting it hard. He fell inside, slamming the door shut behind him.

At the same moment, the creature smashed the door apart.

The door flew off its hinges, splintering across the room. It knocked him backwards into lawn furniture and yard equipment. The broken door crashed down on him as he fell to the dirt floor.

The shriek was now a roar. It was screaming into the open doorway.

Garrahan felt a blast of fetid air coming from the thing's mouth.

The shed opening was too small for it.

The beast threw itself against the doorway. The room shuddered.

The thing's arm reached in. Talons probed wildly, knocking bottles and tools off shelves. Glass shattered as shovels, hoses, and saw blades rained over Garrahan.

The thing felt its way through the debris, tentacle fingers poking—yet not seeing.

Lying still, Garrahan flitted his own fingers around the floor searching for a weapon. They landed on a screwdriver. He grabbed it tightly in his fist.

The monstrous hand clambered over the door panel lying across Garrahan's chest.

Not feeling him, the hand kept going. Seeking something soft.

The talons grasped a plastic gas can. It squeezed tight, shattering the can. Gasoline splashed over the talons and down onto Garrahan. The smell invaded his nostrils.

Soaked in gasoline, the claw hesitated.

Then it stopped. The hand didn't move. It hovered motionless in the dark, gas running along its metallic fingers.

Suddenly, the hand retreated from the shed. The monstrous body moved away from the door.

In the next instant, the creature smashed itself against the roof, cracking the rafters and showering debris over Garrahan.

The roof held.

The Behemoth let out a cry.

Not a roar, nor a sound of anguish.

An animal announcing its presence.

The cry was guttural and sustained, from deep within the beast.

Garrahan's blood turn frigid.

The beast slammed its hands against the side of the shed, causing the one window to shatter inward. Garrahan felt the force of the blow ripple through the ground underneath him.

Looking up to the window, he could see the Behemoth facing the streetlamp. Head flicking, teeth bared, it lurched toward the street.

The monster was gone.

CHAPTER 92
MAY 12
SUNDAY, 4:30 AM

Garrahan laid on the floor for another hour, not able or daring to move. He listened for any sound of the creature. For the sound of anything.

The village was quiet.

No crickets, no cicadas, no frogs broke the silence.

Perhaps they had retreated in fear of the Behemoth.

He slipped quietly into the house and made his way up the stairs. His face and arms were sliced with cuts from the shattered door and the flying glass. He smelled like the underside of a lawn mower.

Abby and Elizabeth were still there, sitting on the floor. They had waited for him.

He flicked on his phone light. Their eyes looked up at him, emotionless.

"You've lived with that . . . that thing, for . . ." he began, his voice jagged. Stuttering. Unsure.

"For our entire lives," Elizabeth said. "Yes, we have."

Garrahan dropped to the floor.

"I had no idea. I mean, who could have? It's not, it can't, I don't . . ."

He had no control over words. His brain couldn't process what he had seen.

The Donahues sat silently, watching him.

He slumped his head into his hands. He felt sticky trails of blood on his face. He looked each of them in the eye.

"I'm sorry. I didn't believe you," he said. "You were telling the truth. I never once believed it. Now . . ." He swept his arm up, to indicate what he had seen only a few feet from where they were sitting. "That's not what I saw under the church. That could have been insects, or something else, I don't know. But this monster," he pointed outside, "It lives. Out there. In the open."

He wanted to ask a million questions. He wanted to babble, to talk, to understand.

But he had all the answers.

He'd been given them. Time and again.

There was nothing that he could ask that he didn't already know.

He had seen the Behemoth. It existed.

As they had told him it did.

Outside of this house, no one would ever believe him.

Ever.

CHAPTER 93
MAY 12
SUNDAY, 5:00 AM

Garrahan wanted to talk. Elizabeth reminded him that the Behemoth might still come back. They had to keep quiet. While it roamed, they were not safe. Not until sunup.

They sat on the stairs. Abby fell asleep on her mother's lap.

Garrahan wanted to know what the thing really was. He couldn't believe it was an emissary of God, a guard dog for people to worship.

The journalist part of him was astounded. *What a find*, he thought to himself. *A creature like no other on Earth.*

The less professional part of him was incredulous. How could a thing like this live for so long, and go undetected except by a select few?

Elizabeth watched him struggle with that. He tapped his fingers on his forehead, he muttered out loud—as if trying to solve a difficult equation.

She dozed off thinking he didn't have much time to figure it out. The Behemoth was back in the village. Malden would want to act quickly.

By the time Garrahan himself fell asleep, he had made no sense of it. He had believed that the creature didn't exist. That helped him keep an objective eye on everything. There had to be something more nefarious behind Bruce's murder.

There wasn't.

Morris was no longer an oddball town mixed up in a strange cover-up of long-ago deaths, doing God knows what to children in the modern day.

The simple story behind it all was true.

What Malden was doing was evil, nonetheless. Killing to protect this creature. And Leonard's killing of Nancy was more evil still. Criminal beyond words. He lingered on thoughts of Nancy: her hair, her smile, her eyes, her scent . . .

His dreams were interrupted by a hard, persistent banging. At first it sounded like the Behemoth trying to get into the house. He jumped to his feet, looking for a place to hide.

Abby and Elizabeth were waking up from their spots in the corner.

The hammering continued. Garrahan heard voices.

As he stumbled towards the door, Elizabeth stopped him. "That could be Mr. Malden. I'll go with you."

Helping her to her feet, they went to the front door.

The hammering continued unabated. Elizabeth checked her watch.

It was almost 7 AM. The sun would be out.

CHAPTER 94
MAY 12
SUNDAY, 7 AM

She opened a shuttered window. Light spilled across the living room floor like a wave of white paint.

Flicking her fingers over the locks, she pulled the door back. More light splashed in, framing the four men standing on the porch.

Malden pushed forward, followed by Ethan, Leonard, and Joel.

It took Malden's eyes a second to adjust to the glare. He made out the forms of Elizabeth and Garrahan.

"Your device called the Behemoth. It came."

Malden said it in measured tones. There was excitement and urgency underneath.

He strutted around the living room. "That device is a signal. It must summon the Behemoth."

Garrahan wasn't so sure. He didn't think the beast was a creature that came when it was called. A Pavlovian dog.

Malden muttered his plans while Garrahan thought to himself.

If it wasn't a call, what was it?

It could be an alarm.

A warning.

It alerted the Behemoth. To something wrong. To something gone awry. To danger.

The device was never mentioned in legends or old writings. Not once. Perhaps it had not been used before. Maybe no one had ever threatened the creature—or the thing in the cave—before.

Until Father Pierce.

He had died with it in his hand.

After calling out to the Behemoth. And the thing under the church.

In a place where very little made sense, this explanation did.

The alarm let the Behemoth know if humans got too close to the beast in the abyss.

Garrahan listened to Malden rant.

"We'll do it again tonight," he said. "We'll summon the Behemoth. We'll be prepared."

"Prepared how?" Garrahan asked.

Malden gave him a disdainful glance. "We'll go to the site of the car crash. Once the Behemoth is inside the boundaries, we'll close it off. Just like the first five priests did."

Garrahan shook his head.

"Last time that happened, a priest had to die at each point. His blood had to be spilled to seal the boundary." Garrahan kept from smiling. "You're not going to find any local priests willing to die like that on such short notice."

Malden cocked his head. He wasn't sure he'd heard correctly.

It was the only time Garrahan had seen Malden taken by surprise.

And speechless.

A scowl, then a worried glaze, passed over Malden's face. His mouth worked a little, trying to form words.

Garrahan was right.

Everyone in the room turned to him, uneasily.

The silence was overwhelming.

Malden sat down on the living room couch. He brought his fingertips together in front of his lips.

He looked at the ceiling, wondering if an answer might present itself up there.

The wheels in Malden's brain turned at hyper speed. He imagined his grandfather in the same position. How he would have reacted to this. What lengths he would go to if the beast was threatened.

"It is up to me, then," Malden said slowly. To no one in particular.

The silence that followed lasted only an instant.

Joel visibly shook. "You can't! We need you to lead the community. You need to . . ."

Malden's eyes turned dark. And strangely sad.

"There's no other way. I have to make it work. As part of my duty. Tonight."

Leonard interjected. "The kid's right. We need you here for . . ."

Malden shut him down. "Joel has completed his studies. He's ready. I'll ordain him this afternoon."

He looked at Joel. "You can run the church."

Joel's eyes widened in shock.

Leonard wanted to say that this was a profoundly bad idea. Instead, he held his tongue.

The Donahues and Garrahan watched without speaking.

"Mr. Garrahan, you will go to the church and start the device at sunset." Malden looked at Garrahan sternly, with no emotion. "Do it inside the church. If the Behemoth comes to us, you will be free to go. I will have Ethan and Joel make sure that . . ." he paused, thinking. "They will make sure all your affairs are in order."

"I hardly think I can believe that," Garrahan said.

Malden's face flushed. "Leonard. Ethan. Joel. Tell me that you will not harm Mr. Garrahan after I'm gone. Tell me that you will attend to the mistake you made in New York. Tell me that you understand that." He looked at each of them.

They nodded somberly.

"What about Elizabeth and Abby?" Garrahan shot back. He was so tired that he was surprised he could come up with anything to say.

"They can stay or go. With the Behemoth returned, it will no longer matter." Malden rubbed his eyes. "It will be under our protection. We can handle that on our own."

He avoided looking at the Donahues. "The town will be done with them."

Leonard shook his head imperceptibly. Garrahan could tell he was seething.

"Joel, what time did the Behemoth return last night?" Malden asked, his gaze focused on a far wall.

"Those who heard it say the time was around 1 AM. Gone by 3 AM." Joel wanted to hedge his bets. "That's not exact or anything."

Malden nodded, dismissively. "Yes, I'm aware it's not exact." He thought a moment. "Everyone will be in position tonight by sundown. That will make for a long evening. I expect it will be time well spent."

"Mr. Garrahan will go to the church. Ethan, you will let him in. Joel, at sundown you and I will stand at the overturned marker. When we know the Behemoth is near the church, I will take the necessary steps to seal the opening."

Meaning he would kill himself.

"Leonard, I need you to patrol the village and make sure everything between the church and the marker is clear." Leonard nodded.

Garrahan felt like he was dreaming. Malden was talking about killing himself—and expecting everyone to go along with it.

In addition, they were all going to be outside and exposed when the monster came back. Presuming it came back.

As of tomorrow morning, everything was supposed to return to normal. Garrahan could get on with his life. So could Elizabeth and Abby. Maybe he was dreaming.

Malden clapped his hands, a rasp of finality. "Get started. We need to be prepared for any eventuality."

He moved swiftly out the door, Ethan and Leonard in tow. Mrs. Bower scooted after them, zipping past Garrahan.

Joel waited behind.

"Did you find out what the device is?" he asked Garrahan.

Garrahan looked up at him, wearily. "No. Did you?

"Uh uh," Joel replied, arching his eyebrows. "Are you going back, uh, underneath the church?"

"Not if I don't have to," he said. "But I'm not the one pointing guns, so that remains to be seen."

Joel left without a word.

The house was empty except for Garrahan, Abby, and Elizabeth. They sat quietly. Garrahan didn't notice how much time had passed, but after a few minutes he realized they hadn't spoken. He couldn't even hear them breathe.

He looked at Elizabeth. She was stroking Abby's hair. Abby was staring out the still-open front door.

Eventually, Elizabeth looked at Garrahan. She was crying.

He hadn't seen her cry since she'd learned of Bruce's murder.

"This might be too much to ask," Elizabeth said, her words soft. "But would it be okay if we went with you to New York tomorrow?" She swallowed hard. "When this is all over?"

Garrahan didn't think it was too much to ask. He also didn't think he had a good answer. He cleared his throat and kept his voice low.

"Despite what you just heard," he said, trying to keep from sounding harsh "I doubt that's going to happen."

Her eyes widened. Abby stiffened in her arms.

Garrahan looked at the sunlight pouring through the door. The day seemed full of promise in its brightness.

"I don't think you will be allowed to leave Morris," he said, crushing her hope.

"If it makes you feel any better, I don't think they'll let me go, either."

CHAPTER 95
MAY 12
SUNDAY, 7:30 AM

The four men strode across the village green. Malden was happy for the first time since those moronic kids had driven into the marker. He had a plan, and it was a good one.

It would be good for the town, and for the Behemoth.

He sent Ethan to the town hall and told Joel to wait for him in the church.

Alone with Leonard, he looked around, making sure no one was nearby. He waved to a couple in the distance, watching them go about their business.

Leonard's eyes darted about the village green. He didn't like the way this was playing out. At all. It was happening too quickly. Malden was making decisions without consulting him.

He wanted to tell Malden they needed to be methodical. Take care of one problem at a time.

That's the way Leonard did it—and it always worked.

"I know you're angry, Leonard, but trust me," Malden intoned. "This will work."

Leonard shrugged. "You do what you have to do," he said, petulantly. "I think this will be a clusterfuck if you don't take care of every last detail."

"By that, I'm presuming you mean Garrahan."

Leonard nodded.

"He'll be dealt with. You and I and Ethan will go over that later. In the meantime, we are not taking chances with the Behemoth. We have to do everything to attract it. That means filling the bowls right away. Get Tom Rossberg's cattle. If he doesn't have enough, take bulls from Bart Mennler's farm. He'll argue but make him come around."

That made Leonard happy. Mennler was a whiny bastard who claimed at village meetings that his farm was too small to participate in feeding the Behemoth. Meanwhile, he was making more per head than anyone else. Taking his bulls by fiat would be a pleasure.

"While Tom and Bart are getting cattle, you need to do something for me. Quietly." Malden scanned the neighborhood for anyone who might stroll by.

Leonard's ears perked up. This was more his style.

"You need to go into the woods and get the altar ready."

That took Leonard by surprise. "Really? You're going to put someone out there?"

"I am. We have to offer something to Behemoth." If the creature came back, it had to be appeased.

Leonard was all in favor. "Thing is, we don't have time for a lottery."

Malden sniffed. "Last I checked, Abby Donahue was next on the list. I don't think anyone in town will have a problem with choosing her."

CHAPTER 96
MAY 12
SUNDAY, 12:22 PM

The sacrificial altar was a quarter of a mile into the woods, north of the church.

Far enough from the village that no one could hear the screams.

A long-trodden path marked the way through the thick trees and overgrown brush. The soil was as hard as concrete from the feet of young girls taken to sacrifice—and the men who led them there.

Malden believed the Behemoth used this same route, but he couldn't be certain. He had never stuck around to see the monster take its sacrifice.

Leonard had. Many times. Years ago, he built a platform high in one of the forest trees. It was a hundred yards from the clearing. With a pair of binoculars he had a perfect view of the ritual.

To protect his view, he came out regularly to prune any branches that got in his way. To protect himself, he carried a high-powered rifle.

Not that the Behemoth had ever come after him. Or even noticed him. It always had the offering in its hands and its teeth.

And not that Leonard was supposed to raise a hand against the creature. He was supposed to protect it. Never harm it. The Behemoth's life was more important than that of anyone in the town.

Fuck that, he thought. If he was in danger, he was sure as Hell going to kill the thing. Kill or be killed, he always told himself. No matter what.

The altar was in the center of the circular clearing. Trees surrounded it like columns reaching to the sky.

Although the people of Morris called it an altar, it was merely a single granite pillar surrounded by flagstones. There was no ornamentation or decoration, save for a thick iron ring hanging off the side of the pillar.

Girls were handcuffed to the ring.

Leonard came out once a month to make sure the ring was rust free. He also tugged on it to make sure it was never in danger of coming loose from the pillar. Couldn't have little ladies pulling free and go running through the woods.

The altar was covered with scratches. Scars from centuries of the desperate clutching of girls.

Clifford Morris had installed the granite pillar and its ring in the early 1700s. Long before he arrived, the site had been used for human sacrifice.

The Vikings had built fires on this spot, throwing the bodies of native tribesmen into the inferno to sate the beast. For thousands of years before that, the ancestors of those same tribesmen had tied women captured from rival tribes to wooden stakes, all for the monster.

Clifford Morris had created a real altar for the English-speaking peoples who settled the region. The pillar was carved and sunk deep into the ground. He claimed it would never be pried from the Earth by anything but God. In three hundred years, it had not moved an inch.

Leonard ran his hands over the grooves made from so many frantic fingers. Fingers that wore themselves down to the actual bone in their fright.

There were deeper grooves. They bore witness to the size of the Behemoth's teeth.

Remembering all the times he'd been here made Leonard's heart speed up. After he handcuffed a girl to the iron ring, she was his to do with as he pleased. That was his little secret. No girl had ever come back to tell. His secret was eternally safe.

Once he'd had his fun, he lit the five torches that marked the perimeter of the clearing. They threw off enough light to let the girls see what was coming their way.

That was when the screaming started in earnest.

By the time that happened, Leonard was safely up on his platform. Binoculars and rifle in hand.

He checked the oil in the torches and made sure his tree ladder was secure. He climbed up and laid his rifle on the platform. He confirmed that his view of the altar was unobstructed.

Everything was ready. Leonard looked at his watch. Abby Donahue had about six hours till he went and got her.

He was extremely excited about that.

CHAPTER 97
MAY 12
SUNDAY, 12:36 PM

Even with the promise of release, Garrahan didn't think he wasn't getting out alive. Or without a fight.

That went for the Donahues, too.

Sitting on the edge of the bed, he went through as many scenarios as he could. None of them had happy endings.

Staring at the floor, something glinted at the edge of the carpet. The ring he'd found under the church. In the whirlwind of activity since yesterday afternoon, he'd forgotten about it. He must have dropped it last night when he fell asleep.

He looked at the inscription again. A gift to Father Pierce. Possibly to celebrate his ordination.

Garrahan hadn't told Ginnie Pierce about the ring.

He called her, standing by the window as he waited for the call to connect.

Ginnie's voice was pleasant when she picked up. "Good to hear from you, Mr. Garrahan," she began. "How's your reading going . . .?"

He interrupted. "Your uncle was right about a lot of things," he said, quietly. "I found a ring that belonged to him. In the church in Morris."

If she was surprised, she didn't let it show. "How do you know the ring is his?"

"The words "Fr. Albert. God Bless" are engraved on it. I don't know anyone else named Father Albert who would have been in the Morris church."

He desperately did not want to tell her he'd gotten the ring off the severed arm of a skeleton.

"Is there a date on it?" she asked, nonplussed.

"No, just those words." He eyed the ring carefully. "I think we're coming to the end here." Like the close of a business deal rather than the end of a monster story.

"That's good," she said. He could hear the smile in her tone. "Can you bring the ring back with the journal when you're done?"

"Of course," he replied, then realized he might not get the chance. "The locals might want me out of here sooner than later. If I can't get to you, I'll leave it here for you to pick up."

Sensing something amiss, she asked "Anything I can do for you? Help out in any way?"

Garrahan watched Ethan walk across the green towards the gas station. "I don't think so," he answered. "I'll leave the ring, and a computer drive, in a bag for you." He scoured the gas station. "There's a planter between two pumps at the Morris gas station. I'll leave it under the planter. If you don't hear from me in the next forty-eight hours, you can get it there." He wanted to apologize.

"That's fine. It'll give me a chance to get out and do some sightseeing," she laughed.

"Well, thank you again," Garrahan said. "I appreciate . . ."

Her turn to interrupt. "One last thing."

"Okay," he said, hesitantly.

"The last pages of the book. Did you read them?"

"I did." He saw Ethan cross the street to the gas station.

"Did you figure out why a group of priests decided to sacrifice themselves for a monster in Morris?"

"I think Father Albert convinced . . ."

"It has to be bullshit, right?" she exclaimed. "That whole suicide part of the story. A Catholic priest, obsessed with something he hates, convinces five priests from different faiths to lay down their lives. For what? A creature worshipped by a strange little village." She made a sound of disgust. "That is utterly absurd."

"Think about what those priests were supposedly doing," she continued. "Each standing alone, out in a field. Each one waiting for a horrifying creature to show up. Does that sound reasonable?" She clucked her tongue. "If you were scared and saw a huge monster—and you had a gun—what would you be inclined to do?" she asked.

"Shoot it," Garrahan answered, hastily.

"Exactly," Ginnie continued. "Doesn't it make more sense that Father Albert sent those priests out to shoot the monster? Instead of asking them to commit suicide?"

"Yes, it does," he replied. "But if . . ."

She wasn't finished. "Morris protected their beast for centuries. Just because Father Albert had a plan doesn't mean they would take a chance on priests shooting it."

Garrahan had come to the same conclusion last night. If she had told him this when he first met her, it might have saved them all some time. But he wasn't going to stop her now.

"Malden would never let the priests carry out a plan to kill the creature. Even if they were determined to do it, he would have a plan of his own to stop them. At least to my mind." She took a deep breath. "I think townspeople followed the priests to their appointed places. They made sure blood was spilled—by shooting those priests dead in their tracks."

She was worked up. "No one would ever suspect. There were no autopsies. No funerals. No one knew what happened. The priests became folk heroes—in Morris—for protecting the creature and protecting the faith."

Garrahan heard banging on the front door. Ethan was ready.

Father Pierce never made it out alive to tell the tale, to reveal the truth.

The story had always been that the priests sacrificed themselves.

That had never been completely explained.

The people of Morris killed the priests.

That was easy to explain.

Ethan pounded again.

"Ginnie, I've got to go. You've been a tremendous help."

He hung up before she could say goodbye.

CHAPTER 98
MAY 12
SUNDAY, 12:47 PM

Garrahan leaned over the bannister. Ethan was talking to Elizabeth. He pointed at Garrahan.

"Mr. Malden wants you to come with me. Guys are digging his plot. He wants you to see he's serious about this."

They drove in Ethan's car. Five men were at the site. All in work clothes with boots and gloves, holding shovels. Father Moynihan's marker still lay on its side.

"Time to get started, boys," Ethan called out. It sounded strange, since all the men were much older than Ethan. "This is Robert Garrahan," he said, jerking his thumb behind him. "He's helping bring the Behemoth back."

There were muttered words and nodded heads. The tallest man spoke up. "What are we digging here, Ethan?"

Ethan had been coached by Malden not to reveal that it was to be Malden's grave. That might get people agitated.

"Another priest has agreed to be part of our mission. He is willing to spill his blood to return the Behemoth to us in accordance with scripture. He will be buried next to Father Moynihan." *That was pretty damned eloquent*, Ethan thought proudly to himself.

He marked out a general area near the original marker. He hoped it was far enough away that they wouldn't uncover Moynihan's bones.

The men dug in quickly, with the force of workers accustomed to using tools on hard ground. In minutes, they were slick with sweat. Ethan and Garrahan stood to the side, watching silently.

Twenty minutes in, the tall man spoke up again. "Malden thinks he figured out how to get the beast back. That right?"

"That's exactly right," replied Ethan. He was now squatting on his haunches.

"Shame it's taken so long to get this under control," said another man as he tossed a rock out of the deepening pit.

There was a general murmuring of agreement. Ethan wanted to say something in Malden's defense, but knew better. These men had been around a lot longer than him. Without Malden around, he couldn't afford to piss them off.

Truth be told, he was nervous about how things were going to be run in town without Malden. The council was a bunch of cranky old people. And Jesus . . . Joel as minister? He was younger and more immature than Ethan.

Didn't matter. None of it was Ethan's call. He would do what he was told.

More silence. The sun baked down.

When the hole was three feet deep, Ethan asked "How much longer you guys think this will be?"

"It'd go a lot faster if you'd get your ass in here and help," the tall man replied.

Ethan felt embarrassed. "Seriously, about how long?"

The tall man wiped his forehead with a dirty glove, leaving a dark smear across his face. "Another hour. Maybe a little longer."

Standing up, Ethan checked the time. "I've got to let Mr. Malden know."

He zigzagged back to the car trying to find a strong cell signal. He left Garrahan alone with the men.

"Shame about Bruce Donahue," Garrahan said, off-handedly.

"Sure is," one of the men said. "He knew the rules. Didn't deserve to die over it, though."

More murmuring. The tall man said, to no one in particular, "They should have brought him back. Bruce would've come back, once he got sense talked into him. Goddamned Leonard and Ethan screwed that up, far as I'm concerned."

"Malden's as much to blame," another chimed in.

"Maybe, maybe not," the tall man replied. "He's scared shitless. Rightly so. He had to do something drastic. Sending Leonard to the big city wasn't the brightest idea, though." They all laughed, as if at an inside joke.

"If this works, it'll all be forgiven," another man said. His shovel clanged against rocky soil.

"Malden's got some answering to do. He's not in control like he should be. None of this should have happened," said the tall man. "I'm not a fan of his. I think the council is feeling the same way."

More nodding. Garrahan watched them work, then turned his gaze to the horizon. Looming above the trees, far off in the distance, was the steeple of the old cathedral.

It stuck out of the forest like a sharpened spike, leaving a dark gash against the bright blue sky.

Something was living beneath that church. Not the thing he had seen last night, but something different. Something that had been walled in. Not allowed to run about in the night.

That thing was more sacred than the Behemoth. Or more threatening. More something.

There were answers in that church. Had to be.

The problem was he didn't know what the goddamned questions were.

Once upon a time, someone had known what was under there. Many someones.

Ethan came back, all smiles. "When we're done, Mr. Malden will meet us at the town hall," he told Garrahan.

The men finished digging. The pit was the appropriate size for a grave: six feet deep and six feet long.

Not big enough for a coffin, but fine for a freshly dead body.

CHAPTER 99

MAY 12
SUNDAY, 1:11 PM

As they climbed into the car, Garrahan said "Let me talk to Malden."

Ethan sighed and hit his speed dial. Malden answered immediately.

"Garrahan wants to talk to you."

"Not now," replied Malden. "I'm getting ready for . . ."

Garrahan grabbed the phone from Ethan's ear. Fuck being polite.

"When was the last time you were in the big church?" he asked Malden.

"When I was four years old."

"Who's been in there since?"

"A few engineers after it collapsed. No one else."

Garrahan thought a moment. "There must be someone who remembers what it was like before it burned down."

Malden was intrigued. "What do you want to know?"

"I want to talk to someone who went to services in the church. Someone who was old enough to understand what went on. Someone who wasn't four years old."

"Why?"

"Because they might remember more about the church than you do." Garrahan tried to put a timeline to his thoughts. "Your grandfather died before the church burned down."

"Yes. And?"

"All his papers, all his instructions. They were destroyed by the fire?"

"I told you they were."

There's more. There has to be, Garrahan thought.

Something must have been written about the thing down in the pit. Maybe that was lost in the fire, too. But the church was built on top of it. The church itself might be part of the myths.

Someone had to know.

Actually, that might not be true. No one had to know. Information from the past was being lost every single day, all over the world. People were taking knowledge with them to their graves.

"Are there older people in Morris who remember what went on in the church?" he asked Malden. "They would have been teenagers or in their early twenties when it collapsed."

Malden didn't know where Garrahan was going with this.

"I'm sure you have reasons for wanting to do this, but we are running out of time. I've got to take care of Joel . . ."

Garrahan cut him off. "Do you want me to follow through on this, or can I just fucking go home right now? Because I'm not doing this for my own enjoym—"

"All right, all right," Malden said, testily. "There are a few people you can talk to. The Stewarts are in their nineties. They might be able to give you something. What that would be, I have no idea. And Bart Mennler's father is still alive. He's in his late eighties. I'll have Ethan take you to visit them."

Garrahan shoved the phone back to Ethan.

They headed towards farms on the other side of town.

CHAPTER 100
MAY 12
SUNDAY, 1:16 PM

Edward Malden sped through Joel's ordination. Mindful of the time.

The younger man didn't notice. He was ecstatic to be joining the priesthood that had served Morris for hundreds of years.

Unfortunately, he wasn't sure he could watch Mr. Malden kill himself without getting sick.

Joel recited the vows he'd been working on for months. He stumbled over a few. Malden didn't correct him.

"You have to be strong for the community, Joel," Malden said, softly. "I know you're young. It's going to feel like a lot of pressure. The expectation will be great. You have to tell yourself that you are ready. And I'm telling you that you're ready."

His words helped Joel's confidence. With each passing moment, Joel knew he was taking on the mantel of the ministry. Yet, the suddenness of it scared him.

Malden noticed. "Don't worry. When the Behemoth returns, things will again be as they should be. Life will be normal. You'll have time to grow into your role." Malden clapped Joel on the shoulder.

"You know where the town documents are. I'll leave other items in my desk."

So much to consider, Joel thought. His head felt like it would explode.

Malden checked the time. "We need to talk to the others. I'll meet you in my office. Tomorrow," he spread his arms expansively, "this will be yours." There was sorrow in his voice.

It struck Joel that Malden would be dead tomorrow. It made him sad, to the point of crying. He held it in and nodded.

Together they walked out of the new church.

CHAPTER 101
MAY 12
SUNDAY, 1:30 PM

The first stop was the Stewart household. It was a nicely kept Victorian house outside the village center. The houses here weren't as close together as in town. Their backyards ran deep into the forest.

Allen and Louise Stewart were sitting on their porch, watching the world go by. Ethan walked up and introduced Garrahan to them. They smiled and politely shook his hand.

"This man has questions about the old church," said Ethan, sounding like a tour guide. "He wants to know if you remember anything about it."

"Not much to tell," laughed Allen. "It was pretty inside."

"Not like this new one," Louise interjected. She scowled. "The old one was more than pretty. It was beautiful. This new one," she harrumphed "barely counts as a church. Looks like a hardware store, if you ask me." She folded her arms across her chest. "And you are asking me."

"Was there anything different about the services in the old church? Anything that didn't make the transition to the new church?" Garrahan asked.

"Not sure about that," Allen said, scratching his head. "It took a long time to get the new church built. We didn't have services for three years. Nothin' formal those days except the ritual. Me and Louise didn't have kids, so we didn't hear much about the ritual, anyway."

"Took too damn long to get services going again," his wife said. "George Malden—that'd be the current Mr. Malden's father—wasn't ready to run the church. He grew up in his father's shadow. Had no idea how to lead the congregation. Then the church burning . . . whew!" Louise threw her arms up into the air. "That was too much for George to handle. Things didn't get done, or they didn't get done right. His boy—our current Mr. Malden—did a better job of taking charge when the time came."

Allen nodded. "George Malden's heart was in the right place, but there were too many things for him to take care of. The church, the town. Plus, his wife and son—they were pistols. Thought very highly of themselves . . ."

"Shush, Allen!" Louise hissed, slapping his arm. "That's nobody's business. And it was long ago." She threw a glance at Garrahan. "Besides, this man wants to know about the church. It was truly gorgeous."

"So I've heard," Garrahan said, not able to help himself.

"One thing they don't have in the new church is the memorial altar!" Allen said, excited at recalling the detail. "The new church isn't big enough for an altar like that." He smiled widely. "It was impressive in the old church. Old Mr. Malden would get up on that thing and preach for hours."

Garrahan tilted his head. "Where was the memorial altar in the old church?" he asked.

"In the middle, towards the entrance," Allen said. "Huge thing. Couldn't miss it. Took up a big space in the church. I'll bet when the building finally falls in, that altar will still be standing." He sat back, pleased with himself.

"You mean the monument to Clifford Morris? The big marble one?"

"Yessir. There isn't any other," said Louise.

"I thought that was his tomb. Or a memorial."

"It was, or is," said Allen. "It was used as the altar every once in a while. Grandpa Malden . . . sorry, Samuel Malden, would climb on top of it. For special occasions, holidays. Or when he wanted to rant."

"How would you know?" Louise asked, haughtily. "You and your brothers always fooled around during services. It's a wonder you remember even being there!"

Allen pressed on, ignoring his wife. "I remember him getting up, above the entire congregation. He would scream and holler like it was the end of days. Impressive." He paused a moment. "Those preachers you see on TV and those stadiums got nothing on him. Not even close."

This time, his wife agreed with him. "It was something to see, that's for sure," she said. "But old Mr. Malden didn't do it often. I saw him do it maybe twice in my life. Both times he was yelling so much you couldn't tell what he was talking about. He scared us."

"Like we don't have enough on Earth to scare us already," replied Allen, gazing out over his lawn.

They chattered for a bit longer, but the Stewarts couldn't remember much else that was different back then.

"If you get a chance, look at the paintings in there. They didn't do those in the new church, either," Allen said, picking at his whiskers. "Real artsy fartsy they were. I think."

"They weren't paintings," his wife said, exasperated. "They were mosaics. Made of tile."

"Well, they didn't put them in the new one, so that's different." Allen nodded at Garrahan. "You should look at them if you get a chance."

Louise was fed up. She turned on her spouse. "He can't look at them! The church is ruined. No one's been in there since you and I were kids!"

Allen waved his wife off and leaned over to Garrahan. "She's just mad that I remember everything better than her."

CHAPTER 102
MAY 12
SUNDAY, 1:35 PM

Ethan drove another mile, deeper into farmland. Even this far out, Garrahan could see the cathedral spire.

"This is the Mennler farm," Ethan remarked as the car slowed. "Bart's not too bad, but his father's a prick. A big one." He looked over at Garrahan. "Just so you know."

They walked from the road to the barn. Cows grazed in a fenced pasture. A horse drank from a trough while chickens pecked at the ground. A bull cooled itself in the shade of a solitary oak.

It would have been idyllic—on any other day and in any other place.

A tractor sat in the barn doorway, framed by freshly painted red walls. As they approached, Garrahan saw two legs sticking out from under the chassis.

"Bart, that you?" called out Ethan, ducking down to see under the tractor shadow.

A voice grunted back. "Bart's not here. He's rounding up fucking cattle for Malden. Don't know when he'll be back."

The sound of tools clinked underneath the tractor engine.

"Actually, Gordon, it's you we came to see."

The tools stopped. "You didn't ask if it was me."

Ethan hemmed and hawed. "I thought Bart might be the one . . . I mean . . ."

The man stayed under the tractor. "Well, I'm not Bart. Do you want me or him? What the fuck do you want?"

Ethan looked at Garrahan, his eyes begging for this encounter to be over. "Mr. Malden sent us to ask you about the old church."

The man scooted into the sunlight. "Who's we?"

Garrahan did a quick once-over. The man was small and thin, wrapped in well-worn jeans and a workshirt. His bare hands were coated with grease. A shock of white hair and a tanned face made him look younger than he was. Garrahan knew he was in his eighties. Maybe older.

Garrahan introduced himself with the simple "Edward Malden sent me." If this guy was really an asshole, there was no point in dancing around with niceties.

Gordon Mennler stood up. He ran his sleeve across his face. "I'm busy, as you can see." He pointed at the tractor. "What does Malden think you're getting from me?" he said disdainfully. "The town's already getting our fucking cattle. There's not much else I'm giving away without cash on my table."

Garrahan marveled at the exchange. For a spry old man, Mennler sounded as hard and menacing as any New York street punk. And they hadn't even started a conversation.

"I'm trying to find out if things in the old church were radically different from the new church. Changes in the . . ."

"Of course it was different," said Mennler, barging in. "That was a fucking church, a cathedral. The new one looks like a nursery school."

Garrahan found it funny that both sets of older people called the current church "the new one." It was over half a century old.

"I understand the physical difference," said Garrahan. "I think things were left behind or forgotten after the fire. The way services were conducted, or elements that had importance in the original . . ."

"Fuck yeah, things changed. George Malden screwed up the new church. He didn't have a big old altar for his sermons. Not like old man Samuel. That altar was a big deal, at least to us kids. George built a little whitewashed shack. Like being stuck in a fuckin' laundromat. No excitement. No . . ." he snapped his fingers agitatedly, "No . . . no theater! That's it."

"The altar was Clifford Morris's tomb, right?" Garrahan asked.

Mennler squinted. Relishing the memories. "Yeah, I think it was. Or some kind of monument to Morris. Old man Malden treated it like his crown jewel." He wiped his face, then grinned. "No one was allowed near it, not even his own kid, George. We were told never to touch it or go near it. Only Samuel Malden was allowed. No one else."

"Why was that?" The story was getting interesting.

"Who the fuck knows?" Mennler cackled. "He told everyone to stay away because it was the most sacred thing in town. More sacred than the Behemoth."

Garrahan would never get used to hearing these people talk so casually about their monster. A Biblical creature that killed humans.

"To us, it was just a white stone block. When old man Malden wasn't looking, we'd touch the marble, run our hands over it. Nothing happened." He made a *pffft* sound, then spat into the dust. "Like we were supposed to vanish if we brushed up against it."

Mennler wiped his hands on his pants. "The old man was out of his mind, sometimes. He'd leap up on that stone and yell at us for hours. I mean hours. About how we needed to respect God's law and worship the Behemoth. How we were all destined for damnation if we didn't do as he said. How we were all inches away from Hell and the abyss as we stood there praying."

He grinned at the thought. "The rest of the time, he was a regular minister. He didn't do the screaming shit that much. But when he did, we'd talk about it at school for fucking days. He was like Jekyll and Hyde."

Mennler's voice changed. "That was long ago. I hadn't thought about it in ages." His face aged. Mennler now looked every bit of his eight decades on the planet.

"Was the altar the only thing that changed after the burning?" Garrahan asked.

Mennler's prickly demeanor returned. "Nah. Everything got all pussied up and dumbed down. After his old man died, George Malden didn't have the balls to tell people what to do and what to build. We ended up with this fucking Vegas wedding chapel. No place for a proper service."

"No one gives a shit about that stuff anymore," he said, angrily. "Besides me, there's probably not a dozen people who even remember the old church. Hell, baby Malden doesn't even remember it."

Garrahan liked that name. "Baby Malden? You mean Edward Malden?"

"Of course I mean Edward Malden," Mennler said, mocking Garrahan with a high-pitched voice. "Keep up with me, if you can, buddy. The old man, the young one, the baby. Grandfather, father, son. Samuel, George, Edward. Edward does okay as the baby these days, but he'll never be like his grandfather. No one will. At least Edward gets more done than his father did." He spat again. "Personally, it'd be nice if he paid for the fuckin' cows he takes from us."

That was as far as Garrahan thought this needed go. "Well, I appreciate your time and . . ."

Mennler wasn't done. He had an audience and he liked it. "You wanna know a perfect example of how lame the new church is? Those pictures on the wall. They get the fuckin' grade schoolers to draw them. Kids' pictures! With fucking crayons! In the old church, there were these pictures, almost like museum paintings. They were real quality. Now kids are doing the drawings. As if kindey-garten art is supposed to make us feel all religious," Mennler snorted. Then he started coughing. It took him nearly a minute to stop. He composed himself.

"Like everything else in the world. The old shit is way better than the new shit." He tapped his ancient tractor with his knuckles.

"What were the pictures of?" Garrahan asked. He wonder how much of Mennler's tirade had any value.

"I don't remember the specifics," the old man said. "Lot of symbolism stuff. Circles and crosses. Stuff about the founding of the church, early Morris shit, Bible images. Like I said, it's been forfuckingever since I was in there. Since anybody was in there."

He laughed then jabbed his finger at Garrahan, as if provoking him. "Hell, you should go in and look at it all."

"Maybe I will," Garrahan said, standing his ground.

"They did it right back then, cared about their work," said Mennler. He sounded like a proud young man. "Craftsmanship in that church was incredible. The paintings, the windows, the pews."

Garrahan could see Mennler's memories coming back. Exactly as they had with the Stewarts.

"Old man Malden even had a set of special stairs he used when he climbed up on the big altar. The thing was made of beautiful wood, like a spiral staircase. 'Cause that altar was up there, almost ten feet high. This stairway, it was amazing. Hand-carved, right down to Bible verses etched into it. And the handrails, they looked like they were alive—snakes or octopus arms or something. They curved up and around, right to the top. Like they were waiting to wrap around him. Old man Malden would march up there, waving his arms, holding a candle or a chalice or some other weird shit . . ."

Mennler let his words trail off, thinking about something. He refocused and kept going.

"When Samuel Malden was up there shouting, you knew he believed it. Every word that came out of his mouth, he believed it. We laughed at him outside of church, but when he was in there, he was an avenging fucking angel. There were a few times, maybe three or four, when he scared the living shit out of every one of us. We were just kids, but I remember a few mothers crying their eyes out right there in the pews."

Mennler squinted into the sun. "All these years later, I don't remember him screaming about anything other than hellfire and damnation crap. Must not have been very important."

He shook his head and stared hard at Garrahan. "So that's what I've got. Nothing else. And unless you've got something for me, then I need to get back to my work." He turned his palms upward. "Got anything for me?"

Garrahan didn't respond. Neither did Ethan.

"Didn't think so. If you change your minds, leave cash in my mailbox." He knelt down next to the tractor and eased himself into his work.

"By the way," Mennler shouted as he disappeared under the oversized tires, "you're fucking welcome."

CHAPTER 103

MAY 12
SUNDAY, 1:59 PM

"I'm going into the church," Garrahan told Ethan as they drove to the Donahue's gas station.

"So?" Ethan replied. He couldn't care less.

"Last time I went in, someone had to open the gate. Like last time, I'm guessing that has to be you."

"Maybe," Ethan replied, sullenly. He hated having to watch over Garrahan. "I'll check with Mr. Malden."

"Check all you want. I'll be there in ten minutes. I want to go in."

"Fine," said Ethan. "No problem."

Garrahan got out. "And get me a huge light. Like a battery-powered work light or a spotlight. I need to be able to see inside."

Ethan grunted nonchalantly and drove off.

As he walked across the gravel, Garrahan glanced to his right. The toolshed stood silently. A gigantic hole punctured the roof as if a huge stone had dropped through it. Broken bits of wood, shingles, and concrete lay scattered around the side yard.

It looked like the remains of a partially finished construction project. He thought of lying inside that shed in the middle of the night, being attacked by a nightmare. A shudder rippled his chest.

Elizabeth and Abby were in the living room. It seemed they were destined to never move from that spot again.

"How are you?" Elizabeth asked.

"Not sure," he replied. He wanted to tell her that things were getting stranger every minute, but she had lived here for years. Strange was a relative term.

"I'm going back to the church."

"For what?"

He shook his head. "I honestly don't know." He couldn't describe his thinking on it. "The church has been shut up for so long that people have forgotten it's even there. They don't know anything about it. Even Malden shrugs it off."

Garrahan gazed out the window at it. "But not too long ago, people knew what was buried under the church. They knew why a stairway led down to whatever the Hell is beneath it."

He stared at Elizabeth and Abby, until he felt awkward. He changed the subject. "Do you have a portable spotlight in the gas station?"

"I'll check," Abby said, rushing out of the room.

Garrahan went to his room and grabbed his bag. He shoved the device into it. He wished he had a gun.

Abby was waiting at the front door, all smiles. She handed him a large emergency flashlight. It would do the job.

Ethan was by the pumps. So was Leonard.

"I'm guessing you didn't find me a spotlight," Garrahan said sarcastically to Ethan.

"Didn't look," Ethan replied. Leonard laughed and slapped Ethan on the back.

Ethan took Garrahan to the cathedral. Garrahan felt déjà vu as the skyscraping steeple loomed over him.

Ethan unlocked the gate clumsily. "Don't do anything stupid this time, okay?" he commanded.

"Don't tell me what to do," Garrahan replied, blandly. "Unless you want to lead me inside."

Ethan's face paled. No way he was walking around inside that wreck. The last thing he wanted was to die in an avalanche of stone and wood, crushed under the remains of a cathedral. They'd probably never bother to dig his body out. "I'm good. You find your own way in."

A minute later, Garrahan was back inside. He didn't have much time. Maybe an hour until he had to leave. The worst part was he had no idea what he was looking for.

He wanted to avoid the rubble and the potential for anything falling on him. Aiming his light across the expanse, it appeared the far wall had held up best. He would stay close to that.

He worked his way to the main altar on his right, opposite the memorial. Swinging his spotlight back and forth, he again got the sense of walking through a European cathedral.

Thousands of lit candles and worshippers in the pews would have completed that scene.

The spotlight landed on the first mosaic. Next to the main altar. Five feet off the ground, a couple of feet wide. Obscured by ash and dust and cobwebs and whatever else decades of neglect had coated it with. The first time he'd been here, Garrahan presumed the mosaics were stations of the cross. Religious images found in every Christian church in the world.

Up close, these mosaics bore no resemblance to anything religious.

CHAPTER 104
MAY 12
SUNDAY, 2:31 PM

Using the sleeve of his shirt, Garrahan wiped the mosaic down. Blowing away dust, he shone the spotlight on the wall.

The tiled image was of a black circle. The circle was surrounded by what appeared to be tongues of flame. To Garrahan, it could have been a black hole ringed with fire.

The mosaic wasn't elaborate, but it was done with exquisite care. The thousands of bits of tile fit together like perfect interlocking puzzle pieces. Garrahan took a picture with his phone.

He edged down the wall to the next mosaic, ten feet farther away. Wiping it off, he saw it was almost identical to the first. Almost. Small details had been added. A white line ran horizontally across the dark circle. The flames now contained tiny circles. They were hard to discern, even with the flashlight glaring on them. They looked like planets, moons, and stars.

Garrahan took another picture and moved on.

The third mosaic was like the first two, with more additions. There was a vertical white line across the black hole, making a cross in the center of the dark circle. The tiny circles of planets had been replaced by little images of people. They were standing on top of the tongues of flames.

The fourth one had the same black center, but more people were in the flames. There were trees and houses among them, like a growing community. Some of the people appeared to be dead. Their bodies were marked with red. There was also a new vertical line in the black circle. It was no longer a cross. It resembled a large capital "H".

Mosaic five added another horizontal line. The tongues of fire were obscured by more houses and people. The flames were being squeezed out by the growing community.

Each of the additional mosaics—thirteen in all—showed more lines across the black circle. The white lines became a grid. People were added in increasing numbers.

On the eleventh mosaic, people were constructing a building. On the twelfth mosaic, the building became the church, positioned above the black hole. Workers climbed its sides.

Garrahan realized that the pattern of white lines was the same as he had seen down in the pit. These white lines represented the metal bars that served as a barrier in the cavern. Or a cage door.

The church was complete in mosaic thirteen. People knelt in front of it. A young girl was illustrated at the bottom. She, too, was kneeling, but she was alone. Her arms were outstretched—they had chains around them.

The row of mosaics told a story. It was the tale of how the church was built. How the abyss was sealed. The origins of the pit were from a time before humans—when God created light out of darkness.

There was no one in town, not even Edward Malden, who had seen these mosaics and knew what they represented. They'd been forgotten a long time ago. Even those who saw the mosaics probably didn't know what they represented.

Unless they'd been beneath the church.

The last mosaic was positioned next to Clifford Morris's memorial. It was as if the tomb marked the end of the story.

Now that he had decent light, Garrahan walked around the tomb and inspected it closely. He searched for markings or signs he might have missed the first time.

Markings had led him into the church's cellar. Regardless of what he found this time, he wasn't going into that subterranean chamber.

Not for anything.

A twisted wreck of wood planks was piled to the side of the tomb. A crumpled staircase. The one old Samuel Malden used to climb on the tomb.

He examined it closely. Gordon Mennler was right. The staircase was marvelously detailed and gorgeously sculpted. The handrails were not in the shape of snakes, though. They were elongated tentacles. Running his fingers along them, he could feel that the tentacles had dozens of mouths carved into them. Each mouth was full of protruding teeth.

He tried to picture Samuel Malden climbing these stairs to get to the top of the tomb. Why did he only occasionally use it as his altar? Why didn't he just use the church's main altar?

He looked over his shoulder. The main altar was dim in the distance. It was much grander than Clifford Morris's resting place. A more fitting altar for a cathedral.

The thing that made the memorial special to Malden, Garrahan guessed, was that the tomb sat directly over the black hole shown on the mosaics. It was the entry way to the hideousness of the abyss.

Being on top of the tomb got the older Malden ranting. Perhaps because he could look down onto the opening from there.

Garrahan set his shoulder bag and the light on the ground. He cautiously dragged the broken staircase to the edge of the tomb. One of the tentacle railings broke off. The lower half remained intact.

He leaned it against the marble. The decrepit stairs reached halfway up the tomb. Good enough.

Grabbing the light and the bag, he climbed the staircase, one wobbling step at a time. He hoisted himself on top of the tomb as if jumping over a wall.

Standing up, Garrahan surveyed the church. From here, Malden gazed over his entire congregation, watching their every move. It was a big stage. All he needed were colored lights and a sound system.

He swept the light around the room. More cracked pews, shattered statues, pieces from the roof. The rest of the church looked the same as thousands of other churches around the world.

Those churches weren't built on top of a creature locked up and buried underneath a holy place.

He aimed his light at the floor. It passed over the circular opening he had pried open a day ago. It flared over the other plaques and then across the top of the tomb. There was a depression in the stone, next to his feet. Letters were carved around it.

He brushed away a thick coat of grime. The depression was perfectly circular. Five inches wide and a couple inches deep. About the size of a hockey puck.

The size of the device.

Grabbing it out of his bag, he placed the device over the depression. It slipped from his fingers and into place.

A perfect fit.

This is where it belonged, Garrahan mused.

For centuries.

Until Father Pierce found it and took it down into the cavern.

The letters around the depression were etched into the marble. In Latin.

PATENT HOMINI AD INFEROS PERPETUO OSTIUM

Garrahan couldn't read Latin. He took a picture. Translation would come later.

He brushed away more grit. It was like a coating of baby powder. Dust whirled into the light and floated languidly into darkness. He swept more away, brushing his hand back and forth like a broom.

There was a picture underneath the dust.

He wiped vigorously.

The image was nearly as big as the entire altar.

Careful not to fall, he swept dirt over the edge.

A large mosaic lay beneath him. Unlike the ones on the wall, this was shiny. The tiles appeared to be made from gold and silver. It gleamed with jewels.

He uncovered the entire picture, then stood up to look at it.

It was the creature in the pit.

CHAPTER 105
MAY 12
SUNDAY, 2:58 PM

The creature on the altar was more horrible than he thought possible.

The tentacles were there, in tiles of blue and green. They came out of a massive body, along with hundreds of tendrils—the things he saw creeping along the floor in the pit. A huge head was sunken into the body, its bulbous skull misshapen and leering. Eyes gilded in bright colors, with pupils of black, stared up at him. Too many eyes to count.

Fangs hung from an open mouth, red with blood. Eight arms, wrapped in tentacles of their own, clutched at groups of humans. All were screaming. All were dying.

It was like a Hieronymus Bosch painting. Grotesque images that shouldn't be part of the natural earth.

No wonder Samuel Malden had gotten worked up on top of this tomb. He was staring at this image, seeing it glisten beneath his feet. He knew the creature existed below him, under the floor of the church.

Garrahan wondered how many ministers had gone before Samuel Malden, how many had known there was a doorway carved into the marble floor. An entry to a festering hole deep in the Earth.

More discomforting, why had a stairway been created at all?

Once that creature was walled up and buried, it should have stayed that way. Covered and caged. Forever. A doorway down meant the builders expected the thing to survive—to remain alive.

So why imprison it?

He wracked his brain. Keeping it locked up, barricaded . . . That's what the people of Morris were doing with the Behemoth.

They wanted to trap the Behemoth, too. To protect it. So they could worship it. So it could do God's bidding.

Were the people who built the church, the original settlers, protecting the thing below them?

No. It was an abomination.

Unless.

They believed it was a creature of God. Placed in this spot to do God's will.

And to be kept safe from the rest of mankind.

Until the time arrived for it to come back to the surface.

Garrahan's head ached from what he was thinking. He checked the time. He had to leave.

He snapped pictures of the creature's image. Each time, its eyes glowed as the flash went off.

Taking a last look around, he picked up the device and placed it in his bag. He climbed off the marble, feet reaching tentatively to the rickety ladder.

Garrahan crept swiftly away and out into the sunlight. He sucked in air with deep breaths.

The afternoon was bright. Birds chirped and clouds dotted the sky. He could not believe, at this very moment, something monstrous lived beneath him.

People had once seen it come out of the pit. To him, that was ghastly beyond his comprehension.

CHAPTER 106
MAY 12
SUNDAY, 4:14 PM

He walked past Ethan, who followed him silently. Garrahan went straight to the Donahue's.

Across the green, Leonard waiting for him between the gas pumps.

Garrahan stopped in the middle of the green, enjoying the warmth of the afternoon. He leaned his head back and basked in it. The beauty of the sky made him think of days like this described as "full of promise."

He took out his phone and looked at the picture of the words inscribed on top of Clifford Morris's tomb. The ones that encircled the device.

"PATENT HOMINI AD INFEROS PERPETUO OSTIUM."

He pasted them into a search engine and hit "translate."

The answer in English came up instantaneously.

Garrahan should have been shocked by what he read. He wasn't. Nothing shocked him anymore.

The words were descriptive and to the point. They told the story of Morris in a single line. The creature, the pit, the black hole under the church.

In English, the words were a warning. And a curse.

"The doorway to hell will forever be open to mankind."

CHAPTER 107
MAY 12
SUNDAY, 5:10 PM

Garrahan sat alone in the bedroom. His mind strangled itself. He didn't want to tell Elizabeth and Abby what he found. He didn't want to talk about it until he sorted his thoughts out. He wasn't going to say anything to Malden, either. Maybe it could be useful information. Then again, maybe not.

While he was sitting on the edge of the bed, staring in a daze at the cathedral, Ethan knocked on the front door.

Time to go.

They walked to Malden's office. Leonard was already there, chatting with Malden. Joel arrived a minute later.

"This is the plan," Malden began. "No one deviates from it."

Garrahan wanted to interrupt. He wanted to explain what they were really up against. It was more than the Behemoth. Much more.

He didn't have the strength to speak up. To speak against them. He felt like he had been drugged.

Malden's plan was simple. At 11 o'clock, an hour before midnight, Ethan would take Garrahan to the church. At the same time, Malden and Joel would drive to the fallen marker and wait.

Leonard, as insurance, would stay with the Donahues. "That is to make sure nothing unexpected happens." Malden looked directly at Garrahan as he said that.

At midnight, Garrahan would turn on the device. Ethan would have a gun to ensure that.

Malden wanted Garrahan to take the device into the pit. That was where Father Pierce had been. However, given Pierce's abrupt demise, Malden agreed to let Garrahan activate the device in the churchyard.

Malden was worried that the device might bring the whole ruined church down upon the Behemoth . . . and whatever was hidden below. Sadly, a it was a chance he had to take.

While the alarm sounded, Malden and Joel would hide in the car by the marker. From there, they should be able to see or hear the Behemoth as it passed.

Joel felt his stomach lurch. Would he finally see the creature he was charged with protecting? The thought was exhilarating and terrifying.

Once the Behemoth passed by—Garrahan imagined them crouching in the back seat—Malden would call Ethan to let him know the creature was heading towards town.

Ethan and Garrahan would go to the library and lock themselves in.

At this point, Malden's voice slowed. "After I contact Ethan, I will walk to the grave that was dug this afternoon. Like five priests before me, I will spill my own blood to keep the Behemoth safe and protected within our borders."

Garrahan saw Malden swallow hard as he spoke.

"Joel will ensure I am placed into the grave. The barrier will once again be in place."

Garrahan would have laughed at this little scenario if he wasn't overwhelmed by its absurdity and violence.

As Malden talked, the others nodded solemnly. As if being given orders on how to seat guests at a reception.

They were, however, listening to Malden talk about shooting himself.

"What about the thing under the church?" Joel asked.

Malden squinted. His face betrayed a struggle. "I don't know, Joel. I really don't. All I can tell you is the Behemoth is our priority. Once it is returned to us, then it will be up to you and the council. You all will determine what exists down there. Use the Book of Revelations, chapter seventeen, to guide you.

Joel wanted to write that admonishment down. He didn't.

They all had their orders. None of them were happy, except Leonard.

Malden told them to go, but Garrahan didn't move. "We still need to resolve some things."

Malden rolled his eyes, like hearing from a petulant child. "I told you that you could leave. Everyone agreed you could go once Joel got back." He waved towards the departing men. "Now, if you'll excuse me, I have affairs to put in order . . ."

"We haven't finished. Nancy is dead."

Leonard stopped, but didn't turn around.

"I told you that people die in holy wars, Mr. Garrahan."

"Fuck your holy wars. You've been holding her body for ransom. I want you to turn it . . ." he almost gagged on the word "I want you to turn her over to me."

"We were going to have her disappear. Without a trace. That seemed most efficient," Malden said, mildly.

"That's not good enough." Garrahan knew he wouldn't get justice for her murder. Malden had that figured out from the moment it happened. Leonard would never be suspected or charged. Malden could make it look like Garrahan was involved in Nancy's death.

"Nancy has, had, a mother and a sister who are going to wonder what happened to her," Garrahan said. "'Disappearing' is not an option."

"What do you propose?"

Leonard remained in the doorway, ears attuned to every word.

Garrahan had been thinking long and hard about this for days. "I know Leonard will not be punished. But I don't want Nancy's family to think a murderer is loose. Even if he is." He turned to look at Leonard, who was grinning. "It has to appear like she died in an accident. A car accident. Her car went off the road. Into the woods. She was found there. After the fact. Something like that." He forced his voice not to quiver. "Something believable."

Malden remained quiet.

"I'm presuming you can make that happen," Garrahan said.

Malden sighed. "It's a little late for me to make it happen. I can ensure that Joel does."

"Then tell him. Now."

Malden called out loudly to Joel, who hurried back into the office. "Help Mr. Garrahan with whatever he needs regarding Leonard's mishap down in New York."

Joel gulped. "Certainly. Yes. I will."

Garrahan looked at Malden, who spread his fingers wide, as if to say "See? It was that easy."

Garrahan wanted to kill Malden right there. He was suddenly pleased by the thought of Malden lying dead in the grave.

Ethan and Leonard waited for Garrahan outside. All three walked to the Donahue house.

"Get packed," Leonard said to him. "Soon as this goes down, you're out of here. And not coming back."

"We're not finished with this," Garrahan mustered. It sounded lame.

"It will be. When I tell you it is." Leonard said.

CHAPTER 108
MAY 12
SUNDAY, 6:30 PM

Garrahan went alone into the house. Abby and Elizabeth were reading a book together. They looked at him, wanting to ask questions.

He explained the plan. Neither of the Donahues said anything; they listened until Garrahan ran out of words.

"In a perfect world, I come back and get you. We go to New York. Immediately. No looking back. Are you ready to do that?"

They nodded.

"In an imperfect world, I only get as far as attracting the Behemoth. Then the story is over . . . for me. You'll be on your own." He paused. "That probably means living here like before, with all that entails. Except Malden will be replaced by Joel."

Abby interjected. "That could be better," she said, cheerily.

"It could," said Garrahan. He looked at her mother. "It could be much better. Leonard and Ethan will still be around, though."

Elizabeth wanted to say something, to agree with him, to explore their options. Any discussion was likely to upset Abby. They avoided the subject with furtive movements of their eyes.

"When do you have to go?" Elizabeth asked.

"Ethan's coming at eleven o'clock." He looked at his phone. "In four hours. Leonard will come with him."

Garrahan didn't know what to do with the time he had. He knew he should plan, but his life was out of his control.

He paced around the room. Shards of the sunset cut through the windows.

This was ridiculous. A goddamned monster and a town full of people determined to protect it. Another priest dying. Absurd. Skull-crunching in its surreality.

He excused himself and went upstairs. After closing the bedroom door, he called Vanukoff. "Did you get anything on the photos I sent you?" he asked.

"Nothing concrete, but I got a boatload of interest. No one at the Smithsonian, the Museum of Natural History, or the Franklin could identify a single marking. But they all want to take a closer look at it. Right away. An up close and personal look."

"That's not going to happen for a while," Garrahan lamented. "No clue at all?"

"Not a one. The woman from Natural History thought it might be someone's art project, until I told her it was a noisemaker you found buried up north. Then she got interested. She called me back and said it was vaguely Scandinavian, but not entirely, whatever that means. So, she wants a look when you get back."

Garrahan's stomach sank. "I'm not sure when I'll get back. Or if."

"What does that mean?"

"I'm thinking this ends badly. In a few hours."

Vanukoff scoffed. "Dude, you're in New England. It's not like a war zone."

"It kind of is," Garrahan lamented. "The locals are barricading themselves in. They're good at doing that. They've done it for centuries."

"What are they going to do? Hit you with a car like they did to the guy down here?"

"No, this will be a lot quieter and no one will know. Except you."

"Then I'm coming up there. We'll work it out together."

"By the time you get here, it'll all be over. With any luck, I'll be on the road home. Without luck, I'll be hidden so far away you'll never know I existed."

Vanukoff clicked his teeth, loudly. "Either way, I'm coming up. This is bullshit. If I don't hear from you, I'll start banging on doors."

"If you end up having to bang on doors, start with a woman named Ginnie Pierce. She lives five miles from my place in Ashford. I'll send you her number. She'll have the background you need. And whatever you hear from her, trust me. It will all be true."

"What do you mean, all true?"

Garrahan was weary. It was an effort to speak. "All the stuff I've been telling you. The monster, the disappearances. All of it." He sighed. "I can't explain it now. I'm too tired."

"Okay, then," said Vanukoff, tentatively. "But I better hear from you in the next couple of hours. Everything's going to work out. It has to."

No, it doesn't have to, Garrahan thought to himself.

None of it has worked out so far.

They said goodbye. Vanukoff immediately went to retrieve his car from the parking garage.

Twenty minutes later he was on the West Side Highway driving out of Manhattan.

An hour after that, he was locked in a traffic jam on the Merritt Parkway cutting through Connecticut. A tractor-trailer truck had gone up the parkway and hit an overpass, blocking everyone from getting through. That included Vanukoff.

By the time he was moving again, people were already dying in Morris.

CHAPTER 109

MAY 12
SUNDAY, 11:00 PM

Leonard and Ethan knocked at the door. Elizabeth and Abby were in bed, presumably asleep.

Garrahan had not bothered to say goodbyes because he was not ready to call an end to it. Or let them think it really was the end.

Leonard barged in, not speaking to Garrahan. He threw himself on the couch and fired up the television.

Ethan led the way back outside.

"You have the noise thing?" he asked, as they stepped into the darkness.

Garrahan held it up so Ethan could see it in the glow of the streetlight. It looked old and worn, dirty and scarred. Garrahan wondered who had created it, where it came from. Why they had made it.

The thought of the thing under the church came unbidden. It made him queasy.

He had a desire to smash the device on the street.

"Hope it works like it's supposed to," Ethan said.

They went onto the green. The church was a black monolith in the moonlight. Darker than the indigo sky.

The streetlights cast scant illumination on the huge offering bowls. Garrahan could smell the heaps of animal carcasses that had been piled up during the past few hours. He wondered briefly how many animals the town had killed for this particular night.

The church loomed over them, its darkness all the more striking by how it blotted out the stars behind it. There was an eeriness that Garrahan had not sensed during the daytime. The church seemed haunted, even malevolent, at this hour of the night.

Knowing what he knew now, he would have agreed with the council. He would have voted against repairing it. He would have gone even further. He would have voted to tear it down. The sooner the better.

They walked to the ruined side. There were more shadows on this side, more hiding places. Garrahan didn't like that.

It clearly made Ethan uneasy. "How far in are you going to go?" he asked, nervously.

They could barely see each other's faces.

"No further than I have to. I'll walk through the chapel to the entrance. Set it off there."

Ethan looked around, as if he expected to see something in the darkness. "I'll wait here."

He unlocked the gate, pulling the chain away. He stopped, remembering what he was there for. "I'll be watching you. Don't think you can get out of this." His voice was more afraid than menacing.

Garrahan didn't bother replying. He turned on the light on his phone, and made his way back into the churchyard, past the empty coffins. There was nothing here that felt remotely like a church. It was dead, old, and abandoned. A decayed skeleton of something from long ago. Waiting for the time when it could crumble into ash.

He checked the time. Quarter to midnight.

He shone the light around. Everything was exactly as it had been yesterday.

The memorial far inside the building, where Clifford Morris was entombed, sat mute and solid.

His light glinted off it. Strangely, he wanted to go to it. To touch it—maybe to descend underneath it.

The thing he had seen under the church was remarkable, despite the horror of it.

He wanted to see the thing up close. For real. To see something that perhaps no one alive had ever seen. Something majestic.

Something that had made people bow down and worship . . .

It was enticing. He took a step in.

Catching himself, he shook his head. Where did those thoughts come from, he wondered.

There was nothing in this ruin he should be seeing. Or hearing. Or touching.

His phone buzzed.

It was midnight.

Fumbling his way along the outside wall of the cathedral, he found an open area. Clear of debris. He knelt down and placed the device on the ground.

Gripping its two halves, he closed his eyes. Took a deep breath. And held it. He spun the top as far as it would go.

Stepping back, he covered his ears.

The shriek was so loud that covering his ears didn't matter. The noise hit him with so much force he saw white flashes inside his eyes. The sound crashed against his skull.

The blast continued for ten seconds. It was longer than either of the previous episodes.

When it stopped, Garrahan opened his eyes.

The cathedral was still intact. He thought he heard bits of stone or plaster dropping in pieces from the roof.

Around him, the world had gone silent. The device seemed to have destroyed everything else that would dare make a sound.

Slowly, he made his way back to the gate.

Ethan was crouched low, ready to run. Malden hadn't called.

CHAPTER 110

MAY 13
MONDAY, 12:01 AM

The creature stirred.

Something was happening, something that probed at its brain.

A sound. A warning.

From where it lay, the creature knew where the sound was coming from.

It rose up from the dark dirt and moved toward the source.

CHAPTER 111

MAY 13
MONDAY, 12:15 AM

It passed Malden's car without slowing, intent on its destination.

The alarm. The sacred place.

Sacrifice. Food.

Joel cowered in the back seat of the car. All he saw was swift and metallic movement cutting through the field.

In daylight, it could have been the shadow of a cloud slicing across the tall grass.

There. And not there.

Malden watched, straining his eyes. "Beautiful," he whispered. "God's greatest creation."

Joel was stunned. He started mumbling the verse from Ecclesiasticus. "There be creatures that are created for vengeance . . ."

This thing was surely created by God to punish man for his sinfulness. His weakness. There could be no other explanation.

Joel wanted to cry. Partly out of joy.

Malden opened the car door. "It's time."

They stepped out. The air was cooler, the night darker than it had been moments ago.

The men walked quickly to the grave. The overturned marker was oddly white, as if phosphorescent. It was brighter than the stars.

The grave itself was darker than everything else.

Malden held his phone up, his face suddenly reflected in its light. Joel feared that the Behemoth might see it and come back. Take retribution on them.

"Ethan, it has returned," Malden said into the phone, his voice a whisper. "It passed us. You must now protect yourself." Malden paused. "May God be with you."

He hung up. Without a word, he walked to the grave.

Joel stepped up next to him, legs quaking.

From his pants pocket, Malden produced a .38 caliber pistol. He could see the outline of the metal barrel, but little else.

His fingers fumbled to get a steady grip on the handle.

"Say a last prayer with me, Joel," Malden whispered.

CHAPTER 112
MAY 13
MONDAY, 12:19 AM

Ethan flicked off the phone. He didn't bother to say a last goodbye to Malden.

"It's here."

He began breathing quickly. "We have to get into the library. Fast. We can't let it see us."

As he pulled the gate shut, Garrahan stopped him. "I'm not leaving the device. We need that."

"No we don't!" Ethan said harshly, whispering and shouting at the same time. "We have to go. Now!" He grabbed Garrahan's sleeve. "There's no time!" He was on the verge of hyperventilating.

Garrahan knocked Ethan's grip away. He made a quick calculation. "I'm getting it. You wait for me in the library. Do not lock the door until I get there."

Fear careened around Ethan's brain. He had seen the Behemoth twice when he was a child. He'd seen the body parts it had left on the altar. He didn't want to ever see the creature again.

Without a word, he ran towards the library. *Fuck Garrahan*, he thought.

Garrahan retraced his steps to the device. He snatched it up with one hand.

He ran through the gate as fast as he could to the front of the cathedral.

Instead of going into the new church and library, he continued straight ahead. In the pale yellow glare of the streetlight, he saw the offering bowl next to the gas station. He beelined for it.

Garrahan didn't think about where the Behemoth might be. This was his chance to get out of town while everyone else was hiding. Running now was his only option.

When he got to the Donahue's, he would set the device off. Again. On the porch. Hopefully it would distract Leonard.

Garrahan might get the chance to overpower him. Or bludgeon him with the device.

As he got close to the house, he saw a light upstairs. That wasn't good. Elizabeth and Abby were supposed to be asleep, and the house was supposed to be closed up and dark. To deter the Behemoth.

A light was also on in the living room, where he'd left Leonard watching TV.

He pulled up short as he reached the gas pumps.

Through the window, he could see Elizabeth. And hear her.

She was on her knees, wailing.

Alone.

Garrahan yanked open the door and stepped in. Elizabeth's right hand was zip-tied to the radiator. Her cheek was purple and bruised. Blood flowed from her lip.

Out of breath, he shouted "What's happening? Where's —?"

"Leonard!" she screamed.

Tears flooded Elizabeth's face, dripping off her cheeks.

"Leonard! He took Abby! He took her to the forest. To the altar!"

CHAPTER 113
MAY 13
MONDAY, 12:20 AM

"Say the Lord's Prayer, Joel," Malden said. His voice was low. Shaking.

Joel nodded.

Malden raised his arm and held the gun to his temple. "Our Father, who art in Heaven . . ." he began.

Joel closed his eyes tight, not wanting to go through this. He had never seen anyone die.

He tried to shut out everything except the prayer.

"Hallowed be thy name," Joel said.

Malden opened his eyes and looked at Joel. The younger man's head was bowed as his lips formed the words to the prayer. His eyes were scrunched shut.

"Thy kingdom come . . ."

Malden extended his arm. He pointed the barrel at Joel's skull.

"Thy will be done . . ."

He pulled the trigger.

Joel's skull vaporized in a dark mist that was red for the briefest instant. When the bullet blew into his brain.

What remained of Joel fell to the ground like a sack of stones.

Malden stood over him and finished the prayer. "And lead us not into temptation, but deliver us from evil . . ."

He bent and placed the gun on the ground.

Turning on his phone light, he held it above Joel's head.

There was no doubt Joel was dead. It had been instantaneous.

Malden was glad Joel hadn't suffered. He wouldn't have minded if Joel had, but he liked the boy. Joel dying quickly obviated any guilt Malden might have allowed himself.

"A priest must shed his blood to make this right," he whispered.

Thank the Lord that Joel was so eager to be ordained. It was almost as if he wanted to take Malden's place in service to the Behemoth.

Joel never knew he would be called upon so soon.

Malden knew, though.

He never had any intention of dying.

It was unthinkable. He was actually dismayed that his minions thought he would go through with suicide.

There was no one qualified to serve the Behemoth as well as Malden. No one. Joel was a mere child, not the least bit prepared to head the congregation. Joel's willingness to believe he was ready was a sign of his unreadiness.

The younger man had had the good grace to die with his body lying on the edge of the pit. Malden rolled Joel into the grave with little effort.

The body fell into the hole unceremoniously, making a thump. It didn't echo or reverberate.

Joel's life had ended quietly. So had his burial.

In the dark, Malden picked up a shovel left behind by the workers. He covered the corpse with a layer of dirt.

The boundary was sealed once again. The blood of a priest blocked the Behemoth's exit, as it had for decades.

Malden got into his car. All he had left was to clean up some loose ends.

CHAPTER 114
MAY 13
MONDAY, 12:22 AM

Garrahan found scissors in the living room desk. He cut Elizabeth's hand free.

She was hysterical and frenzied, flailing her arms and body about.

"He took Abby! We have to go after her!" she shrieked.

"Okay, okay," he said, trying to calm her. "When did they go?"

"Ten minutes ago. Maybe more. He's taking her to the altar!"

Garrahan didn't understand. "They already have the Behemoth back. They don't need a sacrifice."

"Once it's back, it needs a sacrifice! They're giving it a sacrifice to show respect. They're using Abby!"

She rubbed the tears and blood off her face. Leonard had hit her hard.

"I'm going after her," she said, resolutely.

Garrahan shook his head. "I'll go."

He looked around for something to use against Leonard. The device wouldn't be enough. "I need a weapon," he said hurriedly.

She pointed towards the hallway door, which led into the garage and repair shop. "There are lots of things in there . . ." she replied, weakly. Her speech slurred a little. Garrahan was worried about how hard she'd been knocked around.

He ran down the hall and turned on the garage light. The garage was a chaotic jumble of hanging pipes, rubber pieces, tools, and boxes piled to the ceiling. As cluttered a shop as he'd ever seen.

There was no time to be choosy. He saw a fireman's axe on the wall and grabbed it.

"Lock yourself in," he told Elizabeth. He didn't need to tell her why. "I'll get Leonard."

"Drive fast," she said, dropping back to her knees. Her eyes were wide and water-filled. "Please, please. Drive fast." She began crying again.

In the car, he retraced the road in his mind. Joel had driven him here two days ago. It seemed like centuries had passed.

It took five minutes to get to the opening in the woods. Leonard's car was parked on the path, under an overhang of trees.

As soon as Garrahan got out of his car, he could hear the screaming.

CHAPTER 115
MAY 13
MONDAY, 12:25 AM

Ethan sat on the floor of the library, eyes peeking over the windowsill. He could see nothing in the darkness but the tiny glare from distant streetlights.

Garrahan had never shown up at the door. *Fuck him*, thought Ethan. *He waited too long. I'll bet the Behemoth got him. Perfectly fine by me.*

His phone rang, and he jumped to his feet at the sound.

Shit, he thought, *I have got to get hold of myself.* There was a case of beer back at his house. Once this was over, that would calm him down.

"Hello?" he whispered, hoping nothing on the outside could hear him.

"Get yourself over to the Donahue's. Now. And bring Garrahan with you!" Malden was sitting inside his car, barking into his phone. His eyes scanned the darkness in hopes the Behemoth wasn't coming back.

The caller took Ethan by surprise. "Mr. Malden? Is that you?" he asked, stuttering the words. Malden was supposed to be dead by now.

"Yes, of course it is. Get moving."

It wasn't registering in Ethan's brain. "But I thought you . . . I thought Joel was taking over. I thought that . . . the grave . . ."

Malden didn't have time for this and didn't need to explain himself in detail to a moron like Ethan. "Joel made the decision to sacrifice his blood for the Behemoth." Malden gritted his teeth. "He will forever have our prayers."

Ethan didn't know how Joel could have sacrificed himself. That wasn't the plan. It didn't make sense.

"But, Mr. Malden. Isn't Joel supposed to . . .?"

"Joel is dead, you idiot! I just told you that. Now take Garrahan over to the Donahue's. Immediately." Malden could feel his blood pressure rising.

Ethan realized this was not about to go well for him. "I don't have Garrahan, sir. He ran back into the church to get the device after it went off. I tried to stop him, but he ran off into the dark. He said he would hurry. But he never showed up at the library." Ethan cleared his throat. "I guess the Behemoth got him."

"Your guess doesn't count for a single thing, Ethan. You better pray to God that the Behemoth got him." Malden wished for a moment that it was Ethan who was lying dead in the grave. "Go to the Donahue's. I'll meet you there."

"But the Behemoth . . ."

"The creature is certain to be at the altar by now. Move it. I'll be at the house in a few minutes."

Malden drove the back road back into town. Where the Hell could Garrahan have gone? Maybe to the Donahue's, but he would have been too late to get to Abby. Plus, he didn't know what Leonard had planned.

He pounded his hand on the steering wheel. This had gone so well, and fucking Garrahan had found yet another way to muck it up.

That was going to change.

CHAPTER 116
MAY 13
MONDAY, 12:30 AM

Firelight emanated from the same path Garrahan had resisted walking down before.

He hurried toward the clearing, trying to be quiet.

Abby's screams would make it hard for Leonard to hear him coming.

As he got closer, torches lit the surrounding trees. He saw Leonard igniting them with a barbecue lighter.

The flames threw yellow and orange shadows across the open space. It was like a small arena, with a black sky overhead. In the middle, Abby was handcuffed to the stone pillar, thrashing and wailing.

Garrahan aimed straight for Leonard. He was lighting a torch with his back to Garrahan.

Raising the axe in his hand, Garrahan turned it slightly. He was intent on smashing Leonard's skull, but he didn't want to cleave it with the blade. Hitting him with the blunt side would do.

Abby abruptly stopped screaming as Garrahan charged into the clearing. It was enough to make Leonard turn just as Garrahan brought the axe down.

Leonard raised his right arm to deflect the blow. The axe crashed into his forearm. Leonard let out a yell as Garrahan felt the bone shatter at the end of the axe.

Leonard twisted his body and kicked out at Garrahan. His boot caught Garrahan's knee. The force of the kick and the momentum of the axe swing caught Garrahan off balance. He crumpled and dropped to the ground. Leonard toppled next to him.

As he scrambled in the dirt, Garrahan heard Abby screaming again.

Leonard stood up. "You stupid motherfucker! You should've stayed out of this!"

He kicked at Garrahan again, his foot connecting with the same knee. An arc of pain shot up into Garrahan's thigh, bringing him to the ground again.

Garrahan rolled away as Leonard attacked, roaring with his damaged arm hanging by his side.

Leonard raised his leg to kick Garrahan's face. Garrahan scooted back and swung the axe at Leonard.

This time, the sharpened blade sliced into Leonard's calf. It dug all the way into bone. Blood erupted from the leg.

Leonard howled, falling hard on the gash. He howled louder.

Garrahan clambered to his feet and lurched over to Leonard. Checking to make sure the axe was blunt side down, he swung it hard against the side of Leonard's skull.

Leonard's screaming stopped. His body went limp.

Blood spread from Leonard's leg onto the ground. It reflected the light from the torches.

Garrahan stood up straight, trying to catch his breath. His knee felt like it had popped off.

He stumbled to Abby and hugged her.

"Shhh. Shhh. It's okay. We're okay," he said, over and over.

She could only grab him with one arm, squirming to pull the other free from the handcuff.

"We have to go," she pleaded, her voice choked and sobbing. "It will come for me! I don't want it to!"

"Hold on," he told her. He looked at her wrist, inspecting the handcuffs. He tugged on the loop that encircled her arm.

"Did you see where Leonard put the key?" he asked. "Think. Think."

She shook her head wildly. "He had it a few minutes ago. It must be . . . must be in his pocket." She screeched in panic. "I don't know!"

Garrahan limped to Leonard and rummaged through his pockets. He grabbed Leonard's phone from his shirt pocket and threw it into the forest. Then he found a keychain in Leonard's pants. The keys jangled like little xylophones. Leonard didn't move.

There were a dozen keys. Most of them looked like house or car keys. He tried the smallest one in the handcuffs. He had a hard time finding the lock because Abby was huddled close against the stone pillar. "I need some light, Abby. You have to stand up. I can't see . . ."

"Please, please, please hurry," she begged. Her voice was deep now, guttural, fear overriding everything. She had stopped crying, but her eyes were preternaturally wide. Her body shook like it was tethered to an electric fence. Garrahan had never seen such primal fear in his life.

"I am, I am." He worked the little key in the cuff. His fingers shook as he jammed it into place. The metal snapped open.

Abby pulled her hand away. The cuffs fell, dangling from the metal circle on the pillar. They clinked against the stone.

"Move it," he urged. "To the opening. My car is there. Go!"

He pushed her forward and staggered after. He thought his knee might buckle if he went any faster.

It did. He fell halfway along the path. He kept from crying out, but Abby heard him hit the ground. She turned to help him. "Come on!" she hissed.

As he got up on his good knee, they heard a roar of pain and anger from Leonard. "I can't move!" he screamed.

Abby's face was close to Garrahan's. They listened for a moment. Leonard shouted again.

"We can't leave him," Abby said." We can't. Not for the Behemoth."

Garrahan wanted to slap some sense into her, but she started crying. "No one should be left to the Behemoth! Nobody!" The sobs started anew. "That was almost me!" she hollered, the realization striking home.

"But, but . . . he . . ." Garrahan knew he couldn't convince her.

"Please, for me. I don't want to imagine what will happen." She hugged him tightly. Her body racked with great gulps of air and tears. "Please!?!?!?"

Garrahan didn't want to. "I can't carry him back. I'm not strong enough."

"Please!?!?!?"

"All I can do is move him out of the circle, maybe hide him in the bushes."

She clutched at him. "Just try! Please!" The words came out in broken, choking syllables.

"Okay," he said, resigned. He was now truly afraid they were out of time. "You go hide in my car. It's open. Climb in and lock the doors. Don't open them for anybody but me or your mom."

He pushed her, hard, towards the car.

Limping back, he saw Leonard trying to crawl out of the circle. Blood trailed in a steady stream from the gouge in his leg. Garrahan was sure things were flickering in Leonard's head from the crack in his skull.

He hobbled over to Leonard.

"Don't come near me, you fuck!" Leonard shouted.

"Abby wants me to help you," Garrahan said, without conviction.

"Well, when I get out of here, I'm doing to her and her bitch mom what I did to your big city girlfriend." He spat blood at Garrahan and pulled himself up on all fours. His damaged arm hung raggedly. It was bent at an odd angle.

That was it for Garrahan. Something went red behind his eyes.

He stared down at Leonard.

Everything he had been pulled into, the entire mess, focused on and boiled down to this bullet-headed psychopath.

Leonard was going to get away with it all. He always had.

This time he wasn't going to.

Garrahan saw the axe lying where he had dropped it. He picked it up, turned the blade forward and walked over to Leonard.

"Kill me, you pussy," Leonard sneered, glaring up at Garrahan. "You don't have the balls."

Garrahan slashed Leonard's good arm with the axe, ripping flesh and muscle from bone. Leonard's body plowed face first into the dirt.

"I won't kill you, Leonard. Not me. But not because I'm a pussy."

Leonard's pain-gorged bellowing got louder when Garrahan grabbed one of his crippled arms. He dragged Leonard across the circle.

"Fuck you! Fuck you!!!" Leonard shouted, wriggling on the ground as Garrahan pulled him in heaving jerks.

"Only a few more feet, Leonard," he gasped.

With another yank, he had Leonard lying under the stone altar. Blood covered Leonard's leg and arm. Garrahan wondered if he might bleed to death.

"Abby asked me to help you. This is the best help I can give you."

He pulled Leonard's arm to the open cuff and slapped his wrist into the circle.

With a flick of metal, he locked Leonard's arm to the pillar. He closed it down tightly.

Leonard stopped screaming the moment he realized what was happening.

"What the fuck?!?!? You can't . . . !" he blurted. He looked up at the handcuff and started shaking it.

"You can't, you wouldn't . . . I don't . . . !" Leonard's mind reached for something to say, anything that would change the situation he was in. Images of things he had seen the Behemoth do—from his perch in the tree—sloshed inside his head. They blotted out everything except terror.

"Noooooooo!!!!" he shouted at Garrahan, his body suddenly ratcheting around the pillar, trying to dislodge the cuff from the stone.

Even as he thrashed, Leonard knew, deep in his brain, that no one had ever been able to get away. No one. Not in hundreds of years. He wouldn't, either.

Garrahan stepped back. "Like I said, I won't kill you. But not because I'm a pussy." He exhaled loudly. "But because I'd like something else to kill you."

He swung the blunt side of the axe at Leonard's jaw, guiding it like a tennis racket.

The tool hit with a satisfying crunch, and Leonard's shouting stopped. It was reduced to a gurgling moan, uttered through a broken mouth.

Garrahan staggered out of the circle and down the path. He glanced over his shoulder, once. Leonard was already disappearing in the distance. He looked like a tangled marionette, trying desperately to move broken body parts and get away from the pillar.

After a few more steps, Garrahan couldn't hear Leonard's muffled croaks.

When he reached the car, the torchlight was dim behind him. He climbed into the driver's seat, his knee throbbing like it was being hammered. He was sure something had broken or fractured.

"Did you help him?" Abby asked, her cries subsiding.

Garrahan started the car and put it in drive. His heart pounded against his ribcage, making it hard to speak.

"As best I could, Abby. As best I could."

CHAPTER 117
MAY 13
MONDAY, 12:31 AM

Malden's call made Ethan even more nervous. Ethan had planned to stay in the library until he got a call from Leonard telling him the Behemoth was at the altar.

Now he had to slink across the green to meet Mr. Malden. Who was pissed off.

He stepped out of the library. He walked on tiptoes as if trying not to wake someone asleep in a bedroom. The darkness didn't seem as bad as it did earlier. The stars were brighter, and the moon seemed fuller.

Ethan pulled his pistol as he started crossing the green. He should have used the gun to plug Garrahan after the device went off. That would have made him a hero. And he'd be in Mr. Malden's good graces—always a nice thing in this town.

A question popped into his mind: Why was Mr. Malden still alive?

He started to run, wondering what he would say to Mr. Malden. It was probably best to not say anything. Best not to . . .

A blackness cut across the grass ahead of him, darting past a tree.

It moved fast.

For a moment, Ethan thought it was the shadow of a cloud passing in front of the moon. He glanced up. The sky was as clear as it had been all night.

"No fucking way," he whispered aloud.

He stopped and started running back to the library. As he did, he heard growling over his head.

Not able to help himself, he looked up.

Reflected in the moonlight, dripping with wetness, were rows and rows of teeth, like jagged shards of broken glass.

And very bright eyes.

Ethan's instinct was to drop to the ground. He never made it that far.

The Behemoth picked him up in one huge claw, its tentacle fingers wrapping around Ethan's body. It lifted him high off the ground.

As Ethan was pulled into the air, he screamed. He stared down into the mouth, and words from scripture—words he had recited thousands of times as a child—came gushing out of his own mouth.

"The people shall be wasted with hunger, and devoured with burning heat and bitter destruction, and the teeth of beasts will I send upon them."

The words kept coming even as Behemoth devoured Ethan's flesh.

CHAPTER 118
MAY 13
MONDAY, 12:40 AM

Malden pulled his car in front of the Donahue house, as if stopping in to buy gas. Leonard's car was gone, a sign he was out doing the job Malden had ordered him to do.

If that part of this plan was proceeding apace, then young Abby Donahue was giving herself as sacrifice to the Behemoth.

That left Garrahan.

He walked into the Donahue house, gripping his gun firmly.

At the sound of the door creaking, Elizabeth Donahue looked up expectantly from her seat on the floor.

The look faded the moment she saw Malden. It turned to an expression of unrestrained rage and hate.

She leapt off the ground with a snarl, like a wild creature out of a cage. Malden stepped back and raised his gun.

Elizabeth stopped as quickly as an animal who knew the pain of a bullet.

"Sit back down, Elizabeth," he commanded calmly.

She did, her face contorted with wrath and her hands twitching like claws.

"Where is Leonard?" he asked.

"You know where he is!" she spat.

"And Mr. Garrahan. Where is he?"

"I have no idea," she said. Her glare cut into him like razors.

"That's not the answer I want," he said.

The fact that neither Leonard nor Garrahan were here was suddenly quite disturbing. He pulled out his phone out and tried to keep an eye on Elizabeth while he dialed.

"Elizabeth, indulge me and sit in the chair on the other side of the table," he said, flicking his gun towards her. That way, she couldn't get at him without lunging across the room.

She slowly did what he said, placing both her hands on the table. Her eyes did not leave his.

He dialed Leonard. The phone buzzed nine times. No answer. He hung up.

Next, he called Garrahan. No answer there, either.

In the best of all worlds, Leonard was too busy to answer the phone because he was handling Abby. Garrahan was unable to answer the phone because the Behemoth had come upon him.

Life rarely offered the best of all worlds. Malden didn't pin his hopes on perfect scenarios. He would call again in a few minutes.

And where was Ethan? He should have been here already. He tried calling Ethan. No answer.

The only person who was assuredly in the place he'd expected was Elizabeth Donahue. That wasn't a good percentage.

He tried each number again. None of the three men answered.

He wanted to curse, but he wouldn't let Elizabeth see that.

Malden closed the front door and started pacing around the room. He kept the gun pointed at Elizabeth. "We're going to wait for a while," he said.

"Wait for what?" she sneered. "Wait for you to decide that someone else should die?"

Malden shook his head. "Don't start, Elizabeth. You don't understand any of what . . ."

"Really?" she interjected, trying to keep her voice even. Hysteria was rising in her chest. "You've turned this town, our religion, into your personal battle with anything that goes against you. Just so you can keep control."

She stopped, tasting blood from her lip in her mouth. She wiped it away. "You don't care about this town, or any of us. You want to stay in power, no matter the cost. The Behemoth could be dead, and you'd still demand to run the congregation."

He mulled that over. What she said was true. But she was wrong about the Behemoth. He did believe it was God's greatest creature. That belief was what drove him. He felt duty-bound to protect it. If people stood in his way, then he had to put those people in their places.

Bruce Donahue had been one of those people. Garrahan had become one. Other people in town, insistent people who questioned his authority, were becoming similar obstacles.

"Like I said, you don't understand." Malden smiled tightly.

As they were talking, neither heard a car drive silently by.

It passed with its lights off. It slowed near the gas pumps and crept away, heading towards the outskirts of town.

CHAPTER 119
MAY 13
MONDAY, 12:58 AM

Garrahan barely pressed the gas pedal as he cruised back into Morris. He turned off the headlights and the dashboard dials. The car was as invisible as possible.

Abby sat low in the passenger seat, her head resting on the door.

They still had Ethan to deal with. Perhaps Joel. With Leonard indisposed, and Malden gone, the other two would be easier to deal with, but no less dangerous.

The car glided into town. Garrahan swerved out of the path of streetlights, afraid there might be townspeople looking through the cracks in their shutters.

If they believed the Behemoth was back, they wouldn't dare come out.

Garrahan wondered where the Behemoth was. It had come past the marker, or Malden wouldn't have called Ethan. In the imagined safety of the car, his stomach churned over the possibility of encountering the monster.

It was almost one o'clock as they drove close to the house. He was ready to pull in by the pumps when he noticed a car parked behind them.

It was Malden's car. He presumed Joel had driven it over.

Garrahan stopped. Leaning forward in his seat, he looked up into the front window. From this angle, he couldn't see Elizabeth. Or Joel.

Someone walked past the window.

Malden.

"What the fuck???" Garrahan said out loud, not able to help himself.

Abby sat up to see what was happening. Garrahan pushed her back down.

"What's going on?" she asked.

"Shhhh," he answered. He let the car roll gently back to the road and away from the pumps. As soon as they were out of sight of the house, he pressed the accelerator.

"Mr. Garrahan? What's the matter?" Abby repeated.

"I . . . I don't know," he answered. "Mr. Malden is in your house. He's not supposed to be."

"I thought Joel was taking his place," she said, softly.

"He was supposed to." Garrahan let the words trail off.

There had to be someone at the marker, guarding it or . . . Christ.

Garrahan sped up the car.

Joel took Malden's place, he realized. Just not as leader of the congregation.

CHAPTER 120
MAY 13
MONDAY, 1:06 AM

On the way to the marker, Garrahan's phone rang twice. He ignored it. He wasn't communicating with anyone until he saw what had happened at the grave site.

Telling Abby to stay in the car, Garrahan limped to the open grave. It was a dark blotch on the ground. The grass around it was silver in the moonlight.

Standing on the edge, he peered in.

A mound of dirt in the shape of a body. Sprawled out at the bottom of the grave.

It had to be Joel. He was sure of it.

Not completely sure.

His phone rang again. This time he checked it. The caller ID said it was Malden.

Garrahan ignored it.

He considered his options.

Leonard was probably and hopefully dead. There was no guarantee of that.

Malden was at Elizabeth's. Garrahan had no idea why he was there.

Ethan was probably cowering in the library.

Abby was here with him.

That left Joel.

In all likelihood, Joel was below him.

He had to be sure.

Because if Joel was here, then Garrahan finally had a plan.

CHAPTER 121
MAY 13
MONDAY, 1:20 AM

Malden's phone rang.

He'd been pacing in front of Elizabeth Donahue for half an hour. Neither of them had said a word. She sat unmoving and unblinking as he crisscrossed the living room.

He hadn't heard from Ethan or Leonard. That was causing him an insane amount of stress. They were not following orders.

He wanted to scream or hit something. When he considered the gun in his hand, Edward Malden wanted to kill something.

No matter what, he wasn't going to let Elizabeth see him lose control.

He flipped the phone to his ear, not bothering to see who it was. Right now, he wanted to hear from anyone who knew his phone number.

"Yes?" he barked, expecting it to be Leonard on his way back from the altar.

"Well, I didn't expect you'd be answering your own phone," Garrahan said. He sounded cheery. "Ever."

Malden was taken off guard. He recovered quickly. "I need to see you, Mr. Garrahan. There are things to discuss." He made it sound more authoritative than it felt.

"Really? You want to see me?" Garrahan asked. "I actually want to see you. I expected you'd be dead right now. Lying in the bottom of a grave that I saw five men dig today."

"That's one of the things we shall talk about," Malden continued. "Where are you?"

"I'm not dead. And I'm not in the library, if that's what you're wondering."

Malden's patience was worn through. "Cut the shit, Garrahan. Come to the Donahue's right now. I've got Elizabeth here. I'll hurt her if you don't show up immediately."

"Really?" said Garrahan, with exaggeration in his voice. "Well, guess what? I have Abby. And Leonard couldn't be here with us." He held the phone up to Abby. "Say hello to Mr. Malden, Abby."

Abby replied with a soft "Hello, Mr. Malden."

Malden started to demand something, but he choked on the words. His lungs seized as pain ran across his chest.

No Leonard? How did Garrahan get Abby? What the hell happened to Leonard?

"You won't be hearing from Leonard anytime soon. If you're concerned about that," said Garrahan, taunting him.

Malden couldn't think of anything to say. He was adrift, his mind yanked from its anchor of carefully laid-out plans.

"Oh, and I have someone else with me, but he can't say hello," Garrahan continued. He paused, a silence that sounded like a snicker. "It's Joel. So you can guess where I am."

Malden felt dizzy.

For the first time, Garrahan's voice was the sinister one.

"You should come out and see what I got here, Edward. You really should. I'll wait for you."

Garrahan hung up.

CHAPTER 122
MAY 13
MONDAY, 1:24 AM

Malden grabbed Elizabeth and shoved her into his car. As he climbed behind the wheel, he held up his gun. "Do not try to jump out, or anything similarly foolish," he ordered. "I will shoot you. Abby will be left with no parents at all."

Elizabeth slid meekly into her seat.

Malden revved the engine and screeched out of the station. He barely saw the road as he drove. Rage constricted his vision and he steered as if on autopilot. He was at the grave before he realized it.

He could see Garrahan's car parked on the far side of the grave. It was silent, the lights off. He couldn't see Garrahan or Abby. Perhaps they were in the car.

Malden stepped into the darkness and hurried to the passenger side. He jerked Elizabeth out, slamming the door behind her. Together they took a few steps towards the grave.

The headlights of Garrahan's car flared on, flooding the scene with twin arcs of dazzling whiteness.

It blinded Malden. He held his hand up to shield his eyes.

Malden heard Garrahan's car start. Then he heard the car door open. Garrahan's vague shape appeared behind the bright lights.

"Give Abby to me and tell me where Leonard is. Then I'll let Elizabeth go," Malden yelled. His voice was too loud in the silent night. "If you don't, I will shoot Elizabeth."

Garrahan's voice came back, calm and even. "I don't think you want to do that," he intoned.

"Oh, really?" Malden shouted. "If you've seen Joel, then you'll know what happened to him. I must say," he said, waving his gun dramatically, "I've come to an appreciation—even an enjoyment—of this weapon in the last few hours."

Elizabeth flinched, but Malden held her tight by the sleeve of her shirt.

"I'm glad you mentioned Joel," Garrahan retorted. "Because Joel changes everything."

"Yes, he does," Malden said, a smile in his voice. "He was the new priest in town. He has given his life to become the new marker for Morris." Malden was getting charged up. "His grave will be memorialized for centuries to come."

He heard Garrahan laugh.

"Except Joel's not in his grave."

Malden wasn't sure he heard correctly. "What did you say?"

"You haven't looked into the pit, have you?" replied Garrahan. His voice was still low and even. "Go ahead. Look."

Malden took a few steps forward, like a man reluctantly peering over the edge of a very high cliff. He kept Elizabeth in his grip.

In the dark, Malden couldn't see much. But he could see that the layer of dirt he'd thrown over Joel had been piled to the side.

There didn't appear to be anyone in the grave.

"What did you do with him???" Malden shouted. He felt himself coming unglued.

Garrahan wished he could look Malden right in the face, but he couldn't afford to get close to him and his gun. Hiding behind the glare of headlights provided security.

Especially since, after climbing into the grave and back out again, his banged-up knee felt like it was ready to explode.

"It wasn't easy, but I brought Joel up out of the ground. He's safe with me."

That made no sense to Malden. Garrahan sounded unhinged. "Where is Joel? His body belongs in a grave."

"That's probably true. Right now, though, his body is in the trunk of my car."

Malden rubbed his face, trying to concentrate on what he was hearing. It was ludicrous.

"Put him back where you found him, or I will kill Elizabeth. Right where I stand." Malden's anger seethed out of his throat.

He would kill Elizabeth. And then Garrahan. And then Abby.

Silence surrounded them all. Even with the low hum of Garrahan's engine, the night was obscenely quiet.

Garrahan stared at Malden, standing stark in the gleam of headlights. Elizabeth looked like a rag doll next to him, doing everything she could to remain standing.

Garrahan liked this scenario. For the first time since he met Edward Malden, he had the upper hand.

"You're not going to do anything, Edward. Here's why." Garrahan swallowed. He was going to summon up a level of bravado he didn't have. To sound convincing.

"If you hurt Elizabeth, I get into my car. Which you'll notice is running. I speed out to the highway before you get back to your car. You'll be wondering what I intend to do. Then you'll realize that you have a tremendous problem on your hand.

"I'm not the tremendous problem. Joel is. Because Joel is in my trunk and you no longer have a priest in your grave. No holy blood boundary for the Behemoth. We both know you need a dead priest in that grave. And you don't have one. You don't even have any candidates.

"Except one. Yourself."

Garrahan let that sink in.

"The instant I take Joel out of here, you are at the Behemoth's mercy. There is nothing, absolutely nothing, to keep it from running from Morris again. Because there is no priest in the grave. Because I'm driving away with the priest. Because you've hurt Elizabeth."

Malden's thoughts roiled, careening inside his head like a train wreck. Anything he planned to do would be for naught if Garrahan drove off. He had not entertained the possibility that Joel would be moved from the grave. Not by anyone. Least of all Garrahan.

And what happened to Leonard? This is the point at which Malden expected that parasitic toad to come in and resolve the situation.

"You haven't told me about Leonard," Malden shouted.

"Don't stall," Garrahan said. "Put it this way: If I'm not worried about him, you shouldn't be, either."

Silence again. Malden couldn't think straight.

Should he shoot at Garrahan? He could barely see him in silhouette. Should he rush him? If Garrahan did get to the highway, what would he do with Joel? Who would he tell?

"Let Elizabeth go. Now." Garrahan reached into the car and flicked the high beams on, further blinding Malden.

"You can wait as long as you want. The fact is that Joel is locked in my trunk, and the keys to that trunk are in my ignition. If Elizabeth doesn't come over here, Joel and I disappear."

Malden was frozen where he stood.

"Do you need more incentive, Edward?" Garrahan asked, trying to mask his nervousness. He thought Malden would have capitulated by now.

"Look at the long-term scenario. If I take Joel and Abby to New York with me, I'm turning them over to the police. I'm pointing the police back here. With the whole story, except for the monster-in-the-woods part. I give them the names of the guys who dug the grave. I tell them about Bruce Donahue. I even tell them about Nancy, and how Ethan and Leonard fit into all this. At this point, along with Abby, I have enough evidence on my side to drop the weight of guilt on your side. Your townspeople will hate having city cops sniffing around Morris asking upsetting questions."

"The only way you can prevent that is to make a choice."

Garrahan took a deep breath.

"You either put yourself in that fucking hole, or you give me Elizabeth."

CHAPTER 123
MAY 13
MONDAY, 1:36 AM

Garrahan was spent. His heart was racing, and his lungs were heaving.

Malden still didn't move.

Elizabeth started whimpering. Garrahan looked into his car. He saw Abby staring at him from the passenger side floorboard. She was a small black shape dim in the reflected glare of the headlights.

It was the coldest part of the morning, yet Malden felt sweat in his collar. The gun in his left hand was trembling. Elizabeth had stopped twisting in his right.

"If you leave with the Donahues, I will find you. You will regret everything." Malden tried to retake the upper hand. It felt feeble.

Garrahan shook his head, knowing Malden couldn't see it. "That's where you're wrong, Edward. After I leave here with Elizabeth and Abby, I still have three cards to play. And you'll have already folded."

Malden harrumphed. "You won't have any cards. We will find you."

Garrahan clicked his teeth together. It was the sound a disappointed teacher might make.

"You're missing the big picture, Edward. First of all, you won't have Leonard coming after me. And he was always your go-to guy for torture and general unpleasantness. So let's count him out for the moment.

"Second. I'm taking the device with me. We know it summons the Behemoth. I can come here anytime I want and set it off. Anytime at all."

Garrahan paused, letting that sink in.

"And third. I would only set it off after I'd knocked over each and every one of your five markers."

"Imagine that. All your markers down, and the alarm summons the Behemoth to venture back outside the boundaries."

As he spoke, Garrahan found himself pleased with how well this was going.

"When that happens, there is nothing you can do—ever—to bring the Behemoth back. You can't kill yourself, because you're only one priest and you need five. You won't have the device, since I'll have set it off when you least expected it. Worst of all, if the towns around Morris get word there's a wild beast on the loose—say a giant bear—a lot of people will want to put bullets into its hide."

"At that point, the town won't forgive you. I'm guessing that even God won't forgive you."

Garrahan paused. The air was getting cold. He could see his breath as he spoke. "The choice is simple. Let Elizabeth go, or you end up buried in this hole."

"Choose."

CHAPTER 124
MAY 13
MONDAY, 1:40 AM

Malden could not believe it had all gone so wrong. Barely two hours ago, everything had been perfect. The Behemoth had returned to Morris, Abby was heading to the altar with Leonard, Ethan was watching Garrahan, and Joel had taken Malden's place in the grave.

In less than half an hour, it had been reduced to this. To choose between his life and control over the congregation, or Elizabeth Donahue's life.

It wasn't much of a choice.

He had a fleeting impulse to shoot himself and drop into the grave, ending everything. Never to deal with anything again. Blissful release.

The idea left his head as soon as it entered.

He let go of Elizabeth.

She moved uncertainly from him, as if afraid he would shoot her in the back.

Malden motioned with his hand. "Go. It's over." He put the gun on the ground to show her.

Elizabeth ran to Garrahan's car and pulled open the door. When she saw Abby, she enveloped the girl.

"Elizabeth, you've got to get in," Garrahan urged. "I mean it. Quickly."

She pulled Abby to her, and the two squeezed into the passenger seat. She pulled the door closed behind her.

When it slammed, Malden raised his hands to show he was complying with everything. "You have the Donahues. Give me Joel." He peered through the headlights trying to see Garrahan. "You promised."

"I did," Garrahan remarked. He hadn't expected that this would take place. In his mind, he'd envisioned a Mexican standoff. Someone—maybe him, maybe Malden—would be lying dead next to the grave. He was shocked that it hadn't come to that.

"Here's the deal," Garrahan said. "You jump into the grave. Once you're down there, I will put Joel on the ground right here. Then I'll drive off. By the time you get out of the hole, we'll be gone."

"That won't be necessary. I won't . . ."

"Yes, it will be necessary. I don't want you thinking you can shoot at us or charge me while I'm moving Joel out of the trunk." Garrahan was losing his voice. "Get in there. Then you get Joel."

Malden walked to the edge of the grave and sat down. He scooted himself over the side, dropping lightly to the bottom. Garrahan could see Malden's face just over the rim of the pit. He felt like hacking it off with the axe he had in his car.

For a few moments he stared at Malden. What a pitiful prick, he thought. All of this for a monster. A monster that came from who knew where. Something that should be captured and studied.

Garrahan hadn't found any real answers to what the monster was, or why it was here. Yet it embodied every Biblical attribute that Malden and the people of Morris ascribed to it. There was no denying that.

"Can we go?" Elizabeth asked, her voice childlike. Garrahan couldn't see her inside the car; she and Abby were a single huddled shape.

He unlocked the trunk. He grabbed Joel's body by the belt and shirt and lifted him out. He tried to do it with dignity—Joel probably deserved that much—but he was too tired and in too much pain to be gentle.

He placed Joel down next to the car. The body cast a long shadow on the ground.

Garrahan stood over Joel and stared at him sadly. He tried not to look at what was left of Joel's skull.

"He's all yours," Garrahan said to Malden.

Garrahan wanted to say something momentous. Something that would be worthy of remembering for a long time. Something that would change Malden's view of life. Pronounce sentence and pass judgment, as it were. But he knew there was nothing he could say that would change a goddamned thing.

He walked to the front of the car and looked down at Malden. "You have things to take care of. You know what I mean. And I don't want to hear from you again as long as I live."

Garrahan climbed into the driver's seat and shifted the car into drive. It lurched quickly across the field, back through the tall grass. He headed towards the highway along the same path that Terry Moran had driven an eternity ago.

The path where it all started.

CHAPTER 125
MAY 13
MONDAY, 2:22 AM

The creature tore through the woods.

It was engorged from the sacrifice. The human had been strong. It had fought harder than smaller humans.

The creature was also enraged. It was locked in by lines of fresh blood. It was no longer free.

The creature understood its purpose. Make the humans tremble in fear. It had done so for thousands of years.

But over time, it had been mistreated by the humans and their offerings. Tonight, their blood sealed off its world once more. The creature was swollen with hatred at being caged in again.

It would seek a way out.

It would start by devouring the humans in their dwellings.

At night.

When they were asleep.

The humans would never dare hurt the creature in retribution. The Lord forbade it.

"The people shall be wasted with hunger . . . and the teeth of the beast will I send upon them."

If they should attempt to hurt the creature, the humans would suffer the wrath of the beast in the abyss.

The one that lurked in cold emptiness far below the church.

Devastation and terror would crawl out of the earth.

"The beast that you saw once long ago shall ascend out of the pit and create destruction. Those who dwell on the Earth, and whose names have not been written in the Book of Life, will be struck down when they behold the beast that was, and has now come back out of the abyss again."

There would be carnage among the humans.

The creature raced to its lair, far from the church.

For even the Behemoth lived in fear of the thing in the abyss.

— *END* —

ACKNOWLEDGMENTS

Writing a horror novel is a solitary endeavor, best done under the cover of darkness at hours when the rest of the world is sleeping soundly—but not always safely—in their beds. Once the book is ready to be exposed to the light of day, however, it requires other people to give it physical form. The people who accomplished that task for *Behemoth* include my literary agent, Alec Shane, whose interest in all things horror has made this book's very existence possible; Pete Kahle of Bloodshot Books, who saw the potential for a monster story in a modern era; and Mikio Murakami, the artist who worked tirelessly amid much input to capture the essence of this book on its cover. To each of them, I am deeply grateful.

I also want to acknowledge the writers who inspired me to take pen (and later computer) in hand and slither into the dark pits of fear and the human soul: Edgar Allan Poe, H.G. Wells, Richard Matheson, Shirley Jackson, Stephen King, Franz Kafka, Ray Bradbury, H.P. Lovecraft, Mary Shelley, and M.R. James.

Thanks to my parents for their encouragement over all these years, to my brothers and sisters for late nights watching *Creature Feature* on Channel 56, to my daughters Madeline and Katherine for sharing my morbid fascination with places where the light isn't so bright, and to Trini, for always being the light.

Finally, thanks to you for reading this book, and taking the time to find your way into the place where my creatures live.

HP Newquist

ABOUT THE AUTHOR

HP Newquist is the author of more than thirty books on topics ranging from artificial intelligence to the ways in which human beings die.

He lives in Manhattan and resides online at www.newquistbooks.com.

BEHEMOTH is his first novel.

PRAISE FOR BEHEMOTH
THE DEBUT NOVEL FROM
HP NEWQUIST

"Newquist has created a fine horror novel that dares to be called literary/historical fiction and entertains the reader from start to finish."
HORROR REVIEW

"Newquist is a great writer . . . his words vividly stoke the imagination!"
CEMETERY DANCE

"One of the best books I've read in a very long time."
HORROR BOUND

"I'm not a fan of the frequently overused phrase 'unputdownable' but there really is no other way to describe this book. This was easily a 5 star read . . . on my top reads of the year list."
KENDALL REVIEWS

"Newquist is an accomplished writer and it shows on each page of BEHEMOTH. A wild ride that doesn't ease up on tension, this is a must-read for any horror junkie."
FANBASE PRESS

"Genuinely terrifying and filled with dread."
GINGERNUTS OF HORROR

"Dark, sinister . . . truly terrifying."
FUNDINMENTAL

RELAYER BOOKS

Other titles from RELAYER BOOKS:

TEN YEARS GONE

Here There Be Monsters

**GUITAR:
The Instrument That Rocked The World**

**THE BRAIN MAKERS:
The History Of Artificial Intelligence**

BEHEMOTH
SOUNDTRACK

Music to accompany this book can be found at HP Newquist's website: www.newquist.net

and his Soundcloud page

soundcloud.com (search HP Newquist)

Made in United States
North Haven, CT
02 October 2025